The Warden

The Chronicler's Series

Book 1

Matthew Louwers

Greg.

Thank you so much for helping me to achieve my dream!

ISBN: 9781521276433

Printed in the United States of America

For Papa

Prologue

From the desk of the Chronicler
The Fall:

    After many cycles of failed attempts at creating the perfect universe, the Makers came together to examine their work. While some civilizations flourished with technology and rapid growth, others turned to war, aggression, and other acts of extreme violence. The Makers were furious at how quickly their creations always brought chaos and destruction into existence.

    To counteract these growing dangers in the universe, the Makers elected to create a race of all-powerful beings who would act in their stead as a force for good. For thousands of years, this superior race accomplished the impossible task the Makers had placed before them, and they quickly became known throughout the universe as the Wardens.

    However, where unlimited power is concerned, peace is rarely sustained for too long. Many Wardens grew bored with the powers they had been given and, instead, began a journey to seek out the Makers and ask for more.

The voyage across the stars took a nasty toll on many of these Wardens. It twisted and corrupted their minds to the point that, when they finally reached their destination, their lust for power had consumed them.

The Makers, appalled by their creations once again, banished these rogue Wardens and stripped them of their jobs and titles. They were never to return to their homes or speak to any of their friends and families again. The weary travelers, furious at their creators, vowed to one day return and seek their revenge.

However, the Makers were not keen on allowing that to happen, for they had worked too hard to create the peace that had grown amongst the worlds. They reconvened one final time and brought to life the Grand Master, a champion of the Wardens who would possess the powers of all the Wardens combined. The Grand Master would act as the final line of defense should the rogue Wardens ever return.

For many years, the Grand Master's presence frightened the rogue Wardens into hiding, preventing their return. Generations passed and, when the Grand Master grew too old to complete his tasks, a new one would take his place. On and on this cycle went, a shepherd to always watch over his flock.

Evil slowly crept back into the dark corners of the abyss. Whispers spread of a great blackness at the edge of space. This darkness continued to grow and soon, the rogue Wardens resurfaced, only now they took on a new name, one more befitting of their sinister nature: Ravens.

With a vast number of followers, the Ravens looked to make good on their threat. They returned to Haven, the Warden home world, and silently infiltrated the city.

The Warden

Only the Grand Master sensed that something was wrong. Fearing for the lives of his people, the Master summoned his Wardens home from every corner of the universe. Many answered the call and arrived within a few days. Little did the Master know that this would ultimately be his downfall.

The Warden outcasts waited patiently for their former brethren to make their triumphant return and defend their world, but many of their old friends had aged poorly from their countless years away from home and would hardly pose a threat to the healthy and powerful Raven army.

On the eve of what would become known as The Great Warden Massacre, the Grand Master attempted to speak to the Makers. He told them of his suspicions and requested their aid in the coming attack, but the Makers were silent and ignored the Master's pleas. The Wardens would be forced to fight this war alone.

That night, the Ravens silently made their opening move throughout the city, slitting the throats of all the defenseless Wardens they could find. The ambush was a bloodbath. As soon as the screaming started, the true battle began. Explosions of magical energy tore through the streets, sending nearby homes up in flames. The ground shook with anger as the skies opened up above and poured torrential rainfall down upon them.

As the battle raged below, the Grand Master struck from his terrace. Bolts of lightning arced from the sky, instantly killing those it struck. He used the rain to quench the fires and did what he could to save his people, but it would not be enough.

The battle seemed to last for ages, and so many had fallen in the struggle that no side could truly claim victory. The Grand Master looked on in horror as the once beautiful and energetic streets of his home were now drenched in the blood of his family and friends. Paralyzed from the shock, he was unable to prevent the remaining Ravens from retreating into the dawn. What remained of Haven was now buried beneath rotting piles of carcasses. Not even the rats wanted anything to do with them.

The Grand Master knew that his time was at an end. Following a few final words to the departed, he gathered the remaining Wardens. He offered them a choice: join him in hiding, or flee and abandon the Warden mantle forever.

Many left the Master that day and were never seen or heard from again. His more loyal followers retreated to a sacred, hidden location, silently awaiting his commands.

But the commands never came. Darkness returned to the universe, and everything that the Makers had worked so hard to protect was destroyed once again.

Or so we thought.

1

Energy. On this particularly brisk morning the emerald forest, just outside the quaint village of Brimsdale, was filled with it. The long, gnarled branches of the massive white oak trees blew in a synchronized dance with the wind as it gusted through, shaking the morning dew from the leaves and stirring the birds from their slumber. They chirped in excitement, adding their melody to the orchestra of the woods. Small critters exited their homes with vigor, while the nearby river surged as it twisted and turned, flowing into the sapphire waters of the crystal-clear lake deeper in. It was another perfect day for the denizens of the Brimwood.

It was at precisely that moment, as the morning routines of the forest wildlife were just getting underway, that two boys, no older than twenty-five years of age, came storming through the trees. The younger of the two was tall, athletic, but not overly so, and had short, brown hair that barely rose off his head. Specks of dark stubble sprinkled his rough jawline, countering his otherwise soft complexion. His counterpart, however, was much shorter and slightly heavier set, with his long, black hair slicked to the side of his head. His round face was clean shaven but riddled with acne, and his cheeks were flushed, as they always were.

Twigs snapped as the pair burst through the brush, stopping only briefly to catch their breath. The two sported red scrapes up and down both arms, and the shorter boy quickly brushed a few stray leaves from his greasy hair. Either the two were involved in some sort of vigorous exercise routine, or they were running from something.

From deep within the trees the deep, angry roar of a mighty beast pierced the forest's song, sending its inhabitants fleeing in terror back into their dens. The boys took one horrified look at each other and bolted. While the young lads were excellent runners and could navigate the thick vegetation with ease, the creature that had caught their scents was faster and knew the forest better than most. As the boys ran in one direction, the beast took off in another.

"What the hell is it doing?" The tall boy yelled as he shoved a branch out of his face.

"Probably got a good look at that ugly mug of yours and scampered home," the short boy replied jokingly. The two laughed nervously, knowing that the creature was certainly still out there somewhere. "I wouldn't be surprised if we never see-" But the young man couldn't finish his thought because, as if on cue, the giant creature smashed through the trees into the clearing just ahead.

The beast was truly a magnificent sight to behold. Its narrow, wolf-like face and jowl protruded from its husky, bear-shaped torso. Bushy, brown fur blanketed its entire body, and a smooth, whip-like tail dangled from the creature's backside. The sheer size of the beast made it an adversary not to be trifled with, and it towered over the boys as it stood menacingly on its powerful hind legs.

"Shit!" Cursed the smaller boy as the monster let out another ear-splitting roar, spewing its hot saliva all over them. "Mathias! What do we do?"

"Well, brinwolves are territorial. Maybe, if we stand real still, we can convince it we don't mean it any harm," the boy named Mathias replied, but he didn't seem too sure of his idea.

"But we *do* mean it harm!"

"Quiet, Alistair!" Shouted Mathias angrily. "Where the hell is Nat?"

The brinwolf was growing tired of the two puny creatures bickering in front of her. She prepared to charge when a flash of light in the corner of her eye caught her attention. Her head turned just in time to see a large stone barreling straight for her face.

The boys' argument was cut short as the brinwolf howled in pain, the sharp rock striking one of her bright, yellow eyes. Frantically, the two searched for the source of the attack, scanning every tree and bush they could find. Finally, their eyes fell upon a shadow, just barely visible against the dark green brush. It was Natalie.

The girl's head was completely shaved and she wore a pair of small, silver rings through the left side of her nose that matched her cloudy, grey eyes. She was just as tall as Mathias and incredibly skinny, and she was faster and smarter than the two boys combined, or so she claimed. Natalie smiled at the boys as they finally saw her standing there, but her victory was short lived. She now had the brinwolf's full attention.

"Get out of here!" The girl yelled as she took off back into the forest. The beast roared and bounded after her, leaving the quarreling boys alone in the clearing.

"Well, you heard the girl," Alistair said dismissively.

"What? You're not actually considering leaving her, are you?" Replied Mathias hastily, appalled that his friend would even suggest such a thing.

"She said to get out of here, and you know we're no match for that thing. She can handle herself, Mat. I'm not dying today!" Alistair retorted angrily, his flushed face growing an even darker shade of red.

"Ali! She's our friend! We aren't just going to leave her." Mathias was fuming. It was becoming much more obvious why their father no longer wanted Alistair to carry on the Warden legacy.

"She'll be fine. I'm out." And with that, Alistair rushed into the jungle and away from the brinwolf and his friends.

Mathias stood there for a moment, completely flabbergasted. Alistair had only been there at Natalie's request, and Mathias suddenly found himself regretting bringing him along.

A chilling scream pierced the boy's thoughts as it reverberated through the forest.

Hold on, Nat! Mathias thought, quickly devising a plan before sprinting back into the forest.

The monster's path was easy to follow. The white trunks of the oak trees were completely obliterated, and the forest floor was covered in trampled leaves, while large, heavy footprints sank into the mud.

Before he even realized it, Mathias caught up to the brinwolf. The beast stood near an old, gnarled tree, scratching at the bark and roaring into the boughs. Mathias followed the white, twisting trunk up and found Natalie clinging to one of the higher branches. He needed to alert her to the plan before drawing too much of the monster's attention.

High in the treetops, Natalie held on for dear life. The branches grew thinner there and would likely snap at any moment. Fortunately, the brinwolf wasn't making any progress in getting to her, but it wasn't giving up either, and the Makers only knew how long she would be able to hold on to that branch.

"C'mon guys, where are you?" She muttered nervously under her breath as she scanned the forest around her.

Mathias, who has crouched quietly behind a pair of white and yellow bushes, had no idea how he was going to get Natalie's attention, let alone relay the plan to her. So, giving up completely on devising a well thought out plan, he picked up the nearest rock, a jagged piece of black stone that almost seemed like it didn't belong amongst the others scattered about, and hurled it at the beast.

The projectile flew with incredible speed, striking the brinwolf on the side of her face. The creature howled in agony as thick, red drops of blood began to seep from the open wound. She turned to him and growled angrily, her one good eye locking onto his. He now had the brinwolf's full attention.

"Nat!" Mathias yelled as he prepared to run. "Get to The Edge!"

Natalie didn't need any more information than that; she knew the place well. As kids, the two had stumbled upon the narrow, barren cliff completely by accident. The Edge was situated high over the lush valley below, and took on the nickname because, to the two young children, it felt like looking out over the edge of the world.

Natalie understood immediately what Mathias had planned. As the brinwolf bolted after him, she jumped out of the tree and sprinted for the cliff.

Mathias twisted and turned through the forest, the brinwolf just behind him. He pushed through denser areas of vegetation, desperately trying to slow the creature down so that Natalie had enough time to get in place, but he had his doubts that the plan was going to work. The pair had used The Edge several times in the past to throw off pursuers, but the brinwolf seemed smarter than the other denizens of the Brimwood.

The wind whistled loudly as it tore through the trees, and Mathias knew he was nearing the cliff. As he rounded another corner, the creature tight on his heels, he burst out onto the open plateau of The Edge. The dry, cracked ground was brown and dusty, and no trees or other vegetation grew in the dirt around it.

The brinwolf screeched to a stop as it crashed through the opening, growling at the boy as it stepped cautiously out onto The Edge. The chase was finally over.

Mathias crept towards the edge of the cliff and shuffled his feet around in the dirt. He felt the ground shift slightly, as though it was no longer rock beneath his feet. He knew, then, that he had found what he was looking for.

The beast paid no attention to the boy's feet, however. As the brinwolf started to charge, Mathias stomped his foot twice in quick succession and dropped through the ground beneath him. The brinwolf, completely caught off guard as her prey vanished into the ground, was unable to slow herself as she slid over the edge of the cliff and dropped into the valley below.

The Warden

The trap door had saved Mathias once again.

Several years ago, when hunting of the local wildlife became a chore of theirs, Mathias and Natalie decided that they needed an escape route in case they couldn't outrun their pursuer. They spent months digging out a tunnel at The Edge, constructing a winding staircase from the base of the valley all the way up to the cliff and out into the forest above. The upper entrance was hidden behind a tangled mess of vines and old tree stumps, an area of the forest many of the larger creatures tended to avoid. Once the room at the top had been completely carved out, they built the trap door mechanism that would allow anyone standing on it to fall through, as long as someone beneath the door pulled the lever. It was a team effort to pull the trick off, but it never failed.

Mathias sat there in the dim cave, laughing and rubbing his rear. The fall through the door was never a graceful one.

"Well, that wasn't so bad," laughed a sweaty Natalie as she helped Mathias to his feet.

"I keep telling you we need some pillows down here or something," he replied, wiping the dirt from his beige shorts as he stood. "I wasn't sure if you'd make it here in time."

"Please. I stopped for a cup of tea and took a quick nap until I heard you fumbling around up there," Natalie jested, but she chuckled knowing the day had finally been won. Mathias joined in as they began their descent down the twisting staircase.

"What happened to Ali?" Natalie asked, her concern rising.

"What do you think?" Mathias replied, his temper flaring up immediately. "The moment you told us to 'get out' he bolted." Natalie looked down at the crudely carved stairs, clearly upset that her friend, someone she cared about, had left her there to die. "I tried to stop him, but you know how stubborn he is." He paused for a moment before quietly adding, "I'm sorry."

"It's fine..." she replied, but it wasn't. Mathias had known Natalie far too long to know when things weren't fine. He also knew that pressing the issue would not help matters any, but he did it anyway.

"He's always been like this, Nat. Never able to deal when things get tough." He hated to say it, but Mathias knew Alistair better than anyone, and there was nothing uncharacteristic about his actions.

Natalie came to a stop. She gently rested her hand on Mathias's arm and stared into his dark, cobalt eyes. "He never used to be like this, Mat, and you know it." A single tear dripped slowly down her cheek. Mathias wasn't sure if he should wipe it away or not, so he watched as it crept toward her chin, where it dangled only briefly before dropping to the ground. "Everything changed when Aurilean went back on making him a Warden."

Aurilean was Alistair's father and one of the last Wardens left in the galaxy. He was getting on in years, but that did little to diminish his commanding presence. He stood taller than any resident of Brimsdale and was awfully fond of his twisted, ashen beard, as it was the only hair left on his round, wrinkled head. He was a kind and caring old man, and he was the father Mathias never had.

The circumstances surrounding Mathias's parentage were still a complete mystery to him. He did know that his mother had passed away shortly after giving birth to him, and, with no information regarding his father, Aurilean had taken him in and raised him as his own. Alistair was ecstatic to have a younger brother, and Mathias was happy to be part of the family, so the two got along famously.

Then came the day that Aurilean chose Alistair to be his successor as Warden. The boy was overjoyed and accepted without question. Mathias had never been jealous of the old man's decision. Becoming one of the last Wardens sounded difficult, not to mention incredibly dangerous, and he liked his simple, quiet life the way it was.

However, the days of sneaking off with his brother and getting into trouble were at an end. Alistair spent countless hours each day training with his father, learning what it truly meant to be a Warden. Mathias oftentimes found himself bored without his brother around, so he would discover the location of Alistair's sessions and keep watch from a distance.

The years seemed to race by after that. The more Alistair trained, the harder things got and the angrier he became. He struggled with many of the simple tasks his father placed before him and would grow frustrated, usually ending the session in a fit of rage. Mathias felt sorry for his brother. He knew Alistair always gave it his all, but it oftentimes wasn't enough.

Then everything changed. It was a wet day, the rain having just tapered off after a seven-day downpour and, when Alistair arrived at The Edge for his training, the cliff was covered in sloppy mud and a damp haze hung in the air. He sat cross legged in the muck to begin his routine meditation when a bolt of white lightning struck the rock around him. Alistair screamed as the ground began to crumble away. He desperately tried to jump to safety but missed the ledge and started sliding down the side of the cliff. He roared in pain as he grabbed hold of an old root stuck in the rock. But the ledge above was out of reach, and there was nothing but hard ground far below him. He was undeniably stuck.

Mathias, who had been watching the entire thing from a safe distance, jumped out of the forest to come to his brother's aid. He carried a long rope slung over his shoulder, a tool he would often bring to Alistair's training sessions at The Edge.

"Ali!" Mathias yelled as he hastily flung the rope over the edge of the cliff. "Grab hold!"

Knowing that it was against his father's rules to accept any outside help during his sessions, Alistair quickly did as he was told. With a surge of strength and adrenaline, Mathias pulled his brother up the cliff to safety.

"What are you doing here?" Demanded a powerful voice behind them. Mathias's heart leapt into his chest. In all the commotion, he hadn't seen the old man arrive. "Do I need to repeat the question?" Aurilean's voice was stern, and his black eyes never blinked as they burned with a ferocity the likes of which Mathias had never seen.

"It's my fault, father," confessed Alistair before his brother could respond. "I invited Mathias to come watch and keep an eye on me. Lucky for me he did, or I might've been a splattered mess at the base of-" but Aurilean held up his hand, silencing his son before he could finish.

"You knowingly accepted an outsider's aid in this test, my son." Aurilean spoke without emotion, his face hard and unreadable. "This test was designed to assess your reaction to an unpredictable event, and you failed." Alistair hung his head in defeat, clenching his fists at his sides. Mathias could see the rage building inside of him.

"Father, I'm sorry," Alistair said through gritted teeth.

"So am I. You have failed me time and time again, Alistair. You are unable to complete some of the most remedial of tasks, and it seems nearly impossible for you to keep your anger in check. It pains me greatly to say it but, as of this moment, you are no longer my successor."

Alistair's world imploded. Everything he had worked so hard for was suddenly crumbling down around him. He raised his eyes to meet his father's. "What did you just say to me?" He asked, his body shaking uncontrollably.

"It's over, Alistair. You have failed nearly every test I've thrown at you, and you sought outside aid when you were strictly instructed not to." Aurilean's face continued to show no sign emotion, but Mathias could see the sadness buried deep within his dark eyes.

"If not me, then who?" It was more of a statement than a question, and Alistair feared he already knew the answer.

"Your brother will take your place." Aurilean looked at Mathias and, for the briefest of moments, the slightest hint of a grin appeared at the corners of the old man's mouth. Mathias suddenly wondered if this is what Aurilean had wanted all along.

"What? I don't want to be a Warden!" Mathias yelled defiantly.

"He's not even your son!" Roared an angry Alistair, his face burning red at his father's betrayal. Mathias felt a sharp pain at his brother's words. How could he say something so hurtful after everything they had been through, especially after he had just saved the boy's life.

"He is as much my son as you are, Alistair, and he is the one who will carry on my legacy when I'm gone." But Alistair wasn't listening to his father anymore. He faced his brother, his olive-green eyes glossy with tears.

"You! You planned this all along!" Accused Alistair as his brother frantically tried to deny it. "This is why you've been following me, so you could steal what is rightfully mine!" Mathias tried to explain that he wanted nothing to do with the Wardens, but Alistair wasn't listening.

"Brother, please! This was never my intention."

"No! As of this moment, we are no longer brothers. I never want to see your face again!" Alistair screamed and stormed off into the trees.

Many days came and went and, after Mathias explained countless times that he had refused to accept Aurilean's decision, the hatred Alistair had for his brother diminished. Unfortunately, the friendship teetered on the brink and was never meant to last. The two fought constantly, and argued about every little thing. Aurilean's choice had crushed Alistair's spirit and destroyed the young, energetic boy Mathias had known for so long.

"Mathias?" Natalie asked, pulling him from the memory.

"I guess I never realized how much that day changed him."

"Everybody changes eventually," Natalie said sadly. "You changed that day too, you know."

"You think?"

"Even though you didn't want to be a Warden, you started acting like one. You stopped getting into trouble and instead, started helping everyone around you. You really grew up that day, I guess. I just don't understand why you don't want the job. You'd be the perfect Warden, you know, even though you're incredibly slow and dimwitted." Mathias smiled at Natalie's attempt at humor but didn't say anything.

He usually tried not to think about being a Warden, but somehow the thought always managed to creep back into his mind. He oftentimes dreamed of soaring through the skies and protecting numerous worlds from corruption and war

16

with other Wardens at his side. Unfortunately, with the dwindling number of Wardens left in the galaxy, those dreams would remain just that. He also knew that he would lose Alistair for good if he decided to take up his father's mantle.

"Just think about it," Natalie continued. "Aurilean wouldn't have chosen you without a good reason." And she had a good point, but Mathias would have to ponder it later because the two had reached the opening at the bottom of the twisting staircase.

They had finally arrived at the valley, the sun burning bright in the sky as the two exited the musty cave into the forest. The brinwolf had taken a nasty fall off The Edge, so the body should have been somewhere nearby.

"There it is!" Natalie yelled excitedly, as she pointed over a pair of bushy, green and gold shrubs.

"That's weird," Mathias replied as he noted the body's location. "How did it get over there?"

As the two closed in on the brinwolf, Natalie jumped back. "It's still alive!"

She was right. The creature was still breathing and looked to be in decent shape. The only injury Mathias seemed to notice was a front leg bent in a way it shouldn't have been.

"Here," said Natalie as she handed Mathias her knife. "You should be the one to kill it."

The young boy took the blade and hesitantly crept toward the beast. She growled at him as he did, but she was powerless to stop him and rested her head on the ground to accept her fate. That's when Mathias noticed the strange flaps of skin drooping from the creatures back.

"The Makers be damned..."

"What is it?" Natalie yelled, not daring to get any closer than she needed to.

"Nat, this thing has wings!" Mathias shouted back to her.

"What?!" She replied, not quite believing what she had just heard. "Brinwolves don't have wings."

"I know that. This isn't a brinwolf." Mathias couldn't explain it, but he knew that the creature was not native to the Brimwood.

"Not a brinwolf? Then what the hell is it?"

"Do I look like an expert on Brimwood wildlife?" Mathias replied jokingly, but Natalie just glared at him. He looked for any other differences, but everything about it suggested that it was a brinwolf. "What are you?" Mathias whispered to the creature. The beast looked up at him and whimpered.

"Mat, if that thing can fly, how did it fall like this?"

The boy had been wondering that very thing. "It looks like she tried to fly, but was caught off guard. The wings must have slowed her descent and carried her here, but she still hit the ground hard, which explains her leg." The creature put its head back on the ground, continuing to whine as the two figured out what happened to her.

"Well, at this rate, it won't be able to do much on its own," explained Natalie. "We should put it out of its misery." But Mathias couldn't do it. This creature could fly! It didn't deserve to meet its end on the ground.

"Nat, throw me my pack," he yelled at his friend.

"Why?"

"Just do it!"

Natalie grabbed the bag of supplies and tossed it. She watched as Mathias fumbled around inside until he pulled out a roll of bandages. "What the hell are you doing?" She asked nervously.

"Get over here, I need you to help me snap her leg back into place."

The expression on Natalie's face shifted from confusion to a look of sheer terror. "You want me to do WHAT? That thing just tried to kill us, and you want to save it?!"

"Yes. Now get your ass over here!"

Grumbling, Natalie cautiously crept over to her friend. The beast glared at her, but allowed her to near as Mathias instructed her to hold the leg very still so he could snap the bent bone back into place. As soon as it happened, the creature howled in pain, but it didn't attack. It seemed to understand what they had just done for her. After it had been set, Mathias took a thick tree branch and wrapped it around the creature's leg. With sensation finally returning to her limb, the mighty beast attempted to stand, growling as pain streaked through her body, but she was strong and fought through it. Finally, the creature stood tall before them once again.

"Now to thank us for all we've done, it's going to eat us," Natalie said depressingly, but the creature didn't eat them. Instead, it looked Mathias dead in the eyes and nodded her head ever so slightly. Mathias was taken aback by the gesture, but part of him also understood it. As she raised her head, she turned to Natalie and roared like she never had before. The songbirds screeched in horror as they quickly abandoned their nests, while Natalie stumbled backwards onto the ground, covered in chunks of fresh meat and sticky drops of saliva. Then the creature made an entirely new sound, something that sounded to Mathias an awful lot like laughter.

"If you tell anyone about this, I'll kill you," Natalie grumbled while Mathias laughed hysterically.

And with that, the monster spread its wings, each one nearly twice as long as Mathias was tall. The brinwolf that wasn't a brinwolf looked at the boy one final time and, with a swift puff of her wings, took off into the sky. Mathias watched her soar away into the sunlight until he couldn't see her anymore.

"I can't believe we just did that. Alistair will never let us hear the end of it, you know," Natalie grumbled in annoyance.

"Yea, but no creature that can soar above the world deserves to meet its death on the ground."

There it was. Mathias had once again proven to Natalie that he was Warden material after all. She smiled at that, knowing it was only a matter of time before the boy learned who he was really meant to be.

"C'mon Nat, let's get out of here." Mathias offered his hand to Natalie and pulled her to her feet. The two then began the long journey back to the village, dreading the inevitable confrontation with Alistair.

*　　　　*　　　　*

Aurilean watched as the ashwolf disappeared over the horizon. The ashwolves were not native to the Brimwood, that part Mathias had gotten right. Instead, the majestic beasts nested in the dark caverns of Mt. Asher. At least they had before the volcano's untimely eruption. Now, only one ashwolf remained. Aurilean had beamed with pride as his son spared the creature's life. For years, Mathias had always done the right thing when faced with a difficult decision, and this time was no different. He had passed another test, and

Aurilean was sure that the boy would go on to do great things. Unfortunately, the time for tests was coming to an end.

As Aurelian looked out over the valley, he felt a shift in the winds around him. Everything was about to change and, if Mathias didn't accept his fate, the life and everything he had come to know and love would come to a devastating end.

Matthew Louwers

2

The walk back to Brimsdale was a quiet one. Mathias continued to ponder the origins of the mysterious flying creature he had rescued, while Natalie worked, albeit unsuccessfully, to get the beast's saliva and bits of food out of her clothes. She considered burning them, but figured a stern washing would do just fine.

Brimsdale was not a very large place. It was situated at the edge of the Brimwood, a great, lush forest that housed all manner of wildlife and acted as a refuge in case the village was ever threatened. Of course, nothing like that ever happened on Talise. Talise was one of the smallest planets in the galaxy, nestled just outside the dark region of space known as Sanctuary. This great, black expanse was completely void of all stars and planets. Even light from the nearby sun refused to pass through it. Many believed that Sanctuary was a gargantuan black hole, while others insisted it was home to a terrible demon that lied in wait for unsuspecting travelers. Because Talise was so close to this dangerous and mysterious abyss, Brimsdale very seldom had visitors.

Alongside being so close to Sanctuary, Talise wasn't the most hospitable of planets. The air was breathable, of course, but thin. In his earlier years, Mathias would often find himself short of breath while hunting or playing. However, like all inhabitants of Talise, he learned to control his breathing and grew accustomed to the conditions. But that wasn't all that made Talise a dangerous place to call home.

When the planet was still young, Mt. Asher, a volcano that was believed to be permanently dormant, erupted in a violent display of dust and lava and annihilated much of the world. Copious amounts of ash and fire blanketed Talise, killing anyone or anything it touched. The destruction was devastating, but a small civilization of white oak carvers managed to survive the blast. However, with their village in ruins, they were forced to set out to find a new one. Surely there must have been somewhere unaffected by the devastation. The carvers walked for nearly a month, trudging through desolate wastelands and losing many of their number along the way before they stumbled, completely by accident, upon the Brimwood. The lush, emerald valley rested at the bottom of a steep cliff, completely untouched by the cataclysm. With their knowledge of the white oak trees that thrived in the valley below, the carvers began to rebuild. After many years, the village of Brimsdale was born and the Brimwood thrived, completely overtaking the cliff and beyond.

Shortly after The Great Warden Massacre, Aurilean crash landed into the Brimwood. He had only heard of Talise through conversation, and he knew it was a dangerous planet to seek shelter, but he had no other options. Wardens across the universe were being hunted down and slaughtered, or worse, enslaved by the Raven Commander. To survive, he would need to start fresh, and thus worked his way into the everyday life of Brimsdale.

The village was nothing more than a small grain of sand compared to the sprawling metropolis on Malador, but it had a very homey feel to it. The houses and buildings were constructed from the white wood of the oak trees, one of the hardest natural materials known to man. The carvers had perfected the art of molding and shaping the wood to fit their needs, and they were some of the only beings that could.

Brimsdale was a circular town, with a few rings of buildings that wrapped around a magnificent wooden sculpture of a grizzly, bearded man swinging an axe. The outer rings of the town consisted of cozy, single-floor homes, while the inner ring focused more on trade and recreation.

Aurilean was given a small house on the outermost ring of the city, and it was there that he began his life anew. He met and married a lovely young woman who gave birth to a bubbly young Alistair many years later. Unfortunately, she developed an incurable heart condition after the birth and passed away shortly after. Four years would pass before Aurilean would find Mathias and take him in.

Brimsdale was the only home Mathias had ever known. But now, as he trudged along through the winding forest, he dreaded returning to it. He knew he would have to confront Alistair about his actions that morning, and all he could think about was beating his brother's face in.

"So, what are you gonna say to Ali?" As if reading his mind, Natalie finally broke the silence that Mathias had grown comfortable in.

"Not sure I'll *say* anything," Mathias replied through clenched teeth, the anger revealing itself in his eyes. Natalie immediately regretted her question. She knew Mathias was upset and that he wasn't serious about harming Alistair, but something in those dark blue eyes of his made her unsure.

"Funny. Don't let Aurilean catch you two beating each other to death. He may have let it go when you were little, but you're not kids anymore. He'll disown you both."

"Yea..." He trailed off. Natalie was right, but Mathias wasn't sure he would be able to restrain himself.

The sun crept lower into the sky as Brimsdale finally appeared through the trees. The hustle and bustle of village life was usually music to Mathias's ears, but tonight it sounded more like thunder before an approaching storm.

As Mathias and Natalie broke through the trees at the edge of the Brimwood, they could see that the village was indeed alive with energy. The townsfolk were preparing for some sort of celebration, with tables and chairs set up around an extra-large buffet table. Mathias didn't know what was going on, and he didn't have the time to stay and find out.

After parting ways with Natalie and enduring one final 'don't do anything stupid' lecture, Mathias made his way to the rec hall, Alistair's stomping grounds. The building was filled with a vast assortment of books Aurilean had collected over the years, along with several board games, and a fully stocked snack cupboard. It was common knowledge amongst the townsfolk that Alistair spent nearly every minute of every day loafing about inside the rec hall. Today was no exception.

The rec hall sat just outside the town center, and Mathias had to dodge and weave his way through the hectic crowd to get there. He nearly took out a woman balancing a giant tray of steaming vegetables, and hastily yelled his apologies as he sped off, leaving the woman grumbling in annoyance. He reached the rec hall a few minutes later and, with a deep breath, pushed through the tall, wooden door.

The Warden

Sure enough, his brother was slouched in a large red armchair in the far corner of the room, his muddy boots resting on the table in front of him. He held a book in front of his face, so he didn't see Mathias come in. Instead, Alistair yelled without looking up, "Try to keep it down, will ya? Just gettin' to the best part."

Mathias didn't reply, his anger already rising at his brother's complete disrespect. He strode across the room to where the boy was sitting and, just as he got close, Alistair looked up over the top of his book. His eyes grew wide as Mathias slapped the book out of his hands, sending it flying across the room.

The only other occupant of the rec hall was a little girl, no older than twelve years old, who screamed as the leather-bound projectile landed beside her. She bolted from the hall at lightning speed, no doubt running to find somebody to tell, but Mathias didn't care. It was just him and Alistair now.

"What the f-" Alistair started but Mathias never let him finish. No sooner had the book left the boy's hands when Mathias swung in with his right fist. The blow hit Alistair square in the jaw, sending him rolling over the side of the chair.

"What the hell?" Alistair sprang to his feet, his hands now prepared to block any further strikes from his brother. Mathias was breathing hard, his knuckles stinging from the blow. However, judging from the sudden discoloration in Alistair's face, his brother was hurting more.

"Don't play stupid with me, Ali," Mathias started as his brother stood dumbly in front of him, one hand rubbing his jaw. "Your only two friends in the world almost died today, and you don't seem to give a rat's ass!"

"Is that what this is about?" Alistair asked with a callous chuckle "I'm not sitting through another drawn out lecture from you tonight, man."

Mathias stood there fuming as his brother turned away to go after his book.

"LOOK AT ME!" Mathias roared, his voice echoing throughout the great room. Alistair turned slowly, and looked angrily up at his brother. Small scrapes and dried bits of blood adorned Mathias's puffy, red cheeks, a result of running through the trees all day. His eyes were slightly squinted, and his breathing was heavy and fast. Alistair had never seen his brother so enraged.

"What are you gonna do?" Alistair asked, knowing full well that a brawl was not something his brother was willing to risk. Aurilean had made the two swear off fighting after one unfortunate day that put both boys under medical care for a week. He had threatened the pair with banishment if they ever behaved in such a way again.

"I just want to talk," Mathias began, trying incredibly hard to keep his composure.

"Is that what you call talking? Well, go ahead, keep the conversation going!" Alistair edged closer, just inside arm's reach. Mathias knew the boy was just egging him on, hoping he would do something he would regret.

"I'm not here to fight you, brother. I'm here to try and understand why you abandoned us out there."

"Because Natalie's a better hunter than both of us. She could have handled it herself."

"No, Ali, she couldn't have. If I wouldn't have gone after her, she'd be dead, and it would be your fault!"

"Well, it's a damn good thing Warden Mathias was there to save the day."

"The Makers be damned. Ali, you need to let that shit go!" said Mathias, although he had a sneaking suspicion he was wasting his breath.

"Let it go? Are you fucking kidding me?" Alistair was growing scarier by the second. They had finally arrived at the real reason for their disagreement, and things were going to snowball if it wasn't resolved quickly. "You seriously think I can just let something like that go? You betrayed me, asshole!"

"Ali, how many times do I have to tell you? I never asked to be a Warden." Mathias was tired of repeating it.

"I don't fucking care!" Alistair replied. The discussion was rapidly turning into a shouting competition and soon, even with preparations going on outside, the villagers would start to hear them.

"Then you know what, Ali? Be mad at Aurilean! He's the one that called you a failure. He's the one that told you that you weren't ready!"

Alistair's nostrils flared. His brother had a point, and he didn't like it.

"I'm sorry that it happened this way, brother, I truly am."

"Big words for someone who gets to inherit MY birthright. You're not even my actual brother! You're not our blood!" Mathias didn't think the same words could hurt as much the second time around, but he was wrong. He turned away from his brother as a tear formed in his eye. He refused to let Alistair see him show emotion or the whole fight would be over.

"What's done is done, Alistair," Mathias said as he faced the door to the rec hall, wiping away any evidence of the tear. Then he swiveled back to face his brother. "I can't change the past. I can only do my best to work towards the future."

"A future without me. You're not my brother and you never will be." Alistair stormed past and gave Mathias a hard shove with his shoulder.

"We got it, you know," Mathias said, his voice returning to a normal volume.

"Got what?" Alistair replied, his back still turned towards Mathias, but his curiosity piqued.

"The brinwolf. Although it wasn't really a brinwolf. It was something else that-"

"Bull shit. Where is it?" Alistair interrupted as he faced his brother, a sly grin spread across his face that said he didn't believe a word of it.

"We let it go."

"Ha!" Alistair laughed as he rolled his eyes. "You're even dumber than I thought." The boy turned back towards the door and started walking again.

"Do you want to know why?" Mathias asked, hoping his brother would take the bait.

"No."

But Mathias ignored his brother's remark and said, "Because it didn't deserve to die."

Alistair stopped again.

"Sure, we invaded its territory with the sole purpose of tracking it down and killing it. But, as it laid there in the valley at the bottom of the cliff, its leg broken and hope gone, I realized that the creature wasn't angry at me for attacking her. Instead, she was upset at herself for not being smart or fast enough to avoid getting herself into that situation in the first place." Mathias had come to that conclusion on the walk back, but he hadn't realized until now just how relevant it was. "Ali, you're not mad at me. You're not mad at your father. You're only mad at yourself, and you're taking it out on everyone around you, on people that love you." As the words settled, Mathias prepared to go in for the kill. "Brother, you need to show the same restraint I did today, and let this whole Warden thing go."

Alistair stood in silence, staring down at the ground. His brother was right. He had beaten himself up for far too long for not being strong or smart enough to be a Warden. Sure, he hated that his father had chosen his adopted brother over him but, when it came down to it, it was Alistair's own fault.

"Ali?" Mathias asked as he rested a hand on his brother's shoulder.

"Don't touch me!" Alistair snapped as he shrugged off the hand. His brother had weakened his defenses, making him vulnerable and emotional, and Alistair didn't like it. As quickly as it had come down, Alistair put his wall right back up and faced his brother one final time.

"Ali, I'm just trying to make this right," Mathias said, truly sympathetic to his brother's resentment.

"If that's true, then you would never have tried to take what was mine in the first place!"

Mathias had said all that he could. His brother was hopelessly lost in his anger and frustration of his past failures.

"Don't you DARE turn your back on me while I'm talking to you!" Alistair roared as Mathias turned to leave. Things were spiraling out of control and, just as Natalie had predicted, one of them was about to do something incredibly stupid. Alistair grabbed Mathias by the shoulder and whirled him around. Then, without warning, he threw his fist at his brother's face. The attack was thrown with such ferocity that, had it connected, Mathias would have been under medical supervision for a week. Fortunately, the door to the rec hall blasted open followed by a massive burst of wind that rush in and embraced the two quarrelling brothers, pulling them apart and sending them flying in opposite directions.

Mathias landed hard, but quickly sat up, rubbing the spot on his head that had slammed into edge of the wooden table behind him. Meanwhile, Alistair had already jumped to his feet, preparing to make another attack. He stopped dead, however, when a bolt of lightning lit up the dark silhouette now present in the doorway.

Aurilean had arrived. As the menacing thunder clap boomed around them, rattling the very foundation of building, the powerful man stepped into the room.

"That. Is. ENOUGH!" Aurilean bellowed, pausing briefly between each word, his voice echoing off the walls as he demanded his sons' attention.

"Nothing happened!" Alistair instantly yelled in defense. He knew he was in trouble and was already working out a way to avoid being punished. Mathias, however, knew there was no chance of that happening, so he kept his mouth shut.

"You lie about as well as you hunt, Alistair," Aurilean jabbed at his son. Mathias was forced to choke back a laugh as Alistair dropped his gaze to the floor, completely humiliated and at his father's mercy.

"Stand." Aurilean addressed Mathias now, his tone not nearly as harsh. The boy quickly came to his feet and stood next to his brother.

"You two might have been under the impression that this *conversation* of yours was private. It will surprise you, then, to know that the entire village could hear your juvenile bickering." Aurilean glared at them, his black eyes hard and angry. "Explain yourselves."

Alistair glanced at Mathias, unsure of what to tell his father. He had a sneaking suspicion his brother was about to rat him out, and Alistair was not going to have that.

"It's my fault, father," Mathias began, speaking up before Alistair even had a chance. "I was so furious with Ali that I had to confront him and tell him how I was feeling."

Alistair was dumbfounded. After all the hateful things he had just said to his brother, Mathias was still taking the blame.

"If anyone is to be punished for this immature display of emotion, let it be me," Mathias finished, his eyes returning to the floor.

"Your honesty is appreciated, my son," Aurilean replied, the corners of his mouth revealing just a hint of a smile. It instantly vanished as he turned to Alistair, however. "And what about you? Do you have anything to add?"

Alistair was still in shock at his brother's confession. He had been the one screaming and yelling, not Mathias, but his father didn't need to know that. Alistair glared up at Aurilean and simply replied, "No."

"I see," the old man said, a pang of disappointment in his voice. He walked over to Mathias, rested a gentle hand on the boy's shoulder and whispered something into his ear. Mathias nodded when his father had finished, took one last glance at his brother who had his angry, green eyes fixed on the pair of them, and then quickly exited the premises, gently closing the door behind him.

As Mathias stepped out into the streets, the eyes of everyone he knew stared back at him with curiosity and discontent. He was about to explain himself when the building behind him exploded in an eruption of violent words spewed forth from both his father and brother. After only a few moments, the door to the rec hall slammed open and

Alistair stormed out of the building, his face full of red hot rage.

"Get back here!" Aurilean yelled furiously after his son. "I'm not through with you yet!"

"NO!" Alistair roared back, not even bothering to turn around. "I'm done with this shit! You'll regret this day, *Father.*" He nearly choked on that last word, the very fact that Aurilean was his family tearing apart at his insides. In his mind, Alistair no longer had a family, and it was time he moved on.

Mathias stared quietly at his brother as he disappeared into the crowd.

"Let him go, son" Aurilean was suddenly behind him, a hand once again resting on Mathias's shoulder, but he quickly shook it off.

"What did you say to him?" Mathias yelled, his anger mounting as he turned to face his father.

"What?" Aurilean replied, confused at the sudden outburst.

"Why couldn't you have just accepted my apology and left it at that? You didn't need to blow up at him!" Mathias was furious. He had tried so hard to protect his emotional wreck of a brother, but his father had destroyed any chance of that.

"Mathias..."

"What? Are you going to yell at me, too? He didn't deserve this!" Mathias was shaking, his fury getting the better of him. He knew that if he didn't control it, he would end up in as much trouble as his brother, or worse.

The village was silent, all eyes fixed on Mathias and Aurilean. Even the Brimwood was still, the animals afraid to utter even a whisper.

"My son," Aurilean began, not sure how to proceed. "You just don't understand."

"That's where you're wrong. I understand perfectly." And he did. Mathias knew exactly what his brother was feeling. "When you realize that, then we can talk."

Aurilean stood in stunned disarray and watched, for the second time that night, as a son turned his back on him and walked off into the darkness.

Matthew Louwers

3

On any given night of the week, Bjorn's Tavern was the place to be. Bright yellow light beamed through the open windows, while obnoxious laughter echoed through the trees. Bjorn's rickety square tables were oftentimes hastily shoved together to accommodate large parties, and his long, oak bar was always packed with joyful, paying customers. No matter where you were in Brimsdale, you could always tell when Bjorn's was open for business.

On this particular night, however, if you were to walk down the dusty dirt road outside the tavern, you would think the old building had closed years ago. The shutters were sealed so tightly over the windows that not a drop of light shown through, and the battered front door, which normally hung welcomingly open, was pulled shut and locked.

On the inside, the candles burned so low that you would have thought they weren't burning at all. Every table was vacant, save for a small, round black table Bjorn kept in the corner for business purposes. There were four large men huddled around a tattered scrap of paper in the middle of the table. They spoke in hushed voices, and one of the men would occasionally glance over at Bjorn and then quickly back to the paper in front of him.

Bjorn wasn't a big man, by any means, but he could certainly hold his own in a fight. His scruffy black hair refused to obey any of his attempts at styling it, and he wore black fingerless gloves that covered the many cuts and scrapes that adorned his hands. He also sported a dark scar across his left cheek, a scar that he reveled in talking about, should one be unfortunate enough to ask.

Bjorn stood behind the bar, meticulously scrubbing the countertop while keeping an eye on his guests. When the strange men had strolled into the tavern, Bjorn hadn't recognized any of them, and strangers in Brimsdale were never a good thing. The first man, who's red eyes Bjorn noticed immediately, had spoken softly, but firmly, requesting Bjorn close his bar for the night so the men could go about their business in private. When Bjorn refused, the red-eyed man pulled a large sum of coins out of his pocket and slammed them down onto the chipped countertop. The barkeep had never seen so many gold pieces in his life. The money was probably dirty, but he didn't care. He quickly closed shop, locking the door and sealing the windows. He knew business would be slow that night, with Mathias's birthday celebration beginning shortly in the town center, so he didn't feel guilty about closing.

One of the men rose from his chair and made his way to the bar where Bjorn was standing. The man was shorter than his friends, sported a filthy neck beard that had clearly never been groomed, and had sickly green eyes. It frightened Bjorn to stare into them directly, so he continued to look down at the bar as the man approached.

""Nother round," the man said in a husky voice that gurgled in his throat. He clearly hadn't bathed in weeks, and his breath nearly made Bjorn vomit as the stench crawled its way into his nose.

"Right away," Bjorn replied, quickly retreating from the pustule of a man.

"And maybe somethin' ter eat," the man added. Bjorn watched as he stuck his large finger in his nose, dug around for a few seconds, and then flicked the heaping glob of mucus at the wall. The man was repulsive, and Bjorn just wanted him to go away.

"My cook is gone for the night," Bjorn said.

"Why?"

"Big party in town, gave my crew the night off."

"What's the party fer?"

"Who knows?" Bjorn shrugged, not wanting to reveal too much.

"Hey Zeke, I wanna go ter the party," the man said as he turned to his friends.

"That's enough, Jardon," the man named Zeke replied, his red eyes burning in annoyance. "Get the drinks and stop harassing our gracious host."

Bjorn nodded at the man and went back to preparing the drinks. He didn't like any of these strangers, but the money he was making off them being there was enough to keep the tavern up and running for the rest of his life.

Jardon had gone back to digging around in his nose as Bjorn placed the beers down in front of him.

"Took long ernuff." Jardon sniffed, then he turned and shot a massive glob of spit into the ground. Bjorn just smiled at the man and watched him juggle the glasses as he walked back to the table.

When Bjorn had taken the money, his guests had made it very clear that they were not to be interrupted while they conducted their business. So, when a sudden stream of knocks on the door pierced the quiet of the tavern, Bjorn sprang into action.

The mysterious visitors quickly grew silent as their host sped across the room and peered through the small hole in the door.

"Sorry, Ali, but we're closed for the night," Bjorn began as he cracked the door open. "Gonna have to ask you to-"

"I need to clear my head, B," Alistair said before Bjorn could finish. "You're the only guy I know that can help me with that."

As Alistair pushed passed him and beelined straight for the bar, Bjorn could immediately tell something was wrong. The boy had clearly been crying, his eyes a puffy red mess. Bjorn looked over at the men in the corner, all of whom were glaring angrily back at him. The man called Zeke shook his head, but Bjorn ignored him, choosing instead to lock the boy in with the strangers.

"Better make it a double tonight," Alistair sighed as he folded his arms on the counter and rested his head inside them. Bjorn wasted no time bringing Alistair some much needed liquid relief. "Thanks," Alistair said as Bjorn set the translucent, brown liquid in front him.

"That one's on me," replied the barkeep. Alistair nodded as the two shared a mutual moment of respect, but Bjorn's curiosity was getting the better of him so he asked, "Mind if I bother you to tell me what's got ya so down?"

Alistair downed the drink in a single gulp, but didn't say anything. As he clanked the smudged glass back onto the bar, Alistair took a moment to examine the unusual set up around him. The bar was completely empty, except for a small group of men that all had their eyes glued to him. None of them had uttered a word since Alistair had arrived.

"Who are they?" Alistair asked quietly as he turned back to Bjorn.

"Beats me. They paid for privacy, so I gave it to 'em. Business was slow since everyone was at your brother's party," Bjorn replied.

"I don't have a brother," Alistair said angrily as he eyed the bottom of his glass for any remaining drops.

"That bad, huh?" Bjorn asked sympathetically.

"I don't want to talk about it!" Alistair snapped as he slammed his glass down onto the bar, but he immediately regretted lashing out so he added, "I'm sorry. It's just been a long day."

"Nah, it's fine. Shouldn't have asked. Another?" Bjorn was done pushing for information and instead went back to doing his job.

"Make it a round of beers. I'm gonna go see what our guests here are up to."

Bjorn was about to argue, but he didn't want to make Alistair any angrier than he already was. He poured five tall beers and set the foaming glasses on the counter in front of him.

"Thanks, B."

"Don't mention it," Bjorn replied as Alistair reached for the beers. "Just be careful. Somethin' about them ain't right."

Alistair nodded and slowly made his way for the corner table.

"Evening gentlemen," started Alistair as he came to a stop before the men, all of whom still had their eyes locked on him.

"What 'choo want, boy?" Asked Jardon as he stood to face Alistair. He was a full head taller and peered down on the boy with the sourest of grins.

Alistair, instead of fumbling under the intimidation, remained calm, held out one of the beers and said, "I bring drinks, if you'll allow me to join you."

"HA!" Laughed Jardon as he swiped the beer out of the boy's hand. "If he brings booze, he's a friend of mine!" The stinking pustule of a man grabbed a chair from a nearby table and added it to the collection of their own. Alistair slid into the seat and distributed the remaining drinks. After a few seconds of each man guzzling down their stein, he knew it was safe to speak.

"Haven't seen you guys around here before," he began. He had to be careful with his words, knowing full well how dangerous visitors to Talise could be.

"Just got in yesterday," replied Jardon, his mouth wet with foam. He used his stained sleeve to wipe his lips and then went for another swig.

"Oh yea? Where from?" Alistair asked.

"Off world," said one of the other men in a strong accent Alistair didn't recognize. The man, unlike his brethren, had pasty white eyes and dark, black skin under the auburn hood he wore while his braided, black hair funneled out through the sides. While the other three men were indeed frightening, this man scared the crap out of Alistair. He knew exactly what the man was, and he would have to proceed with extreme caution if he was to make it out of this situation alive.

"So, what brings you this close to Sanctuary?" Alistair pressed.

"We be lookin' fa' someone," the hooded man replied.

"So, you're bounty hunters?"

Jardon nearly choked on his beer, coughing it up on the table in front of him. Zeke and the man who had yet to say anything glanced at each other, fear rising in their eyes, while the hooded man slowly moved his hand to the knife at his hip.

"Easy boys, I'm not gonna turn you in or anything," Alistair said quickly, but he wasn't sure the strangers were convinced.

"What makes ya tink we be bounty huntas?" The hooded man asked, his hand glued to the weapon at his side.

"Well, for one, you've come a long ass way to a planet that, for years, had no signs of sustainable life," Alistair continued. If he was going to earn the visitors' trust, it was going to be now. "And I saw the bounty lying on the table when I came in."

Zeke quickly looked down at the piece of paper now tucked away in his cloak. Had the boy really seen that much in the quick second before he had pocketed it?

"You're a perceptive little one." The hooded man had his knife out now, and he pointed it towards Alistair and said, "Give me one reason not to cut ya tiny throat right now."

"Because I can take you to the Warden."

All hell broke loose. The hooded man jumped out of his seat while simultaneously throwing Alistair from his. He came down on top of the boy and rested his blade against Alistair's neck. The weapon was incredibly sharp and drew blood at the first touch. Zeke and the other man, who had remained silent the entire time, also rose to their feet and clambered over the fallen chairs to Alistair. Jardon, who had spent the past few minutes wiping beer off his pants, pulled a blaster pistol from his hip at lightning speed and pointed it at the bar where Bjorn stood, motionless and utterly terrified.

"I'm only gonna ask ya dis once, boy," the hooded man began, keeping the knife pressed against Alistair's neck. "Why do ya tink be huntin' a Warden?"

Alistair wasn't prepared for the chain of events that had followed since the declaration, but he knew he had to play this next move perfectly, or it would be his last.

"Because you're a Magister."

The hooded man seemed to think about the boy's response for a moment, before quickly twirling his knife back to the scabbard at his hip. "Impressive," the man replied. "Not many could tell just by lookin' at me, especially in dis dark a place."

"I wasn't sure at first, but I've read a lot about the Magisters and the betrayal of Artem. It only took a few seconds for me to realize it was true," Alistair said as he breathed a sigh of relief. He had just dodged a bullet, but more were sure to follow.

The Magisters, prior to the Massacre, were known amongst the races as the most holy and religious of beings. These dark-skinned men and women spent day after day in extended periods of prayer, under the belief that their words to the Makers were shaping the very foundations of the universe. Their leader, Artem the Omniscient, was even believed to be a Maker in human form, leading the Magisters down a path of righteousness. However, after the horrible events in Haven, the Magisters decided that the Makers no longer cared for their creations. They felt betrayed by Artem and slit his throat while he slept. Alone and without purpose, the remaining Magisters abandoned their holy mission. With their spirits shattered and their lives in ruin, the Magisters prepared to leave their sacred homes. Then, as if to answer their prayers, came Bravia.

Bravia was once a powerful Raven warrior, and an integral part to the onslaught at Haven. She had slain many Warden soldiers, but took a devastating blast of fire to the face. The flames charred her near-perfect skin and left her completely unrecognizable. She survived long enough to escape with the rest of her people, but found herself being forced into an escape pod. To the other Ravens, Bravia had outgrown her usefulness. The escape pod blasted through space and landed just outside the Magisters' home. The broken men and women saw this as a sign of providence and crowded the woman's pod. They opened the door and found Bravia's mangled body. Her power seeped from every crevice of her once-perfect skin, and the Magisters lapped it up like dogs, thanking the Makers for this second chance. Over time, the power of Bravia was passed from father to son and mother to daughter, and soon, the Magisters had regained their name in the universe, only now it was a name to be feared.

"And I can only assume that if you have a Magister with you, that you're hunting a being equal in strength and ability," Alistair said as he came to his feet.

"I have no equal," the Magister replied, his white eyes gleaming in the candle light.

"Let's get back to the topic at hand, shall we?" Zeke finally spoke up, his voice catching in his throat as he did. It was clear he was afraid to speak out against the Magister.

"Very well," spoke the Magister, but his attention remained on Alistair. "So, da Warden is here?"

"No, that's not how this is going to work," Alistair said slyly, his plan finally coming full circle. "First, you are going to let Bjorn over there go." He hadn't forgotten about Jardon's blaster still pointed at the bartender's face.

"Ali, what are-" Bjorn started.

"Just go, B. Forget everything you've seen here tonight."

Bjorn felt more betrayed than he ever had in his life. He had taken Alistair in when he shouldn't have and treated him, but the boy was throwing that hospitality back in his face. He took the money from the drawer at the counter and, without looking back, walked out of his own bar.

"Now, here's what's going to happen," Alistair continued cautiously, keeping an eye on the Magister's knife which had reappeared and was still dripping blood. "I'm going to tell you how to find the Warden, and you're going to take me with you once we have him."

The Magister reacted instantly, bringing his knife up once again, but the man who had been quiet the entire night interjected before another fight could break out.

"Put the knife away, Zed." And the Magister did. Alistair couldn't imagine who this man was to command a Magister in such a way. "You've impressed me, young one. That's not something that usually happens." The quiet man spoke again. He, too, had a strange accent, but one dissimilar from the Magister's. "You are a man who knows what he wants, and I respect that." His voice was full of energy that both intrigued and frightened Alistair, but things were finally starting to go his way. "If any of these morons had half the brains you do, I would have found the Grand Master ages ago."

The other three bounty hunters simultaneously looked at the ground, embarrassingly admitting their incompetence.

"I accept your conditions, and will gladly permit you to join us, should you deliver on your end of the bargain."

"Oh, don't worry. I know just where he'll be," Alistair responded, the excitement already rising in his voice. He knew the moment he had been waiting for was nearly within his grasp, and soon, Aurilean would rue the day he had ever betrayed his own flesh and blood.

Matthew Louwers

4

Aurilean could sense something was off. The night was dark, but it wasn't your typical darkness. An ominous, black mass of clouds blanketed the horizon, shielding it from any starlight. It was impossible to determine where the dark blades of grass met the skyline. The Brimwood, which was normally abuzz with its many nocturnal occupants, was silent, and the wind rushed by wildly as Aurilean flew. No, this darkness was dangerous. The old man needed to find Mathias as quickly as possible; he would deal with Alistair later.

Just a few miles outside of Brimsdale there rested a mysterious wooden structure that existed long before the construction of the village. It was the only building that seemed to have survived the eruption long ago, and most of the population still had no idea of its existence. Those that did chose to avoid it due to its haunting nature and its rather inaccessible location. It was for those reasons that Mathias oftentimes sought the building out whenever he wanted to be alone. Aurilean knew this.

The building, which resembled a small, rundown chapel, was nestled deep within the Brimwood, surrounded by gnarled vines, ancient, crumbling trees, and thick, brown mud that was always sloppy and wet. The white walls of the building were broken in some places, but the foundation was mostly still intact. The structure was complete with a rustic, golden bell that no longer chimed and a once magnificent stained-glass window that had since lost its luster. The window depicted an image of the Makers breathing life into the first Wardens and sending them out into universe. Aurilean had always admired the craftsmanship that must have gone into creating such a work of art, and he longed to meet the man or woman responsible.

Along with its unwelcoming facade, a mysterious presence seemed to surround the chapel as well, and Aurilean oftentimes wondered if Mathias could sense it. His adopted son had spent so much time there that he was sure the boy knew something about the chapel that he didn't, and that disturbed the old Warden greatly.

The crumbling bell tower slowly poked through the black canopy, and Aurilean began his descent. The air was always cooler here and, as Aurilean exhaled, his breath immediately crystallized. The wind continued to gust violently, and the wooden boards on the chapel's windows rattled angrily. A storm was coming, and Aurilean only hoped Mathias was ready for it.

The old man walked up the crumbling, stone steps to the archaic wooden door that stood slightly ajar and peaked his head inside. Mathias sat alone in an elegantly carved wooden pew a few rows in, hunched over with his face in his hands. There was nobody else in the room with him, but

Aurilean hadn't expected there to be. He slowly pushed open the ancient door which let out a bone-rattling creak as he entered the hall.

Mathias lifted his head abruptly and quickly wiped the tears from his face, before turning to see who had just entered his sanctuary. Aurilean was gliding down the center aisle, his black robe flowing gracefully behind him. He made no eye contact with his son and passed by him, continuing all the way up to the stone altar. He stopped for a moment, glancing slightly left and then slightly right, before turning and heading back towards the boy's location.

"I was just making sure we were alone," Aurilean said quietly, as if reading his son's mind. The old man groaned as he took a seat next to the boy.

"There's never anybody here," Mathias replied, still a bit choked up from crying. "They're all afraid of this place."

"They should be," Aurilean said as he pondered the multitude of mysteries surrounding the establishment.

"What ails you, my son?" Aurilean continued, placing his arm around the boy's shoulder.

"You already know the answer to that."

"I think there's a lot more to this than our disagreement from earlier."

"There's not," Mathias stated, but that wasn't true. There was quite a bit on his mind that night and very little of it revolved around the fight.

"Mathias, you are my son and I love you, but I have grown quite adept at realizing when you are being less than truthful with me," Aurilean said with a knowing smile.

"I never was a very good liar," Mathias said and then chuckled. The wind howled as it blew against the battered walls of the church and a light rain now tapped against the windows.

"Have I ever told you about the day you were born?" Aurilean asked. The mystery of Mathias's birth had always intrigued Aurilean, and it was something that he had never fully discussed with his son.

"Not much, just that I wasted no time coming into this world," Mathias said, wondering why his father would bring this up now.

"Indeed! Your mother was thrilled at how quickly and easily it happened." They both smiled and then Aurilean continued. "What I mean to ask is, do you know *where* you were born?"

Mathias shook his head. "Never really thought about it."

"You were born right here in this monastery," Aurilean revealed.

"Really?"

"Really. It happened just up there, at the foot of the altar." Aurilean extended a bony finger towards the back of the church and then looked back at his son.

"Why here? Why not at the care house?" Mathias asked, his full attention now on Aurilean.

"The night of your birth, the skies were so clear that you could look out into space and see millions of stars in every direction. I'd been tending to a few tedious tasks that night when I noticed a great ball of light appear in the sky." Aurilean spoke faster now, and Mathias just stared at his father in amazement. "The ball grew larger, and I realized it had no intention of slowing its descent. I ushered the villagers to safety and then headed off in the direction of the incoming projectile. I wasn't sure what I was going to find so I prepared for the worst. As the mysterious object came even closer, I noticed a silver, egg-shaped object amidst the bright

yellow flames. I quickly estimated its trajectory and
discerned that it would land somewhere around here."

Mathias frantically scanned the building for any sign
of an impact, but he saw nothing.

"I see you notice our predicament. The object crashed
directly into this building, but instead of breaking through the
ceiling like it should have, it simply passed right through it
and landed gently at the base of the altar."

Mathias was completely blown away. He had always
felt something mysterious about the chapel, but he never
suspected that it had anything to do with him.

"When I arrived, I found that the egg-like object,
which ended up being an old escape pod, had opened up to
reveal a very pregnant young woman. I rushed to her side and
prepared to take her to the care house, but she immediately
went into labor. She used to say that you refused to come out
until I arrived, almost like you had been waiting for me."

Mathias smiled. From the stories Aurilean used to tell
him, his mother had been a beautiful and kind-hearted
woman until the very end. The sickness that eventually took
her was still unknown to the Warden, and it pained Aurilean
every day that he was unable to save her.

"Like I've always said, you popped out of there like a
torpedo, kicking and screaming and ready for anything this
world could throw at you."

Mathias finally began to understand the point of the
story.

"Father, I-" But he was instantly silenced as Aurilean
thrust a hand over his mouth. Something wasn't right. The
rain slammed like bullets against the windows, and the wind
seemed like it was going to rip the walls right off. Aurilean
stared out the front door, which was now banging
rhythmically against the side of the building, into the black

abyss of the storm. He removed his hand from boy's mouth and then firmly gripped his shoulder.

"I need you to listen to me very carefully and do exactly as I say," Aurilean began, his voice shaky and quickening. This wasn't the same man he had been only moments ago. Mathias had never seen his father behave like this before. "Everything is about to change, and I need you to do everything in your power to accept it."

Mathias didn't like this. The sudden change in Aurilean's demeanor sent chills up the young man's spine.

"What are you-"

"Quiet! No more talking! You are a brilliant young man, Mathias. I know that you will go on to do great things and become the man that I could never be." A solitary tear escaped down the old man's cheek. It was the only time Mathias had ever seen his father cry. "You are the son I always hoped you would be, Mathias, and I will always love you." And with that Mathias felt an odd tingling sensation flowing throughout his body. He looked down at his hands, only to find that he had no hands. He could certainly feel them, but he couldn't see anything where a hand should have been. In fact, he couldn't see any of his body. He was completely invisible. "No matter what you see or hear, stay completely still and don't make a sound," Aurilean whispered dangerously.

A bolt of lightning flashed against the darkness, sending luminous rays of light bouncing off the masterfully crafted glass window. The explosion of color was truly breathtaking but, while Mathias was distracted by the window, Aurilean watched as the flash lit up the four silhouettes in the doorway.

"Good evening, gentleman." Aurilean said, his voice shifting from the caring tone of a father to the powerful, authoritative voice of a man not to be trifled with. Mathias wanted to see who Aurilean was talking to, but he remembered he wasn't supposed to move and kept his head straight. "What brings you out here in this weather?"

"We be lookin' fo' someone, mon," said one of the men. He was short of breath and spoke with an accent Mathias had never heard before. "Perhaps ya can help us find him." Sloshy footsteps echoed throughout the great entryway, and the four men slid into the church, each taking a different aisle and strategically surrounding the Warden.

"I will certainly aid you as best I can," Aurilean sneered, already knowing that *he* was the man these intruders were looking for.

"Smart man," said a different voice in a husky growl.

"I have a bounty here for a man of great power and nobility. Tall, lean, and bald, but keeps a well-groomed goatee. Surely there is somebody on this god forsaken rock that matches that description?" A third voice spoke, as if reading off a sheet of paper. Mathias was terrified. These men were obviously after Aurilean.

"It would seem you have found your mark," Aurilean stated as he pulled the black cloak from his back. "You gentlemen should know that you are severely outnumbered."

"Guess again, Warden. Don't reckon ya ever fought against the Magi before," said the first man. Mathias cringed. Magisters were known to travel amongst groups of bounty hunters. They were ruthless beings and would stop at nothing to achieve their goals.

"You would be wrong in that assumption, my friend," Aurilean replied coolly. The Magisters were formidable adversaries but nothing he couldn't handle.

"If you come quietly, we may let you live out the rest of your days as a broken, mindless husk of your former self."

The fourth man finally spoke. He, too, had an accent, but it was different from the first man's. The way he spoke gave Mathias chills. "Assuming the commander allows it, of course."

"I shall give you this one chance. Leave now and nobody dies," Aurilean said dangerously. Mathias could feel the power emanating from his father. It engulfed the pair and was warm as it compressed itself around them

The four men cackled in unison, clearly underestimating the old man.

"Not gonna happen, mon," said the first man. Mathias heard a blade escape from its scabbard and knew things were about to take a turn for the worse.

"Then you leave me no choice." Aurilean sighed sadly and instantly summoned a white-hot streak of lightning from the surrounding storm. The bolt burst through the shining window of the chapel, immediately shattering the great work of art. Shards of colorful glass rained down around them as Aurilean channeled the bolt's energy into himself and then redirected it at the nearest attacker. It caught the gruff man square in the chest and sent him flying through the wall, killing him instantly. The other three attacked without hesitation. The Magister pulled out his knife, a weapon Aurilean knew was just as frightening as the magic the man possessed, and charged across the room. The other two men reached for their weapons, one wielding a crossbow while the other fired two smaller blaster pistols. Aurilean had not been prepared for the sudden counterattack and was knocked off balance by the Magister's powerful charge.

As arrows and hot bursts of blaster fire whizzed by him, Mathias did his best to remain completely still per his father's instruction, but things weren't looking good for Aurilean. If Mathias didn't do something, the visitors would certainly overpower the old man. He began to devise a plan. The men couldn't see him, and they had no idea he was even there to begin with. Mathias decided he would try to flank the men in the back and take each one out so Aurilean could deal with the Magister.

Mathias prepared to move when the strange tingling sensation returned. He glanced down at his hands but they were still invisible. He was wrought with confusion as the world suddenly shifted around him. The dark walls of the church vanished and Mathias was suddenly surrounded by the large oak trees just outside. A drop of water splashed onto his head and he realized that he had been teleported out of the chapel. Aurilean must have sensed the boy's plan and transported him to safety instead.

Mathias went to wipe the rain dripping into his eyes and realized he was also no longer invisible. He had to get back inside and help his father but, as soon as the thought entered his mind, a massive explosion lit up the sky and sent Mathias flying through the air. The church had become a raging inferno of fire and ash. Mathias wasn't sure if his father or the Magister had conjured the blast, but it certainly didn't bode well for either them.

Run, my son! Find the others. Mathias jumped, startled at the sudden voice in his head. Aurilean was still alive! Mathias needed to get back inside.

NO! RUN! Mathias jumped again. The voice was louder this time and more demanding. He had to help his father, but he wasn't going to disobey a direct order from him. With one final glance at the pyre raging behind him, Mathias sprinted into the trees.

Matthew Louwers

5

Alistair jumped from the decaying tree stump he was sitting on as the chapel exploded behind him. His instructions had been to wait just inside the Brimwood while the hunters conducted their business. However, a detonation of that magnitude was not a good sign for his newfound friends.

He quickly scanned the small encampment for supplies, finding a large crossbow, complete with a quiver of barbed arrows, leaning against a nearby tree. It was one of Zeke's bows, left behind for Alistair's protection.

The boy strapped the small quiver of arrows to his hip and prepared to make his way to the burning building when a scream echoed through the storm raging around him. It was a deep voice and one that Alistair was all too familiar with. Deciding against aiding the bounty hunters, Alistair bolted into the jungle.

*   *   *

The excruciating pain that coursed through Mathias's back was unlike anything the young man had ever felt before. It was as if his skin had been ripped clean off and was then prodded with a scorching hot branding iron.

Mathias had been running through the Brimwood as his father had instructed when the sensation suddenly came over him. It wasn't nearly as bad at first, just uncomfortable enough that it slowed him down a bit. Then the burning intensified and Mathias was forced to halt his escape. He screamed as the pain seared through his body.

The boy knelt on the forest floor, his head hung low and his hands at his sides as the pain finally subsided. Steam rose from his back and an eerie sizzling sound sent chills up his spine. He hadn't been burned at the chapel, so why did it feel like his whole body was on fire?

Very carefully, Mathias reached one of his hands around to his back. At first, he felt nothing, no wound or burn mark, no sign to indicate why he had just endured so much pain. However, as he moved his hand towards his neck, he found a raised mound of skin that certainly had never been there before. Strangely, it didn't hurt as he rubbed his fingers over it. He then noticed it was more than just a tiny bump. The raised skin continued to snake along his upper back and slightly onto his right shoulder. Mathis was very confused. He had never carried such a mark before, but then everything clicked into place. It was a Warden's brand.

Every Warden carried a brand. Each brand was different and signified the type of Warden that man or woman was. For example, a Flame Warden would always have two brands, one on each hand that slowly twisted up around the forearm in a fluid design that, naturally, resembled a rising flame. Mathias had spent a great deal of time studying Warden brands, but the brand he felt on himself was never mentioned in any book.

His thoughts were abruptly interrupted as a twig snapped just behind him. He prepared to turn when he heard a sudden twang of a bowstring. A new pain exploded in his back as an arrow pierced his flesh. Mathias roared again, trying to turn to face his attacker. Another snap and a second arrow found its mark slightly higher than the previous shot. Mathias fell to the ground, two arrows deep in his back and an odd cooling sensation suddenly rushing throughout his body.

Poison! Mathias thought, knowing he was suddenly in very deep trouble.

The attacker slowly circled his prey and knelt to examine his work. He pulled Mathias back to his knees and stared him straight in the eyes. It was Alistair.

"Hello, *brother.*" The venom in Alistair's words stung more than the poison coursing through Mathias's veins.

"Ali," Mathias said softly. "What are you doing?"

"Something I should have done a long time ago." Alistair sneered, the half-smile on his face sending a wave of fear through Mathias.

"It was you. You led the bounty hunters here!"

"Of course it was me." Alistair laughed as he paced in front of his brother, swinging his loaded crossbow at his side. "I told him he would regret betraying me, and now he's dead."

"No..." Mathias whispered. But with the explosion at the church and now the brand showing up on his back, he knew Alistair was telling the truth.

"It's just too bad I couldn't have been there to see the look on his face when-"

"You son of a bitch!" Mathias roared as he tried to stand, but Alistair raised the crossbow and pointed it directly at his face.

"Ah, ah. You stay right where you are. I'm under strict orders to take you in alive, but I could always say that you tried to escape." Alistair smiled. Everything was finally going his way.

"Alistair... Don't do this!" Mathias yelled. "You got your revenge on your father. Is that not enough? Must you destroy everyone that's ever cared for you?"

Alistair glared at his brother, the hate slowly diminishing within him. Mathias was right. The man who had betrayed him was gone.

"Please, brother. End this now, and let me go," Mathias pleaded. The pain in his back was subsiding, but he knew it was because his body was growing numb from the poison, and he wouldn't be able to make it very far if he stayed there much longer.

"I'm sorry, Mathias," Alistair said as he prepared to fire the crossbow one final time. Mathias closed his eyes and flinched as the familiar twang of the bow signaled an arrow in flight. He waited for the pain, but it never came. Instead, the arrow whizzed by Mathias's head and stuck into a tree behind him. Confused, he looked to his brother who had shed a single, solitary tear. "You always were there for me. You even stood up to Father for me tonight, even after everything I said to you." Alistair wiped the tear away and put his crossbow on the ground.

"Ali, I-"

"Let me finish," Alistair interrupted. "I'm only giving you a head start. When the hunters return, and they will return, I'll tell them that I wounded you and that you won't make it very far on your own." Loud voices echoed from the direction of the church. The hunters would be on them soon. "You did save my life the day you took everything from me, so consider this debt repaid in full," Alistair said. "Go."

"Thank you, brother," Mathias replied as he slowly wobbled to his feet.

"Don't thank me," Alistair replied, the anger returning to his voice. "If I ever see you again, I will not hesitate to put an arrow through your heart." And with that, Alistair pushed past his brother and walked back into the forest, pulling the arrow from the tree as he went.

Mathias stood motionless for a second, not sure if the poison was having any major lasting effects on him. Then, after a few seconds of testing out his legs, he darted off into the woods, the two arrows still jutting out of his back.

After only a couple minutes of running, his legs burning as his muscles tightened and his face and clothes dripping with rain water, a yell rang out from the darkness behind him. Alistair must have just told the hunters about him, and they would surely be on him soon if he didn't find his way out of the jungle. The only problem was that he had no idea where he was, and it was too dark to find a solid vantage point. So, Mathias did all he could do and kept running. Blood slowly dripped down his back, both arrows digging deeper with each stride.

Mathias crashed through the trees, fallen twigs breaking underfoot with each step. He twisted and turned, avoiding the thick, low branches that jutted out into the path until he rounded a corner and slid to a sudden stop. He was back at The Edge.

"No..." He muttered under his breath. "This can't be happening."

The voices were louder now. The hunters had picked up his trail and would be on him in a matter of minutes, and

Mathias had nowhere left to run. He couldn't even access the trap door since no one was there to control it from below. He frantically searched for any other means of escape, but there was nothing. His freedom was going to be very short lived.

A familiar, blood curdling roar suddenly reverberated through the forest, stirring the birds from their slumber. The brinwolf that wasn't a brinwolf had returned. Mathias wasn't sure what to do as the hunters screamed in the distance.

"Bring it down!" He heard one of the men yell.

"It's too fast!"

Blaster fire erupted and Mathias had to duck in cover as stray shots whizzed by him. The battle was taking place close enough that trying to run would only endanger him further. Another roar pierced the night and the blaster fire stopped.

"Leave him! Concentrate on the monster!"

Mathias could hear the whoosh of arrows as they soared through the air. The beast roared again, this time in pain. It burst forth from the tops of the trees and began flying straight towards him. With nowhere to run, the boy watched in stunned terror as the beast dropped abruptly in front of him. It was the same creature he had helped earlier, as the crude splint still covered her leg.

"Forget about it! Find the boy!" Roared one of the men. They were close now, and Mathias needed to find a way off the cliff and fast, while still avoiding being torn to shreds by the creature in front of him.

Get on. The sudden voice in his head took Mathias completely by surprise. *If you want to live, get on!* The voice returned more demanding this time, and the creature knelt before him. Mathias was sure that the poison had finally taken over, and he was going insane.

Branches snapped as three men jumped out of the trees and onto the barren entrance of The Edge.

"Der you are," said the Magister. He was covered in blood and held his glowing blade tightly in his fist. The other man had his bow pointed at Mathias. Alistair was there as well, with his crossbow aimed at the beast instead.

"Kill da monsta. I'll handle da boy!" The Magister instructed angrily.

Without warning, the beast whipped its large tail around, pushed Mathias off the edge of the cliff, and then leapt up into the sky. Mathias honestly hadn't thought that, out of all possible outcomes, this was how he was going to die. As he fell, he saw the outline of the creature soaring down the mountainside towards him, her wings flapping vigorously. With fantastic grace, the creature swooped under him. Instead of colliding with the cold ground, Mathias landed softly on the fuzzy back of the beast.

Hold on, the creature said. Mathias no longer questioned the voice in his head. He grabbed at the creature's fur as she spun out of the chasm and took off into the skies.

"Shoot it! Shoot it, dammit!" The Magister yelled, but the creature was already too far out of range for the bounty hunters and still gaining speed. The creature made a sudden, sharp drop as a giant ball of purple fire blazed by just above them. The Magister was not going to make their escape easy. Two more blasts of dark purple flames chased after them, but the creature dodged them as well. Mathias could hear the Magister swearing as his attacks failed to find a mark.

"Get back to da ship!" The Magister yelled, and then stormed off back into the jungle. Mathias looked back and saw Alistair still staring at him. Even through the massive distance now between them, the boys' eyes connected for a moment, and then Alistair turned to follow the hunters back into the trees.

He still cares for you. Mathias jumped causing him to nearly lose his grip as the voice rattled around in his head.

"How are you doing that?" He asked, finally accepting that this creature was somehow able to speak to him.

Doing what?

"Talking to me in my head, of course."

I can communicate with the Wardens, and you *are a Warden.* Even though he had felt the brand appear on him earlier, hearing the creature confirm that Mathias was a Warden still surprised him.

The forest below rushed past as the creature soared through the night sky. The rain had subsided and the dark clouds had begun to dissolve back into nothing. Mathias had never seen the world from this vantage before, and it was exhilarating. The trees looked so small, and far off in the distance he could see his home. Unfortunately, the creature was flying away from the town.

Mathias poked the creature and pointed back at the horizon. "Uh, the village is back that way."

We are not going to your home.

"Then where are you taking me?"

To mine.

"You're not going to eat me, are you?" He asked, half-jokingly and half completely serious.

No. The monster made its strange laughing sound again and turned its head back to him. *There are others who wish to see you. They have instructed me to bring you to them.*

Others. Aurilean had mentioned others, but Mathias had no idea what that meant. However, it seemed that he was about to find out.

The two flew for a while before the ground began to change beneath them. The emerald forest ended abruptly, and the pair crossed over into the Broken Lands, the dead expanse that stretched far off into the distance. No trees or other signs of life grew in the barren wasteland devastated by the ancient volcano. The once rushing rivers and shimmering lakes were little more than dried out ravines and craters, and the bones of the those not lucky enough to escape the eruption still littered the area.

"You live here?" Mathias asked, not believing it was possible for any creature to live in such a place.

Not here. There. She nodded her head at the dormant peak in distance, and the boy's jaw dropped. Never had he heard of a creature that could live in a volcano.

A sudden sharp pain in his back interrupted his thoughts and he cried out. He had completely forgotten about the arrows, the adrenaline having overpowered the pain. Unfortunately, that feeling was gone now and the raw throbbing of the two projectiles in his back had returned.

The ashwolf, sensing her passenger's suffering, flapped her wings as hard she could, gaining even more speed. Her home was not far off now, the mountain rapidly growing larger as they made their approach. She spiraled into a dive and pulled up about halfway down the mountainside. There was a small opening in the rock, just large enough for the creature to fit into. It landed on the ledge with what grace it could muster and then slowly helped the boy down.

Mathias found he could barely stand as he slid from the creature's back. He immediately collapsed in the dirt as his feet hit the ground, a cloud of dust billowing up around him. As the dirt settled, he realized his vision was growing blurry, and his head was starting to spin.

Do not fall asleep, the creature said to him and then bounded into the cave, leaving the boy alone in the darkness.

Mathias tried to get a feel for the landscape around him to keep his mind occupied and off the growing pain coursing throughout his body. The volcano was truly massive, towering over everything in the area. Around the base of the mountain were several branching rivers of lava that had hardened over the years. Their flowing, black formations were quite interesting, and Mathias wished he could examine them further.

A light pierced the mouth of the cave and, through his blurred vision, Mathias could just make out a tall, slender figure running towards him. Then a second figure appeared, nearly three times the size of the first. Both strangers wielded torches as they sprinted out of the cave's mouth. The creature was not with them.

"Thank the Makers he's still awake," said the first of the two, a young woman by the sound of it, her voice soothing, but stern, as if she was accustomed to giving commands. Mathias could see her long, auburn-red hair tied in a braid that hung next to her face as she knelt over him.

"Good! More fun for me," replied the second voice in an odd twang that amused Mathias greatly. The huge man knelt beside the woman, his muscles bulging from nearly every part of his body. The man wore only a tattered pair of beige pants and nothing else, but Mathias didn't think this man needed any armor to protect himself.

"Who..." Mathias began but found he didn't have the strength to continue his inquiry.

"Try not to speak." The woman's voice was enchanting, and Mathias found himself doing what she asked without question. "Joel, turn him around."

"On it," replied the large man as he helped Mathias turn his back to them. The damage from the arrows was worsening as the woman wiped the lines of blood from the boy's back.

"Listen to me, Mathias." The woman spoke loudly and enunciated with severe precision. Mathias had no idea how she knew his name, but he liked how it sounded as it rolled off her tongue. "The arrows in your back were laced with a powerful inhibiting toxin that, were your powers more developed, would have crippled you instantly."

Powers? What was she talking about?

"Luckily, the poison hasn't completed its work, which gives us the time we need to cleanse you of it. But to do that, we have to remove the arrows." Mathias suspected there was something she wasn't telling him, but he didn't want to interrupt her. "Hunters use a very specific style of arrow when they want to poison their victim. The tip itself is barbed so that it is nearly impossible to remove, allowing a full dose of the poison to make its way through your system. The shaft of the arrow is also barbed to make pulling it out a difficult process as well."

Mathias was barely listening. Sounds were becoming jumbled, and he could no longer discern any clear shapes or colors. Falling asleep sounded quite wonderful at that moment.

"Mira, kid doesn't even know what you're sayin' anymore. Let's just get it done," the man named Joel said to his counterpart. Mira looked back at him, and then to Mathias. He'd begun to drool, and his eyes were struggling to remain open.

"Fine," she said. "This is going to hurt. On the count of three-"

"THREE!" Joel yelled as he ripped the two barbed projectiles from Mathias's back. Chunks of skin flew off as Joel tossed the arrows out into the ravine below them.

"What the hell was that?" Mira yelled at Joel.

"I find the anticipation far worse than the actual act itself," Joel replied with a goofy grin on his face.

"I hate you." Mira shook her head is annoyance.

Throughout the whole process, Mathias had just sat there quietly. He had noticed the sudden tug at something in his back but felt no pain. The poison had completely inhibited his ability to feel anything. He barely noticed the muffled voices arguing around him and wondered what was going to happen next.

"Well that just ain't true. Why, you'd be lost without me." Joel chuckled as Mira continued to shake her head.

"Let's just get the poison out," she said as she pulled a small knife from her hip. The blade itself was very short and the hilt had a built-in tube that contained a dark red liquid. Without warning, Mira thrust the blade deep into the boy's back. The red liquid rushed out of the knife and into his body.

Mathias was suddenly aware of everything around him. The cloud in his mind was gone, and he could feel his arms and legs again. He also felt a searing fluid rushing throughout his body. His muscles spasmed as the red liquid twisted and turned through his veins, forcing the poison out through his pores. It reached his toes and then snaked back around and headed straight for his face. As soon as it did, Mathias vomited. The red liquid, along with other bits of who-knows-what, went flying from his mouth and out into the canyon. He was finally himself again. He could see clearly for miles out into the forgotten wasteland and could smell the burning wood of the torches the two had left unattended.

The others! Mathias had completely forgotten about them. He tested out his legs and found they worked perfectly. He jumped to his feet and wiped the green residue left by the poison from his arms and legs, then he turned to face his rescuers.

The two stood facing him, both with unimpressed looks on their faces. The woman was devastatingly beautiful under her simple, black robe. The man, on the other hand, had muscles on top of other muscles, along with a nasty scar down the right side of his face. The two looked like they had seen their fair shares of battle.

"Welcome back," said the woman as she gracefully stepped towards him. The way she moved enchanted Mathias and he found he was at a loss for words. She smiled at him, held out her hand and said, "I'm Mira, Warden of Fury."

"Mathias," he replied, taking Mira's hand in his. Her grip was firm, but her skin was tantalizingly smooth. He gazed into her dark, brown eyes and instantly lost himself. He had never met someone so beautiful and dangerous at the same time.

From a few feet away, the burly pile of a man coughed, clearing the phlegm and drawing the attention to himself.

"And this is Joel, Warden of Strength," Mira said, pulling her hand away and gesturing towards her counterpart. Mathias didn't want to take his eyes from Mira, but as she turned away from him he was forced to.

"Pleasure," Joel replied. Mathias didn't think it was possible for a man to be so large as Joel stood there towering over him. He took Joel's hand in his and winced as he immediately found it crushed between the man's massive fingers. Mathias also noticed the block-like brands on both of Joel's arms.

"It's great to meet both of you," the boy began. He had never met any other Wardens before. "But we need to get out of here. The hunters will find us soon."

"I couldn't agree more," replied Mira.

"Let them come!" Joel yelled, startling Mathias as his loud voice echoed across the mountainside. "I'll take 'em all on!"

"They have a Magister with them," Mathias said, his voice growing more serious. "He's the one... the one who killed my father." The two Wardens looked at each other and then back at Mathias. That's when they noticed the speck of light rapidly growing in the distance behind him. The bounty hunters had found them.

"We're leaving," Mira said. No one questioned her. Joel rushed over to Mathias and put his abnormally large hand on the boy's shoulder.

"Hold on, kid. This is gonna feel weird," Joel snickered as a bright white beam of light shot down out of the sky around them. Mathias watched as Mira suddenly disappeared in front of him. He tried to move but Joel had a firm grasp on him. Mathias wasn't going anywhere. He looked down at his hands as the odd sensation overtook him. Bits and pieces of his fingers suddenly disappeared, and Mathias could no longer feel them. Then his whole hand was gone. Finally, without warning, the rest of his body vanished and the white light disappeared, leaving the mountain and the barren wasteland around it in the quenching darkness it was accustomed to.

6

Ardemis swiveled around in his chair as he waited for
word from the others. Mira and Joel had left to retrieve the
Grand Master some time ago, and Ardemis was starting to
worry. He stared out into the black abyss in front of him,
stars twinkling in every direction. Talise was currently
situated between him and the planet's sun, so there was little
light to obstruct his view.

Ardemis sat at the helm of the Longshot, one of the
last Warden starships left in the galaxy. The Longshot was a
smaller vessel when you compared it to something like a
Raven battle cruiser, but it did its job well and could outrun
any of those clunky cruisers any day of the week. At least
that's what Ardemis liked to tell himself. The outside of the
ship had been painted matte black, as all Warden starships
were, to prevent the reflection of light in a battle. Many of
these ships would often remain undetected in a skirmish until
it was too late. The curved triangular wings of the ship were
currently in their relaxed state, folded tightly against the hull,

but, when the time came, they would stretch to nearly equal the ship's length on either side. Three large pulse boosters adorned the back of the ship, while the cockpit, and Ardemis's current location, sat front and center. It was a rather common design, but one that achieved its purpose.

Ardemis gazed out through the glass windshield at the old world rotating slowly in front of him. He had stalled the ship just outside of Talise's gravitational field, but he was still able to keep track of Joel and Mira's location. Per Mira's last report, there had been a great explosion that she feared had involved the Grand Master and his son, Mathias. They had sent the ashwolf to retrieve the two, and that was the last thing Ardemis had heard.

Now the Sky Warden sat alone in his ship, waiting and watching.

We need to get out of here, now! Mira's voice rang loudly in Ardemis's head, causing him to jump a few inches off his fluffy red chair.

What happened? Ardemis replied hoping nothing had gone wrong.

No time. Get us out.

Without hesitation, Ardemis pressed the small blue button on the dash in front of him. He could hear the whirring of the teleportation system as it kicked into gear and acquired a lock on his companions, a process that required sever calculation and timing.

Something bad had happened, Ardemis could sense it. He quickly powered up the Longshot's primary systems and prepared to make a speedy exit.

A loud thump from the rear of the ship told him that one of his companions had arrived, followed quickly by two more thumps. Ardemis waited for the fourth but it never came. He rose out of his chair to investigate but Mira suddenly rounded a corner and almost slammed into him.

"Mira, what-" Ardemis started but was quickly interrupted.

"Hunters. They'll be on us soon."

"The Makers help us," Ardemis prayed under his breath.

"The Makers aren't going to fly this ship, Ardy!"

"Right. To Sanctuary, then?" Ardemis asked, snapping out of his daze and returning to his chair.

"Yes. Let's move."

"Alright, lassie. Setting course for Sanctuary. You may want to tell them to hold on," Ardemis said, rhythmically pressing away at the flashing buttons in front of him. He plotted the course in his chart and prepared to leave.

Mira dashed out of the cockpit and headed for Joel and Mathias. The two had recovered from the journey and had found passenger seats just outside the helm. Both were already strapped in and Mira took an empty seat across from Mathias.

"Let's go!" She yelled to Ardemis.

"Thrusters at full. We're out of here!" Ardemis yelled as the ship took off into space. The force of the launch thrust everyone back into their seats. Mathias had never flown before, so the sensation took him completely by surprise. He let out a gasp as he tried to catch the air escaping from his lungs.

"Stabilizing!" Ardemis's voice rang out over the intercom. Mathias's breath suddenly returned to him, and the force pressing him deep into his chair receded.

"That wasn't so bad, eh?" Joel said to Mathias with a smirk plastered to his face.

"Speak for yourself," Mathias replied. That was something he didn't want to experience again anytime soon.

The cabin they all sat in was not very large, with six black cloth passenger seats separated by a small table and a large, locked storage chest on the opposite side of the room. Behind him was the room where his body had been strangely reassembled from when he had disappeared off the planet's surface. In front of him was a small entryway leading to what must have been the cockpit. A small man suddenly appeared in the hallway and walked towards the group. The man was much shorter than Mathias or the other Wardens. His long blonde hair was tied in a ponytail behind his head, and he had a small limp in his right leg as he walked.

"What are you doing?" Mira asked sharply.

"Put her on autopilot," the man replied, then he turned to Mathias. "How ya doin', lad?"

"I've been better." Mathias was still unable to come to grips with the fact the Aurilean was gone and that he was now aboard a spacecraft with actual Wardens.

"Sorry ta hear that," the little man said, then held out his hand. "Name's Ardemis, but you can call me Ardy."

"Nice to meet you, Ardy." Mathias took the man's hand in his and gave it a good shake. "You're a Warden too?"

"Sure am. You're lookin' at one of the last Sky Wardens around." Ardemis sported a huge smile as he introduced himself.

"A Sky Warden!" Mathias said excitedly. He had always loved hearing the stories of the Sky Wardens when he was young, but he never imagined that he would ever meet one. The Sky Wardens were believed to have been completely wiped out during the Massacre, along with many other classes of Warden. Mathias had always thought that the ability to fly was the most exciting Warden ability, and he was ecstatic to finally meet one of these legendary pilots.

"You're grinnin' like an idiot," Joel said stupidly.

"Sorry," Mathias said, quickly regaining his composure. "I just thought the Sky Wardens were extinct."

"And it's best everyone keeps on thinkin' that," Ardemis replied, taking the seat across from Joel. "So, you must be Mathias."

"That's right," Mathias replied, realizing that he had completely forgotten to introduce himself.

"So, what happened down there? Where's the Master?" Ardemis asked. Mathias immediately lowered his head and stared sadly at the ground. Mira and Joel shared a quick, uneasy glance and then began to explain the situation. After a brief recount of the events, Ardemis got out of his chair and walked over to Mathias.

Ardemis rested a hand on the boy's arm. "I'm so sorry, laddie."

"Me too," Mathias replied, his eyes fixed on a splotch of mud on the floor.

"Well, boosters should get us to Sanctuary soon." Ardemis said awkwardly and then headed back for the cockpit.

"Sanctuary?" Mathias asked, bringing his gaze back to the Wardens. "We're flying into the black hole?"

"Not quite," replied Mira. "The 'black hole' is actually just an illusion created by the first Grand Master as protection for what lies inside. Sanctuary is a planet, complete with its own sun, hidden deep within the void. Only those that know of the planet's existence dare traverse the illusion."

Mathias didn't know what to think. Everything was happening so fast.

"I never wanted this..." Mathias said, his eyes returning to the floor. He thought about the last things his father had said to him, that Mathias would be the man that he could never be. But now Aurilean was gone and, even if Mathias didn't want it, he had no choice but to accept his father's mantle.

"That may be so, but you have a responsibility now, not only to yourself, but to us as well." Mira's tone was sympathetic, but also stern.

"It's not all bad, kid. You could have worse company!" Joel said pointing at himself with a stupid grin on his face.

"Look, I'm sure all of you couldn't wait to become Wardens. You probably spent your entire childhood training for it. But this was never the life I wanted!" Mathias spoke loudly, his voice rising in anger. He never should have saved Alistair that day. Mira glared at him and then firmly stood up out of her chair and turned her back to him, heading straight for the cockpit. "What did I say?" Mathias asked, turning to Joel.

"There ain't a single person on this ship that *wanted* to be here," Joel replied, his eyes locked on Mathias. "We've all been through hell and back to get to where we are today. But don't, for one second, think that we chose this life 'cus it sounded like somethin' fun to do."

"I'm sorry." Mathias was shocked. He had always believed that young people chose to become Wardens.

"Don't have to apologize to me," Joel said as he shrugged his shoulders and then gestured toward Mira.

"What happened to her?"

"Ain't my story to tell," Joel replied shortly.

Mira shifted in the doorway, her back still facing the boys. Mathias had no idea what could have happened to her that was so bad, but he figured it wasn't an issue he wanted to press at the time.

"Entering Sanctuary's atmosphere. Prepare for departure." Ardemis's voice echoed throughout the chamber. The ship barely shook as it broke through the atmosphere, an added perk of its stabilization systems.

Mira turned around and headed straight for Mathias.

"I'm sorry. I shouldn't have assumed anything about any of you," Mathias apologized, standing up as she approached him.

"No, you shouldn't have, but I'll forgive you this time." She smiled at him, a smile that sent a mix of strange feelings rushing throughout his body. "Listen to me, Mathias. I know things are changing for you and it's going to be hard, but you need to put everything you've ever known behind you. You're going to learn that everything you know is wrong. Life on Talise was a beautiful lie. Out here, everything is dangerously different. Just be ready for that." Mira explained this all to him as the ship made its descent into Sanctuary. Snow covered mountaintops passed by, and a bright sun was shining in the blue sky. Not too far below he caught his first glimpse of the planet's surface. A rushing waterfall raged in the distance, and a set of strange white buildings arose on the horizon.

"When we land, there's a ritual that must be performed," Mira said as she commanded his attention once again. "All new Wardens that we have recovered over the years go through the same ritual, and now you must do the same." Mathias was shaking anxiously, unsure of what to think. "It's quite simple. The moment your foot hits the ground, you will not speak. You will walk directly behind me, and Joel and Ardemis will be behind you on either side. You will look straight ahead and your gaze will not wander to the world around you. You will show no emotion whatsoever and make no contact with anyone that tries to speak with you." Mathias must have looked terrified, because Mira put a gentle hand on his shoulder and added, "Relax. Everything will be fine as long as you do as I say. This ritual is meant to free your mind. We'll walk through the gardens until we reach the temple at the end of the road. Once there, you will remain silent until our mentor speaks to you. Nobody knows his true name, so we just stick to calling him Monk. He'll ask you two questions, the nature of which I cannot say as the questions are always different. Only then will you be permitted to speak."

Mathias breathed slowly as he took in all the information Mira was spewing at him. Whoever this Monk was, he sounded incredibly important, and Mathias didn't want to say anything that might upset him. But what kind of questions would he ask?

The Longshot came to an abrupt stop as it made contact with the ground. Mathias firmly kept his feet and then followed behind Mira to the loading bay, a large open room just beyond the teleportation pads. Joel was already there waiting for them.

"No pressure, kid," Joel said slapping the boy on the back. "Just don't screw it up."

Everyone glared annoyedly at the hulking behemoth of a man.

"Ignore him, lad. Just be yourself," Ardemis said as he waddled into the room. Then he walked over to a large red button on the wall and pressed it. The loading ramp creaked as it made its way toward the soft ground beneath it. The fresh air washed over all of them like a tidal wave, and the brightness of the day forced Mathias to shield his eyes.

"Remember what I told you. Free your mind," Mira said as she turned to Mathias. He nodded at her and she smiled, which sent his heart racing once again. How was he supposed to keep a clear head with someone like her walking in front of him? "Alright, let's go," she said and then, with Mathias and the others in tow, began her descent down the ramp.

Matthew Louwers

7

Vibrant rays of yellow sunshine struck the four Wardens as they exited the spacecraft. Not a single cloud tainted the bright, sapphire sky, and the brilliant beams of sunlight reflected off nearly every surface. The towering, emerald trees of the local forests rustled in the light breeze, and a river flowed vigorously, its rushing crystal waters providing a steady stream of background noise to the harmonious chirps and squeaks of the local wildlife.

The moment Mathias's foot hit solid ground, he was unable to contain his wonder. The sky was a perfect shade of blue, vibrant and absolute against the lush green foreground. Flowers and bushes of all different colors littered the gardens around them, and a wide cobblestone path stretched far into the distance. Mathias was in complete awe at the serene beauty of the world he now occupied, but he quickly remembered Mira's words and wiped his face clean of all emotion.

The stone walkway clicked against the Wardens' shoes as they marched along, Mira keeping a steady pace while Mathias did his best to keep up. He desperately wanted to examine the strange world further and so, without Mira realizing it, he permitted his eyes to wander. His gaze immediately fell upon the marvelous columns that lined the stone path. The white, marble structures towered over them, each one masterfully carved into a more intricate design than the last. Some were glorious representations of past Grand Masters, while others resembled great beasts from the legends of old. However, two columns near the end of the path drew his attention from the rest. The pillars mirrored each other and were meticulously detailed, carved into the likeness of the mythical dragon, Chiede. She stood on her powerful hind legs, her massive wings spread wide, creating a magnificent arch over the path. Her snarling jaws were open to the sky, a pillar of flame spewing forth in a permanent state of rage.

Word of the ancient dragon's terror had spread throughout the worlds like wildfire. Chiede, the once benevolent Maker of Life, was horribly betrayed by her siblings and had no choice but to turn against them. It became her goal to destroy all that her brothers had worked to create. Countless worlds fell to her mighty power, until her brothers found and captured her. However, because of her immortality, the Makers had no choice but to imprison their sister for eternity. It was this creature that influenced the formation of the Ravens. Some of the rogue Wardens could even take on a similar guise in an attempt to recreate the devastation wrought by Chiede. It was odd that, in a Warden refuge such as this, these statues had been erected.

A sharp poke in his side snapped him back to reality, the others clearly realizing that his attention was not where it should have been. He returned his eyes forward and noticed the giant building rising in the distance. He was forced to squint as the blinding rays of sunlight reflected off the golden pillars of the temple. The building was circular in nature with its tall columns supporting the shingled, crimson roof overhead. Mathias had never seen anything like it, having only ever known the white oak of his home.

Just outside of the temple sat large, square sparring mats, all of which were occupied by men and women of all different ages. Some fought with long, wooden staves while others used only their own hands and feet. They were also almost impossible to tell apart, as everyone's head was shaved and they all donned the same fluid, white garb. Mathias watched in awe as the strangers fought, fluidly dancing in endless rhythmic battles, neither one ever striking the other.

Several of the strangers stopped the moment they saw the Wardens approaching. Mira kept her pace, and the front staircase leading up to the building was rapidly approaching. Soon, all the men and women had delayed their battles to examine the group, most of their eyes fixed on Mathias. Whispers rose against the rushing waters still present in the background, and Mathias wondered what they were saying about him.

One of the fighters, a young boy no older than sixteen, sprinted up to the temple doors the moment he saw the Wardens coming. He now stood atop the stone staircase, near the entrance to building, next to a massive, golden disc. He raised an equally golden mallet into the sky and then brought it down hard onto the disc's surface. Mathias was not prepared for the burst of sound that suddenly reverberated throughout the land. He had never heard such a sound before, but found that he enjoyed its triumphant resonance.

The young man struck the disc three times, never once struggling to keep the mallet aloft, and then kneeled at the top of the stairs. Mathias hadn't noticed until that moment, but the rest of the men and women were also kneeling around them, honoring them as they passed by. Mathias was confused, as he had never done anything for these people worth honoring.

Finally, the four reached the top of the temple steps and came to a halt before the young boy.

"Sanctuary welcomes you home, Warden Mira. We are pleased to see you and your companions return to us safely," the boy said, his eyes washing over the four of them and finally coming to rest on Mathias. "And to you, Mathias, son of Grand Master Aurilean, Sanctuary is overflowing with excitement to welcome you. We hope to learn much from you in the years to come."

Grand Master? Mathias wasn't sure if he'd heard correctly. Had Aurilean really been the great leader of the Wardens? If so, how could Mathias possibly hope to live up to that? He pushed the thought aside and prepared to thank the young man, but remembered the ritual and stopped himself. Instead, he simply nodded his head at the boy and kept his face firm.

"He will see you now," the boy finished and then made his way to the door in front of them. Mathias could vaguely make out the design that had been intricately carved into the face of the gate. Men and women fought in glorious combat while majestic beasts battled alongside them. He wanted to examine the etching further, but the boy pulled open the heavy doors and Mathias was forced to follow Mira into the waiting darkness of the temple.

The four had only taken a few steps into the building when the great doors slammed shut and the hallway was thrown into complete darkness. Mira stopped, and the rest followed suit. They waited for only a few seconds before a dim, orange light illuminated the corridor. The torches spaced evenly apart along the length of the walls suddenly came to life to light the way. Mathias wasn't sure who or what had lit the torches, but he guessed he would soon find out.

Beautiful, complex murals adorned the walls of the corridor, all equally spaced just like the torches. Each intricate piece depicted an event from the Wardens' history, from the initial creation of the Warden race, to the aftermath of the battle on Haven. While each painting was significantly different from the next, they all seemed to share a common theme: the persistence of life and the inevitability of death.

The hallway ended abruptly, and the group marched out into the middle of an expansive, circular room. The cylinder was completely void of light apart from a faint, red aura emanating from the man in the center of the room. Mira came to another stop, and the rest followed. Mathias could just barely make out the man before him, balancing with one foot atop what appeared to be a long, black staff. His red aura washed over the group, warming and relaxing their stiff bodies. It was an odd, yet mesmerizing feeling.

The realization suddenly clicked in Mathias's head: this man must be a Flame Warden.

The moment the thought crossed his mind, the man before him leapt off his staff. He flipped through the air, a trail of red flames in his wake, mimicking his fluid movements. The staff snapped towards the ground and then rebounded back into the air, also leaving a path of fire behind. The man snatched the weapon out of the air and landed softly in front of the group. The room was suddenly flooded with vibrant torch flame, and Mathias could fully see the Warden standing before him. He was bald, as the men and women outside had been, but he sported a full black beard and glowed with a fiery presence that demanded respect. He wore a comfortable, white robe that had been emblazoncd with sparkling red and orange flames, and his hands stuck out just far enough for Mathias to notice crimson brands swirling in fluid patterns up his arms.

Mathias realized he had dropped his gaze and returned to meet the man's eyes, which now burned with a fiery passion before him.

"Who are you?" The man asked, his burning eyes unmoving and intimidating. His accent was strangely foreign and caught Mathias by surprise, but he kept his head up and prepared to answer his first question.

"I am Mathias, son to Regina and a father I do not know, raised and cared for by Aurilean," Mathias responded, hoping that revealing his true birth parents was the correct response to Monk's question. The man before him squinted, pondering the boy's answer.

"And why, Mathias, are you here?" Monk asked dangerously. Was it a trick question? Mathias had been through so much over the past couple days, having lost the only father figure he'd ever had as well as his brother. His life had been threatened multiple times, and he was practically abducted from the only world he had ever known. The answer to why he was there seemed incredibly complicated.

"I had no choice but to come here after my father was viciously murdered by a group of bounty hunters. Your people saved me and brought me here because they believe I'm some great Warden. But, I'm not. I don't want this power my father has thrust upon me." Mathias replied, the anger evident in his shaky voice.

The Warden

The others looked at each other nervously, not really sure what to make of the boy's responses.

"Leave us." The command was stern, but gentle, Monk's eyes never leaving Mathias. Without question, the others silently exited the room. "For having lived twenty some years, you seem to know very little about who you are," Monk continued. He circled Mathias, examining him from head to toe.

"And you know who I am?" Mathias asked, annoyed at the man's presumption.

"No, I do not. But, I do know who you could be," Monk replied, stopping again and turning to face him.

"My father said something similar just before he died," Mathias continued. "He told me that I needed to become the Warden that he could never be. But, I look around at all these paintings and these statues, and I see the greatness he achieved. How could I possibly live up to a man like that?"

"Your mind is clouded by false assumptions of the man who raised you. Look around you, Mathias. Really look. See the fruits of your father's labors." Monk gestured to the walls of the room that encircled them which were now bathed in light. Another magnificent mural blanketed the entire interior of the room. In the center of the piece, surrounded by smoldering corpses and homes ravaged by war, Mathias found Aurilean. The late Grand Master was kneeling next to a mutilated body, while a mass of dark shapes blocked out the light of the setting sun.

"This can't be right," the boy said, refusing to believe that his father had been the cause of all the destruction he saw before him.

"The Great Warden Massacre destroyed everything that once made Aurilean a brilliant leader. Some even blame him for it. He sent the remaining Wardens into hiding, abandoning them here so he could start his life anew," Monk said, keeping his tone calm and informative.

"Why would he leave them?"

Monk shrugged. "He believed there was nothing left to fight for."

"But what about the Ravens? So many of them got away. How could he just forget about that?"

"They got away because your father let them. He failed the Wardens in their most desperate hour and could not bring himself to lead another charge against them. So, he created this new haven and brought his most loyal followers here. He told us that he needed to leave, but that he would one day return to lead us to victory." Monk was pacing again, using his staff for support. "But, that day never came."

Mathias dropped his gaze to the floor. His whole life he had looked up to Aurilean as a brave and honorable man. Now, as he listened to Monk's revelation, he began to question just how honorable a man Aurilean had really been, Grand Master or not.

"When the Raven army resurfaced, beginning their manhunt for the remaining Wardens, I sent word to your father and pleaded that he return to us, but he refused. He told me that he was training a new generation of Wardens and that he would return only when the time was right. I was told never to contact him again." The pain in Monk's eyes surged with a fiery passion that Mathias was careful to avoid, lest the fire consume them both. "I told his followers that the Grand Master had forsaken them and that any who wished to take the fight to the Ravens were free to do so. Those who left I never saw again."

"We finally received word from your father a few days ago, after many long years of silence. He warned us that his life was in danger and that a new Grand Master would soon take his place. I sent the last of Aurilean's loyal followers, and my closest friends, to retrieve you and your father and return to us. Unfortunately, they arrived too late." At this point, Monk finally averted his gaze. He seemed broken and tired. Too many years in hiding had certainly taken its toll on the man, and it was only a matter of time before the same thing happened to the others.

"But, not all was lost. When Mira sent word that you still yet lived, I was overjoyed and my confidence renewed. A new Warden, one who could lead us against the Ravens, was coming to Sanctuary." Monk's eyes returned. The fire in them still raged and, for a brief moment, Mathias could feel all the hardships this man had faced in his life. Everything Monk had ever done, he had done because of Aurilean. The old man had been forced to make decisions that tore at his spirit, knowingly sending his fellow Wardens to their deaths.

The fire in Mathias continued to grow. Never had he felt so many conflicting emotions within himself, emotions now directed solely at his father.

"So, when I answered your questions, I essentially gave you the worst answers I possibly could have," Mathias said, now understanding the gravity of the ritual he had undergone. He had lost himself in the beauty of his home world and the terrible lie he had refused to accept.

"That you understand that reveals much to me about who you are, young Mathias. You say that you had no choice in coming here and that you wish nothing more from us. If that is what you truly want, though I do not believe that it is, then you are free to go." Monk stated. Mathias was surprised that he didn't feel more relieved. The old man had just offered him exactly what he wanted, but Mathias no longer wished to return to his old life. "But, I see the fire in you,

Mathias. I feel it. It burns in you as it has burned in me for centuries, aching for vengeance against those that have wronged you." Monk revealed an ever-so-slight grin as he spoke. He knew that Mathias had changed his mind, and it was time for him to accept it.

"When I asked you who you were, you told me who your parents were. That tells me nothing about you as a person. Abandon your thoughts of home and the life you once lived. Forget the father that lied to you and betrayed his people. See, now, the man I know you can become!" Monk roared and flames violently erupted around him. The man vanished, but in his place stood a new man, wreathed in flame.

It was Mathias.

The boy stared at the fiery incarnation of himself. This man was almost unrecognizable as he stood there tall, proud and confident.

"This is who you are meant to be, Mathias," Monk said, his voice echoing throughout the room. He couldn't see him, but Mathias knew the old man was still there. "See the power you can possess and the confidence you will wield. Others will follow you simply because they know your name." As the old man listed off attributes, the apparition changed. It showed Mathias soaring through the skies, fighting off waves of fiery enemies. It showed him leading a massive flaming army into battle, all chanting his name as they charged. Could this truly be who Mathias was destined to become?

"Eventually, they will come to love and respect you as the greatest Warden of all time."

Mathias saw the apparition change again, this time showing Mathias hand in hand with Mira, followed closely by Joel and Ardemis and many other Wardens. Was this to be his future? The incarnation suddenly fizzled into nothing and Monk reappeared to take its place. He stared at Mathias, both of them now surrounded by the red, fiery aura.

Mira, Joel and Ardemis had rushed back into the room at the apparition's fiery entrance. They had thought Mathias was in trouble, but instead found him quite safe. Unbeknownst to him, the three stayed in the room to watch the rest of the scene play out. Mira frowned at the vision of the two of them holding hands, while Joel chuckled silently beside her.

"Know this, young Warden: you are not alone. Your friends will stand beside you and will never abandon you as your father did." Monk's voice had risen now. He spoke with such energy that the red glow around him pulsated with each word he uttered. "So, again, I ask you: Who are you?"

"I am Mathias, Grand Master of the Wardens!" Mathias roared, the title solidifying itself as it rolled off his tongue. The fire around him grew, and he could feel the warmth as it enveloped him.

"And why, Grand Master, are you here?"

"To do what my father would not! To learn what I can about my power and to one day, lead the Wardens against the Ravens. Together, we will finally end this war!" Mathias was yelling now, hoping the entire building could hear his exclamation. The fire that had been growing around him finally exploded and he could feel the heat pouring from every corner and crevice of his body. His radiant glow illuminated the entire room and his eyes fell upon the others standing in the corner. Ardemis and Joel nodded at him as his eyes passed over each of them.

Then he saw Mira.

She smiled at him as their eyes connected and deep in his mind, he heard her voice.

Well said.

He returned the smile, imagining the strange future he had seen in the flames. Then he turned back to the Flame Warden.

"Accepting who you are has awakened the power within you," Monk continued. He motioned to the others and, much to Mathias's surprise, large sections of the walls began to twist and rotate, allowing the brightness of the day to pierce the dark of the room. "As Grand Master of the Wardens, you have the inherent abilities of all the Wardens who have existed before you. Those abilities exist within you in a constant state of rest until they manifest," Monk explained. Mathias could certainly feel something powerful within him, but he didn't know how to reach it.

"What causes these abilities to manifest?"

"I'm glad you asked," Monk replied, a large grin spreading over his face.

8

Blinding shafts of white sunlight penetrated the large openings now present around the room. Mathias was enthralled by the building's unique design. One minute the room was shrouded in complete darkness, and the next it was illuminated by the outside world. However, the room was not the only thing that captured the young Warden's attention. Where each of the panels had opened, a dark silhouette now stood silently waiting. There were four men and two women, and each one held a wooden staff in one hand.

"Your first test begins now," Monk stated, a wide grin plastered to his wrinkled face. At his words, the six figures stepped down into the room. He had seen some of these men and women only moments ago in the courtyard, but the one that caught his eye was the young boy that had greeted them at the door. His smile, though, had vanished, and his face showed no sign of emotion. "In battle, you will oftentimes find that your powers alone will not be enough. Some in this galaxy have adapted to the magics the Wardens possess, and your abilities will do little to harm them. You must learn to fight in other ways if you are to succeed."

Mathias was shaking. A bead of sweat slowly dripped down his back as he recalled the fights him and Alistair used to get into when they were little. However, childish bickering was nothing compared to fighting trained warriors.

"There are two sides to every fight," Monk continued, using his staff as a crutch as he paced back and forth. "The attack and the defense. Today, you will focus only on the latter. The fighters you see before you have trained their entire lives for this moment, and they will do everything in their power to take you down."

Mathias stole a glance at each of the faces staring back at him, but none of them showed any sign of fear or doubt.

"Your task is simple: do not let them strike you. You can do whatever you need to avoid their attacks, but you will not retaliate in any way."

To the complete surprise of the entire room, Mathias smiled. The fear in him evaporated and his confidence swelled.

"Did I say something funny?" Monk asked, perplexed by the young boy's reaction.

"You'll see," Mathias responded slyly.

"Very well." Monk motioned to the boy closest to him. Without hesitation, the young man stepped into the middle of the room to face Mathias. It was the boy from before. He stood before Mathias now with only a pair of tattered shorts and his staff, a rather plain looking piece of wood. The boy's finely toned muscles glistened in the sunlight and, for the briefest of moments, Mathias's confidence waivered.

"Begin!" Monk yelled and, without warning, the boy lashed out with his staff. Mathias stumbled back as the tip of the weapon just barely missed the side of his face. The boy gave Mathias no time to recover, already coming at him with another attack. He dodged the blow once again, this time rolling just out of the way and quickly returning to his feet. His opponent was incredibly fast and wasted no time preparing a new method of attack should the previous attempt fail. The boy was masterfully trained and would give everything he had in this encounter.

Mathias continued to dodge the boy's blows, using the entire room to his advantage. His opponent's frustration was growing as he struck with increasing ferocity and abandoned proper planning. This gave Mathias an idea. He wasn't allowed to strike back, but he could certainly relieve his opponent of his weapon.

The boy struck out again with the end of his staff, a move Mathias had familiarized himself with as the fight had dragged on. He had a good idea how the boy would attack next and positioned himself accordingly. The blow came as Mathias expected and, as the boy thrust his weapon forward, Mathias slid to the side and used his attacker's momentum to pull the weapon from his grip. Completely caught off guard by the maneuver, the young boy was thrown forward as Mathias whipped the staff out of his hands.

The room was dead silent as Mathias leapt onto the fallen warrior and brought the staff within an inch of the boy's face. He let the weapon hover there for a few seconds and then backed off, tossing the carved piece of wood back at his opponent. The boy caught it and came to his feet. He looked Mathias in the eyes and bowed. The Warden simply nodded at the boy and turned back to Monk.

The Flame Warden stood wide-eyed at the head of the room, clearly not expecting Mathias to have performed so well. He gestured towards the two warriors on his left. Without hesitation, the two bounded into the room, weapons ready to strike.

Mathias hadn't expected the next round to begin so quickly. His new opponents were both women, their white robes flapping as they moved through the air. Mathias prepared for the assault and jumped out of the way as the first woman swung her staff at his face. He dodged the blow but was immediately attacked by the other woman, who swung her staff at his feet. Mathias rolled over the attack and away from the deadly duo. The two moved with a synchronized grace the likes of which Mathias had never seen. Each woman attacked where the other did not, forcing him to think fast and careful about how to dodge each strike.

While he contemplated the situation, the women attacked at once, one staff coming straight for Mathias's face and the other aimed at his lower back. Mathias, knowing it was the only way to avoid losing the round, leapt backward into the air and twisted himself into the small gap between the two weapons. The staves found only air as the Warden rolled out of his dodge unscathed. The two looked at him in amazement, the maneuver never having failed before. Mathias smiled at them, realizing how he was going to win the round.

The girls wasted no time as they charged back into the fray. The Warden danced his way through the blows, twisting and turning and leaping through the air to avoid every strike they threw at him. He was waiting for the duo to attack simultaneously again, suspecting that they wouldn't leave a gap open this time. The maneuver happened sooner than Mathias expected, but he was ready for it. One of the girls spun rapidly and swung her staff forwards while her counterpart mimicked the move from behind him. Mathias immediately dropped to the ground as the two weapons collided in midair and shattered. He quickly rolled away from the falling shards of wood and came to his feet, preparing for another attack, but it never came. Instead, the women dropped the splintered remains of their weapons and bowed.

The second round was over.

Mathias relaxed, taking a quick moment to catch his breath. He knew what was coming next and needed to prepare. The sweat was pouring out of him, and he decided it was time to lose his shirt, the weight of it having slowed him down in the first two fights. He threw the soaked rag to the side and looked over at Monk, but the Flame Warden just glared back at him. Mathias smiled again and thought about taunting the man when he heard shuffling behind him. He turned just in time to jump out of the way of a powerful blow meant for the back of his head.

The three attackers that closed in around him were all men. They were huge and muscular, nowhere near as large as Joel, but intimidating nevertheless, and Mathias knew just a single strike from one of them would be the end of the round. The men positioned themselves around Mathias and lashed out all at once. The Warden spun around, gracefully dodging each attack as it came at him. The attacks were laced with power, but the men themselves were slower than the others had been. Mathias danced with the blows, fluidly gliding around the staves as they came for him. Each strike was a different step of the dance, a dance Mathias had familiarized himself with years ago. He moved with the attacks, strategically placing himself where he needed to be. One of the men swung at him hard and, as Mathias ducked out of the way, the staff connected with another attacker. The blow sent the man instantly to the ground, blood seeping from his swelling ear. The two that remained roared out in anger and continued their attack. Again, Mathias danced around the blows, positioning himself between the two men. A powerful swing once again came for his face and he dodged the blow with ease. The shear strength of the follow through of his swing caught the man off balance, and his body twisted painfully as he fell to the floor. He landed on the ground so hard that the entire building shook, and bits of dust and rock crumbled from the ceiling. Two of the men were down for the count.

The last man was furious. He charged at Mathias, raising his staff over his head for a final assault. Mathias quickly spun to the ground and brought his leg around into the charging man's path. The warrior tripped over the extended appendage and landed face first on the floor.

Mathias had passed the third round unscathed. He turned once again to the Flame Warden, breathing hard and drenched in sweat.

Monk stood before him, mouth agape in disbelief. The other Wardens were there as well, also in complete shock at the result of the battle. Joel and Ardemis looked at each other in stunned disbelief, while Mira just stared intensely back at Mathias and nodded her head in approval.

"How..." Monk muttered, trying to piece together what had just happened. His warriors trained rigorously day after day and, without ever landing a blow, Mathias had defeated them all.

"You asked me what was funny earlier," Mathias said. He paused to catch his breath and then began to explain. "When I was younger, and my brother was training with my father, I would sneak off to watch their sessions. Alistair could certainly throw a punch, but avoiding one was never his strong suit. Many of their sessions were focused on dodging and using an enemy's momentum against them. I paid close attention to these lessons and, when the two of us would spar, I would use what I learned against him. My brother could never strike me, and that infuriated him. I'll be the first to admit that I'm not the best at returning an attack, but avoiding one I can do."

Everyone stared at him, no one really knowing what to say next. Suddenly, and to everyone's great surprise, Mira stepped forward. She kicked a staff up off the ground and twirled it around in her hands, testing its durability. After she was satisfied, she glided out into the middle of the room, stopping just in front of Mathias. He looked around at the others, but nobody showed any sign of stopping her.

"Pick a number," Mira said to him.

"What?"

"Pick a number." She stood before him with a burning intensity. Mathias looked behind her to Monk, but the old man simply shrugged and said nothing.

"Four," Mathias said with wavering uncertainty.

"So be it," Mira said, a twinge of disappointment in her voice, and then readied herself. She let the black robe fall from her back, and Mathias found his eyes wandering. Her long, red hair had broken out of its braid and fell wildly down to her chest. She wore a brown, leather shirt that cut off at the shoulders and her loose, beige pants still managed to perfectly compliment her figure. Mathias was entranced, but it was short lived as she leapt at him. Mathias jumped out of the way, rolling to the side and then hopping back to his feet. The second attack was already on its way and Mathias was forced to duck to avoid the blow. The third strike came just as quickly as the second. Mathias rolled backward away from the weapon as it came down. Mira, moving with the

momentum of the staff, flipped into the air as Mathias rolled
away from her. She brought the staff down fast and, as he
came out of his roll, Mira landed on top of him bringing the
staff down hard. Mathias noticed the attack far too late and
had nowhere left to go as the weapon sped towards him. For
a moment, Mira considered stopping the attack before it
could connect, but ultimately decided against it. Mathias
watched as the fourth attack found its mark, striking the
Warden directly on the forehead. The boy's head snapped
back onto the ground, and then everything went black.

*   *   *

The sound of laughter brought him back. His head
throbbed as Joel cackled hysterically. Mathias rolled his head
around and found Mira standing over to him. She held out a
hand and hoisted Mathias back to his feet.

"How did I beat you?" She asked as she passed
Mathias his wrinkled shirt. It was still wet with sweat as he
slung it over his shoulder.

"I'd say the same way I beat each of them." Mathias
motioned to the men and women he had just fought. Some
were still unconscious, while the others attentively awaited
instruction. "I watched how each of them fought and adapted
my technique to how they attacked, eventually using those
attacks against them. You watched how I moved and
positioned myself for three rounds, so you knew exactly how
to strike to get me right where you wanted me." Mathias kept
his eye's locked on Mira's the entire time.

"Impressive," she replied with a smile, and Mathias
was overjoyed. Mira had knocked him out, but he couldn't
have asked for a better outcome.

"Impressive indeed," added Monk as he appeared beside Mira. "Never has a new Warden stepped into this temple and done what you just did. Nor have they been able to fully understand the true meaning of this test. You did well."

"Yea, 'til Mira knocked you on your ass!" Joel was on the brink of choking from laughing so hard.

"Perhaps you'd like to try?" Mathias asked the burly man.

"Oh, you have no idea, kid," Joel replied, his laughing quickly subsiding.

"Then let's go," Mathias replied, his temper rising.

Joel made a move to come at him but Monk quickly intervened.

"You two will have plenty of time to beat on each other in the coming weeks," the old man said. "For now, get some rest." Joel grunted before turning and storming out of the room while Mathias chuckled to himself.

"You'd be wise not to antagonize him, lad," Ardemis said from behind.

"I was just having a bit of fun," Mathias replied. He was actually terrified to exchange blows with the giant of a man.

"Trust me, laddie, that would not have been fun," Ardemis said, then added with a chuckle, "For you, anyway." Mathias laughed alongside the Sky Warden and then looked around for Mira, but he didn't see her and decided she must have left.

The rusty creaking of the giant panels twisting back into place echoed throughout the room. The fading light of the day was quickly squelched as the temple was thrust back into darkness. Monk released a few balls of flame towards the door to illuminate the way out.

"I'll be along in a minute," Mathias said as he turned back towards Monk. Ardemis nodded and then skipped out of the room into the darkness.

"You want to know why none of your abilities manifested today." It wasn't a question.

"Well, that was part of the reason for the fight, wasn't it?" Mathias asked. He had been excited to learn that his powers would reveal themselves over time, but was severely disappointed when nothing had happened.

"Patience, young one. It took your predecessors weeks to finally call forth an ability," Monk replied, smiling and placing a hand on the boy's shoulder.

"I guess I just hoped that something would happen today."

"Something *did* happen today!" Monk replied excitedly. "You managed to defeat some of my strongest warriors without ever laying a finger on them. That's something your father was never able to do."

"Really?" Mathias asked, a big smile spreading across his face.

"Aurilean wasn't a fighter. He relied solely on his ability to strike from afar with little regard for finesse. He had no respect for the style of self-defense I teach here. You, on the other hand, see everything around you. You move like the wind and dance with the flow of battle. If I had to guess, I'd say we'll see something very interesting in the next few days."

Mathias was beaming, his confidence completely restored.

"Thanks," he said as he held out his hand. Monk took it and shook firmly. The Flame Warden's hand was incredibly warm, but not overly so.

"Run along now. I've no doubt the others are waiting for you." Mathias nodded at the old man and made his way out of the circular room. As he reached the entrance to the hallway, he turned back and saw that the old had returned to balancing atop his staff. A small hum echoed across the room as he meditated, and Mathias wondered if, one day, he too would find peace like that.

The sun was just beginning to set as the young Warden stepped out of the dark temple. For the first time since he had arrived on Sanctuary, he could truly take in the beauty of his surroundings. Rays of red and orange light glinted off the twin dragon statues in the courtyard as the sun dipped below the horizon. The emerald blades of grass swayed as the gentle breeze wafted over them, and the songbirds resolved their tunes and settled in for the night as the green trees rustled with the wind. Monstrous, snow-covered mountains provided a scenic backdrop in every direction, completing the picturesque landscape.

Finally, his eyes fells upon Ardemis. The small man was leaning against a golden statue of a lion just at the bottom of the stairs. Mathias made his way down to the man, rubbing the throbbing lump on his forehead. Ardemis had one foot against the statue, his other firmly on the ground. He turned his head as Mathias approached, but the rest of his body remained still.

"So, he answer all your questions?" The small man asked.

"Yea. Told me exactly what I needed to hear."

"He does that. Quite good at it, actually." The smile on the man's face stretched from ear to ear.

"So, what now?" Mathias asked, eagerly hoping sleep was in the near future.

"Put this on," Ardemis said slyly and threw a black sack in the boy's direction.

"What?" Mathias carefully examined the dark piece of fabric he now held in his hands.

"Trust me, lad. Just put it over your head."

Mathias assumed this was some sort of initiation ritual, so he played along. He pulled the black sack over his head and was immediately shrouded in darkness. He couldn't see a thing, but he found that he could breathe with ease.

"You look absolutely ridiculous, laddie," Ardemis chortled. Mathias laughed alongside him nervously, wondering what the rest of the night would hold. "Alright, lad. Put your hand on my shoulder and do your best to keep up."

9

The ascent up the mountain path was a slow one. Ardemis knew the road by heart, but guiding the new Warden blindly up the trail was far more difficult than he had anticipated. Joel was usually the one to lead the new recruits up the mountain. His size alone made it nearly impossible for his follower to lose him, and, should the recruit be unable to make the journey, Joel was strong enough to carry him or her the rest of the way. Ardemis had volunteered for the task today, however, knowing that Mathias could make the trek himself.

The Warden had his eyes closed as he strolled along behind Ardemis. Keeping them open under the black hood seemed unnecessary, so he decided to let his other senses do the work for him. He could feel the earth changing around him as he walked, the steep incline of the path wearing on his muscles. The wind blowing against the pair was quite cool, and Mathias was sure, had he not been wearing the mask, his breath would have been visible in the evening air.

"Not too much further, lad," Ardemis said, his breathing heavy. The little man's body wasn't accustomed to such journeys on the ground. Mathias chose not to reply, keeping his hand glued to Ardemis's shoulder.

A new scent slowly drifted through the stitching of the dark hood. The smell of ash and burning wood signaled that a fire was nearby and that the two were nearing their destination. As Mathias continued to wonder about the reason for his journey, Ardemis made an abrupt turn and the Warden, doing his best to follow suit, turned with him and caught his foot on a nearby rock jutting out into the path. With what grace he could muster, he quickly forced his other foot forward and spun himself into the air, avoiding the painful fall that awaited him. Ardemis looked back just in time to see Mathias land on both feet before him.

"Y'alright, laddie?" Ardemis asked curiously.

"You sure you're not trying to kill me?" Mathias joked. The two laughed for a moment and then he stuck his arm back out and found Ardemis's shoulder once more.

Night had finally set in, and not a single cloud hung in the black, star studded sky. As he rounded another corner, Ardemis saw the other Wardens sitting near a small fire along the mountainside. He led Mathias beyond the pair and stopped just before the edge of the cliff. Mira and Joel abandoned the flames and came to stand with him. When everyone had positioned themselves appropriately, Ardemis pulled the hood from Mathias's head.

Opening his eyes for the first time since the temple, Mathias found he was speechless as he gazed out into the expanse before him. Snow covered mountain ranges stretched on for miles in every direction, while millions of bright, twinkling stars littered the night sky.

"He journeyed well," Ardemis said, speaking to the other Wardens.

"Prolly took the easy path," Joel replied, crossing his arms against his chest. "He'd have begged me to carry him had he come with me."

"We took the broken path, actually. The boy only tripped up once and managed to keep his feet in the process." Ardemis beamed as he defended the new Warden. Joel grumbled something inaudible under his breath, and Mathias was still staring out into the canyon as the big man stepped in front of him.

"You've proven to Monk that you have the willpower and the fortitude to assume the role of Grand Master," Joel began. He spoke as if reading from a piece of paper. Mathias assumed he had given this speech, or something similar, many times before. "But you still gotta prove yourself to us."

"As our leader, you must understand that we will follow you anywhere, even into oblivion," Mira stepped forward, replacing Joel. "As we place our lives in your hands, so must you place your life in ours."

Mathias had only just met the Wardens earlier that day, and now they swore complete loyalty to him. Never before had he felt a bond as strong as he did now.

"You must now take a leap of faith so that the bond of trust can be established." It was Ardemis that spoke now, once again taking the place of the previous Warden. "The chasm before you is wide and endless, leading into a deep, unknown darkness that will swallow you whole. We ask you now to step into that darkness and trust in us to show you the light."

Mathias had wondered what strange request the group would ask of him, but he never expected something so extreme. He was cold from the frigid wind biting at his neck, and falling through that chill into darkness was not something that appealed to him at that moment. He looked around at the faces staring back at him. Each was stern, revealing no signs of emotion. However, Mathias discovered the slightest hint of a smile on Mira's face. She nodded at him and then placed both of her hands behind her back, awaiting the Grand Master's response.

"Before I do this, I just want you all to know that I've never had anyone so quickly put their faith in me. We've only just met and already you're willing to give your lives for me. Truthfully, I don't really know what to say," Mathias said shakily as the cold sent shivers throughout his body. Without thinking any further about what-ifs and the dangers of jumping off a mountain, he moved to the edge, his toes just barely dangling out into the chasm. "I suppose there's only one thing left to do."

Looking over at Joel, he gave the big man a huge grin, smacked him in the shoulder, and then jumped out into the night. He hung in the air for only the briefest of seconds, enjoying the sudden laughter coming from Mira and Ardemis, but then he started to fall. The air was freezing as it rushed past him, the mountains growing as Mathias fell towards their roots. The dark abyss before him grew closer and closer, and he was sure he was about to discover what lied within. Just as the blackness began to swallow him up, Ardemis flew in out of nowhere and snatched Mathias out of the air, just as the ashwolf had done back on Talise.

Mathias cheered in exhilaration as the two flew, soaring back up into the mountains. Ardemis was overjoyed by the boy's excitement. He would never have been able to carry Mathias up the mountain pass but, out here in the night sky, weight was of no concern to the Sky Warden. The two were as light as feathers drifting in the wind.

At Mathias's request, the two circled around the mountain's peak a few times before finally heading back toward the cliff. As the pair landed, Mira came up to Mathias and gave him a gentle hug. The way her body pressed against his own sent his heart racing. She pulled away far sooner than Mathias would have liked, and Joel made his way over to him.

"I'll get you back tomorrow, kid," Joel said with a smile, holding out his hand. Mathias was hesitant at first, remembering how crushed his fingers had been from the last handshake with the man, but eventually took Joel's hand in his. The shake was firm, but not nearly as painful as before.

"Thank you, all of you. That was exactly what I needed." Mathias smiled at each of them. "But now I have a request to make of you." The group looked around at each other in confusion. "When we first met, I wrongfully assumed things about each of you that I know I shouldn't have. I'd like to know how you all came to be here."

"It's freezin' up here, kid!"

"I believe I can help with that!" Ardemis chimed in. With a sudden clap of his hands, a burst of air puffed out around them, forcing any remnants of cold out into the night. Then, Ardemis swept his hands in a circular motion, swirling the air into a sphere around them. Faster and faster the ball of air spun, and the cliff around the fire was suddenly warm and toasty, completely void of any cold winds.

"Cool!" Mathias said under his breath.

"C'mon, Joel, it'll be good for you," Mira said as she grabbed the man's bulging arm and pulled him towards the fire.

"And I suppose you'll be the first to tell your story?" Joel replied, immediately wiping the smile from Mira's face. She glared at him, but continued to pull him along. The two sat down around the fire, which continued to burn with vigor before them. Each time the wood cracked, a splash of sparks would leap into the air and get caught in the spinning ball of wind around them, keeping the cliff warm and comfortable in the cool night breeze.

"I suppose it's only fair that I tell you a bit about myself," Mathias said. Each of the Wardens' eyes were on him, his face illuminated by the glowing flames. Mathias started by going into detail about Talise. He talked about his childhood with Alistair and the day Aurilean chose him to be Warden. He told them about the lightning and how Alistair had lost his father's faith. He recounted the battle with the brinwolf that wasn't a brinwolf, a story which Joel had to interrupt to explain the creature's true identity. Mathias sadly recounted the events that had transpired at the chapel. Ardemis was most interested when Mathias began to discuss the details of his birth, particularly when the silver pod was mentioned. He couldn't help but ask what the model of the pod was and the type of ship that must have sent the pod in the first place. Mathias smiled at the Warden's enthusiasm, but he couldn't give the little man the answers he sought.

"...and now here I am, sitting around a fire with some of the most powerful and dangerous people I've ever met." Mathias smiled at each of them. He could see a twinge of sadness in both Mira's and Ardemis's eyes. Joel, on the other hand, stood up and began pacing back and forth before them.

"You ok, big man?" Mathias asked, pondering Joel's strange behavior.

"Dangerous don't even begin to describe what we are," Joel replied. He walked over to Mathias and sat down beside him, placing his massive arm around the boy's shoulders.

"Under the right circumstances, I guess. You all seem fairly calm right now."

"Ain't no one tryin' to kill us right now," Joel replied.

"Are people usually trying to kill you?"

"Nah, not always. Things used to be easier." Joel stared fiercely into the fire. "Back when me and Damien were kids."

"Damien?" Mathias asked.

"His twin brother," Ardemis chimed in.

"Twin? Does that mean-"

"Yup. Dad split the power 'tween us, didn't think any one person should control it. Damien was the shield, sportin' the toughest skin of anyone I knew. Could take a punch fired from a canon and shrug it off like it was nothin'. I, on the other hand, was the sword. Could lift ten times my own weight, and I had a mean right hook. Me and him, we were unstoppable."

"Were?"

"Yea. Damien and I had different beliefs when it came to family. See, my older brother, Jon, got into some trouble. We tracked him down, but we were too late. Damien set out to avenge him, leavin' me to care for our grievin' mother. Ain't seen him since."

"Have you ever tried to find him?"

"Oh, I know where he is. Got a lab on Malador. Stonewall or somethin'. But, he's made it pretty damn clear that he doesn't wanna see me. So, came here instead."

"I'm sorry," Mathias said sadly.

"Eh, it is what it is. I actually feel better talkin' 'bout it," Joel replied with a smile, slapping Mathias on the back.

"Good! And who knows? Maybe you guys will work everything out one day."

"Maybe," was all Joel said as he returned his gaze to the fire. The stars twinkled even brighter in the night sky, and the air shield continued to keep the group warm against the frigid winds.

"I should warn ya, lad, my tale isn't much brighter," Ardemis said sadly.

"That's alright, Ardy. And if you don't feel like sharing, I understand," Mathias replied.

"Nah, I'll tell ya. Like the big lummox said, I'll feel better afterwards." Ardemis chuckled to himself, but Joel ignored the jab. Mathias readjusted the patch of dirt he was sitting on.

"I don't think any of you lads know this, but I was one of the original Sky Wardens."

"You mean to tell me, when the Makers created the Wardens, you were one of 'em?" Joel asked, clearly in complete surprise. Mathias was more shocked that neither of the other Wardens knew this about the man.

"Indeed. Me and my best friend, Emily. Because we were some of the first to be created by the Makers, neither of us had any parents or family. Like most Wardens at that time, we also aged at a rate far slower than the Wardens of today."

"So how old does that make you?" Mathias had to ask.

"Ya know, lad, I've honestly lost count."

Mathias was disappointed, but at the same time he couldn't believe he was sitting in the presence of one of the original Wardens.

"Anyway, Emily and I were immediately chosen as Sky Wardens, along with hundreds of other Wardens that fit the bill. Together, Emily and I quickly rose to become two of the first Sky Captains. You see, lad, not all Sky Wardens got their own starship. Many Sky Wardens were sent to watch over a planet and could only fly within that planet's atmosphere and without the means of a spacecraft. For those Wardens that could master their abilities of the air and sky, a promotion to Sky Captain was what followed. My ship at the time was called Arrowhead, while Emily flew the Longshot. Together, we used our knowledge of the sky to serve and protect wherever we were needed. Emily was a far superior pilot to me, and she became the first Sky Captain ever to be promoted to Sky Commander, a position that entitled her to her own battalion of Sky Captains."

"Sounds like you kids knew what you were doin'," Joel interrupted.

"We certainly did, laddie. Em commanded our battalion for years, and eventually I rose in status enough to become a Sky Commander me'self. Emily was upset when I left her division, but I promised her our two companies would fly together."

"It seems like you and Emily were close," Mathias said with a grin.

"We were indeed, lad. Very close. There was nothin' in the sky that could tear us apart. At least until the Massacre. You see, we'd been fightin' in the War of Three Stars when Aurilean summoned us to Haven."

"You fought in the War of Three Stars?!" Mathias asked excitedly. He had read all about the War of Three Stars as a kid, and he knew that the war had been one of the biggest turning points in terms of peace for the galaxy. It took place hundreds of years ago just outside the planet of Telyaveen, a uniquely lush world filled with a wide assortment of wildlife and many thriving civilizations. The planet was unique in that it received its light from three different stars positioned in a perfect triangle around the planet. The planet didn't revolve around any of the stars, the clashing gravities causing it to remain firmly in place. The planet did, however, still rotate on its axis leading to three short night and day cycles.

As time passed on Telyaveen, its distinct ability to maintain life and vegetation became highly sought after by others around the sector. When the people of Telyaveen refused to accommodate more and more civilizations, a large-scale war broke out, and civilizations from across the sector brought immense fleets to duke it out in the stars above. The initial onslaught lasted for quite a while before the Wardens arrived. It was said that the Sky Commanders came without warning, ended the hostility in a matter of hours and brought peace to all civilizations involved. Then they vanished without a trace. It was a mystery many still pondered to this day.

"I use the term 'fighting' loosely, lad. You see, when we arrived at the battle, hundreds of starships had already been destroyed and the planet was in danger of being ravaged by the destruction as well. Emily commanded her battalion to strike at the opposing forces, while my division oversaw the sweeping of the area, keeping debris and the like from entering the planet's atmosphere. It was arduous work, but we pulled it off. Emily'd pushed back the opposition and demanded a cease fire. She was in the middle of negotiations when Aurilean reached out to us, commanding us to return to Haven as fast as we could. I was prepared to leave immediately, but Emily refused. She said that she needed to stay and see the negotiations through. I argued with her about the importance of our duties, but she believed the peace at Telyaveen was far more important than the security of Haven. So, I stayed with her and we ended the hostility in the sector."

"Wow!" Mathias was unable to contain his amazement any longer.

"Unfortunately, because of our decision, Haven was lost when the Ravens attacked. Had we been there for the battle, we might have defended the city and prevented everything that happened that day. Instead, we abandoned the Wardens. Aurilean was furious with us. When we finally arrived at Haven, Aurilean refused to let us land and instead, commanded the remaining Wardens to attack us on sight. With no other choice, Emily and I fled Sanctuary with nowhere to go. Many years passed and, as the Raven presence grew, our battalions shrunk. I even lost the Arrowhead in a rather vicious ambush. Luckily, I was able to get to the Longshot before I could be gunned down."

"Wait. You could fly through space without a space craft?" Mathias couldn't believe what he was hearing.

"Only a Sky Warden with full control of the air can fly through space unharmed, without the aid of a suit or a ship. Luckily for me, laddie, I was one of those masters. Emily scooped me up, and we escaped the Raven fighters. With the Arrowhead lost and our companies shattered, we exiled ourselves. We flew to the desert world of Rashim where we lived for a year out of our ship. But the time away from what we knew took its toll on Emily, and her thirst for battle became unquenchable.

Much to my dismay, I awoke one morning to find us cruising through space, far away from desert world we had called home. Emily was on the hunt for any Raven cruiser she could find, and there was nothin' I could do to stop her. We finally ended up near Ravendra, the Raven home world. Emily'd found a large Raven battle cruiser in orbit around one of Ravendra's moons. Without thinking or any proper planning, she tried to take the ship. There was very little the

Longshot could do against a massive warship like that. During the attack, a laser blast from the cruiser broke through the Longshot's shields and shot straight through Emily's chest. She died instantaneously. I was overcome by sadness and anger, but mostly anger, and in that anger, I managed to destroy the Raven battle cruiser and escape in one piece."

Mathias held his breath, the details of the story keeping him on the edge of his seat. The others seemed just as interested in the tale as he was.

"I released Emily's body into space so that she could float for eternity amongst the stars. It felt like the only right way to let her go. After that, I learned that Aurilean had abandoned the other Wardens here and decided it was time to end my exile. Monk welcomed me with open arms, and I've been here ever since."

Mathias didn't know what to say. His mind was spinning with all the information he had just absorbed. Joel had to deal with his twin brother turning on him, and Ardemis had watched the only person he ever cared for succumb to fatal madness. Mathias was almost too nervous to hear what Mira had to say.

"I'm sorry you had to go through that, my friend," Mathias said sadly, placing his hand on Ardemis's shoulder.

"It's what makes us who we are, lad," Ardemis replied, smiling and placing his hand on the boy's. Mathias returned the smile and then turned to Mira, who's face had grown very dim, even in the light of the ever-burning flames. She looked back at him, a gaze that penetrated his very soul. There was something dark there, and Mathias wasn't sure he was ready for it.

"This has been enough sadness for one night, friends," she began, keeping her eyes fixed on Mathias. "I will tell you my story one day, Mathias, but not today."

"Big surprise there," Joel said, rolling his eyes and laying down to rest his head on the soft, warm ground.

"Hey, if she doesn't want to share, I understand and won't force her to. But, I am glad to have learned more about the two of you."

"It was my pleasure, lad. I rather enjoyed sharing with everyone, actually."

"I guess I did too, but don't get used it, kid." Joel rolled over, turning his back away from the group.

As everyone settled down, Ardemis pulled some of the wind from the spinning sphere and blew the fire out. The Wardens were quickly shrouded in darkness, but the air shield continued to spin, keeping the heat in constant motion around them. As Mathias's eyes began to close and his thoughts drifted off into the night, a quiet voice entered his mind. He knew it was her right away and a tiny smile fell upon his lips as the two soft words echoed inside his head.

Thank you.

Matthew Louwers

10

The small transport ship shook aggressively as it began its docking procedure. The stubby square wings folded into the craft's sides as the air lock pressurized against the seals of the larger space station. None of the passengers were in a particularly pleasant mood. Of their original group of four, only two remained, along with the recruit they picked up on the planet's surface.

Things certainly had not gone as Zed originally planned. The Magister had heard that the Grand Master was supposed to be somewhere in the sector, but he figured it would be just another wild goose chase. They had been preparing to leave Talise when that kid had busted into the bar, ranting to the barkeep about his personal issues. Zeke had been very clear about keeping the hunters' presence on Talise a secret, but the young boy didn't seem to care. In fact, he had strolled right over the table and revealed the whereabouts of the Warden, a man they'd been hunting for years. Zed dismissed the news as to be too good to be true but, as they entered the small chapel later that night, everything had changed.

Now, as Ezekiel slowly maneuvered the transport into The Hammer's docking bay, Zed couldn't help but question everything that had happened. He thought mainly about their new passenger, who hadn't said a word since the three had left Talise. Zed was having a hard time getting a read on the kid. He would occasionally turn back to check on him, but the boy's gaze was always fixed on the black nothingness that surrounded them and refused to acknowledge the Magister in any way. Ultimately, he decided it was better to the let the kid be. However, as the airlocks hissed outside, confirming that the transport had successfully docked, Zed knew he would need to explain some things to the recruit.

Alistair continued to stare blankly out the window as Zed made his way into the passenger bay.

"Time ta' go," the Magister said, attempting to draw the boy from his trance. Alistair turned to look at Zed and, for the first time, realized how truly frightening the Magister was. The man wore a dark leather jumpsuit that stuck tight to his skin, revealing the man's unusually large muscles bulging from his arms, legs and chest. He wore two short swords at his hip, one on either side, and kept a dagger sheathed against his lower back. The swords looked brand new, but the dagger's grip was worn and the blade was caked in dried blood. It was obviously the man's weapon of choice. The Magister's long, dirty dreadlocks hung over his shoulders and his bright, white eyes stood out against his jet-black skin.

Alistair swallowed, burying any fear or doubt that remained, and stood to follow Zed out of the transport and into The Hammer. The Magister towered over Alistair at nearly three times the boy's size, making him a truly intimidating sight to behold.

As the two made their way to the exit, Ezekiel rushed through the airlock and off into the larger ship.

"What's his hurry?" Alistair asked the dangerous man beside him.

"Has ta' take care of sometin'. Won't be long," Zed replied, keeping his eyes forward and ducking as he passed through the airlock.

Alistair was short enough that he could pass through the hall with ease and, as he came out the other side, he was instantly met with a flight of stairs. The Magister took the steps three at a time, continuing to keep his head lowered as he climbed.

The first thing Alistair thought as he entered the central hub of The Hammer was that there was no way a space station could be this massive. There were swarms of people everywhere, some of them in a hurry while others stood around chatting. Small, two-wheeled vehicles rushed past, horns blaring loudly. One nearly clipped Alistair, and he was forced to jump out of the way. There were small, crudely constructed buildings and houses in every direction, all scattered around the central square. A grated, metal ceiling rested about ten stories up, but the city didn't end there. Another collection of buildings was built atop the grate, and even more beyond that. These layers of civilization signified the class structure on The Hammer, with the top layer belonging to only the most powerful of hunters. At the very center of the great dome was the winding, spiral staircase that extended through a hole in the ceiling all the way to the top of the dome

"Da control center is at da top," Zed said, following Alistair's gaze. "Dat's where we be headed."

"Why?" Alistair asked. He still wasn't sure what they were doing on the station in the first place.

"Need ta speak ta Rolan. He runs dis place and sets all da' bounties for us huntas. He'll want to know about da Grand Master, and he'll want ta meet ya. We don't usually take on new recruits in the middle of a hunt."

Alistair wasn't sure about meeting the hunter leader so soon, but he decided it was better than sitting around while Mathias was off saving the galaxy. The very thought of it made him sick. He could have easily ended his brother's life, but instead he had let the boy go. It was a decision that he was slowly beginning to regret.

"Look, boy, der's sometin' ya need ta know," Zed began, stopping at the base of a large metal staircase. "Dis ain't a charity. Sullivan brought ya in because he saw sometin' in ya. I don't know what it was and now dat he's dead, it don't really matta. You'll be expected ta pull ya weight."

"I wouldn't have joined if I wasn't ready to work," Alistair replied. He didn't like the Magister presuming to know anything about him.

"Good. Der's gonna be lots of it, mon. De always give da new ones cleanin' duty," Zed said with a chuckle, then began the long climb to the command center.

"I didn't come here to clean stalls, Zed."

"Of course not. Ya came for da' money. Da' glory. It don't happen ovanight, mon. Ya gotta work for it."

"I just want to hunt Wardens. I can't do that if I'm cleaning up after your shits," Alistair declared, the two chuckling in unison. It was a weird thing for the pair to laugh about, but it was better than Zed telling Alistair what he could or could not do.

"All I'm sayin' is don't expect Rolan ta make ya a hunta right away. Hell, it took Zeke nearly three years of cleanin' shit 'fore Rolan added him ta my team."

Three years. Alistair didn't have that kind of time.

The two continued to climb, Zed never tiring of the endless ascent. Alistair's legs had started to cramp, but he persevered and kept climbing. The two passed through every layer of the ship on their way up the staircase. As they neared the top, they came to the floor where the elite hunters lived. Many of those men and women were standing around as they passed by. Some of them shook hands with Zed, while others jokingly cursed at him and called him names. All of them, however, gave Alistair some rather unnerving looks of disapproval.

"Who's the kid, Zed, your new maid?" One of the men yelled. The others broke into laughter, some pretending to sweep the floor while others mimicked cleaning a toilet and gagging. Alistair ignored them. He knew the hunters were just trying to antagonize him, and he wasn't going to let them know it was working.

The man who had spoken stepped between the two, stopping Alistair in his tracks. He was nowhere near as large as Zed, but he was still bigger than anyone Alistair was accustomed to.

"What's your name, maid?" The large man asked, the snickering of the other men echoing around him.

"What's it to you?" Alistair responded in annoyance, but it was the wrong thing to say. Two men jumped at Alistair from either side, grabbing his arms and holding him in place. Alistair tried to move, but he was trapped. He looked for Zed beyond the large man in front of him, but the Magister was gone.

"Let me explain somethin' to you, maid. Around here, when I ask you a question, you give me a fucking answer!" The man yelled and slammed his fist into Alistair's stomach. The other men laughed as the boy coughed violently.

Alistair looked up into the dark brown eyes of his assailant and, knowing it would probably get him killed, spit in the man's face. The response was instantaneous. The attacker threw a powerful punch directly at Alistair's chin, sending the boy flying. He landed a few feet away as his head snapped back onto the metal grate. He could taste blood in his mouth and realized he had bitten off part of his own tongue. He tried to stand, but the large man jumped on him, quickly unsheathing the small knife at his hip and bringing it to Alistair's neck.

"I'm going to kill you for that." The man grinned, slowly pressing his knife into the skin around Alistair's neck. Blood seeped from the fresh cut and down onto the grate. It was a rather stupid way to die, he thought. He could have just given the man his name and none of this would have happened. He was about to speak when he heard the familiar twang of a bowstring from the distance. Blood suddenly splattered against his face as an arrow pierced his assailant's neck. The man on top of him grunted, choking on his own blood as he desperately gasped for air, but it wouldn't come. Alistair shoved the dying man off him and watched as he flailed around for a few seconds before finally going still.

"That's enough fun for one day, I think," a voice said as the remaining hunters scattered into the darkness like roaches. Alistair's head was still fuzzy as his rescuer drew closer, but he could see that it was Zeke who had saved him.

"Damn good thing you showed up," Alistair said as he took Ezekiel's outstretched hand. Zeke pulled the boy to his feet and slipped a rag from his pocket to wipe the blood from Alistair's neck.

"Where the hell is Zed?" Ezekiel asked, looking around the now barren vicinity.

"No idea. Just disappeared after those idiots grabbed me."

"Typical," Ezekiel replied angrily. "Well, c'mon." Alistair was glad Ezekiel had showed up when he did, but his rescuer didn't seem too thrilled. "Word will spread of what happened here, kid," Zeke continued. He was moving quickly and Alistair, having just climbed hundreds of stairs, was struggling to keep up.

"What will they do to you?" Alistair asked, hoping his new friend wasn't about to be in a heap of trouble.

"To me? Nothing. Rolan will probably send you away, though, for inciting violence and picking fights with his top hunters."

"But, I didn't-"

"It doesn't matter what you did or didn't do. For all Rolan knows, you started that fight and you ended it."

Alistair had never seen people behave in such a way before. He'd only just arrived on The Hammer and, if this Rolan person got word of what had transpired on the landing, he would be leaving just as quickly.

The two finally reached the top of the dome and came upon the strange, octagonal command center that hung out over the entire city. From up here, Alistair could see everything going on down below, and it made him appreciate the hunters' ingenuity.

As the two approached the entrance, one of the glass doors swung out at them.

"Da' hell took ya so long?" Zed asked as he stepped out into the light.

"Made some new friends," Alistair responded, but Zed's white eyes were fixed on the blood spattered across Alistair's face.

"Is Rolan ready for us?" Zeke asked impatiently.

"Yea, but he's not in da best mood. So, I'd keep ya snide remarks to yourself, mon." Zed turned around and walked back into the building. Zeke held the door open as Alistair followed Zed into the darkness. The lobby of the command center was exceptionally clean. The dim bulbs in the ceiling barely provided any actual lighting and the only object in the room was a smooth desk positioned in the very center. A stunningly attractive young woman sat at the desk furiously typing away at a computer, her long, blonde hair wrapped in a tight knot behind her head.

The three walked right past the woman without saying anything and into the bright room behind her. The walls were made of thick, double panned glass that allowed for a completely unobstructed view of the city below. There was another desk, also made of glass, in the middle of the room, along with two glass chairs, each equipped with a spotless white cushion, directly in front of it. The desk was unoccupied at the present. Instead, the man the three had come to see was standing against the far wall observing the city below.

"Sir," Ezekiel began.

"It would seem I have a mess to clean up." The man spoke with his back to the group. His voice was deep and rough, as if he had spent most his life barking orders at people.

"That would be my fault, sir," Alistair began, stepping in front of his two comrades. "I provoked one of your men, and he attacked me. Obviously, you know the rest." Rolan turned and locked eyes with Alistair. He was tall, muscular, and sported a thick black beard that matched his short, professionally trimmed black hair. His eyes were also black and, as they connected with Alistair's, a sense of dread washed over him.

"Honesty," Rolan said, walking slowly towards the group. "It's a trait I admire in my men, and it's also a trait your companions here seem to lack."

"Rolan, we-" Zed began but Rolan stepped up to the man and punched him square in the face.

"You will not speak to me!" Rolan yelled at the Magister. In the short time Alistair had known him, he had never seen Zed cower the way he did now. Rolan must have had incredible power over these men.

"Don't worry about the man who attacked you," Rolan began, taking his eyes from Zed and returning them to rest on Alistair. "He's had that coming for some time now." Alistair breathed a sigh of relief, but he wasn't sure how long that feeling would last. "You're far too young to be the Grand Master," Rolan continued. He was now slowly circling Alistair, examining him from head to toe.

"The Grand Master was my father," Alistair said hesitantly.

"Was?" Rolan asked, his ears perking up like a dog's after you offered it a treat.

"Your men killed him. Fortunately, before he died, he transferred the power to my brother, Mathias." Alistair decided it was best to tell this man the whole truth.

Rolan's eyes opened wide in anger and he rapidly whirled around to face Zed.

"You *killed* him?!" Rolan yelled, his voice reverberating off the glass walls.

"He attacked us and-" Zed tried to explain but Rolan punched the man again.

"What were your orders?" Rolan was fuming. He held a long knife clenched tightly in his right hand. Upon closer inspection, Alistair discovered that the bounty hunter's hand was actually made of some kind of metal.

"Ta bring da Warden back alive," Zed replied, as if he had repeated the order several times before. He could barely stand as he hung his head low in shame.

"So then help me to understand this: you find the Warden we've been hunting for years, he attacks you, and you decide to kill him. Then, you let his successor, a mere child, get away, and you decide that your best course of action is to return here empty handed?!" Rolan's blood red face was mere inches from Zed's, the deadly blade clenched tightly at his side.

"Dey had some kinda beast. It musta' been protectin' da boy. It killed Sullivan!"

"Yes, well, you're going to wish it had killed you too," Rolan replied and without hesitation, sliced the blade across Zed's throat. Alistair flinched and his eyes went wide with fear, but he didn't look away. As the Magister crumpled to the floor in front of them, his dark, stolen power began to seep into the room. The black magic hung in the air for a brief moment and then dissipated into nothing. The Magister was dead. Rolan used Zed's black pants to wipe the fresh, purple blood from his knife and then turned to face the two remaining men, both of whom stood in complete terror before him.

"Magisters," Rolan said, clearly annoyed at the situation, then took a seat at his desk. The violet puddle of blood around Zed was growing by the second. "Have a seat, friends." Rolan motioned to the two chairs before him. Reluctantly, the two each picked a chair and sat down.

"Now, tell me about this brother of yours." Rolan said to Alistair. With concise detail, Alistair recounted the events that had transpired on Talise. Rolan remained quiet throughout the entire tale, and only when Alistair had finished did he speak again. "So, you have no idea where he is now?"

"Well, that's not entirely true, sir." Alistair replied. He had been trying to remember something his father had told him a long time ago, about a refuge for the remaining Wardens. He wasn't sure if that's where Mathias had gone, but he figured it was worth mentioning. "My father spoke to me once of a small planet within the black hole outside of Talise known as Sanctuary. The planet is supposed to be safe from outside interference as only those who know of its existence ever go looking for it."

"And you think your brother is there?" Rolan asked.

"Don't really think he'd be anywhere else."

Rolan looked down at the bounty laying on his desk. It was a copy of the one he had given to Zed, the bounty for Aurilean. Commander Jax, leader of the remaining Raven forces on Ravendra, had submitted the bounty for the Grand Master many years prior, but the hunters had never been able to find him. Now, the bounty was suddenly much more obtainable, and the reward for the young boy's capture would be astronomical.

"If I were to ask you to take me to this Sanctuary, do you think you could do it?" Rolan asked Alistair.

"Yea. I think I could," Alistair responded slowly. He was starting to remember bits and pieces from his training with his father. He also recalled many other Warden secrets the old man had told him, but he decided to keep those to himself.

"Excellent. I'll assemble a team. We leave within the hour," Rolan stated and then turned to Ezekiel. "You are grounded until further notice. Be glad your punishment is not more severe."

Ezekiel knew better than to argue and simply hung his head in shame. Alistair didn't think it was a good idea to press his luck, but he couldn't leave behind the man who had just saved his life.

"Sir? Zeke has saved my life twice now. I'd like to request that you let him stay on the team."

Rolan raised an eyebrow at Alistair. He wasn't sure what to make of this child sitting before him. If anyone else had just asked what Alistair had, Rolan would have probably pulled his knife back out. But there was something about the boy that Rolan liked. He couldn't quite place his finger on what it was, but he decided to agree to Alistair's terms.

"Very well. Keep this one close, Zeke. Seems he owes you a life or two," Rolan said and then stood up from his desk. "Meet me at Bay 21 in an hour. If you're not there, I'll assume you've betrayed me and will send every hunter in this place to find you. Do you understand?" The two nodded simultaneously and watched as Rolan exited his office, taking care to sidestep the decaying corpse on the floor.

"Thanks," Zeke started. He had never had anyone stick up for him before.

"No problem, man. Gotta have someone watching my back, ya know?" Alistair laughed, and slapped Zeke on the shoulder.

"Yea, that's true," Zeke smiled. It was nice to have a friend. "You think you can really find Sanctuary?"

"I do," Alistair replied, a wicked smile coming over his face. "The Wardens will never see it coming."

11

The early morning wind gusted through the valley as Mathias instinctively ducked to avoid his opponent's attack. The Grand Master was sparring against the young boy he had met a few days before. He had expertly passed a couple more defense and maneuverability tests, and had started working on fighting back. His current lesson dealt with exploiting enemy weaknesses and opportunistic strikes. However, unlike his success from the previous days, Mathias had already suffered several blows to his chest and back and one blow to the side of his head, resulting in a rather nasty bruise near his right eye.

His opponent, whose name Mathias had learned was Kris, had met the group of Wardens outside their lodgings. He escorted the four to the training square just outside the entrance of the temple where the rest of the group awaited them.

"Welcome, friends!" Monk had said, speaking vociferously to the groggy Wardens. "We gather once again to continue the training of our new Grand Master!"

Great, Mathias thought as he stretched out his muscles. He suspected that the sessions would only grow more difficult as his time on Sanctuary progressed, and his head was still sore from his lesson with Mira.

"Over the past few days, we have learned that a fight can be won without ever landing a single blow on your opponent," Monk continued, his voiced echoing across the valley. "But what happens when your opponent matches your skills in defense? What happens when you are forced to mix that defense with a series of precise and quick attacks? Step into the ring, young Warden, and we shall see."

Mathias had reluctantly stepped onto the spongy, white sparring mat, throwing his dirty, tattered shirt aside. Kris stepped into the ring opposite him and tossed Mathias a staff. The shaved piece of wood felt incredibly light and well-balanced as he twirled it between his fingers.

Nearly two hours later and Mathias had yet to land a single blow on his agile opponent. With a weapon thrown into the mix, he was having a painfully difficult time balancing his defense with his offense. All Kris had to do was wait for an opening, and there were many.

Mathias quickly jumped back, feeling the wind whip against his face as his opponent's staff came within an inch of his nose. Feeling that he had a sudden advantage, Mathias brought the long staff around and launched an attack at the boy's head. Kris immediately spun his body down to the ground, expertly dodging the attack. It was a move that, had Mathias blinked, he might have missed entirely. Before the Warden could react, the young boy continued forward and slammed his staff hard into the Warden's stomach. Mathias dropped to his knees, coughing furiously as he gasped for air.

"And that would be the seventeenth time Kris has killed you," Monk said impatiently. After the boy's riveting display in the days prior, the Flame Warden had high hopes for the boy. But, as the spectators that now bordered the square were acutely aware, that was certainly not the case.

Joel howled with laughter from the sidelines, while Mira and Ardemis stood in uneasy silence. The two had been shouting words of encouragement to Mathias during the fight, but it had gotten so distracting that he had yelled at them to stop. In that moment, Kris used the opportunity to whip Mathias along the side of his head. Joel had cried from laughing so hard at that one.

"Kris, take a break," Monk said as he limped to the middle of the ring. Mathias was still coughing as the old man used his staff to kneel beside him. "What's wrong, Mathias?" He spoke quietly so none of the other Wardens could hear him.

"He's too... damn fast..." Mathias said, the coughing finally subsiding. "I don't have any time to think."

"Well, right there is your problem. Don't think." Monk smiled, but Mathias was even more confused.

"Huh?"

"You're far too preoccupied worrying about what you need to do," Monk replied. "Kris is able to beat you not because he's faster than you, but because he doesn't spend his valuable time thinking about how he's going to beat you. He simply reacts to the way that you move and uses what openings he can find to strike. You must do the same. Instead of thinking about how the whole battle will play out, focus your energy on what's happening now."

Mathias rubbed his jaw, the pain still present from Kris's earlier blow. What Monk said made sense, but Mathias still didn't fully grasp the concept. If he stopped thinking and simply reacted to each blow, he still had to figure out how to get the staff where he needed it to be.

"But what about the weapon?" Mathias asked, bringing his thought to life. "How do I make sure it's moving in the way that I need it to?"

"You stop thinking of it as a weapon," Monk replied, as if he had known what Mathias was about to ask.

"What is it then?"

"It is part of you. Do not think of the staff as a foreign object that you must constantly keep tabs of. Instead, think of it as an extension of yourself."

Mathias picked the weapon up off the ground and tossed it into the air a few times.

"The staff exists to extend your reach. You can use it to knock fruit from the tallest tree, or perhaps pull a friend out of a deep hole. When you use it in battle, it is a way for you to strike your opponent while keeping yourself out of harm's way. Let it dance with you in the same way that you would dance with your opponent. Do you understand?"

"I think so," Mathias replied. He looked at the solid piece of wood in his hand and considered for a moment everything the man had told him. Then he jumped to his feet and yelled to Kris at the side of the square. "Alright, let's do this!" He spun the weapon around in his fingers, allowing it to become a part of him. He considered how the staff would move with his arm as he danced across the mat, dodging and ducking to avoid any attack his opponent would throw at him.

Kris hastily jumped back into the ring and also twirled his weapon in his fingers. The two bowed to each other and then, without warning, Kris attacked, the end of his staff already headed straight for Mathias's head. The Warden performed a quick diving roll backward to avoid the blow. However, as soon as Kris failed to connect, he continued forward with his assault. Mathias jumped out of the way again, dodging another attack. Every time he avoided a blow, Kris was right there swinging in for another one. If the fight continued at this rate, Mathias would lose for sure. He needed to change his technique and become the aggressive attacker Monk expected him to be.

Mathias spun to the ground as Kris came in for another attack, but this time the Warden was ready for him. The young boy had been favoring that particular move, and Mathias knew he could use it to throw his opponent off balance. As soon as Kris whipped his staff through the air, Mathias used his own staff to sweep at Kris's feet. Kris managed to jump over the attack, but the strike caught him off guard. The Warden didn't wait around for the boy to analyze the maneuver. With a sudden surge of confidence, Mathias rushed at his opponent. He felt the staff in his hand, the powerful extension of himself, and knew what he needed to do.

Kris saw the attack coming and prepared to defend himself. Mathias charged in and swung straight for the boy's head. Kris had seen the move many times before and prepared to counter the attack with a strike of his own. As Kris spun out of the way, he brought his staff around with him. It was a perfectly timed swing, as Mathias was still recovering from his assault. However, instead of a connecting with his attacker, Kris's staff found only air. Mathias had managed to use the momentum of his first swing to carry his body forward in a circle around Kris, causing the counterattack to fail. As Kris frantically searched for his attacker, he felt a sudden whack in the back of his head. The power behind the strike sent the boy flying forward, his face slamming into the padded mat around him. His head was throbbing, but he knew he had to get up and finish the fight. He rolled from his stomach to his back but, just as he was about to stand, Mathias was on top of him. Just as the Warden had done a few days before, Mathias brought his weapon within an inch of the boy's face. Kris, knowing full well that he had lost, tapped the padding twice signaling his surrender.

Mathias backed off the young boy and extended his staff, pulling his smiling opponent to his feet. The crowd had grown since the fight had begun, and everyone was cheering at Mathias's victory. Monk had a smile hidden beneath his beard, and he nodded as Mathias's eyes fell upon his own. Ardemis cheered wildly with the others, but Joel seemed to have vanished. The big man was probably upset that Mathias had finally succeeded in his battle. He still had two more rounds to go, though, and he wasn't sure if he could keep his winning streak alive.

As Mathias made his way over to his friends, a large silhouette appeared atop the temple. It took the Warden less than a second to recognize the hulking figure as Joel.

"Grand Master!" Joel yelled, his deep voice reverberating across the valley. "I challenge you!" The massive figure jumped high into the air and came crashing down to the training square beneath him. He landed perfectly in the center, shaking the very ground beneath his feet.

Mira uttered something about Joel always needing to make an entrance, and the trio burst into a fit of laughter. Mathias quickly calmed himself, though, and turned from the sidelines, slowly walking to the center where Joel now stood. The Warden of Strength was truly an intimidating sight as he stood in the center of the ring, the sunlight gleaming off his exposed muscles. Joel was equipped with his usual attire: a tattered pair of beige shorts and nothing else. The brands on his arms and legs seemed to glow against his tan skin.

"'Bout time," Mathias began. He knew Joel had been itching to spar with him since the moment the two had met. There was a competitive tension between the two, and a fight was just what the boys needed.

"You know I'm 'bout to kick your hind parts off this rock, right?" Joel asked and then charged. Mathias knew the assault would be swift, but he hadn't expected the massive Warden to move as fast as he did. Mathias dropped under Joel's punch but was instantly thrown forward as the man's leg swung around and connected with his backside.

"HA! Hind parts. I crack myself up." Joel cackled at his own joke, and Mathias was sure this was only the beginning of it. Without waiting around for Joel to ready himself again, Mathias leapt off the ground and sprinted towards the man. He spun his staff around and aimed it straight for Joel's exposed face. The moment before the staff found its mark, Joel slid to the side, grabbing the weapon as he did, and flung Mathias face first into the mat. Joel roared with laughter as the Grand Master scrambled back to his feet.

"This is impossible..." Mathias muttered in frustration.

He's using his size against ya, lad. A voice instantly said, echoing inside the recesses of Mathias's mind. Ardemis was trying to help him! *Try to turn it into his weakness.* The Warden looked over to the edge of the square where Ardemis stood. The little man nodded at him and gave Mathias a huge grin and a thumbs-up.

"Quit your stallin'!" Joel yelled and then chucked the staff back at Mathias. The boy snatched the weapon out of the air and then bounded across the square. He was barely half Joel's size and could move around in ways the hulking behemoth could not. As he came up on the man, Mathias dropped to his knees, using the growing momentum of the staff to spin him under the punch Joel had launched his way. He jumped up behind the big man and slammed his staff hard into Joel's back. However, instead of inflicting any damage to his opponent, the weapon simply bounced off Joel's massive body.

Mathias looked down at his weapon and found that a small crack had formed where it had connected with Joel. The man was so huge that he had broken the weapon without having to do anything.

"Was that it?" Joel asked, laughing as he turned to face the Warden. "You're gonna have to do better than that, kid."

Now what? Mathias asked, reaching out with his mind to communicate with Ardemis.

Same advice as before, lad. His size is going to beat you every time. You need to find a way use that against him. But Mathias had already tried that. What else could he possibly do?

The wind gusted fiercely around them forcing the clouds above to race through the skies. Mathias watched them for a brief a moment and then returned his gaze to Joel. The man stood against the wind like a brick wall, never permitting it to shake his foundation. At that moment, an idea suddenly sprang into Mathias's head. He wasn't sure how to do it, or even if he could, but he had run out of options. Spinning the staff around in his hands, he prepared for another round with the Warden of Strength. The wind caught the staff as Mathias spun it and pushed it forward with great speed, spinning it faster and faster.

Joel wasn't sure what the boy had planned, and he was tired of waiting. It was time to end the battle for good. The snaky brands on Joel's legs suddenly lit up with a bright yellow light and, using his Warden-like speed, he roared with vigor and charged.

Mathias hoped that Joel would grow impatient enough to attack on his own and, as the man rapidly closed the gap between them, he prepared his defense. The Grand Master hadn't expected Joel to use his power against him, so the attack came much faster than Mathias anticipated. However, at the speed Joel was traveling, he would fall into the trap much sooner.

The staff in the Warden's hand was now spinning so fast that he could feel the wind blowing around him. It blew across his body, breezed through the small hairs on his head and chest, and danced around him as he danced around his opponents. The wind was his to control, and he would use it to break his opponent's steadfast fortification.

The blocky brands lit up Joel's bulging biceps as the man swung his fist in for the blow he'd ached to land since first meeting the boy. Mathias watched the fist close in on his face and, in one swift motion, ducked under the attack and spun around the massive man. Then, using the winds now caught in the spinning staff, Mathias swung the weapon at Joel's exposed back once again. The sheer force of the gale, along with the growing speed of the staff, crashed into the Warden's body and sent the massive figure flying into the air. Mathias watched in awe as Joel slammed into the temple walls, shaking the very building itself. The entire mass of people that had gathered to watch was now dead silent.

Mathias breathed heavily as he stood alone in the ring. The wind that had thrown Joel into the building had returned to Mathias and was now swirling around him in a gentle breeze. Mathias wasn't sure how, but he'd managed to command the wind around him.

The crowd erupted in a wild uproar of cheering and yelling. Monk was even clapping wildly in approval. Mira and Ardemis ran out into the center of the ring, completely ignoring Joel's groans of pain.

"I knew it! I told you!" Ardemis was yelling.

"So you did," Mira said, a hint of surprise in her voice. "I'm glad you won, Mathias, but don't think you're off the hook. He'll make it his life goal to beat you now." But Mathias didn't care. Mira flashed him the biggest smile and it sent all sorts of strange feelings rushing through him.

Joel was finally on his feet and stumbling slowly back towards the square. The crowd grew silent as the large man pushed his way onto the mat. Mathias stood firm, the staff in his hands and Mira and Ardemis at his sides. There was a small trickle of dark red blood oozing from a scratch in Joel's head, and it seemed like he was prepared to start the fight all over again. Instead, and catching everyone completely by surprise, Joel stretched out his hand. Mathias took it in his and shook firmly.

"You're alright, kid," Joel said as he used his other arm to wipe the blood from his face.

"Joel!" Ardemis suddenly yelled. "I told you it would be me!"

"Dammit, you did. Kid, you owe me fifty silver pieces," Joel said to Mathias as he released him from the handshake.

"What are you talking about?" Mathias asked.

"It appears that something interesting has happened today. The power of the Sky Wardens has manifested within you." Monk stepped out into the ring to join the others. "I'm impressed. Many of the previous Master's spent years learning to attune themselves to the air around them, a feat you've managed to accomplish in a matter of days."

Mathias was in shock. But, as quickly as it had come, the surprise vanished, and Mathias finally realized what Monk was talking about. The wind. Mathias had called upon it for aid in the battle, using it to propel his victim through the air. Now, the breeze continued to blow around him, acting as a shield and preparing for when it would be called upon again.

"And I told you it would be me!" Ardemis yelled again, dancing around the group and pumping his fists into the air.

"That you did, my friend," Monk replied, patting Ardemis on the back.

"So, what does that mean? What do I do now?" Mathias asked excitedly. He was already aching to learn how to fly as Ardemis did.

"It means that your sparring sessions are over for today," Mira said, a wicked grin spreading across her face. A grin that made Mathias feel incredibly uneasy.

Matthew Louwers

12

Ardemis could hardly contain his excitement as he dragged the Grand Master away from the temple. His massive grin spread from ear to ear, and he couldn't stop muttering, 'I knew it!' under his breath, but just loud enough so the others behind him could hear.

Mathias's mind was swirling with questions, but he was given only shady grins and responses like, 'you'll find out.' He decided that he would just have to go with the flow and see if the answers he was looking for would reveal themselves along the way.

The day had grown quite warm as the sun beat its rays upon the group. The wind still rushed furiously through the valley, and it continued to swirl around Mathias as they arrived at the hidden path Ardemis had told him about it. The entrance to the path was covered in long, tangling vines so gnarled that Mathias had no idea how they were going to get through. Beyond the vines, Mathias could just barely make out a winding dirt trail that led deeper into the valley.

"Here we are!" Ardemis exclaimed as the group came to a screeching halt. "Friends, the time has come once again to lead another down the Master's Path," Ardemis began. Mathias could have sworn the little man looked taller than usual. "As we all know, the Path hasn't been used in several years. The valley has sealed this ancient trail away until the day it would be needed once again." Ardemis looked to Mathias and added, "That day is today."

The group cheered loudly behind him, and Mathias could do little to hide his nerves. He was still having a hard time convincing himself that this wasn't some elaborate dream. Everything was happening so fast, and he needed some time to catch up.

The wind whistled melodiously as it breezed through the trees around them, and Mathias snapped out of his daze. Ardemis performed a series of beautifully fluid movements, commanding the very wind that swirled around them. The trees danced as the air blasted by, swirling faster and faster around Ardemis. Then, with a sharp and direct snap of his wrists, Ardemis fired a blade of air towards the wall of vines. At first, Mathias didn't think anything had happened. The vines remained firmly in place and hardly budged as the wind passed through. However, Ardemis moved to the wall and pushed on the gnarled mess, shattering the blockage with ease. The wind had cut perfectly through the vines. Another cheer went up from the crowd, and the Grand Master found himself cheering along with them.

"Mathias, the ability to command the wind has manifested within you, and it's best to begin training as soon as that happens. Because of that, I have re-opened the Master's Path and will be your teacher in the days to come." Ardemis was having an impossible time restraining his excitement.

Mathias was jittery with anticipation, as well. He couldn't believe that his first ability to manifest was control over the wind. It was hardly a huge surprise, however, as Mathias always dreamed of flying amongst the other denizens of the air.

"Now, Grand Master, we depart. Do try to keep up, if you can," Ardemis said with a grin and then blasted down the dusty trail into the valley. For a little guy, the Sky Warden sure could run. Mathias chuckled for a moment as he finally understood the expression, 'running like the wind.'

"Whatchu waitin' for?!" Joel yelled from the clump of spectators behind him.

Mathias glanced back at the Warden of Strength and returned a sly grin. Then, as he turned to run, he felt the wind pick up speed around him. Without giving it a second thought, Mathias bolted after Ardemis. It took only seconds to realize that he was faster than he had ever been. The wind he now commanded blew against his back at incredible speeds, pushing the young boy along. He moved with such speed that the bright green leaves of the trees broke free from their branches as he passed, catching in the gusts and trailing just behind him.

The dark, dirt covered path was winding, but fairly easy to follow, and Mathias realized that it was leading him uphill. The trees grew thinner as he continued, and the sun began to poke its rays through the branches. Up and up the Warden went, but he still hadn't caught up with Ardemis. There were no forks in the trail, at least none that Mathias could see, so he couldn't have deviated from the correct path.

Before he knew it, Mathias burst forth from the jungle and out onto a wide, rocky cliff. He hadn't noticed it while he had been running, but the rushing of the nearby river now drew his attention. The sapphire waters were crystal clear and moving nearly as fast as Mathias had been. The Warden followed the river to the edge of the cliff and gasped as the rushing water reached its end and opened into the canyon. It crashed into the rocks far below and thrashed as it splashed around in its new world.

"Beautiful, isn't it?" Ardemis said. Mathias jumped at the voice and faced his teacher, his heart pounding hard in his chest.

"It is. How does the river flow up the mountain like that?" Mathias asked. It was a detail he had only just noticed.

"Not a clue, lad. Just always has," Ardemis explained, a fact Mathias found incredibly odd. Curious, he turned back to the edge of the cliff. Just off in the distance, he could see the group he had left behind not too long ago. They gathered on a smaller plateau across the valley and were now cheering and waving at him.

"You did well to get here as quickly as you did, but I bet you could have gone even faster. You might have even been able to beat me. Now wouldn't that have been exciting!" Ardemis laughed. His deep belly chuckle reminded Mathias a lot of Aurilean.

"Why did the wind help me? I didn't call upon it," Mathias asked. It was only the tip of the iceberg of questions the Warden had piled up in his head.

"The wind is in a constant state of flux around us. You can always feel it brushing against your cheek, or each time you inhale. Whether you call upon it or not, it's always there. You simply need to mold it to your needs."

"I see," Mathias said excitedly, but he was still eager to learn more. "Now what?"

"Now, we fly," Ardemis said with a grin. Mathias tried to keep his composure, but he couldn't help letting out a small hoot of excitement.

148

"I can't tell you how ready I am for this!" And he meant it.

"Good," Ardemis replied and, without giving Mathias any warning, pushed the boy off the cliff.

It wasn't a very long fall, but long enough that Mathias had time to wonder what the hell had just happened. He decided that thinking too much about the situation would likely get him killed so, instead, he reached out for the air around him. It rushed past him as he plummeted towards the gushing waters below. It pushed at his back and pulled the Warden down faster. Before he could ask the wind for aid, he crashed into the splashing river. He was lucky that he missed the rocks at the base of the falls, but something told him there was more than luck involved.

As soon as Mathias poked his head through the surface, he could hear the dreadful howl of laughter coming from Joel on the cliff above. Some of the others were laughing with him, but Mathias didn't care.

Much to the boy's surprise, his entire body rose out of the water and floated back towards the top of the waterfall. Ardemis stood there chuckling to himself as he commanded the wind around Mathias. When the boy reached the top of the cliff, he continued to hover in mid-air, the wind blowing fiercely around him.

"I thought you said you were ready?" Ardemis asked, a sly smirk plastered to his face.

"Yea, for you to teach me! Not for you to throw me off the mountain!" Mathias yelled through the gust around him. The hairs on his arms stood on end as the cool wind blew against the water dripping off him.

"I find that one learns best in the moment," Ardemis replied and dropped his hands. The wind around Mathias dissipated, and he found himself falling once again.

Fortunately, Mathias had a suspicion this would happen and was ready for it. He put his arms out and felt for the wind around him. This time, however, the Grand Master called out to it. He let the breeze wash over every part of his body, feeling the rush as it weaved in between his fingers and toes. As soon as he was sure that the wind would obey, he asked it to stop his fall. But the wind ignored him, and Mathias found himself once again crashing into the water's surface.

Ardemis wasted no time pulling the Grand Master back up the cliff.

"I think I almost had it that time!" Mathias yelled.

"Not even a little bit, laddie," Ardemis replied with another chuckle.

"What?!"

"Listen, lad. The wind isn't something you can just control. It heeds no commands and can be quite unpredictable at times. Constant state of flux, remember?"

"Then how do I get it to do what I want?" Mathias asked.

"You don't. You do what *it* wants," Ardemis said and once again sent Mathias plummeting towards the water.

Let everything go. Mira's melodic voice suddenly echoed inside the Warden's head. *The wind is a free-spirit, and so must you be.*

That's when it all finally made sense. His battle with Joel earlier that day and his run up the mountain were both times when Mathis was forced to let go of everything he had ever known. The wind was always there to help him but was never truly his to control. As soon as he came to grips with that realization, he closed his eyes and let the fear of crashing into the water go. Every doubt that had ever crossed his mind he set free into the afternoon breeze. When he no longer had any worries or cares weighing him down, Mathias felt like a feather on the wind. He slowly opened his eyes and realized he was no longer falling. Instead, the Grand Master hovered just above the water's surface. He reached out and brushed his hand through the waves, sending ripples through the reflection starting back at him.

The crowd on the cliff roared with excitement and Mathias could feel the wind blowing around him and forcing his body ever higher. Without even giving it a second thought, he pushed off against the air and blasted himself past the cliff where Ardemis stood cheering and punching his fist into the air.

Higher and higher Mathias climbed, always feeling the air around him. The higher he travelled, the cooler it got and the harder it became for him to breathe. However, having lived on Talise for so long, the young Warden was accustomed to the thin air. He quickly banked and darted straight for the nearest cloud. He had always wondered what it would be like to fly through one. The cool mist rushed against him and he soared through it at lightning speed, coming out the other side covered in ice crystals and shivering furiously. Clouds were apparently very cold and very wet.

"Well done, lad," Ardemis yelled as he suddenly appeared beside Mathias.

"Ardy, this is amazing!" Mathias was overcome with glee. He had always envied those that could soar through the skies, but now he could fly among them as well. It was almost too good to be true.

"It truly is, laddie."

"Wait here. I'll be right back!" Mathias yelled and suddenly dropped out of the sky. He let his body freefall as it dropped back towards the ground, the wind rushing past. Then, just as the Warden was about to collide with the rocks beneath him, he swooped out of his dive and blasted back into the air.

As he rose, he saw the group from the temple had begun to dissipate. Joel and Mira both had their backs turned as Mathias slammed down onto the cliff behind them.

"Hey!" Mathias yelled. The two stopped and turned around in unison to face the Warden. They watched as the Grand Master approached, covered from head to toe in melting ice crystals.

Mathias stopped just before the beautiful woman in front of him and, without paying any attention to the hulking man beside her, gave Mira the biggest hug he had ever given anyone. Mira's eyes grew incredibly wide as the icy wave washed over her. Just as Mathias began to pull away, he stopped and looked Mira dead in the eyes.

"Thank you," he said, and laid a gentle kiss on Mira's cheek.

Joel was suddenly very afraid for the young boy who, unbeknownst to him, had just crossed a very dangerous line. He knew how Mira felt about other men getting close to her, so he prepared for the worst, but it never came. Instead, the young woman burst into laughter as Mathias took off into the air. He spun rapidly, spewing droplets of icy water in every direction, then sped off into the distance.

Joel was in utter amazement as he watched the Warden fly off. He was inclined to question Mira over what just happened, but saw her with her hand on her cheek in the exact spot Mathias had kissed her. Joel decided it was better not to upset her. He hesitantly turned away from the cliff and began his trip back to the temple.

Mathias couldn't believe what he'd just done. He never expected Mira to let him hug her, let alone plant a gentle kiss on her cheek. But, today was a day full of big changes, and Mathias was ready for more. He found Ardemis where he had left him only moments ago.

"What was that about?" Ardemis asked curiously.

"She gave me some pretty good advice back there. Had to thank her."

"Surprised she didn't knock you on your ass again, honestly." And he meant it. Mira wasn't known for her caring and gentle nature. The Grand Master simply shrugged.

"So, what now?" There was no slowing Mathias down. He wanted to learn as much as he could all at once.

"It's still a wee bit early to take you off world," Ardemis continued. Mathias let out a groan of disappointment. He really wanted to learn how the Sky Wardens could survive in the dark, starlit void of space. "How about a race?"

As soon as the words left Ardemis's mouth, the Grand Master's ears perked up. A race would be the perfect way to test out his new abilities.

"Let's do it!" Mathias responded enthusiastically, punching the air as he did.

"Ha! Don't get too excited, lad. I'll have you know this Sky Warden has *never* lost a race," Ardemis said, putting a little extra emphasis on the word 'never.'

"Then it's time we change that!"

"Alight lad, you see that tall mountain out there? The one where the peak climbs higher than all the others?"

Mathias squinted in the sunlight, searching around for the mountain Ardemis spoke of. It towered over all the others around it, its peak reaching high into the clouds. "I see it."

"Good," Ardemis replied and then blasted off towards the mountain, leaving Mathias spinning in circles. Instead of trying to regain his balance in the wind, Mathias used the spinning to launch himself after Ardemis. The maneuver had

153

the desired effect, as Mathias now sped through the bright, blue sky. Far off in the distance he could see Ardemis weaving in between the clouds, flying with a grace the likes of which Mathias had never seen before.

The Warden decided, if he was going to beat his friend in this race, he would need to think outside the box. He dropped into a dive, pulling a massive current of air down with him. He plummeted rapidly, adjusting his course for the raging river below. Faster and faster he flew, gaining speed as he continued to dive. The water was approaching rapidly and, just as he was about to crash into it, Mathias pulled up into a glide across the river's surface.

The maneuver had certainly put some distance between him and Ardemis but, if his plan worked, it wouldn't matter. He continued to push against the wind behind him, forcing his body to fly faster and faster. Because of his incredible speed, drops of water from river floated up and got caught in the trail of wind behind him. But it wasn't enough. If his plan was to succeed, he would need more than just water. That's when he remembered the mountains. The snow near the peaks of some of the smaller ones would work perfectly.

Gathering what remaining water he could, Mathias pulled up and shot towards the nearest peak. It was a smaller mountain, but it still had plenty of snow around the top. As he neared the peak, Mathias began to circle the mountain. Faster and faster he spun, creating a cyclone that pulled the snow from the mountaintop. As soon as he had enough, Mathias broke the circle and sped off after Ardemis, a trail of ice and water following closely behind.

Ardemis continued to fly with style, dodging and weaving between the mountaintops while avoiding the other denizens of the sky. He realized he was far enough ahead that he could rest a moment and see how his opponent was fairing. He slowed his speed and spun around, scanning the horizon for Mathias, but the Grand Master was nowhere to be seen. Ardemis hoped nothing had happened to the boy, and he was about to call off the race when he suddenly noticed a blazing ball of white light hurtling up at him from one of the smaller mountains. He couldn't make out exactly what it was, but it was moving far too fast to be a cloud or a bird. Squinting against the bright sunlight, he noticed a black blur at the center of the light, and that's when everything clicked. Mathias was heading straight for him! He couldn't believe that the boy had already performed the Comet Tail, a tactic Ardemis himself had used several times before. Wasting no more time admiring his protégé, Ardemis turned and sped off into the sky.

Mathias was rapidly gaining on his opponent, the ice-cold trail of snow behind him seemingly pushing him on even faster, instead of dragging him down. Using that to his advantage, Mathias climbed higher, positioning himself above Ardemis. The Warden continued to gain speed, while Ardemis only seemed to be maintaining his. As soon as he had closed the gap just enough, Mathias dove once again, except this time he stopped just in front of Ardemis. The trail of ice behind him slammed down into the Sky Warden, catching him completely off guard.

Ardemis was flabbergasted. There was no way the boy could already perform a stunt like that.

The remaining drops of water froze to Ardemis's skin slowing the Sky Warden down immensely. He couldn't stay in the comet's tail forever, but every time he tried to dip down Mathias would follow suit, keeping him cold and sluggish.

The final peak was so close now and Mathias was sure the victory was about to be his. He couldn't believe that he had just bested a master Sky Warden at his own game. In his overconfidence, Mathias failed to notice the change in the air around him. His trail of snow had vanished and the air around him became nearly unbreathable.

He spun around and noticed Artemis had stopped flying. Instead, the little man appeared to be pulling the wind toward him and away from Mathias. He tried to make a break for the peak, but it didn't work. He couldn't move, and there was hardly any air left to breathe.

"I didn't want to have to resort to this, lad," Ardemis yelled, but Mathias couldn't hear him. In fact, the Grand Master couldn't hear anything, even his own attempts at breathing. That's when he realized what Ardemis had done. The Sky Warden had created a vacuum. Mathias was trapped as he floated in place, unable to move. Ardemis dropped his hands and immediately darted for the peak. All Mathias could do was watch as the Sky Warden sped to victory. That's when something strange happened. Mathias felt a brush of air against his cheek. It wasn't much, but it was enough for Mathias to push off of. The push accelerated him just enough that he began to slowly drift towards the gusting wall of the vacuum. As soon as he pierced the wall, the vacuum broke and everything came rushing back. Mathias wasted no time and darted off after Ardemis once again.

The Sky Warden was only moments away from the peak when he felt a surge of air rush past him. The force from the wind caused his body to spin a few times before he could stabilize himself. When he did, he noticed a dark shadow standing atop the frozen peak.

It was Mathias.

Impossible! Ardemis thought to himself. He couldn't believe the Grand Master had broken free of his trap. Very few had ever been able to do that. Faced with defeat, Ardemis drifted up towards the peak where Mathias stood with his hands on his hips.

"What took you so long?" Mathias jested.

"I don't know how you did it, lad, but I applaud you." Ardemis stroked the red scruff on his chin and wiped away the bits of ice still clinging to his shirt.

"I don't know either, Ardy. I felt a brush of air in the vacuum and used it to push myself out," the boy explained, still looking genuinely confused as to how he managed the feat.

"Seems like we should have gone off world after all," Ardemis chuckled.

"We still have time!" The Warden's eyes twinkled with excitement.

"Well, I don't see why not."

Y'all need to get back here, now! The loud voice rang in both Wardens' heads. It was Joel, and something was very wrong.

Matthew Louwers

13

The battlecruiser appeared out of nowhere. The group of trainees, who had just returned from the Grand Master's first real lesson, were dispersing for the evening when the jet-black ship materialized above the temple. The initial shock of the unexpected visitors paralyzed the few that saw it. A few seconds later, the foreign craft lowered its front guns and, without any warning, unloaded a barrage of energy bolts into the temple. The resulting explosion was instantaneous as bits of wood, glass and metallic debris blasted in every direction. Anyone unlucky enough to be inside the temple was immediately crushed, while those further away managed to just barely escape with their lives.

Mira was the first to react to the situation. She quickly gathered the trainees that remained and began prepping them for battle, passing each of them a wooden staff or spear. While Mira continued to usher the others away from the temple, Joel tried to reach the other Wardens.

Y'all need to get back here, now!

What's wrong, laddie? Ardemis's voice echoed inside Joel's head.

Temple was just attacked.

What?!

Yea… We need you and the kid now!

On our way! And that was the last Joel heard from Ardemis. The Wardens were coming, and he needed to buy them some time.

Joel waited at the edge of the seared field as the black ship touched down just beyond what remained of the sacred hall. The loading ramp slammed into the dirt and a plethora of armor clad figures stormed out of the aircraft. They all wielded blaster rifles and positioned themselves in a wide semi-circle in front of their ship. Joel considered the best form of approach, which usually consisted of a head-on assault.

Don't go in alone! Mira's voiced boomed in Joel's head, but he ignored her. The brands on both his arms and legs were alight, signaling he was prepared to fight with or without backup. The Warden of Strength bounded towards the ramp where the strangers were still pouring out, but he was immediately met with waves of blaster fire. Without his brother around to absorb the blasts, Joel was forced to find cover. He dove behind a nearby pile of debris and waited for the bolts of energy to subside, but the blasts kept coming. A ray of sparks violently exploded around him as a shot found its mark, obliterating the debris pile he was hiding behind.

"Joel!" A voice yelled from the distance. The other trainees had arrived, and Kris was leading the pack, spinning his staff in hand, deflecting the bolts of energy that now came for them. The carved weapons had been specifically designed to repel common weapon fire and very rarely splintered under the pressure of continued exposure. Kris made his way to where Joel was crouching, continuing to deflect any attacks that came his way. The rest of the trainees ran headstrong into the fray, making their way across the debris covered field.

"Nice timin', kid," Joel said as Kris helped him find new cover. Fortunately, the blasts of energy died down as the trainees engaged the enemy in melee combat. The invaders were forced to shed their guns for the swords many of them had strung at their hips.

"Who are they, Warden Joel?"

"Hunters by the looks of 'em. Prolly here for the kid," Joel replied through gritted teeth.

"But how did they find us?" Kris inquired, but Joel didn't have an answer for him. Only those who knew of Sanctuary's location could find it, and everyone that knew of its location was currently on Sanctuary. It didn't make sense.

"I don't know, kid, but I ain't waitin' around to find out." And with that, Joel jumped from cover and darted into the fray. A few hunters from the backline continued firing their blasters in his direction, but Joel was moving too fast for any of the shots to have been fired with any accuracy. He slammed into the nearest hunter, sending the poor man flying into the distance. If the sheer force of the blow didn't killed him, the fall certainly would. But Joel didn't pay it any attention as he ducked under a blade that nearly severed his head. He came out of his dodge with his fist and shattered his attacker's face.

Men and women from both sides were falling quickly. Some of the younger trainees, while still adept at their craft, were too inexperienced in an actual fight and quickly met their demise, and the hunters were relentless. None of them cared if the man or woman next to them fell. Instead, they would simply shove the fallen body aside and continue fighting without remorse. The battle was rapidly becoming a bloodbath with no clear sign of who would claim victory.

As the battle continued to rage, Mira and the last of the trainees finally arrived. Knowing full well that unleashing her power here would be a complete disaster, the Warden of Fury picked up a staff from the ground and did her best to aid the others. As one hunter fell, two more descended from the ship to take his place. The Wardens were vastly outnumbered.

Then, as all hope seemed to fade, a massive ball of fire appeared out of nowhere, flying toward the battlefield. Mira and Joel pushed their friends aside as the great ball of energy slammed into the hunters caught in its path. The flames exploded on contact, sending smaller, but equally powerful, balls of red hot fire in every direction. The tables had turned as Monk limped his way towards them, using his staff as a crutch to traverse the field of debris before him.

Much to everyone's surprise, the hunters backed off and retreated to the black ramp where the final three men now stepped out. Joel and Mira, along with what trainees remained, returned to formation behind the Flame Warden. The two groups glared angrily at each other, a burning pile of carcasses smoking between them.

"What is the meaning of this intrusion?" Monk yelled across the field. The three men, clearly the ones in charge, stepped in front of the others. Monk immediately recognized one of them as Rolan, the ruthless leader of the bounty hunters. He towered over the two men beside him and was equipped from head to toe with all manner of weapons and armor. He wore blaster rifles on each hip, swords across his back, a belt of grenades around his waist, and daggers pretty much everywhere else. Monk knew Rolan to be a man not to be trifled with, and he was not about to take any chances.

"We've come for the Grand Master," Rolan began, his deep voice echoing across the battlefield.

"Sorry to disappoint you, friend, but we've not seen or heard from the Grand Master in many, many years," Monk replied, his face stern and emotionless.

"Is that so?" Rolan stepped out in front of his comrades and onto the blackened battlefield. "You see, I have it on good authority that you have."

"If he was here, I would know," the old Warden replied, unwavering. Mira and Joel watched carefully as Rolan carelessly stepped over the smoldering bodies before him.

"You're not lying to me, are you? I do hate being lied to," Rolan said, a small grin spreading on his face. He knew Monk was lying. Joel clenched his fists and powered up the brands on his arms as Rolan stopped just in front of them. Mira kept her power at bay, but was ready to call upon it if necessary.

"Now, now, no need for that," Rolan said as he turned to face Joel, pulling the blaster from his hip and pointing it at Joel's groin. "All I did was ask the old man here a simple question. However, if he continues to lie to me, things could get very, very ugly."

"Things are already ugly," Mira said dangerously. She could feel the power within her rising, and she wouldn't be able to restrain it much longer.

"So they are." Rolan smiled.

"Like I said, Rolan, the Grand Master is not here. Now if you would kindly-" but Monk was cut short as two figures suddenly dropped out of the sky. The group had been so busy arguing that no one had noticed that the wind had picked up. Dark clouds swirled overhead as the gusts blew in every direction. Ardemis was the first to land, slamming into the ground and blowing Rolan back. Mathias followed suit, hitting the ground just as hard and knocking Rolan from his feet. The bounty hunter was down for only a second before he jumped back and marched straight up to Mathias. The young Warden held his ground, refusing to move even an inch as Rolan stood face to face with him.

"And who are you? I don't believe we've met," Rolan asked suspiciously.

"It doesn't matter who I am," Mathias began, careful to avoid revealing his identity to the stranger. "What does matter is that you are trespassing on sacred ground. You destroyed our temple and killed our people!"

"How observant of you," Rolan replied sarcastically.

"Now tell me what the hell you want!" Mathias was fuming. Too many had already died on his account, and he would have no more of it.

"And who are you to make such demands of me? Someone important, yes? Someone… Grand?"

He knew. These were bounty hunters, Mathias was sure of it. He glanced past Rolan to the mass of people behind him. He recognized only one of them from the struggle on Talise, and standing next to him was none other than Alistair.

"No…" Mathias muttered under his breath. He couldn't believe his brother was there, but then everything suddenly made sense. Aurilean must have informed Alistair of Sanctuary's location long ago, and the boy now used that information to betray his family once again.

Rolan noticed the Warden's sudden lack of attention and turned to follow his gaze, his eyes landing upon the recruit.

"Ah, yes, I'd almost forgotten," Rolan said, walking back toward his people. Alistair shifted, straightening his posture as Rolan strolled up to him. "I'd like to introduce you to my newest and most loyal protégé, Alistair of Talise."

Joel and Mira exchanged worried glances, while Mathias stood firm, his fists clenched tightly at his side.

"You see, Warden, young Alistair here told me all about this place. He also told me about his traitorous brother that became the Grand Master after he betrayed his father. Quite the tale, wouldn't you agree?" Rolan asked, the wide smile plastered to his face.

Mathias said nothing, but the pain in his eyes spoke louder than any words could have.

"Easy, lad," Ardemis said quietly as the wind continued to swirl around them.

"Alistair promised me that he would gladly point out his brother to me once we landed," Rolan continued, slowly circling the boy. "While I believe the answer to that question is now painfully apparent, I think I'll ask him anyways, just for fun."

Mathias finally snapped. He roared out in anger and, feeling for the wind around him, launched a gust of air straight at the hunters. Alistair pushed Rolan out of the way and then jumped aside himself. The blade of wind just barely missed them, instead splitting an unfortunate man behind them clean in half. Mathias now understood how Ardemis had cleared the vines at the hidden path. He prepared to launch another attack, but the hunters immediately raised their guns, each one pointing directly at the Grand Master.

"There you are," Rolan said victoriously.

"What do you want?" Mathias yelled, his fists still clenched and prepared to fight.

"It's simple, really. Surrender yourself to me and we'll leave this planet forever." Rolan was still smiling, but now Alistair had joined in. The hunters knew they had won, and they had no problem showing it.

"I'll never come with you!" Mathias roared.

"I thought not," Rolan replied and raised his gun, firing only a single burst of energy. Mathias had no time to react before the laser found its target. Kris, the young boy who had worked so diligently with Mathias over the past few days, roared in pain as the bolt pierced his heart.

"No!" Mathias yelled and moved towards the boy, but Rolan fired a second shot that landed just near the Warden's feet, stopping him in place.

"Ah, ah. You stay right where you are," Rolan said, his smile now completely gone.

Mathias! Mira's voice jumped into the boy's head. *Just give the word and we'll end these hunters for good!*

At what cost, Mira? Mathias replied. He refused to let anyone else die on his account.

Then how're we gonna to stop 'em?! Joel suddenly chimed in, adding his voice to mix.

The only way I know how. Mathias replied, and then stepped forward.

"I'm only going to say this one more time, Warden," Rolan said, his blaster rifle now pointed directly at Mathias. "Surrender yourself to me, or we kill every last one you." Each hunter was poised and ready to fire should Rolan give the command. Even with all their strengths, they wouldn't be able to survive that much firepower. Mathias just couldn't risk that.

"Very well. I submit," Mathias stated sadly.

What are you doing?! Mira suddenly yelled in his head. *Mathias, we can take them! Don't do this!*

I have no choice, Mira. I won't let you sacrifice your lives for mine, not when I can resolve this peacefully.

There is no peace with them, lad, Ardemis replied. *But, I understand.*

"Excellent!" Rolan yelled, clapping his hands. "Alistair, tie him up and bring him to me."

"With pleasure," the recruit replied and made his way across the field. The smile he sported as he approached Mathias sent shivers up the Warden's spine. Mathias was sure that, in that moment, Alistair couldn't have been happier.

"Brother," Mathias said, but Alistair refused to look him in the eyes.

"I told you not to call me that anymore." His voice was lush with hatred and sadness. There was no sign of the boy Mathias had once known.

"You're right. You have a new family now."

"One that doesn't betray me!" Alistair jabbed as he finished wrapping the boy's wrists. The knot was so tight that the blood flow to his hands was already dropping.

"Not yet." And then Mathias said nothing more. Alistair turned away from him and yanked on the rope, pulling Mathias face first into the charred ground. The hunters burst into laughter, while Mira had to hold Joel back from charging at the boy. Mathias pushed off the ground and came to his feet. He refused to look back as he was pulled along by his brother.

This is stupid! Joel thought angrily.

It's the only way, Mathias replied. He followed Alistair to the ramp of the ship where Rolan now stood.

"Thank you, Alistair," Rolan said. The boy nodded smugly and awaited further instruction. "Now then, the basics…" Rolan began and before Mathias could react, Rolan whipped a dagger from its sheath and stabbed Mathias in the leg. The pain was instantaneous. He howled as the blade pierced his skin, a familiar tingling sensation once again spreading throughout his body.

"Wayne," Mathias heard Rolan quietly say, "I'm leaving the transport behind. Take twenty men and destroy this place after we leave.

"You… You said you would leave in peace!" Mathias yelled angrily.

"Did I? Memory isn't what it used to be." Rolan laughed and disappeared into the black cruiser.

I can't talk long. I can feel the poison repressing my abilities, Mathias thought to the others, his rage only causing the poison to act faster.

You're an idiot, kid, Joel instantly replied, but Mathias ignored him.

Just listen to me! He's leaving behind a squad to destroy what's left. Take them out, but use the one called Wayne as leverage to negotiate my release. Rolan seems to favor him, so he may be willing to make the trade.

And if he's not? Mira asked.

Then get rid of him. But don't endanger anymore of the others. We've lost too many- But that was all Mathias could muster. The poison worked much faster than it had before, and he could no longer feel the bond between himself and the other Wardens, nor could he feel the wind blowing around him as he boarded the ship.

The ramp led up into a dark hallway, where many of the other hunters stood guard. The ship was immensely larger than the Longshot but, with the poison working its way through his veins, Mathias doubted he would remember any of it.

Alistair led Mathias deeper into the dark recesses of the craft. Finally, they came to a small room with a solitary chair situated in the center. Mathias was so woozy from the poison that Alistair had to practically carry him to it. He felt himself slam into the cold, hard surface of the seat, but he felt no pain from it. His whole body was numb and his brain no longer functioned properly.

"You were wise to come with us," Rolan said from the shadows, but the Warden could barely understand the words. "Don't worry. The poison won't kill you. It's only there to maintain control and keep you from breaking free. As you can imagine, the Grand Master free aboard this ship would be total chaos."

Mathias tried to speak, but only gibberish and drool escaped his lips.

"Look at you. Grand Master of the Wardens, incapable of coherent speech," Rolan said happily and then flicked a nearby radio switch. "The boy's secure. Take us out." Mathias felt a sudden jolt as the ship started up its engines. "Now, my friend, sit back and relax. We'll land on Ravendra within a couple days, and I have no doubt that Commander Jax will be happy to see you," Rolan said and strolled out of the room, laughing all the way down the hall. Alistair followed suit, flashing Mathias another wicked grin before slamming the metal door, sending the room into total darkness.

Matthew Louwers

14

There was fire everywhere. Mathias sprinted through the cobblestone streets, weaving between the panicking citizens. Every house was ablaze, but there was nothing he could do to stop the fire from spreading. Summoning forth the wind would only help the flames to spread faster. There was no hope for these people.

"Look out!" A woman's voice cried from the distance. Mathias turned just in time to see a man in a black hood running straight for him. The hooded man wielded a long, blood-drenched sword and, as he charged at Mathias, appeared to have every intention of using it. Feeling for the wind around him, Mathias stretched out his hand and called forth a rushing gust of air. But, instead of air, a bright arc of white lightning burst forth from the Warden's fingertips. The hooded man took the blast square in the chest and instantly fell to the ground. As his attacker lay there, steam rising from the hole in his back, Mathias raised his hand to examine it.

He had never conjured lightning before, nor did he even know how.

"Excellent shot, sir," a voice said. It was the same voice from before and he turned to face its origin. Mira was walking up to him, a slim, elegant sword in her right hand and a ruby hilted dagger in her left. She was also covered from head to toe in blood. This was not the Mira he knew. She had short, choppy hair and was dressed from the shoulders down in tarnished red battle armor.

"Mira? What are you doing here?" Mathias asked, but he was surprised to hear that it wasn't his voice that came out.

"Looking for you," she replied, then turned and stared off towards the courtyard. "They've broken through the front gates. We've also found a bunch of them scattered throughout the city, like they were just waiting for the attack to happen."

Mathias had no clue what Mira was talking about, nor did he know why his voice didn't sound like his own.

"I see," Mathias said. This time his body spoke without his consent. Something was very wrong. "I need to return to the Golden Hall. Can you hold this position alone?"

"I will hold it for as long as I can, sir." Mira replied as she nodded her head in assurance.

"Good. Fight well, young one," Mathias said again, and that's when it all made sense. This was the Warden Massacre, and Mathias was seeing through the eyes of Aurilean.

Without warning, Mathias leapt into the air and soared away from Mira. As one, Mathias and Aurilean darted over the crumbling city below. Mathias hadn't realized just how massive the great city of Haven had been.

Every street they flew over contained Wardens and Ravens fighting for their lives. The sheer number of them was unfathomable. He desperately tried to alter their course to aid those below, but Aurilean wouldn't budge. Mathias was trapped in his father's body.

Something in the sky ahead of them caught the boy's attention. An ominous, dark spot covered the stars, and it was growing rapidly. Mathias tried to warn his host of the coming darkness, but Aurilean couldn't hear him. Closer and closer the dark mass came until it was near enough that Mathias could make out its shape. It was a bird, larger than any he had ever seen.

An explosion below suddenly illuminated the night sky and Mathias saw before him what he had only heard stories about: a dread raven. The monstrosity cawed loudly, the shrill scream sending a shiver running down the Warden's spine. Then, using its dark, violet wings to propel itself forward, the dread raven attacked. Aurilean didn't react as the raven's beak came at him. The bird clamped its jaws around Aurilean's arm and Mathias screamed in pain. As the raven pulled, attempting to rip the limb clean off, Mathias felt his host call forth some form of energy. A sudden explosion of fire erupted from the man's other hand and the bird screamed in agony as its feathers began to burn. In its anger, the dread raven struck again. Aurilean was still unable to see the beast as it came for him and this time, the bird attacked with full force. It opened its beak wide as it neared and Mathias braced for another attack. The raven struck Aurilean with such force that it knocked the man unconscious. Mathias panicked as his father's body began to fall. He tried to take over, searching for the wind around him, but it was useless. He couldn't do anything to stop their rapid descent.

In the distance, Mathias heard another caw from the raven, a shrill cry of victory as it took off into the night. All that was left for the Warden and his host was the cold, hard ground that was quickly approaching. It was odd. This was not the Massacre he had read about; Aurilean wasn't supposed to die. But, before another thought could cross his mind, Aurilean's unconscious body slammed into the ground, and then there was only darkness.

*   *   *

Mathias jumped as he awoke, beads of sweat adorning his brow. He breathed a short sigh of relief, realizing that his battle with the dread raven had simply been a dream. He thought it strange, though, how vivid the dream had been. It was almost as if he had just experienced a vision of Aurilean's past. However, if that were case, then the bit about the dread raven worried him greatly.

He was happy to find that he was no longer under the influence of the hunter's toxin. He could think and see clearly and, although he was tied to the chair, could wiggle his appendages with ease. The only thing bothering him was his memory. He couldn't seem to remember what had happened since Rolan stabbed him.

Glancing around the room, Mathias realized just how much trouble he was in. The door and walls were both solid metal, there was a drain in the floor beneath his feet stained a dark red, and a small table and sink sat near the door with strange, sharp looking tools, many of which were rusted and clearly worn from extensive use.

The metal door screeched against the floor as it was pushed open from the outside.

"Ah, you're awake," said Rolan, closing the door behind him. It clanged as the metal banged against metal and then reverberated ominously throughout the steel cell. Mathias was certain that nothing good would follow.

"Where are we going?" He asked. His voice was scratchy, and his throat burned as he spoke.

"Ravendra," Rolan replied. He was busy meddling with something on the table. Mathias knew about Ravendra from his studies and that the planet itself was a massive swirling ball of noxious fumes that made living there nearly impossible. The gas was so potent that it surrounded the planet with a dark violet halo. However, breathable air shields had been constructed in certain areas where the gas was thinner. Because of the potential danger of the air, along with the ever-growing Raven presence, Ravendra rarely had visitors. The only people to ever come and go were hunters claiming their rewards.

"So, you're handing me over to the Ravens." It wasn't a question. He wondered how much they had offered for him to be returned alive.

"Naturally," Rolan replied, keeping his back towards his prisoner.

"Why?"

"Why do we do anything? The price on your head is enough to set me and my crew up for the rest of our lives. Would *you* pass up that opportunity?" Rolan finally turned, a look of annoyance plastered to his face and a dagger dripping with green goop held firmly in his hand.

"I'm not like you," Mathias replied through gritted teeth.

"Of course not," Rolan began. "You're young and naive to the ways of the galaxy. You don't understand how things happen outside of your perfect little world."

"Neither do you if you're turning me over to the Ravens," Mathias replied, his voice rising in anger. The louder he talked, the more his throat burned, but he didn't care.

"Please. There are scarier things than birds hiding in the dark, boy."

"Like what?"

"It doesn't matter. You won't be alive much longer to worry about it."

"What do you have against the Wardens, huh? What did they ever do to you?"

"What?" Rolan stopped his advance. No one had ever asked him that before.

"Why do you devote your life to hunting down the people trying to protect you?"

"Protect me? Do you know what it's like to be betrayed by those closest to you, Warden?" Rolan asked, placing the knife back onto the table behind him.

"Yes, actually, I do. Alistair, the man you hired, betrayed his father. Betrayed me." Mathias knew Rolan was already aware of the boys' circumstance, so why was he asking?

"What I mean is, do you know what it's like to be betrayed by someone you love, someone who you thought loved you unconditionally and forever?" Rolan continued, the confidence in his voice teetering ever so slightly.

"No, I've never felt that way about anybody before," Mathias replied. Natalie was the only girl that Mathias had ever been close to, but he never thought of her in a romantic way. And Mira he had only just met.

"Then you couldn't possibly understand why I do what I do," Rolan said and picked the knife back up.

"No, wait! I want to know," Mathias replied
frantically. He was growing more interested in Rolan as the
conversation went on, and he wanted to know more, not to
mention the growing fear of what Rolan was going to do with
the knife.

"Why do you even care?" Rolan said sadly.

"It's simple. You're a smart man, Rolan. I don't think
you chose to become a hunter for the fun of it. I think there's
more to it. I just want to know what happened to you, what
the Wardens did to you."

"Very well. I was married before I joined the
hunters," Rolan began. He had once again set the knife down
and was now leaning against the table, his arms folded across
his chest. "She was a spunky little thing, always running
around, full of energy. She, like you, was a Warden, one of
the younger ones. I was but a simple man working salvage
missions on Earth when we met."

"You've been to Earth?!" Mathias asked excitedly.
His father used to tell him stories of the human home world
when he was young. He used to say that Earth was a mystical
world full of strange happenings and interesting people. That
is until the humans killed themselves off.

Some of Earth's most brilliant minds had come
together and created a vaccine able to cure and further
prevent every disease known to humankind. For many years,
the people of Earth rejoiced and hostilities amongst nations
were ended. However, as the years passed, the population of
the earth continued to rise. With sickness no longer possible
and the humans breeding like rabbits, the world was suddenly
a much smaller place. People killed other people just to make
room for more people. It was a vicious, never-ending cycle.
War and destruction returned to the world and soon, the
killing just wouldn't stop. Aurilean would always say that

nobody knew who dropped the last bomb. The battle became known as The Last War to the humans who managed to escape the planet. It was believed that those men and women drifted off into the stars searching for a new home, but human technology was only so advanced, and their craft ran out of food and oxygen long before they could find anything. It always made Mathias sad when his father would tell him the story, but Aurilean would explain that understanding the past was crucial for maintaining the future. Only, at the end of his life, would Mathias truly understand what his father had meant.

"It's not as great as everyone thinks it is," Rolan continued. "The world is flooded with radiation and dust storms. We had to wear these protective suits that sealed us from the harmful gases of the planet."

"What were you looking for?" Mathias asked.

"Anything we could find, really, but specifically the Relics." Mathias knew it. Scavengers and collectors alike would spend billions of gold pieces funding Relic salvage missions, but they always came back empty handed. The Lost Relics were simple objects from Earth's past that were said to contain mystical powers. One of these items was what the humans had referred to as a Mirror. Throughout the universe, reflections existed everywhere, but the humans had unknowingly created a device that opened doors to other worlds. For some time, the Mirror had been used to traverse alternate realities and explore new regions of space. But the Ravens learned of its power and stole the door. A small team of Wardens, knowing that the Mirror's power was far too great for the Ravens to possess, took it upon themselves to find the Relic and destroy it. They succeeded in their mission, but none of them returned from it. The Lost Relics were soon outlawed by the Enforcers of Malador, and anyone found in possession of one would be locked away and the Relic, destroyed.

"Did you find one?" Mathias asked enthusiastically.

"Not me, personally," Rolan said with disappointment. "But what we did find was another salvage team, and *they* had found something: a small, glass orb that they could look into and see anywhere and anytime in the universe."

Mathias couldn't believe that something like that even existed.

"We met up to examine the orb and, being the naïve people that we were, we started asking it silly questions. It was all fun and games until one of our men asked it when he would die. The orb showed a young woman stabbing the man through the heart on the surface of the Earth. It was then that we noticed that a member of the other crew was missing. Only moments later, a smoke grenade went off and the whole camp was blinded. That's when the screaming started. One by one, the assassin slaughtered her entire crew."

"But she didn't stop there. The assailant came for my crew next. We tried to fight her, but we couldn't see anything, and it was impossible to breathe properly. The woman burst through the fog at me, but someone jumped at her and pushed her out of the way. She slammed into a sharp rock in the dirt, tearing a hole in her suit. The toxic gas and radiation immediately infiltrated the suit, and she was dead within seconds. I turned to thank my rescuer and saw Warden Marie for the first time. I'd no idea that she was a Warden at the time, however, and I treated her like I would have anyone else who'd just saved my life."

"We recovered the orb and returned to our ship, leaving Earth's cold embrace behind. Marie told me that she'd been tasked with watching over any Relic salvage missions on Earth. She'd seen so many lives lost over the fight for possession of a relic that she told me I could keep the orb upon returning if my team and I kept its existence a secret."

"Long story short, a bit after we returned Marie and I were wed. We spent many wonderful years together and eventually wanted to have children. Marie decided to ask the orb how many kids she would have, but the orb remained blank. We thought the Relic was broken, so we tried asking it something else. The orb immediately returned an answer. But Marie was heartbroken. The orb had revealed to her that she was unable to bear children." Rolan sniffed and rubbed at his eyes. He wouldn't be caught dead crying in front of his prisoner. "Things got bad after that, Warden. There were times when I would find her sitting and talking to the orb in the middle of the night, stroking it as if it were the child she could never have. It tormented her, and it upset me greatly to see her in such a state."

Mathias suddenly felt himself sympathizing with the man. He had known the Lost Relics to be powerful, but never had he imagined that they could torment a person so, especially a Warden.

"So, what happened?" Mathias asked.

"One night, I woke to a crash in the living room. I ran out to find Marie hunched over, a knife in hand dripping with blood. I ran to her to see if she was ok and, as I came to face her, I could see that the blood was her own. There was a rather large puncture wound in her stomach and she was steadily dripping blood onto the floor. I looked to Marie and asked her what she'd done. She told me that she had asked the orb about my children, instead of hers, and saw three young boys running and playing in the fields behind our home. I loved Marie and would never have betrayed her so, but she took it as a sign of unfaithfulness and, in her rage, she charged at me. I'd never understood how strong a Warden could be until that moment. She slammed into me at full force, cracking several of my ribs, and I was thrown into the wall behind me. But her assault didn't stop there. She sped across the room and landed on top of me, knife raised and ready to strike. I didn't want to hurt her, but I wasn't going to let her kill me. I reached around for anything I could use to defend myself and my fingers closed around the orb. I immediately swung the glass ball into the side of her head." Rolan stopped for a moment, closing his eyes and rubbing the hair standing on end on his arms. "The orb shattered and a shard of glass pierced her temple, killing her instantly."

Mathias, who had his eyes locked on Rolan throughout the entire story, sadly dropped his gaze to the cold floor at his feet.

"It was at that moment that I realized why the orb had shown her only darkness. It wasn't because she was incapable of having children, but because I was going to kill her before she ever could. It's a very dangerous thing, looking into the future." Rolan stopped.

"I'm so sorry." Mathias muttered, his voice full of sadness.

"I'm not. The Relic had driven her to madness. She betrayed our love and acted irrationally. I did what I had to do, what anyone would do."

"Yea..." Mathias replied, but he wasn't sure he would have acted the same way.

"Anyway, now you kno-"

"Sir! Are you there?" A voice crackled through the intercom along the wall.

"I'm here, Carter, what is it?"

"We're being hailed, sir. It's one of the Wardens from Sanctuary. They... They have Wayne, sir."

Rolan turned to his prisoner who now sat tall, listening to every word of the conversation.

"Put them on in here. I'll speak to them, personally," Rolan replied and pressed a small button near the door. A sudden screeching echoed throughout the room as a metal panel slid away to reveal a screen hidden in the wall. As soon as the panel came to a halt, the screen lit up and there, standing aboard the Longshot, was Mira.

"Well, well, Warden Mira. What can-"

"You listen to me, Rolan, and you listen well. You took something of ours, and we want it back," Mira began. She was standing in the cargo hold, just outside the small airlock for side docking. The door to the airlock was open and inside stood the man Mathias recognized as Wayne. His arms were tied tightly behind his back and his feet were bound at his ankles. "It just so happens, we found something that belongs to you. I would like to propose a trade."

Rolan was fuming. Mathias remembered that there had been about twenty other men Wayne had chosen to stay behind. Mira had done as Mathias had requested and kept the hunter alive as a bargaining chip.

"And if I refuse?" Rolan replied, his eyes glowing with anger.

"Then your friend here goes for a little ride." Mira pressed a button near the air lock and the door closed behind her, trapping Wayne inside.

"You wouldn't dare!" Rolan roared.

"You clearly don't know me very well," Mira replied coldly and moved her hand to the door release button. Rolan turned to Mathias.

"Please, Rolan. Do as she asks. Nobody else has to die," Mathias said hopefully.

Rolan seemed to ponder the Warden's request for a moment, and Mathias was sure that his plan had worked. However, the bounty hunter turned toward the camera and said, "I'm sorry, Wayne. Go to hell, Mira!"

Mira sighed and then, much to Mathias's surprise, pressed the button. The air lock opened and Wayne was sucked out in the dark nothing of space. Rolan roared and ran towards the intercom.

"Get us to Ravendra, now!" Rolan yelled into the radio and then, using all his strength, flipped the table by the door through the air. It crashed into the wall, spilling weapons, tools and strange liquids all over the place. The screen had gone dark as Mira closed the channel between them. Mathias was upset that it had come to this, but they had given Rolan multiple chances now to walk away. Mathias realized, however, as the hunter grabbed the knife off the floor and headed straight for him, that Rolan would never walk away.

"And the Wardens call *us* monsters," Rolan said through gritted teeth and raised the poisoned blade into the air. Mathias braced for blow, but it did nothing to dull the pain as the blade came down and pierced his leg. The poison's effects were instantaneous as Mathias once again began to lose control of his senses. "You should know that I don't give a damn what the commander does to you and the rest of your villainous band of traitors. Frankly, I hope he takes your power and uses it to destroy this entire shit hole of a galaxy because, by that time, I'll be far away from it!" And just like that, Rolan stormed out of the room, slamming the metal door as he went.

Mira! Mathias reached out.

I'm sorry, Mathias. I had-

Poisoned. Ravendra... And that was all he could think before the toxins overtook his brain and he fell into blackness once again.

15

The slender, shadowy figure appeared to glide as he made his way down the lengthy corridor. The dim hallway housed several tall, wooden doors, all leading off to different parts of the complex, but the mysterious man wasn't interested in those doors. His gaze was fixed on the solid steel wall at the end of the passage. He moved with an elegance only a man of his stature could, his long, black robe flowing behind him.

A scream pierced the darkness and echoed throughout the corridor. The man smiled a wide, toothy grin, but never stopped moving. Everyone knew he loved the screaming.

The man came to a stop as he reached the metal wall before him. He pulled a small knife from his hip and, using his black robe as a rag, wiped the fresh blood from the blade. The knife was quite extravagant for what appeared to be a simple weapon, but the man knew that the blade was so much more. The purple crystal in the hilt glinted as the dim light from above reflected off it.

The stranger knocked twice on the metal wall and a small panel slid aside to reveal a pair of eyes staring through. Recognition washed over the man behind the wall and, as he closed the small panel, another sheet of metal the size of a door began to slide open.

"Commander! We've been waiting for you," croaked the man behind the wall as the stranger made his way into the room. The chamber where they stood was a cramped, square cell with sheets of steel on all four walls. There were chains and shackles strung up around the room, and there was a young man at the back currently occupying a pair of them. He hung from his wrists and sported a collection of bruises plastered all over his body. The boy raised his head as the stranger entered, and the door man closed the wall behind him. A look of fear washed over the boy's face as he laid eyes upon his visitor. The commander simply stared right back until the boy was forced to avert his gaze, causing the man's grin to spread even further.

"This is the other one?" The commander asked, his silky-smooth voice echoing throughout the chamber.

"It is, sir. Did his counterpart give you anything?" The door man inquired hopefully.

"No. He was quite keen on protecting his friend, here," the stranger replied.

"Pity."

"Quite. What's this one's status?" The commander asked.

"He hasn't said much. Says he saw us coming, so I assume he has some kind of enhanced vision ability."

"That could be useful."

"Indeed. Shall I depart?" The doorman asked as he gathered his things.

"That won't be necessary," the stranger replied.

"Sir?" The doorman questioned, but the commander had already moved towards the prisoner. The boy breathed heavily as the man neared, the fear running its course through his veins.

"Do you know who I am, child?" The commander asked. The boy ignored the question and kept his eyes on the floor. Annoyed by the prisoner's lack of response, the tall man clenched his fist and slammed it hard into the boy's gut. The boy let out a loud grunt as the air quickly fled his lungs. He tried to hunch his body over to dull the pain, but the chains prevented any such movement. "I'll ask you again: do you know who I am?"

"Commander Jax," the boy replied, his voice a scratchy mess as he tried to breathe.

"Now, was that so hard?" Jax taunted. The boy, already feeling defeated, kept his head down. "Who are you?"

"Cyrus," the boy replied reluctantly.

"And are you a Warden, Cyrus?" Jax asked, although the commander already knew the answer.

"Yes."

"And what, Warden Cyrus, brings you to Ravendra?" Again, Jax already knew the answer, but he thoroughly enjoyed breaking his prisoners.

"I can't…" Cyrus muttered.

"Oh, come now, boy, you can tell me. I'm rather good at keeping secrets." The Commander was smiling as Cyrus raised his head. Up close, Jax didn't seem nearly as frightening. He had a fair complexion and his smile only made the man more handsome. His long, blonde hair was tied up behind his head and his brilliant blue eyes appeared friendly as Cyrus peered into them. Maybe the Wardens had been wrong about Commander Jax.

"I w-was sent here to scout th-the city," Cyrus stammered, his body still ripe with fear.

"You're a long way from the city, Cyrus." Commander Jax averted his gaze and began to pace in front of the boy. "This little outpost was built long ago by my father as a kind of holding facility. This is where we process visitors and, for lack of a better word, dismiss uninvited guests."

Cyrus returned his gaze to the floor. It was obvious which category he fell into.

"Your friend was quite keen on keeping your mission a secret from me. For that, he was punished." Jax gestured to the splotch of red on his robe. "You, on the other hand, are smart, aren't you?" He was toying with the boy now. It was only a matter of time before he got what he wanted.

"Y-Yes sir," Cyrus managed to say as he held back tears.

"I thought so. Now tell me, Cyrus, why did my men find you and your friend scouting the outpost?"

Cyrus knew that the people he worked for would banish him if he revealed any further information to the Raven commander, but he also suspected Jax would kill him if he didn't answer his questions. He decided he would tell Jax what he needed to know and deal with the Wardens later.

"The initial mission was to scout the city, sir," Cyrus began. Jax stopped pacing and turned to face the boy. "Thomas and I were never very good fighters, but we were excellent observers."

Except we managed to catch you, Jax thought, but he let the boy continue.

"Tom could hear things from miles away, and I can see things about that same distance. So, as you can imagine, we made a pretty good team." Jax had to keep himself from laughing at the sheer naiveté of the boy. "Our mission was simply to observe and not get involved. We were told to scout the city and report back within a few days' time. The mission started off fine. We remained undetected for two days, observing the movements of your people. On the third day, we saw a ship coming in and watched it land here, near the outpost. Thomas told me to ignore it, but I wanted a closer look. The spacecraft was not a typical Raven ship so we knew it had to be something else."

Jax knew the craft Cyrus was referring to. A Magister had stopped by with word of potential movements of the Grand Master. The leads had proven to be false, however, so Jax had the Magister hung by his ankles and gutted till he bled out. He didn't like it when people fed him bad information.

"We changed our position to get a better view of the incoming craft and that's when we were captured. I suspect Thomas was upset with me after that. It was, after all, my idea."

"The Wardens who sent you here, who are they?" Jax asked, hoping the Grand Master was among them.

"We're all stragglers and refugees. Most of us refused to follow the Grand Master after the Massacre, so we left and sought new lives for ourselves."

"You're just a boy. You couldn't possibly have fought in the war."

"You're right, sir. I was born many years later, and my power was passed on to me when my mother died." A tear dripped down Cyrus's cheek. It always upset him to talk about his mother.

"I must say that I am pleased with you, boy. You have just revealed to me far more than any Warden I have ever captured. You are to be commended," Jax said with a grin and turned his back to the boy.

The Wardens would certainly exile Cyrus for betraying them, but at least he would still have his life. As he breathed a sigh of relief, Commander Jax strolled over to the door man. The two spoke softly to each other, but Cyrus was unable to catch a word of what was said. As soon as the pair finished conversing, Jax made his way back towards the boy.

"What happens now?" Cyrus asked hopefully.

"Do you know what this is?" Jax replied, holding up his dagger. The purple gemstone gleamed in the bright light of the room. Cyrus's eyes grew wide as recognition flooded over him.

"No! Please, no!" The boy cried out.

"Ah, so you do. Saves me from a lengthy explanation." Jax and the door man chuckled in unison.

"You said if I told you-"

"I never said anything. You told me everything because you didn't want to end up like your friend. And don't worry, you won't. Young Thomas is still alive, a slave to my every whim and without control of his body or mind, but alive." The smile on Jax's face continued to grow.

"No! Why are you doing this?!" Cyrus yelled as Jax closed the distance between them.

"Because I can't have someone who betrays their own people as my slave, now can I?"

"Stop! This wasn't supposed to be like this!"

"You and your friend were foolish to come here, Warden Cyrus," Jax continued, finally stopping just before the boy. He had dealt with Sight Wardens before and knew their brands were marked on their eyes. The boy would endure a great deal of pain for his betrayal.

"Please… Don't…" But Cyrus knew there was no negotiating with Commander Jax.

"Now, Warden Cyrus, I free you of your power." Jax raised the gemmed knife into the air and was about to bring it down when a loud knock came from the wall behind him. The doorman moved to the slot and opened it.

"A message for the commander," a voice said urgently and Jax turned his head to see the visitor pass a note through the slot.

"What's it say?" Jax asked the doorman. As the man read through the note, his eyes grew wide and his mouth fell open.

"You're going to want to read it for yourself, sir."

"Now?!" Jax yelled. He hated interruptions.

"Yes, now!" Normally, the doorman would never have spoken to the commander in such a way, but this message was about to change everything. Jax grumbled as he lowered his weapon. Cyrus breathed another sigh of relief, but he knew his death was only being delayed.

Jax snatched the note out of the door man's hand and began to read. Just as the man before him, the commander's eye's widened and a new grin spread across his face.

"Is it true, sir? Could they really have found him?" The doorman asked.

"Rolan has never given me a reason to doubt him. I think the bastard might have actually pulled it off."

"Shall I inform the others?"

"No. I have another task for you." And Jax began to whisper into the doorman's ear. Cyrus had only heard bits and pieces of the conversation, but he recognized the name Rolan. The Wardens used to tell him that Rolan was a bounty hunter who dedicated his life to the capture of the Grand

Master. If Rolan was on his way with a prisoner, Cyrus had no doubt who it was.

"Are you sure?" The doorman asked, hesitant about the instructions he was just given.

"Completely," Jax replied and then turned back towards his captive. "You're in luck, young Cyrus. I suddenly find myself in a good mood, and I won't be taking your power today after all."

Cyrus was suddenly more relieved than he had ever been in his entire life.

"However, I cannot say the same for my friend here." A wave of dread washed over Cyrus once again as his brief glimmer of hope was suddenly shattered.

"You can't do this!" Cyrus yelled, clenching his fists and yanking on his chains.

"Shall I start with his tongue?" the doorman asked.

"No. I want to hear his screams all the way to the main hall. Do not go easy on the boy, Pietrus, or I will know."

"Yes, sir." And with that, Commander Jax stepped out of the room. The door slid closed behind him and he started towards the entrance. A howl of pain erupted from the room, piercing the quiet of the dark hallway, and Jax smiled. Everyone knew he loved the screaming.

16

The icy splash of dirty water yanked him from his slumber. There were no dreams this time, at least none that he could remember, but that wasn't what worried him at the moment. The engines had stopped, and Mathias had no doubt that they had finally landed on Ravendra. He was still woozy as he adjusted his eyes to the dark room. Rolan had used an increased poison dosage the second time around.

"Get up," a nearby voice commanded. Mathias squinted as he scanned the darkness and finally laid eyes upon a dark silhouette leaning against the doorway. He should've known who it was from the voice but, in his current state, his senses were still impaired and voice recognition was proving difficult. However, as his eyes adjusted to the blackness around him, he pieced together his brother standing before him, an empty bucket dangling from his fingers.

"Ali..." Mathias began but quickly found his voice missing in action. His throat burned like he had just swallowed an entire bonfire, logs and all.

"I said get up."

Mathias squirmed in his seat and glanced down at his legs. His right leg was covered in dried blood and his stab wound had been stitched up, albeit somewhat poorly and with great haste. Both legs were numb, but the feeling was slowly beginning to return, a feeling he could only describe as being stabbed repeatedly with a small needle. He wasn't sure if he would be able to stand but, if he didn't act soon, Alistair would no doubt force him up in other, more physical ways. He stretched out his fingers, the prickling sensation present in them as well, and grabbed the arms of the chair. Using his own arms for support, he pushed his body off the hard seat and tried to stand. He wobbled briefly as he straightened his legs, but quickly found his balance and stood tall once again.

"Let's go," Alistair said as he turned his back to Mathias and strolled out of the room. The Warden slowly stepped forward with his right leg, the needle-like poking finally subsiding. He found himself leaning too far to the right and had to put his arms out to balance himself. No matter how drugged he was, there was no way he was going to let himself fall in front of his brother. He took another step, and then another, slowly regaining his ability to walk. After a few seconds, he was outside of his cell and moving through the ship.

While it was much larger than the Longshot, the hunter ship used a similar layout. The cell where he had been kept was located next to the craft's medical bay, and the rec room and sleeping quarters were just beyond that. He passed through both on his way towards the ramp, following just far enough behind Alistair that he wasn't yelled at to keep up. Mathias was taken aback as he entered the craft's cargo hold, however. It was an incredibly massive room, home to several smaller space crafts. There were also small, barred cells along the walls of the room, and crates upon crates towered dangerously around them. Guns, grenades, swords, and other weapons were scattered around the base of these crates, many of them covered in dried blood. Mathias wondered how many people these hunters had killed on their journey to find him.

Alistair stopped at the ramp, which had yet to drop to the planet's surface, and turned to speak to Rolan who was waiting patiently for them. They spoke amongst themselves briefly before Rolan turned to his prisoner.

"Hold out your arms," Alistair yelled from the ramp. Mathias did as he was told and felt a cold snap around his wrists. The cuffs were metallic and grooved just enough that if Mathias wasn't careful, the small slits would cut into his skin. It was a barbaric contraption, but it served its purpose well.

"In a few moments, you'll be in Raven custody, and we'll be long gone from this place," Rolan began. "You'd be wise to refrain from upsetting your new host. I've no doubt that you've conceived some manner of escape attempt, but I'd advise you to forget it. There's no escaping from Commander Jax." He finished his statement with a wide grin, but Mathias kept his face free of emotion. There was indeed a plan of escape, but he wasn't about to let anyone know that.

"You were fools to bring me here," Mathias managed to say, his throat burning with each word.

"Say what you will, Warden. It doesn't matter. Let's go!" Rolan said through gritted teeth and turned his back to Mathias. A loud clang echoed throughout the massive hold as the ramp began its descent. A sudden wave of icy air rushed

195

up the ramp and into the room. The unexpected chill caused the hairs on the Warden's arms to stand on end. He was unaccustomed to such freezing temperatures.

The ramp came to a halt as it rested upon the cold earth below. Several other hunters, dressed from head to toe in black battle gear and wielding blaster rifles, exited the craft first. Rolan clearly wasn't taking any chances. It was the only smart thing the man had done thus far.

Rolan was next to make his exit followed by Alistair and Mathias. The Grand Master's footsteps echoed with each wobbly step he took as the rush of the evening air brushed against his face. His mind was clearer now, but he knew the poison was still coursing through his veins. The hunters were taking every precaution they could. An accident would mean the end of their negotiations and would likely result in their deaths. Rolan's confidence was just a front. The hunters feared the Ravens just as much as everyone else.

The ominous purple haze of the planet drifted into sight as Mathias neared the bottom of the ramp. He quickly scanned the horizon, his eyes falling upon the dark silhouette of a city far off in the distance, a city he assumed was the Raven capital, Corvia. He had never seen anything like it in his life and, with his focus elsewhere, he nearly tripped as his feet touched solid ground. The earth beneath him was hard and cracked, a clear sign that nothing would ever grow in this desolate land. He pulled his gaze from the capital and found that he was surrounded by several dark, hooded figures. Only Rolan now stood between Mathias and his new hosts.

"Commander Jax, it's been quite a while!" Rolan said as he strode toward the tall man at the center of the hooded strangers, his hand outstretched and his gait long.

"Rolan," Jax replied, taking the hunter's hand firmly in his. "It's good to see you again." The two appeared as old friends, reuniting after years of time spent apart, but Mathias knew better. These were simply the pleasantries exchanged between two powerful men.

"It appears that you received my message?" It was more of a statement than a question.

"Indeed. Where is he?" Jax asked, looking around the large group at the base of ship. Mathias was confused, as he was currently in plain sight of the commander.

"Sir?" Rolan asked, equally confused.

"I was told you were in possession of the Grand Master, yes? Yet you present only this child before me. Where is Aurilean?" Jax asked, his impatience growing. He had no idea that Aurilean was dead.

"The boy *is* the Grand Master, sir," Rolan replied hesitantly. He knew this detail could prove to be a slight complication in the exchange, but he hoped Jax would overlook it.

"If that's true, then am I to assume Aurilean is dead?"

"Yes. He engaged my men before they could bring him in, killing one of them before detonating the last of his power and passing his brand along. The boy standing before you now is Aurilean's adopted son, while his trueborn son stands next to him." Rolan pointed to Mathias and Alistair as he spoke, and Mathias cringed as Jax's eyes fell upon his own. They were a bright, vibrant blue that appeared welcoming and did much to hide the darkness lurking inside. Mathias stared back at the commander, but said nothing.

"I see," Jax said as he stepped forward and made his way to Mathias. He circled the boy once, examining the brand on his back and giving him a quick look-over before stopping just in front of him. "What is your name, child?"

Mathias ignored the question, maintaining eye contact but refusing to speak. He wasn't about to give this man his name or any other personal information that could be used against him. Instead, he stood as tall as he could and sported the harshest glare he could muster.

"His name's Mathias, son to a father he's never met and a mother who wasn't around long enough to care for him. He's also a traitor," Alistair said angrily, but Mathias had stopped caring what his brother thought of him. His words no longer carried any weight.

"And you," Jax continued, turning his attention to Alistair. "You are Aurilean's son and the rightful heir to his power?"

"Yes, sir. I was his original choice before he-"

"If you speak another word to me, I will personally see to it that you never speak again." Jax removed his gaze from Alistair and returned to Mathias. Alistair immediately shut his mouth and dropped his eyes to the ground, utterly humiliated.

"Mathias, Grand Master of the Wardens. It does have a nice ring to it," Jax said with a chuckle. The other hooded figures chortled along with him, but stopped when Jax began to speak again. "Do you know why my friends have brought you here, Mathias?"

Again, the Warden refused to answer the Raven's question. He hated the way his name sounded as it oozed off the commander's tongue.

"Oh, come now, Warden. Ignoring my questions will not prolong your life, if that's what you're thinking." Jax was still smiling his friendly smile, but it had no effect on Mathias. "What it will do is save you from a great deal of pain. You're wrong to think that you can withstand such pain, of course, for we have mastered that particular art." More laughing sprang forth from the circle, and Mathias began to question if remaining silent was truly the best idea.

198

"Yea, I know why I'm here," Mathias said, his voice no longer shaky from the poison. He spoke with confidence, never dropping eye contact.

"Tell me," Jax demanded.

"For years, your people have sought the power of the Wardens. Your ancestors abandoned them in the early years and slaughtered them on Haven. You hunt us down so you can take a power that isn't yours and rule a universe that cannot be ruled. I'm here because you want what I have. So, go ahead, *Commander*. Torture me. Take my power and use it to destroy everyone and everything that's ever lived. But, know that someone, somewhere in this god forsaken universe, will stop you." Mathias breathed heavily as he finished. He could feel the heat of his anger growing in his chest and he wondered if a new ability was on the verge of revealing itself. He quickly calmed himself, letting the fire diminish and return to its place of origin.

"Spoken as if reading from a history book," Jax chuckled as he brushed a wisp of blonde hair from his eye. The surrounding Ravens laughed once again, but Mathias remained unwavering. "In time, my young Warden, you will come to see things in a different light."

"You and I will never see eye to eye, Jax. Never." Mathias continued to glare at his host, hoping the man would get the message.

"Do not make the mistake in thinking that you are in control here, *Warden*," Jax said, his tone turning far more dangerous, the smile vanishing from his face. "I could drain the power from you right here and now. I could put an end to your short, pathetic existence and, how did you put it, destroy everyone and everything in the universe."

"Then do it," Mathias challenged. He suspected Jax had bigger plans than simply gutting the boy out in the open.

But, as Jax's hand grasped the blade at his hip, a sudden surge of fear raced through the Warden's body. Jax quickly closed the gap between Mathias and himself, the jeweled knife held firmly in hand. Mathias swallowed and prepared for the end.

"You'd like that, wouldn't you?" Jax asked, quickly regaining control. He whispered now as he held his blade up in the light of setting sun. "Take a good look at this blade, Warden. See how it glows with the energy of your fallen brothers and sisters?" Mathias shifted his eyes to the rustic weapon. Jax had clearly wielded it for some time, and the purple gem in the hilt glowed as the commander had said. "They fought for their lives until their final breaths, and only then did they realize just how futile it was. When your time comes, Mathias, you will fight as they did. You will give every ounce of your being to survive, and you will fail, just as they failed."

"You're wrong if you think you can intimidate me, Commander. You gave me some advice, now let me return the favor. Release me. Let me go and everyone here walks away with their lives." He had given the same chance to the bounty hunters, but Rolan had squandered it.

The laughter that erupted from the circle came from Raven and hunter alike. Mathias had to admit that his chances of survival were slim at this point, but he had to try. He knew the Wardens were on their way, and they would do everything in their power to secure Mathias's freedom.

"I like you, Mathias," Jax said, the wicked smile appearing on his face once more. "I may just let you live as my slave, simply to entertain me with your hopes and dreams." Mathias no longer cared what the Raven had to say, and he returned to his state of silence. "Take him to holding," Jax said to the nearest hooded figures. Two men broke from the circle and moved towards Mathias. Each placed a cold hand on his shoulders and gave a firm shove. Mathias had to step forward quickly to keep from falling over. "Do me a favor, gentlemen, and take our guest past the *others*. He may enjoy seeing what happens to his brothers and sisters when they become... overconfident." Jax and the Ravens laughed again and then he added, "I'll be along shortly after I've paid our associates here."

Money. That's all the bounty hunters cared about. They didn't care that they had just handed Mathias over to the most dangerous beings in the universe, but none of that mattered now.

Mathias? A faint voice suddenly chimed into his head. The poison had nearly gone from his system now, and the mental link between him and his friends was returning. *Mathias, can you hear me?*

Mira?

Thank the Makers! We've been trying to reach you for about a day now.

The poison prevented me from communicating with you. The effects seem to be wearing off now, though.

Good timing, then. We're on approach to Ravendra now. Where are they taking you?

Two Ravens are escorting me to a prison complex a fair distance outside of Corvia. Jax and the hunters are on their way to Corvia now to draw up the payment. They won't be gone long, though.

Then we'll have to do this quickly. What's the plan? Mira asked hastily. Mathias prepared to respond when the Ravens stopped him. One of them shoved his left shoulder and turned him to face the nearest cell. He'd been so focused on communicating with Mira that he hadn't even noticed that he now stood inside the prison. The air was damp and cool and reeked of rotting flesh. The only source of light was a small torch hanging from the solid stone walls. Mathias squinted as he peered into the black cell. Far in the corner he could just make out a group of shapes, all huddled together. One of the Ravens pulled a small piece of bread from his robe and tossed it into the cage. The reaction was immediate. At least eight people sprang forth from the darkness for the scrap of food. They pushed and shoved each other out of the way, each one longing for the small piece of sustenance. But, as quickly as it had begun, the fight ended. The victor, a rather muscular woman, feasted upon the scraps with glee as the others returned to the corner to sulk.

Mathias was appalled. The prisoners behaved like animals that had been locked away for too long, relying solely on their primal instinct to survive.

"These are Wardens?" He asked, the shock very prevalent in his tone.

"They used to be," one of the men said. His voice was gruff and contained no signs of sympathy or remorse. "They belong to the commander now."

"He doesn't kill them?"

"Not always. The ones that really piss him off he keeps alive as slaves with no minds of their own. They answer only to him." The other man spoke now, his voice deep and apathetic.

"This is despicable." Mathias couldn't believe how nonchalantly these men spoke of the situation.

"You keep talking to the commander like you did today and you'll find yourself in there, too." The first man gave Mathias another shove and they continued along through the dark corridor.

Mira, Mathias began again in his head, *they have other Wardens here.*

What?! That's not possible. Mathias could hear the surprise in her voice. The others hadn't heard from any other Wardens in many, many years. The fact that some still lived, especially on Ravendra, came as a tremendous shock.

It is possible. I just saw them. They've had their power stripped away by Jax, left to rot in a cell.

Then they are lost to us, Mathias. There's nothing we can do.

We can bring them with us.

Mathias...

They come with us, or I stay.

You can't be serious! Jax will destroy you!

I'm aware of what Jax will do. Mathias was disappointed that Mira was so ready to pass the other Wardens by. He couldn't let these people suffer any more than they already had. *Jax has already made it very clear what he plans on doing to me. He'll take my power and turn me into a mindless slave. But, I have to believe that some of them can be saved. Even if we save one, that would still be better than saving none of them.* His mind was quiet for a moment, the only sound coming from the echo of his footsteps against the cold floor. The two men finally stopped and turned Mathias once again. He faced an empty cell, one he assumed was his own.

"Home sweet home," one of the men grunted and shoved Mathias hard into the darkness. The Warden quickly put his hands out to break his fall, but the cold ground came up fast and the stone floor tore at his knees. The men laughed as they slammed the barred iron door closed.

"I wouldn't use your powers, if I were you," the second man stated. "The last Warden who tried lost his hands." And then the two were gone, laughing as they went. Mathias had no intention of using his power on the cell walls.

Instead, the boy sat in the center of the room with his legs crossed, waiting for a reply from Mira. He waited for what seemed like an hour before her response finally came.

We have a plan. Things are going to get messy, and you may not like everything we've decided. Be prepared to act fast. We are coming.

Mathias smiled for the first time since he had arrived on Ravendra. He closed his eyes, rested his shackled hands in his lap, and waited.

17

Long before its corruption by the Raven exiles, Ravendra was a world ruled by industry. In those times, the planet was better known as Drastem 3, the third in a chain of planets that once housed a very plentiful natural resource: steam. Where most planets were dominated mainly by water, Drastem 3 was almost one hundred percent land, home to only a few small ponds. The rest of the water was hidden deep below ground. Because of the naturally dry nature of the planet and very short daily access to sunlight, there was almost no vegetation on Drastem 3. Instead, the ground was riddled with cracks and holes. It was a dusty, barren wasteland.

Over time, the immense pressure growing inside the planet would force the boiling water out through the cracks, creating geysers. More time passed and soon, steam had become a much-desired resource throughout parts of the universe. Steam collectors, or Steamers as they were called, flocked to Drastem 3 when they discovered its secret.

Drastem 1 and 2 had become so overpopulated that the discovery of a third, hospitable steam based planet came as excellent news. The first Steamers to arrive on Drastem 3 were tasked with the painstaking mission of constructing a central hub around the most powerful of the planet's geysers. It took the Steamers nearly a decade to finish the project, but the city that emerged was magnificent. Unlike Malador's technologically savvy design, Corvia was blocky and rigid, with many buildings constructed directly over the steam vents. These geysers blew straight into the factories, keeping the buildings in peak working condition. There had never been a better time to be in steam collection. But then the Ravens came.

It was a small force in the beginning, the first of the rogue Wardens to be exiled from Haven. The Steamers, fearing for their lives, imprisoned the visitors in a small holding facility they constructed just outside the city. The facility was nothing special at the time, just a small, stone complex with a few barred cells. It would have kept any normal person locked away for life, but it was never meant to contain a Warden, let alone a group of them. Shortly after their incarceration, the Wardens broke free and lashed out at the people of Corvia. They were ruthless and showed no restraint as they annihilated every Steamer in the city.

Shortly after the planet's downfall, the leaders sent a message to their remaining followers. Hundreds of Ravens flocked to Drastem 3 seeking refuge following the Massacre. With nearly the entire Raven population now gathered in Corvia, they began to rebuild the city to suit their desires. The steam factories became polluted with dark energy, spewing toxic gas into the air. Air shields were designed specifically to counteract the abundant poison supply that had begun to infect the populace. The Ravens unfortunate enough to have been infected by the air transformed into mutated monstrosities and were either killed on sight or quarantined for study. What remained of the Raven population seized complete control of the planet, a planet they appropriately renamed Ravendra. From that day forward, Ravendra was the most feared planet in the galaxy.

Rolan had been aware of Ravendra's chaotic history when he had first met Commander Jax, but the money was too good to pass up. Jax had heard of Rolan's success as one of the galaxy's finest hunters and summoned the man to meet in person. They gathered in a massive, stone conference building just inside the city walls. The entryway was supported by magnificent black columns on either side of the cracked stairway. The white doors of the building were equally as magnificent, a giant raven carved intricately into the wood. However, the moment you stepped inside, you forgot all about the beauty of the exterior. There was nothing inside the hollow room save for a wide, round table in the center. In varying locations around the table were a wide variety of chairs, each a different color and style befitting of its owner.

Now, Rolan found himself entering that very same room where it all began several years ago. He thought about all the people he had brought to this planet over the years. So many of them had been innocent, young minds that the hunter had condemned to death. But, he shrugged off any regret he felt. He was a businessman, and retrieving people for Jax was never a personal affair. Rolan simply did what he had to do to survive.

As they always did, the doors to the expansive room slammed shut as Alistair brought up the rear of the pack. Rolan was impressed with how well the boy had handled himself thus far, even if Jax had humiliated him in front of everyone. The boy had suffered enough, and Rolan would do his best to keep Alistair at his side.

"Have a seat, gentlemen," Jax offered, extending his hand towards the round table. Rolan slouched into his usual seat: a forest green armchair with a bright, neon green pillow. He didn't know what had drawn him to the chair originally, but it always stuck out in his mind as unique. Alistair sat next to him, taking the wobbly, faded yellow stool that everyone always seemed to neglect. Across the table Jax gracefully lowered himself into his chair, a black throne detailed extensively with intricate carvings of birds and feathers. There was also a soft, violet cushion upon which to sit. It was the perfect chair for the commander of the Raven army.

"Now, as you are no doubt aware, I've brought you to Corvia to draw up payment for the delivery of the Grand Master," Jax began. With a snap of his fingers, one of the commander's associates laid a tattered document on the table. "You'll notice that the original order I placed was for Aurilean. While you have still succeeded in bringing me his successor, I am forced to deduct from the original payment as the specimen that arrived is, in fact, not Aurilean. Fair?" Jax asked, raising his head and offering his sincerest smile.

"Yea," Rolan grumbled in reply. He suspected Jax would short him, he just hoped it wasn't too much.

"As for the status of the delivery, the boy was visually unharmed and showed no signs of tampering. He was awake and aware of his surroundings, but was still impaired from the effects of the toxin you used to inhibit his abilities. No deductions to speak of there. Excellent work, as always," Jax said with a gentle nod of his head. With another snap of his fingers, another servant plopped a locked, brown chest onto the table. The box jingled as it settled, the contents rattling around inside. Jax opened the box and Rolan was sure, as he was every time, that the gold shown with a light all its own. Very carefully, Commander Jax began to pluck coins from the box. He removed nearly a hundred gold pieces before gently closing the lid. He then pushed hard on the chest and sent it sliding across the table towards Rolan. "A one-hundred-piece deduction for delivery of the wrong Grand Master. I assume this offer will suffice?"

Rolan opened his mouth to confirm but stopped as a knock on the door took the entire table by surprise. He spun in his chair as another, more abrupt knock followed shortly after the first. There had never, in all his times in this room, been a knock on that door. Something was very wrong.

Jax nodded to the two men standing beside him. The hulking figures abandoned their master's side and made their way to the giant entryway. All eyes were on them as one of the men unlocked the latch that sealed the group inside. Almost instantly, the ivory gates of the hall were blown open by a massive wave of red fire. One servant was now a flattened mess against the wall. The other had jumped out of the way just in time, but doing so caused the flames to leap onto the man's robes. In an effort to quench the fire, the man fell to the floor and began to roll frantically. However, instead of diminishing the inferno, the flames grew larger and larger. They continued to grow until the man on the floor ceased his spastic seizure.

The men at the table now stood attentively, eagerly awaiting the flames to die and reveal the identity of the intruder. Rolan gasped as a dark silhouette strolled through the flames like they were nothing. The man was far older than Rolan had expected, and he leaned on an intricately designed staff as we walked. He appeared incredibly tired, like a man who had seen more than his fair share of pain and suffering.

"Well, well, well, what a pleasant surprise," Jax taunted. He hadn't thought it possible, but his day had just gotten better.

"Hello, Jax," the old man replied. The moment the man spoke, Rolan was overcome with recognition. This was the man that had set his troops ablaze back on Sanctuary.

"What are *you* doing here?" Rolan asked, his anger rising. He clenched his metal fist at his side and prepared to engage the old man.

"The years have been good to you, *Commander*," the old man said to Jax, completely ignoring Rolan's question. His quarrel was not with the hunter.

"I wish I could say the same of you, old friend." Jax returned the jest and moved towards the end of the table. "Why are you here, Bastian? Or is it, Monk? I can never keep your names straight."

"Either will do, *old friend*. I am here to request that you release the boy," Bastian replied. He knew the Raven would never relinquish his prize, but he needed to keep Jax distracted.

"Of course you are," Jax said with a sad smile. "Never just a simple social visit, is it?"

"I'm afraid not, child."

"So be it. I assume the rest of your people are here as well?" Jax asked. He decided that the time for niceties was over.

"Indeed. You can thank your friend here for that," Bastian said as he pointed his staff at the bounty hunter. Rolan's eyes grew wide as Jax turned his angry features on him. "The hunter was kind enough to reveal his entire plan to young Mathias while his mental link was still functional."

"You did what?!" Jax yelled as he walked right up to Rolan, his eyes burning with intensity.

"I didn't think-" Rolan began but was immediately cut off as Jax slammed his fist into the side of Rolan's face.

"No, you didn't think! I thought you were different, Rolan. I thought you were smart!" Jax punched the man again, this time aiming for Rolan's stomach. The blow sent the bounty hunter instantly to the floor. "But you're not different, are you? You're just like every other slimy, money grabber out there!" Jax slammed his foot into Rolan's face, blood spewing from the man's nose and mouth.

Rolan's face swelled up like a balloon, and he could feel the wet blood dripping down his cheek and onto the floor. Though one of his eyes had swollen shut, he could see Alistair and Zeke still standing next to the table, a look of sheer horror plastered to their faces. He wanted to tell the boys that he was sorry for what was about to happen, but he couldn't.

"You useless pile of shit! I had a nice evening of torture planned, and now I have to deal with an entire squad of Wardens." Jax was fuming, but he refrained from attacking Rolan further. "Don't get me wrong, I'm glad that I will have a whole slew of Warden powers to choose from, but you know, it's the principle of the thing." Jax said as he stared down at the bleeding mess on the floor. He turned to Bastian, who had been waiting patiently for the commander to finish and said, "I apologize for the delay."

"Do what you need to do," Bastian replied with a shrug. The more time Jax spent here was less time he spent fighting off the others.

"You know what happens now, don't you Rolan?" Jax bent over and kneeled next to the hunter. Rolan simply waited there as he prepared for what was coming. Jax stood and signaled to his associates at the table. "Take them down to Reconstruction."

"No…" Rolan managed to say as his eyes, even his swollen one, grew nearly three times their size. He had thought Jax was just going to kill them. Instead, he was sending them to the most horrifying place in Corvia. He had seen firsthand the monstrosities that came out of Reconstruction, and he knew that death would have been the preferable alternative.

"Yes, Rolan! You've been good to me, but this betrayal I simply cannot abide. Take them away, and then see to our guests." Jax waved his hand and the remaining servants grabbed each of the bounty hunters at the table. Many tried to fight off the brutish figures but were knocked unconscious. Alistair looked to Rolan for a sign of what to do, but the man simply shook his head. He watched as the boy was yanked from his feet and dragged out of the room. This wasn't how he had expected this day would go, but Rolan knew that things rarely went according to plan. Four massive hands pull him to his feet and positioned him face to face with Jax.

"It was a pleasure doing business with you, Rolan." Jax smiled his wickedest smile and turned his back to the hunter. He grinned from ear to ear as Rolan was dragged off into the darkness.

"Is this how you handle all of your business nowadays?" Bastian asked, his eyes deep with sorrow.

"I do what I must. I seem to recall learning that from you, *master,*" Jax said, spitting at the ground near his feet.

"I find it hard to believe you learned anything from me, Jax."

"Would you like to see what I have learned, Bastian? Would you like to see what your training has accomplished?" Jax asked with a grin. He dropped the elegant black robe from his back and stood before Bastian with nothing but a loose pair of black pants.

"That is why I have come," Bastian replied sadly. He, too, dropped his billowing white cloak from his back and stood shirtless before Jax. The two were almost complete opposites of each other. Jax stood tall and confident, his muscles rippling across his arms and chest while his golden hair dangled in a tail behind his head. Bastian slouched against his staff, his age clearly weighing on the physicality of his body. His skin sagged in random places and there were wrinkles everywhere. The only groomed hair on the man's body was his perfectly sculpted black beard that glistened in the light of the rabid pyre behind him. Instead of dying as the conversation progressed, the flames in the doorway had grown stronger, preventing anyone from entering the building.

"Then you have come to your death," Jax said fiercely. He held his hand open at his side and a mass of dark purple energy began to swirl around his arm. The magic worked its way towards Jax's hand and, much to Bastian's humor, began to craft a sword hilt. The energy continued to swirl outward, building a long blade for the weapon. When the magic finished, Jax held an incredibly long sword in his hands, a sword that pulsed with unpredictable dark energy.

"I see you managed to learn one thing from me," Bastian said with a slight smile. He firmly grasped the black staff at his side and prepared for the confrontation.

"The only thing that mattered." Jax twirled the blade through the air, gathering a feel for the weapon that had materialized out of nothing.

"Shall we?" Bastian asked, his staff at the ready.

"We shall," Jax replied and then launched himself across the room. The commander brought his blade down hard as he landed, but Bastian slapped the blow aside with his staff. Wasting no time, Jax brought the sword around aiming for Bastian's neck. Again, Bastian brought his wooden staff up and stopped the blow before it could reach him. Jax had prepared for the block and used his free hand to send a blast of dark, purple energy straight into Bastian's chest. The old man flew into the nearby wall, cracking the structure and sending bits of debris flying. As he slid down the crumbling stone, Bastian conjured a blast of fire from his fingers and pushed himself off the wall and through the air. Jax simply watched as his former master glided over him. The moment Bastian landed Jax was on him, swinging his blade left and right, over and over. Each strike Jax threw was met with a powerful block from Bastian's black staff. Jax launched his strikes again and again, continuously trying new methods of attack, but Bastian was always prepared, blocking the blow, but never returning it.

Jax knew what his former teacher was trying to do, so he decided it was time to change up his game. He dropped a blast of energy at his feet and propelled himself away from the monk. He plunged his sword into the floor and began to channel his darker power. He felt the black energy begin to swirl around him and immediately lashed out with it. The black magic struck at Bastian like a whip striking a horse, forcing the old man to leap out of the way. But where one whip of the energy missed, another quickly took its place, shattering the stone floor all around them. Dust and debris shot through the air as the magic continued to hammer the ground.

Bastian was growing incredibly tired as he continued to jump out of the way of Jax's attacks. The years had indeed not been kind to him, and he could feel the muscles in his legs beginning to tire. He wouldn't be able to keep his defense up much longer. As soon as that thought crossed his mind, a black whip of energy found its mark, slamming Bastian into the floor. The old man screamed out in pain as the magic coursed through his body. The sound of Jax laughing in the distance was enough motivation to force Bastian back to his feet but, as soon as he stood, another wave of energy sent him straight back to the ground. He coughed violently as shattered bits of rock found their way into his lungs. As he struggled to return to his feet, he felt the black magic vigorously wrap itself around both of his arms. Their grip on him was impossibly firm and quickly cut off all circulation to his hands. Then, much to his displeasure, the magic pulled Bastian into the air. His fingers had grown so numb that he was forced to drop his staff. The weapon bounced once as it hit the ground and then settled.

"I must say that I am disappointed, old friend," Jax said sadly.

"You will never learn, child," Bastian croaked and then closed his eyes. He channeled all of his inner rage and anger into one simple thought and, without hesitation, brought the fire forth. Much to Jax's surprise, Bastian's entire body was suddenly engulfed in flame. He glowed with a confidence that sent a brief pang of fear through the commander, and then he was burning. Bastian sent waves of fire coursing through the whips that held him in place and back to their master. Jax screamed in pain as the inferno overtook him, burning away all the black energy around him.

Savoring his small victory, Bastian used the fire that engulfed him to extend his reach, grabbing his ancient weapon from the rubble at his feet. He hovered a few inches off the ground as the raging inferno burned around him. He then turned his attention to Jax, who had finally managed to calm the flames. The Raven screamed in rage and pulled his sword from the ground. He quickly called more dark energy from within himself and used it to strengthen the blade. Then, letting out another angry yell, Jax charged at the burning man. Bastian wasted no time mounting an offensive, launching continuous balls of fire at Jax as he closed the distance between them. One of them caught Jax in the shoulder and another found its mark in his chest, but the Raven shook the blows off like they were nothing. Jax was far more powerful than he used to be.

The Raven let out a nail biting screech as he zeroed in on Bastian, swinging his sword with every ounce of his being. Bastian raised his flaming weapon to block the strike as he had before, only this time, when the shadow infused weapon connected with the staff, the wooden core shattered. Bastian panicked as the reverberation of the shattering weapon sent a shockwave through his hands. He howled with rage as the weapon he had carried for so long disintegrated back into the fire around him. However, before the old man could react to the situation, he felt a sharp pain erupt in his chest. The flames around him suddenly evaporated, and Bastian fell to his knees in defeat, the longsword having pierced his heart.

"Now, what did you learn?" Jax asked victoriously, sliding his sword out of the man's body. Bastian had always asked that same question at the end of every lesson. It seemed only fitting for Jax to ask it now. The commander circled his kneeling foe and laid his blood drenched blade across Bastian's neck.

"That you are not… the man… you once were…" Bastian managed to say, taking sharp breaths every couple words. The fire in the doorway had vanished and Ravens from all over Corvia had gathered to see what the commotion was about. What they now saw was one of the most ancient of Wardens, a Warden who several of the Ravens had trained under, kneeling to Jax in defeat. It was something many of them had never thought they would see.

"That man disappeared long ago, Bastian. He died when you sided with the Wardens. You abandoned us. Abandoned me!" Jax roared.

"We... are all... Wardens..." Bastian could hardly find the strength to speak anymore, the blood rapidly draining from his body, his heart no longer functioning.

"No! We are better than Wardens! We are the ones who will save this universe!"

"Save it... from who?" Bastian asked with his final breaths.

"From you," Jax said spitefully and raised his sword high into the air. He took a deep breath and then let out a roar as he brought the blade down.

Bastian had always known this moment would come, and just as he felt the cold steel break the skin of his neck, he managed to relay one final message to the others.

The fire is extinguished. Jax is coming.

Matthew Louwers

18

He had been asleep for a couple of hours when the words burst into his mind followed directly by a searing pain in his heart. Mathias grabbed at his chest hoping to dull the pain, but the fire continued to rage within him. He wasn't sure what was going on, but he knew something bad had happened.

The fire is extinguished. Jax is coming.

The words continued to echo inside Mathias's head as the inferno burned away at his insides. The voice, Mathias was sure, could have only been one man. But why Monk was contacting him now remained a mystery. The old man had stayed behind on Sanctuary to clean up the wreckage. Unless, of course, he hadn't.

An earthshaking crash echoed through the long, stone corridor of the prison. Someone, or something, had just smashed through the solid iron doors at the front of the building. The pain in his chest began to subside as Mathias waited patiently in the darkness, listening to the quick footsteps growing progressively louder. Mathias remained calm as a dark silhouette appeared in front of the cage and the sound of footsteps ceased.

"You just gonna sit there?" A burly voice asked from the darkness. Mathias cracked a smile as he instantly recognized the intruder.

"Well, I was having a nice little nap," Mathias replied jokingly.

"Could come back later if you'd prefer?"

"No point, I'm awake now," Mathias said with a chuckle.

"Stand back then," the hulking man said as he placed his two massive hands on the cold bars of the cell door. Mathias stood and leaned against the cold, stone wall at his back. The man's arms suddenly illuminated the cell with a bright yellow light and Mathias watched in amazement as his rescuer ripped the door from its hinges. The resulting crash of metal and rock was music to the Warden's ears, and he breathed a sigh of relief as the man easily tossed the door aside.

"It's good to see you, Joel," Mathias said as he stretched out his arms and exited the cell.

"Yea, I reckon it is," the Warden replied, brushing the dirt from his hands. Joel then looked Mathias in the eyes and added, "Monk is dead."

"What?" Mathias asked, but part of him knew it was true. The message he received had been the old man's final words to the four of them, and the fire in his chest was the power deep inside him reacting to the man's death. The Wardens were all connected and, when one of them fell, the others knew it.

"We need to get outta-"

"What happened?" The Grand Master asked.

"He volunteered to distract Jax while I came for you. I was against his plan, but there ain't no point in arguin' with him." Joel was in a lot more pain than he was letting on. His usual scowl was extra frowny and he spoke with the sadness of a man who kept losing people close to him.

"Did you get the same message?"

"Yea. Jax is comin'. Which is why we need to go!" Joel's patience was wearing thin.

"After you," Mathias replied and the two Wardens darted off into the darkness. They passed several empty cells before they came upon the broken Wardens Mathias had seen earlier. The Grand Master stopped and Joel was forced to as well.

"Mathias, we don't have time-"

"They come, or I stay. Decide." Mathias stared intently into Joel's hard eyes and hoped his friend would make the right decision. Only a few seconds passed before Joel averted his gaze and let out a massive, and quite childish, groan. He grabbed the iron bars of the cell door and called upon his power once again. The door came free with ease, screeching as Joel chucked it down the hallway.

"Can we go now?" Joel asked hastily.

"In a moment," Mathias responded and then walked into the cell. Many of the cage's inhabitants stood as Joel pried the door from its home, while the sicker captives simply turned where they sat to examine the development. The ones able to stand moved towards Mathias as he entered the cell. "Listen to me, and listen well, we don't have a lot of time. Commander Jax has taken your lives from you, but I'm here to give them back."

Joel looked on in annoyance as Mathias spoke.

"Today, I free you from your bonds. You are no longer Jax's slaves!" Mathias was shaking, but he smiled as many of the faces staring back at him glowed with approval. Some of them even bent over to help the sicker and older captives to their feet. "While you're free to go wherever you'd like, I offer you a life with us. Come with me and my friends, and we'll take you to others like you. We can show you that there is still a reason to live!"

The cage exploded with excitement. Mathias was confused at first, as these were very different behaviors than the ones he had witnessed earlier that day, but he was too distracted and determined to give it any deeper thought.

"Come with us now, and stay close! Your former masters will be upon us soon, and we may have to fight for our lives. Come, now, to freedom!" The prisoners cheered and many sprinted straight out of the cage while others helped the sicker men and women onto their backs for easier transport. Mathias was amazed at how simple it was to convince these prisoners to abandon their masters. It was almost too easy.

"Quite the motivational speaker, ain't ya?" Joel said as he placed a hand on the boy's shoulder.

"I just hope I can deliver on my promise to see them to safety." Mathias shuddered at the thought of these slaves dying at Raven hands only moments after they had been freed.

"Then we'd better get movin'. Ardy put the Longshot down some ways off to avoid bein' seen. There were also a few Ravens perched outside that I had to take care of, but there'll be more."

"Alright everyone, this hulking behemoth is Joel," Mathias said as he motioned to the Warden at his side. "He's going to lead you to our ship. Stay as close to him as you can and do your best to keep up. I'll be in the back to make sure no one is left behind. Now, let's move!" And with that Joel took off, leading the pack towards the entrance. Mathias waited a few seconds as each of the prisoners ran after him and, as the last man burst free from the cell, Mathias started to run.

The prison wasn't very large so it was only a short distance to the exit. Mathias was surprised at how quickly everyone seemed to be moving, especially since so many of them had been locked in a cage for years. This was going to be easier than he thought.

Mathias heard shouting from the front of the pack and realized that they had just crossed the threshold of the building. Some of the prisoners were seeing the outside world for the first time in years. However, as Mathias neared the exit and burst out into the darkness, he realized what the shouting had really been about. Dark shapes were moving against the night sky, and Mathias knew that they were about to have company.

"Run!" The Grand Master yelled, and the pack began the long trek to freedom.

*   *   *

Mira paced across the cold ground as she waited for any sign of the others. Joel and Monk had left almost an hour ago, and one of them had met their end at Raven hands. Mira had been so furious when she received Monk's message that she almost ran off to Corvia on her own. However, after some brutal counseling from Ardemis, she refrained from taking that pointless action. Instead, she distanced herself from Ardemis and waited impatiently for Joel and Mathias.

We're on our way! Joel's voice rang out in her head, and she immediately stopped her pacing.

Is Mathias with you? She asked hopefully.

Duh! The other Wardens, too. Joel replied, and Mira cursed. She had told Joel to get Mathias out of there as fast as he could instead of wasting time on the prisoners. It was a decision she hadn't made lightly, but one she knew was necessary if they were to survive.

Where are you now? Mira asked as she peered off into the night sky.

I don't know! We just passed a big rock, does that help?

Mira didn't so much as crack a smile.

There's Ravens, Mira. They'll be on us in seconds!

Mira swore again. She had known this would happen if Mathias stayed to free the others. He put everyone in danger to save a group of prisoners he knew nothing about. She turned and, as quickly as she could, sprinted into the ship. She found Ardemis sitting in his chair in the cockpit, his legs stretched out on the dash in front of him. He looked surprised as he turned to face her.

"What's wrong, lassie?" Ardemis asked.

"They stayed to free the damn prisoners, and now they're about to be swarmed. I'm going to go buy them some time." Mira looked angrier than Ardemis had ever seen her.

"You against an entire flock?" Ardemis questioned. "You're good, lass, but you're not *that* good."

"I have to, Ardy." Mira knew it was the only way to save them. "Listen to me, the moment everyone from the prison is aboard this ship, you take off and you don't look back. If I haven't returned, don't you dare come looking for me."

"You know the lad will never let that happen, don't you?" Ardemis said sadly.

"Ignore him. Just get him out of here," Mira said and ran off. She didn't have time to waste arguing with Ardemis.

Be careful, lass. Ardemis's voice rang in her head as she stormed out into the night. The cool air brushed against her face as she prepared for what she needed to do. Reaching for the pain she had suffered as a little girl, she retreated into her thoughts. The wind billowed around her, rapidly gaining speed. Mira closed her eyes and waited for the power to take over. It took only a few seconds for the red-hot fury to flood through Mira's body. Her eyes opened abruptly but, instead of her usual brown, both eyes now glowed bright red. Her brand, which she had never shown to anyone, was also radiating with vibrant red light as the power assumed complete control, burning away her clothing. The Warden of Fury had arrived. With a bone chilling scream, Mira sprinted into the darkness.

*　　　　　*　　　　　*

The scream that pierced the evening air brought Mathias to an abrupt halt. The rest of the group seemed unaffected by the noise, but something about it seemed vaguely familiar to the Grand Master. He scanned the area for any sign of the sound's origin, but saw nothing.

A blast of dark shadow energy suddenly whizzed past Mathias's head and he was forced to continue running. They were making excellent time, but the Ravens were still gaining on them. The ones that had closed in were launching bolts of purple energy in their direction, but Mathias deflected the blasts away from the group, calling upon the wind to act as their shield.

A red streak against the horizon caught the Warden's attention. He wasn't sure what he had just seen, but he couldn't afford to stop again. As they continued, weaving through blazing hot geysers and deep cracks in the earth,

Mathias noticed that the Raven attacks on them had almost completely diminished, and he stopped to see what was going on. Facing the Raven horde, Mathias saw a streak of red light weaving through a mass of black and purple. He had never seen anything like it. He wanted to get a closer look, but a voice in his head snapped him back to reality.

Let's go, kid! The ship is just ahead. Mathias turned on the spot and called upon the wind once more to speed him along. He caught up to the pack almost instantly and breathed a sigh of a relief as the Longshot appeared, hidden just behind a nearby rock formation. The loading ramp was down and Joel stopped as he approached it. He hastily ushered each of the prisoners onto the ship. When the last of the Wardens was on board, Joel jumped up the ramp and Mathias followed suit.

"Ardy!" Joel yelled as he sprinted towards the cockpit. "Get us the hell outta here!"

Mathias was helping the prisoners to find a safe place to sit when ship began to shake, signaling takeoff. As the ship began to climb and gain speed, Mathias had a gnawing feeling that something was wrong. He jumped up and sprinted towards the cockpit.

"Where's Mira?" He asked quickly, hoping nothing had happened to her. Joel ignored the question and Ardemis pushed forward on his controls, urging the ship on faster. "I'll ask again, and I'd better get an answer. Where the hell is Mira?!"

"Giving us the time we need, lad," was all Ardemis could say, but he couldn't bring himself to look Mathias in the eye.

"No…" Mathias replied and dashed back towards the cargo hold.

"Don't do it, kid!" Joel yelled as he chased Mathias through the ship.

"You're just going to leave her behind?!" The Grand Master yelled angrily as he approached the loading ramp.

"She specifically said not to go after her."

"If you know anything about me, then you know I can't let that happen!" Mathias roared and pushed the ramp drop button. The ramp resisted at first, but opened, releasing the growing pressure in the hold.

"Mathias, look at me!" Joel yelled over the noise. The wind howled and the roaring of the engine made it nearly impossible to hear anything, but Mathias turned to face the Warden anyway. "She ain't herself. She won't recognize friend from foe. She'll kill ya!"

"No, she won't," Mathias replied, and then he jumped out of the aircraft. The air immediately tasted sour as it brushed against his lips. He assumed he was outside of the planet's air shields, which meant he was in serious trouble. He watched the Longshot grow smaller and smaller as he rapidly made his descent. He dropped for a few moments before the strange taste in the air vanished, and he passed into the safety of an air shield. He spun abruptly in midair and pushed off against the night, propelling himself toward the battle raging below.

The first thing he saw was the glowing red blur of light moving at incredible speeds amongst the Raven flock. Another scream pierced the night and Mathias now understood why it seemed so familiar. The red blur was Mira. Mathias had always wondered what her power was, and now, as he flew into the fray, he wasn't sure he wanted to find out.

He slammed down hard on the outskirts of the battle, knocking two nearby Ravens to the ground. Unfortunately, his landing drew more attention than he hoped, and many of

the Ravens turned from Mira to him. Mathias dodged a blast
of purple energy as it blew past him and returned the attack
with a blast of wind, launching his attacker into the air.
Another ball of energy came at him from the side, and
Mathias called the wind to him, deflecting the attack and
redirecting it back. The raven jumped out of the way and then
charged at Mathias, a silver dagger in hand. It was very
similar to the one Jax had shown him, but the crystal in the
hilt shined with an eerie green light instead of purple. The
Raven was on him in seconds, swinging and striking with the
blade where he could, but Mathias dodged each blow,
dancing around the Raven with ease. Two other Ravens
suddenly approached him from behind. Each one grabbed
one of Mathias's arms and held him firmly in place. Mathias
swore under his breath for letting his guard down.

"You shouldn't have come back, *Warden*," grunted
the man he had been fighting. He approached Mathias with
the knife and prepared to plunge it into his chest when
another knife flew in out of nowhere. The ruby dagger caught
the Raven in the side of the head, piercing his skull. He
instantly crumpled to the ground and was gone. Mathias took
the sudden distraction to call the wind to him, and then
instantly pushed it away, freeing himself of the other two
Ravens. With all his strength, Mathias sent sharp crests of air
towards the two men, splitting each of them in half.

Another red dagger suddenly appeared out of
nowhere, only this time it was thrown directly at Mathias
himself. The Warden dodged the blade just in time, but he
was shocked to see that it was Mira who had thrown it. He
was more shocked, however, to see that Mira was standing
completely naked before him. Her dark red hair billowed out
in the wind as she suddenly charged at him, another scarlet
knife having appeared in her hand. Mathias panicked and

jumped to the side to avoid the attack. That's when he
noticed that Mira hadn't been aiming for him after all, as she
sliced the neck of a Raven who had been just about to strike
Mathias from behind. The Grand Master was confused. Joel
had seemed confident that Mira wasn't in control, but already
she had saved his life twice.

A sudden hum overhead drew the Warden's attention
away from the battle. The Longshot had returned and the
loading ramp was open.

The Ravens around them had closed in and Mathias
knew there was only one way the two of them were going to
make it out of the battle alive. He pushed off the ground hard
and flew directly at his counterpart. Mira screamed wildly as
Mathias grabbed her and pulled her into the sky. The Ravens
below howled in anger and launched blasts of energy their
way, but Mathias dodged them all. Mira struggled to break
free, swinging her knife angrily around, but Mathias held her
tight. He needed to get her to the ship.

*Mathias! If you bring her aboard like that, we're all
dead!* Joel yelled into the boy's head, but the Grand Master
ignored him. There was no time to figure out how to stop the
power that controlled Mira's body. He made a quick turn to
fly straight into the ship when another blast of dark magic
was fired his way. He normally would have dodged the
attack with ease, but he was moving too fast. If he
maneuvered away from the ball of energy, he and Mira
would crash into the side of the ship. Mathias twisted himself
so that as the black magic approached it crashed into his back
instead of Mira's. He screamed in agony as the energy tore at
his body. Ardemis, seeing that the Warden was off course,
angled the ship so that Mathias dropped straight into the
Longshot's cargo hold. Joel was there with some of the other

Wardens that they had rescued earlier and jumped on top of Mira before she could get up.

"Hold her arms down!" Joel yelled at one of the men, and then he turned to another. "You! Hold her feet!" But the men were instantly thrown off as Mira tossed them aside like dolls. She wailed as she stood and slammed her fist into Joel's gut, launching him backwards. Everyone in the cargo hold crawled to hide from the rampaging Warden now fuming in the center of the room. Mira screamed again as Mathias jumped at her, knocking her down once more.

Ardy! Take us to Vega! Mathias said to his friend.

What?! You can't be-

Just do it! Mathias thought and blocked him out. The Warden of Fury was fighting ferociously beneath him. He didn't have time to argue with Ardemis.

Joel quickly appeared back in the fray and secured Mira's arms above her head. She was still kicking with all her might, but Mathias managed to keep her pinned down.

Mira, he said in his mind. *I need you to come back to us now. I need you to remember who you are.* He wasn't sure if his idea was even going to work, but he needed to try something. *I know you can hear me, Mira. You're safe now.*

Mira's legs suddenly stopped kicking, and the red glow of her eyes began to fade.

"What the hell did you do?" Joel asked in amazement, but Mathias didn't respond. Mira was still twitching and fighting to break free, only less violently. Mathias smiled down at his friend as she ever so slowly quelled her struggle.

"Let go," Mathias said to Joel. The Warden was about to object but Mathias glared at him before he could speak. Reluctantly, Joel removed his hands from Mira's wrists. The red of her eyes had nearly gone and the hazel color was returning. He breathed a sigh of relief as he relaxed his hold on her and, at that moment, Mira reached up and grabbed the Warden's throat. Joel rushed back in but Mathias waved him away. Her grasp was unbelievably strong and she lifted Mathias off the ground as she stood. She stared deep into his eyes, as if she was looking for something. Mathias struggled for air, but found none as Mira's hand closed off his throat.

"Who are you to speak to me in such a way?" Mira asked, but it wasn't her voice that spoke. It was deeper and distorted, and it echoed throughout the hold with an eerie vibrance.

Mira, come back. Mathias repeated in his mind, ignoring the creature that had spoken to him, but the darkness was taking over. If Mira didn't let go, he would die. Without warning, and much to Mathias's surprise, Mira screamed one final time and threw Mathias across the room. The Grand Master slammed into the steel wall of the ship and then fell to the ground with a thud. He tried to fight the urge to pass out, but failed miserably as the black abyss of unconsciousness took over.

Matthew Louwers

19

The Warden was nearly blinded as he opened his
eyes. Sunlight radiated throughout the hold, illuminating
even the darkest of nooks and crevices. His eyelids slammed
shut immediately, and he let out a quiet groan as he
discovered a new pain throbbing against the back of his head.
That's when it all came back to him: Mira's hand around his
throat, the collision with the wall of the ship, and the fade to
black. He opened his eyes once more, just slow enough to
gradually let the piercing rays of light in. At first, he could
hardly make out anything around him, but his vision quickly
returned and he could examine his surroundings with greater
care. He was growing tired of waking up this way.

The first thing the boy noticed was that the cargo hold
was void of life. There wasn't a single person anywhere
around, nor could he hear any voices from any other areas of
the ship. In fact, the Longshot itself also showed no signs of

life. Mathias wondered if Mira had caused the Longshot to crash, or if Ardemis had managed to land the ship in time.

The sudden whistle of a songbird snapped Mathias out of his daze. He turned his attention to the loading ramp and noticed bright green grass blowing in the wind just below it. Without thinking, Mathias pushed off against the ground and tried to stand, but a wave of dizziness rushed over him and he clumsily fell to the ground with a thud.

"Whoa, easy lad," a voice echoed throughout the room. Mathias turned his head towards the voice and saw Ardemis quickly jogging over to him.

"Ardy? What happened? Where are we?" The questions poured from the boy's mouth.

"It would seem Mira has a knack for, quite literally, knocking you off your feet," Ardemis replied with a chuckle. Mathias groaned, the pain in his head growing with each intake of air. "As for where we are, I managed to put 'er down on Vega like ya asked. Can't imagine why you picked this particular planet, laddie, but I figured you had your reasons."

"My father once told me that if I ever found myself in need of refuge, I could come here. It was the only place I could think of at the time." Mathias rubbed the bridge of his nose as he tried to force the swelling down. Mira must have thrown him incredibly hard to have caused this much pain.

"Well, if the Ravens don't get us, the monstrous wildlife surely will. Can't decide which way I'd rather go, to be completely honest with you," Ardemis replied with a smile. Mathias laughed, enduring the pain it brought. The little Sky Warden excelled at cheering him up.

"You don't think we were followed, do you?" The Warden asked with a sudden twinge of fear.

"Not that I could see, lad. No ships have appeared on radar, but we've only been here a couple days."

"Wait, what? A couple days?!"

"Joel tried to wake you, laddie, but you wouldn't come to. So, we took the others off the ship and found a small cave to hole up in. Been treating some of the sicker Wardens, while some of the stronger ones look for food." Ardemis continued to glance at the ramp as he spoke.

"And Mira?"

"She's fine. A little banged up, but she'll survive. She blacked out the moment you did. Was kinda weird, now that I think about it. But she's been helping the others look for food."

"Is she mad at me?"

"What do you think?" Ardemis replied, suspecting Mathias already knew the answer. When Mira had woken up, she'd been surprised to see that she was still alive. She screamed angrily at Ardemis for disobeying her orders and stormed off into the jungle. Only a couple hours later did she return, seemingly calmer about the situation.

"And the other Wardens? They're all okay?" Mathias asked hopefully.

"Surprisingly, I might say. Many of them seemed to have healed overnight, their wounds vanishing without a trace and their minds rapidly returning to a functioning state. It's quite unbelievable, actually," Ardemis said, the shock apparent in his tone. Mathias smiled knowing that he had succeeded in rescuing the Wardens from a grim fate. "Would you like to see them?"

"I would. I think I've seen enough of this ship." The throbbing in his head dwindled as the two spoke, and Mathias was starting to feel like himself again.

"Take my hand, laddie," Ardemis said. Mathias grabbed the man's small, outstretched hand and pulled himself upward. There was no pain this time, and he found himself standing firm and balanced.

"Lead on," Mathias was quite anxious to see the others, especially Mira. Ardemis walked towards the ramp while Mathias followed closely behind. The foreign air that blew into the hold bore an unusual salty taste that Mathias found quite interesting as it snuck into his mouth. "The air is strange here."

"I noticed it as well. The others didn't seem to, but I tasted it right away. Don't think it's anything to worry about, though," Ardemis said as they began their descent down the ramp. The wind blew steadily and a choir of birds sang from the massive trees all around them, a melody that seemed a tad foreboding.

The first thing Mathias saw as he cleared the ramp was Joel running towards them.

"Look who finally decided to join us," Joel said as he stopped before them. "Have any good dreams about me?"

"Can't say that I did," Mathias replied with a chuckle.

"Too bad. Some of the other Wardens were just askin' 'bout ya. Figured I'd swing by and see how you were doin'."

"Well that's awfully kind of you," Mathias replied with a grin. "We were just on our way to see them."

"Good deal. I'll head back and let 'em know you're comin'," Joel said then sprinted back into the trees.

"You know, lad, sometimes I wonder about him," Ardemis said and then burst into laughter. Mathias joined in as the two began their walk through the woods.

The jungle was a thick mass of overgrown vegetation. The trees grew taller than any Mathias had ever seen and the canopy completely prohibited any sunlight from entering the

236

jungle. Dark, jade vines twisted and tangled their way over the branches and down the thick brown trunks, many snaking across the squishy ground. Peculiar assortments of multi-colored plants and flowers littered the area. Some were striped and bore vivid yellow and gold centers, while others had bright red and white polka-dots that lined each drooping petal. Mathias yelped as an abnormally large beetle flew past him and landed atop a purple and blue spotted flower and then gasped in amazement as the flower opened and revealed a gaping maw filled with at least twenty razor sharp teeth. The flower gobbled the insect whole. Mathias was in complete awe as he watched the bug slowly fall through the flower's stem into the ground.

"Had a young boy, first day we were here, lose a finger to one of those bad boys. Bit it clean off, bone and everything," Ardemis said as he noticed Mathias had stopped to examine the plant.

"Makes you wonder what else is out there."

"We decided it was better not to think about that." Ardemis turned back towards the path and pressed on. Mathias tried to stay his curiosity, but that was like placing a big red button in front of a child and telling them not to press it.

The tales surrounding the exotic wildlife on Vega were numerous. Some of them were so extravagant that Mathias could hardly believe they were true at all. From monstrous fiends as tall as skyscrapers, to microscopic water leeches that would latch onto you and drain your very life force, there was always something lurking in the darkness.

As one of the three planets in a cluster known as the Dead Worlds, Vega was the only one to contradict that name. The planet was bursting with vegetation and housed millions of different species of wildlife. Many of the creatures on

Vega, however, were nearly as large as an average sized home and would normally attack unfamiliar visitors on sight. It was because of these monstrous beings that many civilizations had failed to thrive on Vega. The creatures aggressively defended their homes and destroyed everything the people worked so hard to build. Vega became the third Dead World simply because it was uninhabitable by anything that didn't already live there.

The other two Dead Worlds held true to their name. Mal'Rashim, the sister world to the desert planet Rashim, was a barren, desolate wasteland completely covered in sand. Water was impossible to find anywhere on the surface, but you were more likely to die from the sweltering heat before digging deep enough to find any. Nothing grew in the sand, and no animal could survive long enough in the heat to thrive. Aquillian, however, was the exact opposite. The entire planet was one, endless ocean. However, where most oceans were home to billions of species of fish and other aquatic life, the water on Aquillian was so toxic that no living creature could survive in it, and there was no land upon which to build.

The Dead Worlds were clustered together on the outskirts of Solace, the region of space home to Ravendra and many other minor planets and star systems. However, as powerful as they were, the Ravens avoided the Dead Worlds just like everyone else, making Vega the perfect place to hide.

A monstrous roar in the distance took the two Wardens by surprise. A nearby flock of birds abandoned their homes and took off into the sky, squawking in fear.

"Stop," Ardemis commanded quietly. The two held their ground and waited, listening for any signs of movement. Mathias scanned the darkness, silently hoping that the other

Wardens were okay wherever they were holed up. Leaves crunched some ways off, and a twig snapped. There was something out there. A gleam of light from a dark purple bush in the distance caught the Warden's eye. As soon as he turned to alert Ardemis the bush exploded in a violent eruption of purple leaves and twigs, and a colossal, black shadow bounded across the jungle floor towards them. The creature moved with lightning speed, its long, blood drenched fangs glistening in the dim light of the forest.

"Run!" Mathias yelled as he took off into the trees.

"Forget that, lad," Ardemis replied and grabbed at Mathias as he ran by. The moment Ardemis had Mathias's arm firmly in hand, he pushed off the spongy earth and blasted into the air. The explosion of wind knocked the creature back into the trees. It spun in the air, landing on its feet like a cat, but it was too late. Within seconds, the Wardens broke through the dense canopy and into the blinding sunlight. The cat-like monstrosity howled with rage below as Ardemis and Mathias joined in laughter. The green canopy stretched on for miles and miles in every direction, and the other two Dead Worlds looked as if they had been painted onto the bright blue canvas of the afternoon sky.

"And I wanted to run," Mathias said with a chuckle. He was so accustomed to running from monsters in the forests of Talise that it was his first instinct. He had completely forgotten that he could fly.

"Why do you think you keep me around, laddie," Ardemis said with a sly grin. Mathias didn't know what he would do without the little Sky Warden.

"How much further to the cave?"

"Not far actually. We'll make good time up here as opposed to trekking through the jungle." Ardemis was already pushing off into the sky as he finished speaking and

239

Mathias took off after him. The two flew well together, weaving between the stray whiffs of clouds and using each other's streams to propel themselves forward. It was exhilarating to fly alongside the Sky Warden.

A break in the trees below caught Mathias's attention. He swooped down to examine the earth below and found a wide, rushing river snaking its way alongside the jungle. There were a few smaller, less-threatening animals drinking on the far side, but it was the two men gathering buckets of water from the stream on the near side that interested him.

"Two of the men you rescued," Ardemis said as he dropped in behind Mathias.

"They look incredibly well for having spent so much time in a dungeon."

"Like I said before, lad, it's very strange."

"Maybe all they needed was some fresh air."

"Maybe." But Ardemis didn't sound convinced.

"Well, let's get down there." Mathias descended behind Ardemis as they landed near the river. They followed quietly behind the other Wardens, who had yet to notice them, and kept an eye out for anything strange. The men moved quickly, but carefully so as not to spill any of the precious resource they had just obtained. They arrived at the mouth of the cave without incident, and Mathias let out a small gasp of amazement as he took in the sight of it. The entrance was so large that the Longshot itself could have fit inside two times over. Mathias hoped that he would never meet the creatures that needed a cave that size.

"Mathias!" A young boy came running out of the shadowy recesses of the cave and hugged the Grand Master around his waist. The two men before them turned in surprise, one of them nearly spilling his bucket. Mathias looked down at the boy before him. He was covered from head to toe in dirt, his shirt and pants were nearly ripped to shreds, and his left hand was covered in bandages. This must have been the boy that Ardemis had told him about.

"Pick a fight with a flower?" Mathias asked jokingly. The boy giggled hysterically and threw a gentle punch at the Warden's leg. Mathias bent over and began to tickle the boy ferociously. The boy squealed with laughter, fighting off the fingers poking at him. "Choose your fights more carefully next time," Mathias chuckled as he let the boy go. The boy ran a few paces away before turning and sticking his tongue out. Then he turned back towards the darkness and disappeared.

"What a peculiar young lad," Ardemis said with a chortle. Mathias smiled and turned towards the two men they had been following.

"How's everyone doing?"

"Very well, sir," the taller man replied, but he kept his eyes on the ground. He was thinner than his counterpart, and stood nearly a whole head over him.

"Thanks to you, sir," the other man said. He too stared at the ground as he spoke.

"You and your people have nothing to fear from us," Mathias replied, hoping to ease the strange tension that had suddenly appeared between them.

"I know, sir," the first man said. "We've never been in the presence of one such as you before, though. The masters always made us look at the ground when we spoke to them."

"Well, I will have no more of that," Mathias said and lifted the man's head up. The tall man smiled as his dark, blue eyes fell upon the Grand Master's face.

"How adorable," a voice suddenly chimed in from the entryway. Mathias turned and saw Joel leaning against the rock wall.

"You're next, big man," Mathias said jokingly to which Joel howled in laughter.

"Spare me," he replied. Just behind him Mathias noticed about four or five other Wardens. Some of them were bloodied and cut, and they all held firmly onto a massive, white deer-like creature. "Watch the antlers!" Joel yelled as they carried the animal past him and deeper into cave.

"Where's Mira?" Mathias asked worriedly.

"Up there," Joel replied and pointed to a dirt path that seemed to wrap upwards around the cave. "Said she wanted to talk when you got here."

"Alright," Mathias said and turned to the men he'd just been speaking to. "You're free now. You can do whatever you want and be whoever you want. Forget what the Ravens told you and live your lives."

"Yes, sir," the tall man replied.

"Thank you, sir," said the smaller man with an awkward smile.

"Now, if you gentlemen will excuse me, I must go find Warden Mira. We'll speak again when I return." The two men bowed and turned to leave but Mathias stopped them. "What were your names?"

"Pius, sir," said the shorter man.

"And I am Pietrus," replied the taller man.

"Pius and Pietrus, it's a pleasure to meet you."

"No, sir," Pietrus replied, the faintest grin spreading on his face. "The pleasure is ours."

20

    The jade leaves of the jungle trees rustled in the wind as Mathias made his way up the path. The golden sun was still high in the sky, its rays beating harshly down upon the him. The trees were sparse around the cave and the hill, so the shade he and Ardemis had enjoyed earlier was but a distant memory. He kept an eye out for the creature that had attacked him before, while staying far away from any carnivorous plant life. He still couldn't believe that he was currently standing on one of the Dead Worlds. These were the most uninhabitable planets in the universe, yet here they all were. He just hoped the Ravens wouldn't think to look for them here.

    He found Mira sitting on a gnarled, fallen tree as he neared the top of the hill. The tree looked as if it had always been there, growing sideways along the ground instead of high into the sky. The hill was also much higher than Mathias realized. From the top, he could see nothing but treetops in every direction.

Mira was staring intently out into the endless sea of green as Mathias quietly sat down beside her. She didn't so much as blink as the old tree creaked beneath her with the added weight.

"It's beautiful up here," Mathias said, breaking the silence between them. "You could sit for days and finally know what it means to be at peace."

"Until the Ravens find you." Mira didn't turn to look at him. She wanted to scream and yell but was having a difficult time finding the words.

"Why would they look for us here? We haven't done anything to-"

"You should have left me there, Mathias," Mira said callously. The Grand Master could feel the anger in her words. Even the way she spoke his name felt painfully cold.

"Left you there to what? Die?"

"You could've escaped! You could be far away from this entire system right now. Instead, you came back for me, possibly giving the Ravens enough time to board a second ship in complete secret and follow us to this very location. For all we know, Mathias, they're tearing the cave apart right now." Mira had finally turned to look at him. Her dark, brown eyes were hateful and angry, and Mathias swore he saw steam rising from her as she spoke.

"I think if they were attacking the cave, we would know."

"That's not the point, and you know it." Mira glared at him.

"Do you want to die, Mira? Does your life mean so little to you that you're willing to just throw it away?" Mathias asked. The anger in him was rising again, the fire that burned away at his insides, and he tried to remain calm.

"I want you to live!" Mira replied quickly. "Instead, you wasted valuable time saving those prisoners and then coming back for me. You brought me aboard the Longshot while I was still without control, and I nearly tore it apart trying to kill you." The Warden of Fury was fuming, and Mathias had to admit that she was rather frightening when she was angry. He also knew that she was making complete sense.

"I only-"

"We took a vow, Mathias, to put your life and the lives of others before our own," Mira said calmly. "That means that sometimes we die because of that choice. Monk knew that. It's going to happen, and there's nothing you can do about it."

"But I *can* do something about it," Mathias replied. The two were staring intensely at each other, but the rage in Mira's eyes seemed to subside. "Do you remember the story I told when we were on the mountain?"

"I don't see how that's relevant." Mira averted her gaze, clearly understanding more than she was letting on.

"My friend Natalie told us to run. To leave her behind. If we would've done as she said, we would've avoided the confrontation with the creature and escaped unharmed. But, I refused to abandon her, Mira. Because of that, we *all* escaped to live another day. Sacrifice, while a noble gesture, isn't always necessary."

His words struck home. Mira had no rebuttal to the Grand Master's argument. She stared off once more into the vast forest before her. She felt strange. She hated Mathias for coming back for her, but she was also glad that he had. There was something there, a feeling she told herself long ago that she would refuse to have again.

"Why do you want to die, Mira? What's so terrible in your life that death would be a relief?" Mathias suspected there was more to this than Mira was letting on.

"You saw me down there on Ravendra. You saw what happens when I lose control," Mira said, keeping her eyes on the trees. "I tried to kill you, Mathias, and I could have killed everyone on that ship."

"But you didn't." Mathias adjusted his seat on the tree and turned his body to face Mira. "Down on Ravendra, I thought you were trying to kill me. But every time you came at me with an attack, it was to strike at someone behind or beside me. You saved my life twice, so some part of you must have known that I was there to help."

"That's not how it works, Mathias," Mira replied sadly.

"Then explain it to me."

"I must've decided that the Ravens were the more pressing threat to my existence and therefore, the power chose them over you."

"Now you sound like a machine. C'mon, Mira, help me understand."

"You really want to know?" She had to ask. It was her final attempt at keeping him from the truth.

"Only if you want me to know."

"Just promise me one thing?"

"Anything."

"Don't think of me any differently." Mira finally turned to face Mathias again and stared deep into his eyes.

"I couldn't even if I tried," Mathias replied. Mira smiled only for a moment and then turned back to the wide-open space before her.

"I suppose it would be easiest to start from the beginning," Mira said as she cleared her throat. "My grandmother was the first in my family to have the power of the Wardens. She was a Life Warden, a powerful healer of our people. Anytime a comrade of hers was wounded, she would bestow upon them restorative energies. She was said to have immense power and was oftentimes considered the wisest of all the Wardens."

"She was wonderful, Mathias. I only knew her towards the end of her life, but I remember the stories of how magnificent she was in her prime. She could keep the Wardens in her unit fighting for days if it was necessary. But, as the years wore on her, so did her power. You see, the power of a Life Warden is unique in that it demands a price from its wielder. Every single time my grandmother would use her gifts to heal a wound or mend a broken bone, a small bit her soul would leave her and spread its power amongst the injured man or woman. In exchange, an equally small piece of the victim's soul was transferred to her. It was a trade of life for death, of pain for peace."

"Sounds like something that would take its toll in the long run," Mathias interjected. He couldn't imagine the burden of carrying so many damaged souls around within your own.

"And it did. In her final years, my grandmother could barely remember who she was. She oftentimes spoke of memories that weren't hers and of people she had never met. She had so many souls inside of her that she'd even forgotten her own name."

"It was only a few years prior to her death that I was born, and it was an incredibly messy birth. They say I came into this world the wrong way and nearly killed my mother because of it. Fortunately, she survived the process, but she was told that another child would be the end of her. My father, who had always dreamed of having a son, was furious. He immediately sought the aid of a Life Warden: my grandmother. He begged and pleaded for her to cure my mother, but she wouldn't do it. She told my father that no force in existence could fix what had happened to my mom. My father refused to listen and sought out the other Life Wardens, but they all told him the same thing."

"Defeated and broken, my father returned home empty handed to a daughter he couldn't care less about. The years passed and Grandmother neared the end of her life. Father continued to ignore me while Mother did her best to raise me on her own. You would have liked the little girl I was back then, so full of energy, always giving my mother a hard time. Sometimes, I wish I had behaved a little more."

"I'd say you turned out okay," Mathias said with a smile. Mira smiled as well, but only briefly.

"Everything changed, though, the day Grandmother passed away. She called for us in her final moments and, as we stood around her death bed, I watched in blissful awe as she transferred the power to my father. Her last words to him haunt me to this day: 'use it well.' That was the beginning of the end for us. From that moment on, my father did everything but heed Grandmother's final request. That first night he tried to use the power on my mother. She refused at first, so he waited till she was asleep. I remember because Mother screamed so loudly that I was sure the world was ending. My father, who had no respect for the power he now controlled, ripped apart my mother's soul that night. He tried to heal her, but instead took more of her than he should have. That poor, kind woman died howling in agony."

"I'm so sorry," Mathias said, placing a hand on Mira's shoulder. To his surprise, she didn't shrug it off.

"It only got worse after that, Mathias. With my mother gone, it fell on my father's shoulders to care for me.

So, really, it was up to me. On the rare occasions that he would acknowledge my existence, he would yell at me for what I did to Mother, blaming me for her death. I tried my hardest to ignore him, and there were so many nights where I cried myself to sleep."

"Things changed as I grew older, though. My body filled out and some of the other Wardens took notice of me. Suddenly, I didn't feel so alone. Unfortunately, my father also noticed the changes, and he took it upon himself to scare off anyone that ever got close to me. He had become so overprotective of me, and I eventually figured out why. He wanted me for himself."

Mathias wasn't sure if he had heard correctly.

"One night, he slammed the door open and stormed into my room. He'd never set foot inside my room before so I was confused and utterly terrified. He sat down on the bed next to me and told me that he would have a son, one way or another. I tried to run, Mathias, I really did, but the old man was too strong. He slammed my head against the wall twice and threw me back onto the bed. I writhed in agony as my father climbed on top of me. He tore my clothes off and threw them aside. I could do nothing but cry as my head exploded with pain. I could feel the cool trickle of blood as it slid down my neck and onto the bed. Before I knew what was happening, his clothes were off and I felt a sudden, sharp thrust in my groin. I screamed for help, but we lived just outside the city and there was no one around to hear me, and my father knew it. Shit, he probably got off to the screaming."

"A few thrusts later and the man was done. He embarrassingly climbed off of me and wobbled to the door. I frantically grabbed for my sheets and pulled them over me, tears streaming endlessly down my face. Just before he left, he turned to me and said, 'you *will* give me a son.' I've never cried so hard in my life."

Mathias didn't know what to say. He pulled himself closer to Mira, extending his hand to her other shoulder and pulling her towards him. She was tense and resisted at first, but eventually gave in, resting her head on the Warden's shoulder.

"The next morning, I thought about making a break for Haven and finding someone to help me, but my father was waiting for me and refused to let me out of the house. I called him every foul name I could think of before storming back to my room. He boarded up the windows and put powerful locks on all the doors. I had become a prisoner in my own home. He came for me again that night, and the night after that. On and on this went until the night I finally became pregnant with his child. You see, something strange had been happening to me over the course of these encounters. Every time my father came for me, he would pour a large amount of his soul into me, while removing a small piece of mine. His power was acting without him even realizing it. I would always wake up the next morning fully healed from whatever cuts and bruises I endured the night before, and I would feel a little stronger. After about a week or so, I could finally start to feel a strange power brewing inside of me. I didn't know what it was, but I could tell that it wanted to help. The more my father raped me, the stronger I became."

"On his final night, he came to me as he always did, but something was different. I could tell that the power had almost completely abandoned him and had turned him into an empty, soulless husk. I decided that this would be the last time he would ever come near me. He climbed on top of me, mumbling about a son and drooling all over me, his breath reeking of alcohol, and I immediately threw a punch at his face. I was amazed at the power behind the swing about as much as my father was when it connected with his cheek. The attack had little effect after that, however, as he instantly returned the favor and hit me so hard that I immediately blacked out."

"When I awoke a few hours later, my door was still open, the hallway light shining brightly into the room. It was odd because my father had a habit of slamming it shut when he left. I rolled over and stepped off the bed. However, instead of a warm, wood floor beneath my feet, I stepped in a cool puddle of liquid. I looked down and gasped at the massive pool of blood slowly spreading across the room. I frantically searched myself for any injuries but found none. Afraid of what I might find, I slowly made my way around the bed. That's when I found him. He was lying on the ground near the window, and there was still blood slowly oozing out of him. I could see puncture wounds all over his body, but there was no sign of a knife or sword anywhere. I rolled the old man over and almost screamed. His face was mutilated beyond recognition and he had been viciously castrated."

"Do you want to know what I did then, Mathias? I laughed. I laughed so hard that I scared myself at the sheer evil of it. But, I didn't care. The man who had tortured me since my birth was dead. I knew I'd had some part to play in his death, but I didn't know exactly what I'd done. I could feel the strange power coursing through me, but I didn't know how to channel it. Fortunately, there were people that did."

Mathias was still processing everything. He was glad Mira's father was dead, or he would have made it his life's goal to find the man and end him.

"When I arrived at Haven, I was immediately taken into custody. I failed to notice that I was covered in blood, blood that clearly wasn't my own. They locked me in special chains that caused the power within me to subside and put me in a bright room to wait. Only a few minutes passed before the door opened again. A bald man with a silly goatee strolled into the room and sat down in front of me."

"Aurilean," Mathias said, immediately recognizing his father's description.

"Yes. It was like he knew right away what happened, because he came over to me, removed his cloak and wrapped me in it and then told me how sorry he was. That's when he told me that my asshole father had succeeded. There was a life growing inside of me along with the Warden power. I asked him if there was a way to prevent it from ever being born, but he told me that all life is to be treasured, even if it comes from a dark place.

While I carried the child, Aurilean took me under his wing and explained to me what had happened to the power inside me. My father had slowly been transferring it to me over the course of our interactions. The power had grown so corrupted by hate and anger that it became twisted and took control of me as I blacked out. The power killed my father that night, but it was my hands that wielded the blade. Aurilean showed me how some abilities can summon forth physical objects, like weapons, to use temporarily. It explained why there was no weapon at the scene when I awoke.

For months, Aurilean tried to teach me to control my power, but he never succeeded. During one of our sessions, I grew so angry that I lost control and nearly took the old man's head off. I think he felt defeated at that point, because we never had another session after that"

"Then came the day that the baby was born. I was off training by myself when I felt something cool rush down my leg. The child was coming far sooner than any child had ever come before. I screamed in agony as the being inside of me started to claw its way out. I labored for only a few moments before the child was lying in the grass in front of me. I picked him up and wiped the dirt and blood from his face. It was then that I realized that the boy was the spitting image of my father, except he had bright red eyes instead of brown. There was no way I could ever look at that child's face and not think about what happened to me. I'm ashamed to admit it, but I thought about letting the power take over to kill the boy. It would've been quick and I could've said that it was an accident. But, Aurilean's words rang inside my head, and I knew I could never take this innocent child's life, but I also decided that I wouldn't be the one to raise it. I took it to the House of Healers in Haven and begged them to find it a good home. That was the last time I ever saw him."

"Is he still alive?" Mathias felt a tear drop onto the hand in his lap. He vaguely remembered someone in Rolan's group of bounty hunters with red eyes but, if Mira hadn't recognized him there on Sanctuary, it must have been someone else.

"I think so. They say a mother always knows, and I can still feel him. He's out there somewhere."

"Would you recognize him if you saw him?"

"I don't know. I'm afraid that one day our paths will cross and he'll look down at me the same way I once looked down at him. I don't know what I would do." Another tear dropped to Mathias's hand and he pulled Mira tighter.

"You are the bravest woman I've ever met, Warden Mira," Mathias said as he rubbed her shoulder. She had endured so much but refused to give up the child's life. It was no wonder she hardly valued her own.

"You don't hate me?" Mira asked as she pulled away from Mathias. Her eyes were wet, and her cheeks were red and puffy.

"Mira, I don't think I could ever hate you. When I look at you, I don't see this horrible person that you think you are. I see the brave and caring Warden that would risk her life a thousand times over for her friends. I see someone who will do whatever it takes to ensure the lives of others. That is a quality far too rare in this day and age."

A sudden hint of a smile broke across Mira's face.

"The past makes us who we are. I would not have you any other way." Mathias found that he, too, was smiling. A sudden rush of emotions flooded through him, and Mira moved in closer to him. Mathias panicked. What was she doing? Did she want him to kiss her? These thoughts rushed through his head, but the sudden rustle of leaves behind her caught his attention. Without warning, Mathias grabbed Mira and rolled from the log just as a massive, dark shape leapt out of the bushes towards them.

21

The first thing Alistair noticed was the smell. The sewers beneath Corvia reeked of death and rotten eggs. The boy tried to cover his nose but found that silver shackles around his wrists prevented any such movement.

A small, dimming lantern in the nearby corner of the stone room was the only source of light, and it was a poor source at that. The flame flickered in and out on the verge of extinction while the glass around it was so caked in dirt and fecal matter that it was a surprise any light passed through it at all. However, in the fading glow of the lantern, Alistair noticed Rolan chained to the wall across from him.

"Not their finest accommodations," Rolan began. His voice was scratchier than normal, a result of his struggle with Jax, no doubt. "But, I can honestly say that it could be worse." The bounty hunter chuckled to himself, but Alistair remained quiet. He had followed Rolan to Corvia with expectations of a completely different outcome. However, instead of riches and revenge, he was rewarded with imprisonment. Things were not going well for him, and it didn't look like his situation was about to improve any time soon. The shackles on his wrists grinded against his bones as he tried to adjust his position against the wall, and he let out a groan in response.

"What's wrong, boy?" Rolan wheezed from across the room. "Chains too tight? I'll call the guards to come loosen them for you." Rolan was laughing again at his attempt at humor but Alistair, again, said nothing. He was done with Rolan and, if he managed to escape, would abandon the hunters altogether and seek out new meaning in his life. Unfortunately, escape wasn't an option given his present condition.

A flickering orange light outside the room slowly illuminated a nearby archway. It surprised Alistair to learn that they were being held in a room without a locked door. Of course, the cuffs on his wrist prevented him from going anywhere, but he still found it strange.

The light slowly flooded into the dungeon as the man who had grabbed Alistair before appeared, a flaming torch in his hand. Alistair's eyes grew wide with horror as the rest of the room came into focus. There were more men and women chained to the walls around the entire room, a room that seemed to extend further back than Alistair could see. Much to his dismay, many of the prisoners were already dead, their rotten, decaying corpses drooping sadly from their chains. It looked as though they had been locked up months ago and forgotten about. Many of the decrepit bodies were missing various limbs as well, and Alistair wondered if this is where mutilated Ravens were sent to die.

The rattling of chains broke his train of thought, and he jumped as the shackles dropped from his hands. He grabbed his wrists and rubbed at his bones, attempting to dull the pain.

"Don't do anything stupid," the Raven said grumpily. Alistair stood in silence as he watched his counterpart drop to the floor as well. It was at that moment that he wondered where Zeke and the other hunters were. He recognized none of the others chained to the wall, so they had to be somewhere nearby. But, for all Alistair knew, they were already dead.

"Are you scared, boy?" Rolan asked as he came to his feet.

"No talking!" The Raven blurted out and slapped Rolan upside his head. Rolan laughed hysterically; the man had clearly lost his mind. "Follow me. If you wander off or try to run, I'll chop off your legs and make you crawl the rest of the way."

"Not if I chop yours off first," Rolan chuckled. The Raven moved so fast that Alistair could barely see what happened. The blazing torch fell to the ground as the Raven pulled a knife from his belt and grabbed Rolan's throat. In the blink of an eye, the Raven pulled Rolan's tongue from his mouth and sliced it clean off. The bounty hunter howled in pain as blood poured onto the ground.

"I said no talking." The hulking Raven wiped the blood of his knife against his pants and then sheathed it while bending to pick up his torch. Alistair was paralyzed with fear as Rolan continued to howl in agony. "Let's go," the Raven said and made his way through the archway. Alistair followed closely behind, leaving the leader of the bounty hunters to bleed out on the floor behind him.

The sewer system was unlike anything Alistair had ever seen. Every tunnel they passed seemed to go on for miles, and every few seconds he swore he smelled something fouler than the odors that already occupied his nose. It made getting used to the stench nearly impossible.

The Raven would occasionally stop and forcibly push Alistair to the wall to allow a swarm of rats to pass by. The packs usually consisted of twenty to thirty vermin, but sometimes he would see a pack of nearly a hundred. The Raven explained that the rats were incredibly territorial, and they would attack in full force if they felt threatened. Alistair was shocked to learn that no Raven or Warden power had any effect on the nasty creatures. Only brute strength could kill the rats.

The two men trudged through the damp darkness for nearly an hour before finally arriving at a large sheet of metal resting against the sewer walls. Alistair noticed bits of broken machine parts scattered around the vicinity. He was confused, but refrained from asking any questions.

"Hold this," the Raven muttered as he handed Alistair the torch. He thought it strange that his jailer would freely offer him a weapon, but the Raven knew Alistair wouldn't be foolish enough to attack him. The large man grabbed the sheet of metal with both hands and pulled fiercely, yanking it free from the wall. A gust of musty air blew out at them, and a pungent aroma nearly caused Alistair to vomit. The Raven snatched the torch back from Alistair and walked straight into the new hallway. Not wanting to fall behind, Alistair followed suit, keeping one hand over his nose.

The narrow corridor felt different to Alistair than the rest of the sewer system. The further down the passageway they got, the more random bits of metal he saw strewn about on the floor. Bloodstains adorned the walls in magnificent but horrifying patterns, and Alistair stopped to examine a large gash in the rock.

"Do not linger, boy," the Raven called from ahead without turning. It was eerie how the man knew Alistair had stopped without ever looking back. He jogged through the soupy air to catch up and then slowed to a walk as he neared.

The sudden clang of metal against stone caught Alistair's attention. The ringing echoed throughout the long hallway, but its origin was unclear. Alistair tried to look past the large man in front of him, but found that the passage had grown too narrow to see anything. Another bang reverberated through the tunnel, this time a result of steel against steel, followed directly by a bloodcurdling scream. The howl of pain sent shivers throughout Alistair's entire body. He wanted to be out of that tunnel very badly, but he fought the urge to turn and run. As quickly as the screaming had started, however, it ended. Alistair jumped as he heard a crash, as if millions of tiny pieces of metal had been thrown across the room, followed by hysterical laughter. He was so distracted by the foreign sounds that he nearly collided with the Raven as they came to a halt.

"Wait here." Without ever looking back, the Raven pushed against a small, wooden door ahead of him. He had to duck as he went through and gently closed it once he was on the other side. In the short time that it was open, Alistair caught a glimpse of a short, balding man wielding some sort of metal object. The man turned to Alistair, and their eyes met ever so briefly before the door was pulled shut.

Alistair trembled as he stood at the door trying to make sense of the muffled voices coming from the room behind it. Something bad was about to happen to him, he was sure of it. The thought of running back out into the sewers and trying to find the exit popped into his mind, but he had no knowledge of the pipe system and would more likely die to a host of rats before coming anywhere close to the surface.

No, he had dug this hole for himself and would deal with whatever consequences that entailed.

The creaking of the door snapped him back to reality. Alistair looked on in horror as the full details of the room came into view. There were bits and pieces of flesh strewn about across the floor, not to mention the lines of blood cascading towards the drain in the center of the room. Chains hung from the ceiling, and Alistair noticed an arm, with no body attached, stuck in a shackle at the end of one of the chains. There was also a stained, padded chair in the center of the room where the two men stood and an eerie green lamp hanging just above it that barely provided any light. A table sat next to the chair with a stainless-steel tray that held an assortment of rusted tools, most of which were covered in fresh blood.

"Come, child," the balding man croaked. Alistair had reactively taken a step back, but remembered that escape was no longer an option. Swallowing his uncertainty, he slowly stepped into the putrid, green room. The smell, Alistair found, didn't improve from one side of the door to the other. In fact, this room was probably the foulest smelling area of the entire sewer system. The combination of sweat, feces, blood and death crawled aggressively into Alistair's nostrils and latched onto him. He was certain this wretched stink would be with him the rest of life, however long that would be.

"This is Doctor Krause," the Raven said lazily as he motioned to the stumpy man next to him. The first thing Alistair noticed about the man was how lopsided he was. The man's right leg appeared shorter than his left which resulted in the doctor's crooked posture. However, to counteract his imperfection, in place of his right arm there was a long, metallic beam that stretched to the floor. The fixture was attached at the man's shoulder and was acting as a cane to keep him standing properly, although Alistair felt like it really wasn't working as the doctor had intended.

"A pleasure, child," Krause said as he used his left hand to slick back what little of his thin, black hair remained atop his egg-shaped head. The doctor was a complete mess, and he frightened Alistair more than the Raven did.

"W-Why am I here?" Alistair asked hesitantly.

"Why, to be reborn, of course!" The doctor said enthusiastically, although Alistair didn't like the sound of it. He remembered Jax saying something about reconstruction, but he had no idea what that entailed. However, as Alistair glimpsed the robotic limbs scattered amongst the Raven ones, he began to understand.

"I don't need to be reborn," Alistair replied. He knew it was pointless, though, as the doctor burst into laughter. The Raven moved to the door, closed it gently, and then positioned himself firmly in front of it to further prevent any possible escape.

"But, of course you do, child!" The doctor said as his maniacal laughter subsided. "We are all born into this world as soft, fleshy beings that keel over and die at the first sign of injury." Krause limped around the room, using his cane-arm for support every time his right foot stepped down.

"Some of us are stronger than others," Alistair replied confidently.

"How right you are, child. That is why Commander Jax has handpicked you for his revolutionary Reconstruction Project!" Krause said vigorously. Alistair, again, took a step back at the mention of reconstruction, but found a firm hand pushing against his shoulder. The Raven had abandoned his post at the door and had positioned himself just behind the boy.

"And what exactly is this Reconstruction Project?" Alistair asked, his voice shaky with fear.

"Why, I'm so glad you asked!" The doctor replied loudly. He stood at the back of the room near a large, steel cabinet. He fiddled briefly with a lock on the rusted doors and then pulled hard. Alistair was confused as the contents of the cabinet were revealed. There was a strange, metallic man standing motionless inside. "Do you like it?" The doctor asked hopefully.

"It's... nice?" Alistair replied nervously. He wasn't sure how else to respond.

"Why, I'm so happy to hear you say that, child. This is the Hunter-Y, a new and improved version of the Hunter-X that we recalled just last year." The man spoke as if everyone in the room already knew exactly what he was talking about. Alistair had never seen a robot in person before. It looked so lifelike that he could hardly tell that it wasn't an actual person. "You see, child, Jax has grown quite frustrated with you bounty hunters over the years. You're all so eager for your payout that you pay little attention to the logistics of your hunt."

Alistair was beginning to make sense of his situation. Jax had been secretly working on making all bounty hunters obsolete by replacing them with machines. A machine would never question its orders, nor would it ever need payment.

"The Hunter-X was designed as a superior killing machine. However, where it succeeded in eliminating a target, it failed to comprehend the more... delicate aspects of the hunt. It couldn't ask the right questions, or move stealthily enough to go unnoticed." Krause pulled a long, metal coil from the cabinet towards the chair in the center of the room. "We then asked ourselves, 'how can we make it think like a hunter?' Then it all clicked! We give it a brain."

"Like a computerized brain?" Alistair asked curiously. He knew almost nothing about technology.

"No, child. We give it a living, working brain!" Krause replied as he plugged the coil into a socket in the back of the chair. The socket sparked briefly, and then the chair began to buzz with a slow and steady hum. "A robot is just a machine without emotions and the inability to make complex, moral decisions. It does what it's programmed to do and will never stray from its predetermined set of protocols. It can't create new methods of operation unless we physically go in and change the programming. But, imagine for a second, if a robot thought like we do, if it could make a spur of the moment decision that we never taught it!" Krause was clearly excited at his discovery, but Alistair still didn't understand how a living brain could function inside of a metal suit.

"How does a brain exist outside of the body?"

"Oh, it doesn't. It would take a whole fleshy system implanted into the machine to contain the actual brain, which would be terribly counterintuitive. No, what I do is take the essence of the brain, every thought, memory, and decision that has ever been made, and implant it into the memory core of the Hunter-Y. I transfer the entire consciousness of the person into the mind of the machine."

"You can do that?"

"Theoretically, yes," Krause said with a wicked grin.

"Wait, you've never actually done this before?"

"Unfortunately, my first few attempts ended disastrously. One of the robots shorted out from memory overload, while the others simply rejected the fusion. But, I believe that it takes a strong, willing mind to achieve full conversion. I have faith that your mind will finally be the one that succeeds!"

263

Alistair was suddenly being pushed towards the chair by the large Raven at his back. He struggled at first, but eventually forced his legs to move forward.

"Why, don't be afraid, child. You will be reborn! You will be better than you ever were." Krause prepared a syringe of bluish-green fluid as Alistair was forced into the chair. The Raven tightly strapped down the boy's arms and legs, rendering him completely immobile. Alistair breathed heavily. He had no desire to be turned into a cold, emotionless machine.

"What will happen to my body?" The bounty hunter asked, the fear evident in his voice.

"Without a functioning brain, the rest of your organs will shut down. Your body will be dead, but your mind and your consciousness will be very much alive in there." Krause replied as he motioned towards the man in the cabinet. "You'll be faster, stronger, smarter. Nothing will stand in your way."

Alistair was beginning to fear the procedure more and more. What if things didn't work? What if the machine rejected him as it had for the others?

"For this to succeed, you must be willing. You must make the decision of your own free will. However, do not think that denying us will prevent us from attempting the reconstruction. We will do so regardless, but we'd prefer you to be a willing participant." Krause stood over him with the syringe, the green light creating an eerie halo around him. Alistair finally understood that there was no way out of this and, if he wanted to live, his best chance was to go along with these men.

"Then I submit. I willingly accept this procedure." Alistair couldn't believe that the words had even come out of his mouth, but he knew it was his only remaining option. He secretly hoped his brother would storm in and free him from this madness, but he knew that was not likely to happen. If this was to be his end, he would at least accept it.

"You will?! Wonderful!" Krause cheered in victory. "They will tell stories of your bravery, child. Everyone will know your name."

"Just get on with it," Alistair replied. He didn't want to be famous. He just wanted everything to be over with.

"As you wish," Krause said from above. He lowered the syringe into Alistair's arm and injected him with the fluid, resulting in immediate paralysis. "You must be awake for the entire procedure to keep your brain activity at maximum. However, there will be quite a bit of pain involved so I had to make sure you wouldn't flail about." Krause was smiling as he looked down at Alistair. The boy assumed there would be pain, but the way the doctor smiled frightened Alistair more than anything the man said. He tried to close his eyes, but the serum wouldn't let him. He would have to watch everything the doctor did to him.

Krause moved over to the cabinet and grabbed another long coil. On the end of the coil was a thick, sharp needle nearly half a foot long.

"The moment this enters your brain, you will experience incredible discomfort. You will not be able to scream or cry out, nor will you be able to bite down on anything. Why, you must simply endure it. If you die before the conversion is complete, then the experiment won't work, and I will have failed once again. Do not make me a failure, child."

Alistair's mind was racing. He didn't know if he had the strength to endure such pain, but he knew that if he wanted revenge on Commander Jax, he would have to survive. It was the only way.

"Shall we begin?" The doctor placed the cold needle against the back of Alistair's head. Krause slowly counted down from three and, on one, thrust the needle into Alistair's skull. The pain was instantaneous. Alistair couldn't move as the feeling of his skull being ripped apart took over.

Krause stepped away from the boy and flipped a few switches at the back of the cabinet. A large humming suddenly drowned out any other noises in the room, and the conversion began. A single tear dripped down Alistair's cheek as his world was thrust into darkness.

22

He first noticed they were being watched just as Mira began her tale. He caught a quick gleam of the creature's eyes flashing in the bushes and then it was gone, leaving only rustling leaves in its wake. Having spent much of his childhood in the Brimwood, the Warden had grown accustomed to the distinct sounds of a wild animal stalking its prey. He memorized how different predators moved and learned how they chose the opportune moment to strike. Mathias hadn't been sure what manner of monster had been hunting them but, as the large, black cat-like creature launched itself at the pair of them, the memory of a similar attack earlier that day came rushing back. Mathias had to admire the beast's persistence considering it had managed to track him this far into the jungle. This was certainly no ordinary creature.

Mathias and Mira quickly rolled away from the cliff's edge and then, in unison, jumped back to their feet. The feral feline flashed its ivory fangs as it stood only feet away, hunched over and poised to strike again. Its short, black fur stood on end as it carefully watched the two Wardens. The beast's eyes were truly captivating. The different shades of green and yellow swirled together in harmony, never mixing but always changing. They were unlike anything the Warden had ever seen.

Mira stepped forward, a glinting red dagger in her hand as she prepared to strike at the beast. Thinking it strange that the creature hadn't attacked again, Mathias grabbed Mira before she could get very far and pulled her back.

"Wait!" he yelled as Mira looked back at him with a confused and slightly annoyed glare. "If it wanted to kill us, it would have done so already." Mira turned back to the creature and found it unmoving, simply staring at the pair of them. She had to admit that it was odd behavior for a predator such as this.

"Fine," Mira replied hesitantly. "But if it attacks us again-"

"It won't," Mathias said confidently. He had a feeling he knew what and, more importantly, who this creature was. "Great Spirit of the Forest, I beg your forgiveness for our trespassing upon your land and humbly ask that you grant us shelter for a few more days. Several of our group are injured and recovering with nowhere else to go. Do us this favor and we will leave this place in peace." As he spoke, he maintained constant eye contact with the beast, never once looking away. The jungle cat's eyes sparkled in the sunlight, but they seemed to grow less hostile as Mathias finished his speech. Suddenly, and a bit unexpectedly, the creature let out a peculiar coughing sound.

"Is it... laughing?" Mira asked in surprise. Mathias simply shrugged in response, and he was about to speak to the creature again when something even stranger occurred.

The cat before them began to change. Its fangs that hung
menacingly from the creature's upper jaw began to shrink,
while the claws on each of its four legs dulled and retracted.
Within a matter of seconds, where the agile hunter once
stood, there was now a towering behemoth of a man. The
stranger's muscles bulged from nearly every inch of his giant,
hairy body and, if Mathias had to guess, he stood about a
head taller than Joel. He was also completely naked. His
boisterous laughter echoed through the trees as the final
patches of black fur fell from his body like pine needles.

"Great Spirit of the Forest?" The strange man said
with a chuckle. His accent was so peculiar that Mathias
nearly broke into laughter himself. "Now that's one I've never
heard before. Well done, mate."

Mathias and Mira exchanged confused looks.

"Are you… a Shifter?" Mira asked hesitantly.

"I am. The one and only," the odd man said. His
laughing had finally subsided and his eyes had grown far
more serious. "Now who the hell are you?"

Mathias looked to Mira again. She shrugged and gave
him little suggestion with how to proceed. As he turned his
gaze back upon the man, Mathias noticed that the Shifter was
eyeing him suspiciously. He stood with his arms crossed over
his dark, hairy chest. He also sported a thin, dark brown
mohawk down the center of his otherwise shaven head, along
with a full, and quite messy, brownish beard that hung about
an inch off his face. The mysterious man was dangerously
intimidating as he stood unmoving before them.

"My name is Mathias, and this is Mira," the Grand
Master said motioning to the woman beside him. "We're-"
but Mira grabbed his arm, stopping him before he could
reveal anything else.

"Wardens," the stranger said knowingly. Mathias and Mira looked at each other again, this time in horror as a smile appeared on the Shifter's face. The Shifters were once a proud race of skin changers, able to transform their humanoid figures into all sorts of creatures from birds and cats, to larger animals like bears and wolves. The Shifters used their beastly abilities for all sorts of tasks including construction, transportation, and even espionage. But, like many other races before them, the Shifters met an untimely end at Raven hands. During a particularly informative Raven war council a Shifter, disguised as a lowly rat scurrying across the floor, was discovered. The Raven in charge of the meeting, an overlord by the name of Malik, forced the Shifter into his humanoid form and then publicly executed him while declaring war on the rest of his people. No Shifter survived the onslaught that followed, or so everyone believed.

"Don't look so surprised," the stranger continued. "I'd recognize a Warden anywhere. Plus, you made it fairly obvious after you took off into the sky earlier." Mathias didn't have to look at Mira to know that she was glaring furiously at him.

"You didn't really leave me much of a choice," Mathias replied in defense.

"Well, you were skulking about in places you shouldn't have. What are you doing here?"

"My father once told me that the Spirit of Vega would help me if I ever needed somewhere to hide. So, when circumstances arose, I made a quick decision to come here," Mathias explained. In the first few days after Mathias had taken Alistair's place as Warden, Aurilean sat Mathias down and revealed many useful bits of information to him, from places he could hide and people he could trust to special phrases that would grant him access to certain hidden locations.

"Your father was mistaken, mate. I don't help children that trudge uninvited across my lands." The man spoke angrily, and Mathias swore he saw the cat-like claws protruding from the stranger's fingertips.

"Please, you must help us! There are injured Wardens back at the cave that need time to heal," Mathias pleaded.

"Not my problem. Vega is a Dead World for a reason, Warden. I'll permit you to leave unharmed, but don't ever return to this place," the man said sharply and then turned to leave.

"Mathias," Mira said gently as she touched his arm again. "Are you sure it was Vega that he told you about?"

"I know it was! Aurilean was always very-" but Mathias was unable to finish his thought as the stranger whirled around and marched straight up to him.

"How do you know that name?" the man asked aggressively.

"Aurilean? He was my father."

The stranger's eyes narrowed as he contemplated the boy's response. Then, much to the Wardens' surprise, the stranger burst into laughter once again. The Shifter laughed with every ounce of his being, the deep bellow reverberating out into the valley below. Then, when he realized that Mathias didn't find the fact nearly as humorous, he stopped. "Wait. You're serious?"

"Completely," Mathias replied confidently. The Shifter continued to eye the Warden in disbelief, but Mathias held his ground.

"Prove it." The Shifter crossed his hairy, burly arms across his equally hairy chest and glared at the Grand Master.

Be careful what you tell him, Mira said as her voice popped into Mathias's head. He quickly recalled all the bits of information Aurilean had given him about Vega and the Great Spirit. After only a few seconds, Mathias knew what he needed to say.

"The debt has yet to be paid, two favors still remain." Mathias spoke the words with as much confidence as he could muster as he recalled his father's story. The words seemed to have the desired effect. The Shifter's eyes grew wide with shock and he slowly uncrossed his arms.

"You... You can't possibly know that," he said, his voice shaky with uncertainty. The debt was something only him and Aurilean knew about, but now this child stood before him speaking of it. Could he truly be the son of the Grand Master? There was still one final test he could give. "What was the first favor?"

"He asked you to become a protector." Mathias had expected the stranger to inquire further and had his answer already prepared. The moment Mathias uttered the words, the Shifter instantly fell to his knees.

"You *are* his son..." The Shifter trailed off, a tear forming in the corner of his eye.

"Not by blood, but he took me in after my mother died," Mathias explained.

"And if you're a Warden, then that means that he..." but the Shifter couldn't finish the sentence. It was suddenly very clear to Mathias just how important Aurilean had been to this man.

"I'm so sorry, friend, but he's gone." Mathias rested a gentle hand on the man's massive shoulder. Even kneeling down, the man was still taller than the Warden.

"Marcus," the stranger said. "Name's Marcus."

"It's a pleasure to meet you, Marcus. I'm sorry that you had to find out this way."

"What happened?" Marcus asked as he wiped away the lines of tears from his face. Mathias quickly explained how the bounty hunters had ambushed them and how Aurilean had exploded in a raging ball of fire. "At least he took a few of the bastards with him." Marcus returned to his feet and Mathias followed suit.

"You guys were pretty close, huh?"

"He saved my life more than a few times, mate. Don't know why, but your father always looked out for me. Three favors ain't nearly enough to make up for everything he did for me and my people."

"We are talking about the same Aurilean here, right?" Mira asked sarcastically. She had been so quiet that Mathias had almost forgotten she was there.

"I know many people didn't approve of the man and his actions, but he was always kind to me." Marcus was firm as he spoke and stared Mira down until she was forced to avert her gaze.

"Sorry," she uttered in defeat. Marcus simply nodded at her in response. His demeanor had changed completely, and he now appeared far more welcoming.

"Now, I may be able to help you. Your father must've known that he'd never live to see the debt repaid, so he must have meant for me to aid *you*, his son. There is something I can do to help your sick and wounded friends."

"Really?!" Mathias asked excitedly.

"As you are already aware, your father tasked me with the painfully solitary job of being a protector. I've spent nearly the last one thousand years on this forsaken rock guarding a powerful and highly sought-after artifact."

"No..." Mira said under her breath, but loud enough for Mathias to hear. "It can't be here."

"I call it the Life Waters, but I believe it's more commonly known as the-"

"Well of Travelers," Mira finished.

"Ah, so you know of the Well?" Marcus asked the Warden of Fury.

"I know that no one has ever been able to locate it. How has it been here all this time?" Mira could hardly contain her excitement. It was as if a childhood dream of hers was finally coming true.

"You've no doubt noticed how large and ferocious the wildlife on Vega has become. This is because they drink from the well and, with its power, dedicate their lives to protecting it. But, should they ever fail, it falls to me to make sure no one ever discovers it." Marcus dropped his gaze.

"You're the reason early civilizations could never settle here," Mathias said. It wasn't a question.

"I am. It haunts me greatly. Many of those young civs had incredible potential."

"You did what you had to do."

"I suppose..." Marcus muttered.

"So, if Aurilean tasked you with its protection, why are you telling us about it?" Mira asked sternly.

"Because I trust you, and because I owe it to Aurilean to help you and your friends." Marcus was smiling now.

"This means more than you could possibly know!" Mathias exclaimed, and he meant it.

"Slow down, mate. There are some things about the well you need to know," Marcus said. His cheerful manner dwindled and he spoke with a far more serious tone. "I'm not the well's only defense mechanism, you see. Aside from the leviathans that protect its gates, the Well of Travelers has other means of making sure nobody ever finds it." Mathias and Mira listened intently, afraid they might miss even one small detail. "Firstly, any who drink of its waters will soon forget that they ever had. Their sickness will be gone and their mind will be cleansed, but they'll have no recollection of the well or its location."

"How soon after they drink do they forget, and how much of their memory will be affected?" Mathias asked.

"It'll take a few hours. The drinker will be cured almost instantly, but shortly after they will fall into a short, but deep sleep. During this time, the magic will erase any memory with a connection to the Well of Travelers or its whereabouts."

"Sounds unpredictable," Mira interjected.

"I never said it would be safe, Warden Mira, only that it would help," Marcus said firmly. Mira nodded at the Shifter and refrained from questioning him further.

"Then we'll have to take that risk, we just-" Mathias began but Marcus held up his hand to silence him.

"The Well of Travelers also requests something of the drinker in return for its power. The fate of the soul that drinks of the waters will be bound to the fate of the soul of the Traveler."

"We don't have time for riddles, Shifter," Mira said impatiently.

"It's not a riddle. It means that if the well were to die and its waters dried up, then any who drank of its gift would meet the same end. It's a life pact, mate," Marcus said, but kept his eyes on Mathias.

"Mathias, we should consider other options. The well demands too much. We can't ask them to give up their souls." Mira stepped between Mathias and the Shifter. The Grand Master understood her concern. The Well of Travelers did indeed demand quite a price for its power. Unfortunately, Mathias didn't see any other alternative.

"We have no choice, Mira," Mathias started. "We don't have the luxury to take them anywhere else right now. Many would die before we made it anywhere that could help them. Not to mention Commander Jax who probably has eyes everywhere looking for us. No, this is our only option."

Mira hated to admit it, but Mathias was right. Part of her still wished he had never freed the others from that cell.

"Talk it over with your people. This decision must be theirs and theirs alone. I'll make for the gates and clear it of its guardians. I can meet you at the entrance to the cave your people are hiding in by nightfall. Hopefully, you'll have made your decision by then." Marcus finished what he needed to say and, much to Mathias's continued surprise, transformed into a magnificent black feathered eagle. The bird took off into the sky and disappeared into the day's fading light.

"Come on, let's go tell the others," Mathias said and began his descent towards the cave. Mira eyed her friend carefully and wondered if he truly understood the price the well demanded. She knew Mathias would do anything to save their people, but she wondered if this was pushing it too far. Mathias skipped along ahead, and she pushed the thought to the back of her mind and followed Mathias down the mountain.

23

```
Initializing...
Startup Sequence Engaged...
Auditory Systems: Online.
```

The whirring of the nearby life support machine was the first sound Alistair heard as he awoke, followed by the splashing of the dirty sewage water rushing through the pipes around him. The tiny footsteps of rats scurrying across the wet, stone floor, echoed throughout the chamber, and a man was yelling somewhere far away.

```
Booting Memory Core...
Calibrating...
```

Where am I? Am I dead? Is this... Hell? What happened to me?! Hello? Is... Is anyone there?

```
Memory Core Overload.
```

```
Rebooting...
Retrieving Memories... Standby...
```

It worked! Krause told me it would work, but I didn't believe him. Where is Krause? I have to tell him that the transition was a success. But, where am I? What am I?

```
Memory Calibration Complete.
Booting Primary Systems...
Booting Visual Recognition Software...
Booting Basic Motor Functions...
```

The room around Alistair was suddenly flooded with light, but the brightness of it had no effect on his new eyes, the metallic orbs moving sporadically about inside his head as he took in his environment. He could see everything from the eerie green ooze seeping from the walls to the tiny, brown pellets of rat excrement scattered about across the floor. He scanned the room for Krause, but saw no sign of the crazy doctor from inside his box. Instead, his eyes fell upon a pale body in the middle of the room. His body. A vessel he no longer occupied.

```
Loading HUD... Standby...
```

The message appeared against the laboratory backdrop and caught Alistair completely off guard. He attempted to yell in surprise but found no voice with which to speak. A few seconds later his vision changed completely. He noticed a steadily lit power monitor in the upper right of his line of sight. No matter where he looked in the room, the solid white, "100%" was always visible and impossible to ignore. Alistair assumed this number was important and would require constant monitoring. On the opposite side of the battery he noticed an option for "Normal Sight" selected from a cycling list of other options like "Infrared," "X-Ray," and "Heat." He tried to cycle to some of the other options but a new message appeared.

```
ERROR... Access Denied.
```

Denied? Why would I have limited access to my own systems?

```
Access to Secondary Systems Restricted...
Please Consult Administrator.
```

"That would be me," a voice rang out breaking the harmony of the other noises around him. Alistair tried to turn his head but found it locked firmly in place. There was no mistaking that voice, though. It was Krause. As the crippled doctor limped into Alistair's line of sight, a red indicator circle appeared around the man. A small box containing the man's full name and a brief bio appeared next to it. Alistair had never seen someone with such a name before.

```
Doctor Greggory E. Krause
Former Professor of Applied Sciences at
Malador Technical Institute. Job termination
following perverse experimental practices on
students and staff.
Clinical Diagnosis: Insane.
```

Alistair could hardly believe that Krause had once taught at an institution.

"I see your biographic reader is functioning properly," Krause said eerily. "Don't be alarmed. I can see everything that you see from my small monitor here." The doctor held up a strange tablet device that currently displayed an identical copy of everything Alistair was seeing. Alistair tried to locate a means of communication but, in his current state of paralysis, the attempt was futile.

"Ah, forgive me. I forgot to enable your voice functions," Krause said, although Alistair didn't think he had forgotten anything at all. The small man tapped a few times on his tablet, and a new message appeared before Alistair's eyes.

```
Loading "Voice Box" Program...
```

Alistair felt a sudden tingling vibration reverberating around in what he assumed was his throat. He thought it very strange how similar this new, robotic shell felt to his old body. In fact, he was beginning to prefer it.

```
"Voice Box" Activated...
Please speak your name for our Records...
```

"Alistair," the boy stated. He was shocked when the voice that came out of him wasn't his own. It was cold and emotionless, and it had a strange metallic ring to it.

```
Name Recorded... Thank you!
Loading Voice Options... Standby...
```

Alistair's vision was suddenly cluttered with hundreds of different voice selections and descriptions.

"Choose one that you think suits you and we will continue," Krause said patiently. Alistair skimmed through many of the options, stopping to try out a few. The "Burly" voice was far too deep for his liking and the "Suave" voice was incredibly cocky. Eventually, his eyes rested upon a selection labeled, "Vengeful." Without even trying it out first, Alistair confirmed his selection.

"This will do," Alistair said in his new voice. He loved the subtle threatening nature of it and how smoothly it reverberated in his throat. It was full and well balanced, and it had an angry, yet persistent undertone to it. If vengeance could speak, this is truly how Alistair believed it would sound.

"An excellent choice, if I do say so myself," Krause began again. "Now, how do you feel?"

Alistair prepared to respond when he stopped himself. That was suddenly a very strange question. He knew the meaning of the emotions he should be feeling, but he didn't seem to care.

"I don't feel anything," he said slowly.

"Oh, come now boy! You must feel something!" Krause set his tablet down on the metal stand next to him and limped up to Alistair. "I put you in there! I made you this way! Surely you feel some sort of anger towards me."

And then it all came back to him: the hunters, his brother, the Ravens and the Wardens, everything that had led him to this point. The emotion that suddenly flooded through his system was nothing more than unbridled rage. Without even understanding how he had done it, Alistair rapidly brought his arm up and clenched his metal fingers firmly around the doctor's throat.

"YOU did this to me!" Alistair roared, his voice ringing out around the room.

"How did you-" Krause started but Alistair tightened his grip cutting off the man's voice.

```
WARNING!
Primary Motor Functions Engaged...
Secondary Motor Functions Engaged...
```

Alistair felt his entire body come to life. He could feel his legs and how they connected at his hip. His arms felt stronger than they ever had, and he could finally turn his head. He was so distracted by his new body that he had forgotten about the man struggling for air in his hand. He quickly released his grasp and dropped Krause to the floor. The doctor gasped as he rubbed his throbbing neck.

"I knew... you were... in there... somewhere..." Krause wheezed as he desperately tried to catch his breath. Alistair slowly stepped out of his box and past the sniveling doctor. He stopped next to the tablet on the table and picked it up. "Stop... you don't know... what you're doing..."

"Not really. But, I'm sure I can figure it out," Alistair said, his tone frightening. He poked a few buttons until he found the administrator panel. A small box appeared requiring a password.

"If it's asking you for the password then you're out of luck. I'll never tell you." Krause had finally gotten back to his feet and was limping towards him, but Alistair didn't have time for games. He set the tablet down and marched over to the crippled doctor. Without warning, he grabbed the man's metallic limb and yanked, ripping the arm from the man's shoulder. Krause howled in agony as he crumpled to the floor.

The laboratory door slammed open as the massive Raven guard stormed in. Alistair wasted no time. He bounded across the room at lightning speed, moving faster than he ever had before. The large Raven fired blasts of shadow energy at him, but they merely deflected off his metallic coating. Alistair closed the gap between them almost instantly and, with his newfound strength, shoved the doctor's metal arm into the Raven's heart, pinning him against the wall. The massive Raven was dead within seconds.

"You... What have you done?" Krause whined from the floor across the room.

"Only what you made me for," Alistair said. He loved the way his voice echoed dangerously around the room. "Now give me the password."

"And then what? You'll never make it out of the sewers, let alone the city."

"Maybe not. But I'll die out there before I become your slave in here. Give me the password, and I'll let you keep your other arm," Alistair said as he knelt before the doctor. Krause's eyes grew wide in horror, and he realized he had been beaten.

"Adrianne," Krause muttered. "The password is Adrianne."

Alistair punched the word in the tablet, chuckling to himself at its simplicity. After a second of processing, the box disappeared and the administrator panel was accessible. If he had normal eyes, they would have grown wide at the number of functions that were currently disabled for him. He began to switch everything over to "Enabled" and, as he did, felt more tingling sensations throughout his body.

```
Weapon Systems Enabled...
Enhanced Vision Filters Enabled...
Camouflage Systems Enabled...
Flight Thrusters Enabled...
Voice Recognition Software Enabled...
Memory Data Core: Access Granted...
```

Alistair had never felt more alive. He would certainly need to experiment with his new systems later, but first he had to take care of Krause. He threw the tablet down onto the floor and slammed his metallic foot into the glass, making sure it was no longer functional. The doctor sat against the cold, seeping wall. Blood spilled from where his arm had been removed, and Alistair knew the man would be dead soon.

"You are more than I could have ever hoped for, child," Krause said slowly. Alistair could see that he was in a great deal of pain, but killing him quickly would be a mercy and, unfortunately, mercy was never his strong suit. Alistair turned his back on the old man and headed for the open door. A swarm of rats had made their way into the room and had already nearly devoured the Raven's corpse. They would soon move on to their next meal. Without even a last glance at his old body, Alistair made for the door, stopping just outside the room, his metal feet clanging with every stepped. He looked around at the disgusting hallway he had been led down only days ago and laughed to himself as he could no longer smell its foulness.

A scream of pain erupted from behind him and he turned to see that the rats had indeed made their way to Krause. Alistair rested his glowing yellow eyes on Krause's and, with as much of a smile as he could muster on his robotic face, slammed the door closed.

24

For Mathias, the trip back down the hill was a quick one. He was overjoyed that he now had a way to help the other Wardens. Mira, on the other hand, was far more concerned. The cost of the well's power was far greater than she had ever imagined, and she wasn't sure the others would be as thrilled about it as Mathias was. She was still salty with him for saving them, but she knew deep down that it had been the right thing to do. She didn't know how he did it, but Mathias always found a way to help Mira understand why he did the things he did. Since their creation, the Wardens had always done things a very specific way, but Mathias never seemed to care. He was always looking for a solution that prevented the suffering of all parties involved. There were no heroes or villains in his eyes. There were only people that stood on opposite sides of a coin unable to see what the other saw.

I can't believe I almost kissed him! Mira thought to herself. *What the hell was I thinking?* But, buried deep within her heart, she knew that what she felt for him was different than anything she had ever felt before. She both hated his stubbornness and adored his kind and caring soul. She knew, and it frightened her greatly, that she was beginning to fall for him.

"You comin'?" Mathias yelled. Mira had been so deep in thought that she hadn't realized she had stopped.

"Yea," she replied quietly and continued her descent.

The sun had set a great distance by the time the pair returned to the others. Ardemis was waiting for them on a smoothed rock just outside the mouth of the cave while Joel paced anxiously beside him.

"The hell took you so long?" Joel asked suspiciously. He was eyeing the grass and dirt that now covered Mathias and Mira's clothes. Mathias quickly explained what happened on the hilltop with Marcus. After revealing the information about the well, Joel's eyes grew wide and his jaw nearly hit the floor. Ardemis, however, had no reaction whatsoever. Mathias began to explain the rest of the details, but Joel couldn't remain quiet any longer.

"Are you insane?!" The Warden of Strength yelled. He stepped uncomfortably close to Mathias, but the Grand Master held his ground.

"It's our only option right now, Joel." Mathias did his best to keep calm. The last thing he wanted to do was start another fight with the Warden of Strength.

"You," Joel said looking past Mathias to the Warden of Fury. "Tell me you ain't okay with this!" But Mira only shrugged and dropped her gaze to the jagged stones at her feet.

"The boy's right, laddie," Ardemis said as he stood. Joel spun rapidly to face him. "The closest medical facility is on Malador, and you know, as well as I, that it would be suicide to try and take them there. Mathias has found a solution to that problem that could save everyone." Joel looked like he was about to rip Ardemis's head off, but he slowly turned back towards Mathias.

"Do what you want, but I'll have no part in this," Joel stated and then stormed off into the jungle. Mira called after him twice, but the big man ignored her.

"Let him go, lass," Ardemis said patiently. "He'll come back." Mira knew it was true, but it would require some convincing.

"I'm surprised the two of you don't feel the same way," Mathias said sadly.

"Don't get me wrong, laddie. I think exposing the others to the well is a terrible idea," Ardemis replied quietly as he slid his hands into his pockets. "That said, we made a vow to trust you, so we know you've considered all options and have come to an appropriate course of action."

"Thank you," Mathias replied with a smile. He had forgotten about that first night on Sanctuary. The others had sworn to trust him in every decision he would make, but now that burden weighed heavily on him. "I need to talk to Joel."

"I'll go with you, lad," Ardemis said almost instantly.

"No. I need you and Mira to explain the plan to the others and be ready to leave when we return. Hopefully, I won't be gone long." Mathias turned to leave but stopped as he felt a soft hand on his arm.

"Be careful," Mira said quietly. Mathias nodded and then sprinted off into the night. He only hoped Joel hadn't strayed too far.

After what seemed like an hour of trudging through dense, swampy jungle, Mathias stumbled into a clearing. The emerald blades of grass danced at his feet as the gentle breeze brushed coolly against his cheek. Mathias was surprised by how bright this section of the forest was. The trees emitted a mysterious blue glow that seemed to bring the entire area to life. He was so caught up in the serene beauty of it that he almost didn't see Joel laying in the grass a few feet away.

"Beautiful, ain't it?" The Warden of Strength asked as he stared into the evening sky.

"It is," Mathias replied calmly. He sat down next to Joel and stretched his legs out. The grass was soft underneath him and Mathias thought about how easy it would be to fall asleep on the spot and just forget about all his problems.

"You do realize that revealin' the location of the Well of Travelers means that this place will never be the same? Some of them will choose not to drink. How do you know that they'll keep it secret?"

"Honestly? I don't," Mathias said sadly. He hadn't fully considered the consequences of telling the others. He was too concerned with keeping them alive at this point. "I guess I'm trusting them to do the right thing. They are Wardens after all."

"Not all Wardens are good," Joel said sadly. He exhaled slowly and closed his eyes, letting the sounds of the growing night envelop him.

"I know. But until they give me a reason not to trust them, I have to believe that they are."

"Ha! That kinda thinkin' will likely get you killed one day, kid. But, I guess that's why Aurilean chose you." Mathias swore he saw the big man crack a smile, but he didn't say anything about it.

"I need you with me on this, Joel," Mathias said as the Warden next to him came to his feet.

"I *am* with you, kid. I just hope you know what you're doin'." Joel stretched out his massive hand and hoisted Mathias up.

"So do I," the Grand Master muttered under his breath. With the conflict between the two resolved, Mathias and Joel quickly made their way back to the cave.

As the pair arrived they found the rest of the group waiting anxiously at the entrance of the cave. Mathias was shocked to see how seriously ill many of them now looked. An older man wobbled as he slowly moved towards them using the cave wall as a crutch. A younger woman was hunched over in a corner vomiting ferociously, while the little boy that had so eagerly greeted Mathias earlier that day was now coughing up a storm in his mother's arms. The Grand Master needed to get these people to the well as soon as possible.

"Is it true?" a voice called from the crowd. Mathias saw the man that had introduced himself as Pietrus pushing his way through the mass of people. "Is the Well of Travelers really here?"

"It is," Mathias replied, but he found the man's excitement a bit unnerving. "Mira explained the details?"

"She did. I admit the price is steep, but for some it is necessary. Most of our people have agreed to drink."

"Will you partake as well?" Mathias prodded.

"Thankfully, I was fortunate enough to remain healthy during my short incarceration. While I am indeed intrigued by the well's power, I'll not need to drink of its waters." Pietrus continued to sport an eerie smile that gave Mathias chills, but before the Grand Master could question the man further a wave of excitement washed over the crowd. Mathis followed a young woman's outstretched finger into the night sky. A dark shape was rapidly descending upon them. As the silhouette neared, Mathias could just make out a massive black eagle. It was the same eagle he had seen Marcus transform into just that afternoon.

The Grand Master quickly assured everyone that the bird wasn't going to harm them and then turned his eyes back to the sky, but the feathered monstrosity was no longer present. Instead, Marcus now stood before them, once again completely nude. Everyone stared at the man in awe, while Joel shifted uncomfortably beside Mathias.

"Why's he naked?" The Warden of Strength asked. Mathias was going to respond but Marcus beat him to it.

"Oh. My apologies, mate," the Shifter began. "I forget that I'm no longer alone here." Much to everyone's surprise, the burly man before them suddenly began to grow hair all over his body, covering his chest, back, arms and legs. Within a matter of seconds, the shifter appeared fully clothed. "Now, are you all ready to go?"

Mathias took one last look at the faces staring back at him, many of them nodding their heads in agreement, before responding with a firm, "Yes."

"Very well. The journey will not take long, and I've ensured that the road ahead will be clear. However, I must warn you not to stray from the path or fall behind. The creatures of this forest are not as understanding of intruders as I am." Marcus certainly wasn't subtle as he explained the dangers of the jungle to the others, but Mathias found comfort in the man's blunt warning. "Alright then, everyone stay close."

Joel and Mira led the front of the group away from the cave while Mathias and Ardemis brought up the rear. Mathias was glad the others had all come to peace with his plan. He just hoped it would all be worth it.

The Warden

The path through the jungle was narrow and drenched in darkness. The strange, glowing trees Mathias had seen in the clearing didn't seem to grow in this part of the jungle. The path before them was draped with damp clusters of fallen leaves, and the dark green vegetation had quickly grown frighteningly dense. There were many times where the road would branch off in several different directions, each one equally as ominous as the next. It was becoming more and more clear why the well had never been found.

Deeper and deeper into the savage jungle they went. Mathias was growing uneasy, and he swore something was watching them from the darkness, but he kept his eyes forward on the group. They were moving too slow, and Mathias feared some would collapse before ever reaching the well.

However, before the thought had even left his mind, the group came to a stop in front of him. He was going to call ahead when a blinding white light illuminated the area. The quick scurrying of the small, curious creatures that had been following them signaled their retreat into the darkness. As his eyes finally adjusted to the light, Mathias could see a tall, stone wall draped with thick, dark green vines that had swung open as if on hinges. Not far beyond did he finally discover the source of the light. He had no idea how it was possible, but the crystal-clear waters in the center of the room shown with a golden vibrance the likes of which he had never seen.

"Welcome, my friends, to the Well of Travelers," Marcus announced proudly. He had watched over this sacred room for hundreds of years. It felt relaxing to finally share its secret with others. As the group slowly trickled into the room, Mathias could see why no one had ever found it. The sanctuary was built like a fortress, with only one way in and

291

no windows to the outside world. The massive stone walls along the circular perimeter of the room towered over them and met sharply with a solid stone ceiling overhead. Mathias assumed that, on any other day, the well was also swarming with monstrous creatures that would do everything in their power to protect the ancient waters.

"Can you believe this, laddie?" Ardemis whispered excitedly to Mathias, but the Grand Master said nothing. He had never seen anything like this in his entire life. The waters seemed to sing to him as he followed the rest of the group into the chamber.

"Those of you who wish to drink please follow me. The rest of you will remain here," Marcus stated as he ushered the injured Warden's forward. Mathias and the others stayed put, as well as Pietrus and his friend Pius. The two stood awkwardly off to the side away from Mathias and the others. They watched silently as their companions were led one by one towards the sparkling waters.

Mathias had never witnessed such an intense ritual. As each of the injured Wardens were led to the pool, Marcus would stop them and ask them a series of questions, to which each person would respond with a confident, "I do." They were then offered a rustic, golden chalice that had been dipped into the pool and housed the prolific waters. Each took only a small sip and then handed the chalice back to Marcus. They were then led to a nearby patch of grass to rest while the well worked its magic.

The Grand Master watched for only a few moments before he turned his attention elsewhere. The two men standing quietly apart from them interested him far more than the life-giving waters.

"Pretty amazing, isn't it?" Mathias asked as he appeared behind them. Neither man flinched at his sudden arrival, but their unease was apparent.

"Indeed," Pietrus said quietly and without turning around.

"It just dawned on me," Mathias continued. "I don't really know anything about any of you." The two men quickly shared an uneasy glance before turning to face the Grand Master.

"Whadyu wanna know?" Pius asked. He was clearly annoyed by something, but Mathias couldn't figure out what.

"Where are you from? Are you all from the same planet? How did you end up on Ravendra? Where-"

"Whoa, slow down," Pietrus chuckled. "We come from a planet called Scarlett, named for its red, rocky surface and dusty, ruby atmosphere." Scarlett. It wasn't a planet Mathias was familiar with, and he had researched quite a bit of planets. "Pius and I watched over the royal families there. With our help, the kings kept Scarlett a place of peace for millennia." Pietrus spoke confidently, but he couldn't hide the shakiness in his voice. Something wasn't right.

"Why were you assigned to Scarlett originally?" Mathias questioned.

"Assigned?" Pius replied with a look of pure confusion.

"Yes. Why did the Wardens send you there?" Mathias found it incredibly odd that the man hadn't understood his question. All Wardens were assigned a specific location upon completing their initiation. That's not something one would easily forget.

"Oh. Right. Well, there was a feud between the two ruling families. We were sent to intervene and reach an agreement."

"The situation was terrible when we arrived, but we managed to calm both groups down so they could reach an accord." Pietrus took over, eyeing his friend suspiciously. Mathias didn't know why he got such a bad feeling about the two men, but he could feel deep down in his gut that something was off about their story. Nearly all of the Wardens' accomplishments over the years had been logged in Aurilean's archives, but Mathias had never seen a reference anywhere to the feud on Scarlett.

"It's not something we like to talk about," Pius said sheepishly. It was clear the Warden's questioning had irked the smaller man.

"I understand," Mathias replied gingerly. "I'm just glad you were able to bring them peace." The Grand Master realized he would likely get no further information from the two. He rested a hand on each man's shoulder and then swiveled on his heels and quickly returned to his friends.

"The hell was that about?" Joel asked loudly.

"Have any of you ever heard of a planet called Scarlett?" Mathias wasted no time probing the others for answers.

"Scarlett? Like the color?" Joel asked. Mathias simply nodded his head in response. "Ain't ever heard of a planet bein' named after a color, kid."

"Did they happen to say what region of space it was located?" Mira chimed in.

"No. In fact they didn't say much about it at all. Something about their story just seemed… Weird." Things had grown eerily quiet around them. Marcus was helping the final Warden with the well, and the two mysterious men were suddenly nowhere to be found.

"What about the Longshot's records?" Mira suggested. "She's been around quite a while. Maybe there's some information on the planet in the logs."

"I can shoot back and do some digging, although I'm fairly certain I've never seen anything about the planet in question." Ardemis folded his arms across his chest, while the others stared blankly at him. "I suppose it wouldn't hurt to double check. I'll head that way now."

"Keep an eye out," Mathias cautioned as he rested a hand on his friend's shoulder. "Something is definitely off about those two." Ardemis nodded and stepped through the stone doorway into the black jungle, and then he was gone.

Matthew Louwers

25

The paranoia had finally set in. Only a couple hours had passed since the last Wardens had drunk of the well, and Pietrus and Pius were still missing. As soon as he had finished, Marcus volunteered to scout the surrounding area for any sign of the men, but he had yet to return. Much to their displeasure, Mathias sent Joel and Mira to find the Shifter, leaving him alone with the sleeping Wardens.

Ardy, any luck with the logs? Mathias still thought it was weird that he could communicate with the others telepathically, but it was an ability he could perform with ease.

Nothin' yet, laddie, Ardemis replied almost instantly. *It's a wee bit strange, actually. Should've found something by now.*

Alright. I'll check back soon-

Wait! Ardemis's thought chimed in excitedly. *Here it is!*

What's it say?

The Feud of Fallen Families: A civil war between the two ruling kingdoms of Scarlett. Ardemis paused, a signal

Mathias assumed meant that he was skimming through the document for any information regarding the two Wardens. *Mathias, the contents of this log are sealed. I... I don't have access.*

How's that possible? The Grand Master asked. He still didn't fully understand how the Wardens operated, but Mathias was sure the logs were public record, accessible to anyone at any time.

That's just it, laddie. It shouldn't be *possible.* Ardemis's voice was shaky with fear as it rattled around in Mathias's head. *My guess is that the records have been tampered with.*

But who would do that? Mathias was certain, however, that he already knew the answer.

Someone who doesn't want anyone else to know what actually happened on that mission. I'm gonna see if I can crack into these, lad. Standby.

Mathias didn't like this. His friends were still missing, and the log detailing the events of the war on Scarlett was locked. He was about to request a status update from Mira when movement near the stone entryway caught his eye.

It was Pietrus.

The slender man was covered in dirt and bore small scrapes all over his arms. He had clearly been running from someone, or something.

Mathias! The urgent ringing of Ardemis's voice blasted back into the Grand Master's head.

What did you find?

I was able to bypass the security. Was pretty faulty programming if you ask me. Looks like someone did the job hastily and without double checking their work. Mathias smiled ever so slightly. The Sky Warden was easily distracted. *Anyway, you were right to suspect something about those two. Turns out their 'solution' to preventing civil strife amongst the families was to infiltrate both kingdoms simultaneously and slaughter them from the inside. It doesn't say how they did it, only that the kingdoms never saw it coming. Mathias, this could make those two-"*

"Ravens," the Grand Master muttered out loud. His eyes were now glued to Pietrus as the stranger closed the gap between them.

They must have tampered with the file knowing you'd question them. Ardemis was spewing thoughts faster now, the fear rising.

You need to get out of there, Mathias replied urgently.
Don't worry, lad, I'm-

Ardy? Ardemis?! Mathias was trying his hardest not to panic, but there were no further messages from the Sky Warden.

Forget the Shifter! Mathias now focused his thoughts towards Mira and Joel. *You both need to get back here, now!* Neither of the Wardens responded, however. Mathias had never been more frightened than he was at that moment.

"Everything alright, Grand Master?" Pietrus asked slyly as he finally came to a halt in front of Mathias. "You look like you've just seen a ghost."

"No," the Warden responded angrily. "Just a corpse."

"Ah, so you know, then. Excellent. I was growing tired of this charade." Pietrus waved his hand through the air and, within seconds, every Warden resting peacefully in the grass disappeared into thin air.

"What did you do?!" Mathias yelled in horror.

"The illusions have outgrown their usefulness. I'm proud to say that maintaining them for as long as I have set a new record for me. Jax didn't think I could do it, but I proved him wrong, eh?" Pietrus chuckled to himself as he shoved his hands into his pockets.

"Illusions?"

"Ghosts, phantoms, soulless husks. Call them whatever you want, but it changes nothing." The smirk plastered to Pietrus's face was hauntingly sinister. "I created them to serve a purpose, and that purpose has been fulfilled."

"They weren't real? So, the well-"

"Did absolutely nothing to them. The Shifter no doubt noticed something was wrong, but he shrugged it off. Not very bright, your friend."

"What have you done with him?" Mathias demanded, his tone shifting violently.

"Nothing that you wouldn't have done were our roles reversed. He tried to follow me into the jungle, so I sent a few illusions after him. I was, however, attacked by a pair of monstrous creatures and forced to flee back here. Considering neither the illusions nor the Shifter have returned, I'd say the job was taken care of. If I were you, I'd be a little more concerned about the stout little Warden fighting for his life back at your ship." Pietrus's smile widened as the expression on the Grand Master's face shifted from anger to horror.

"If you do anything-"

"Oh, it's not me, Mathias. Pius, on the other hand, is quite adept at dealing with Sky Wardens. Took several of them out during the war. He's the one that-" But before the Raven could finish taunting the Warden a massive blast shook the entire room, followed by a shower of rock and dust as the stone ceiling shattered into pieces above them. Mathias and Pietrus quickly dove away from the falling debris. Out of the corner of his eye, the Warden caught a glimpse of a massive, black object falling amongst the rocks. It landed with a thud and then burst forth from the billowing cloud of dirt. Mathias's jaw dropped as he laid eyes on the monstrous black gorilla rampaging across the room. The primate was nearly five times Mathias's size and sported massive fangs that glistened in the lone ray of light that now shone dimly through the hole in the ceiling.

The gargantuan ape roared ferociously as it charged for Mathias and Pietrus, both of whom were still in the process of coming to their feet. The creature closed the gap between them almost instantly and, much to the Grand Master's surprise, slammed his giant hairy fist into Pietrus, leaving Mathias completely untouched. The Raven flew across the room and slammed into the wall with such incredible force that surviving was completely out of the question. The man's body crumpled to the ground and didn't move again. The gorilla snorted victoriously and faced Mathias.

"Marcus?" The Grand Master asked hesitantly. The gorilla flashed a wide toothy grin, signaling that it was indeed the Shifter standing before him. "Thank the Makers. Stay here and wait for the others. I'm going after Ardemis." And before Marcus could argue, Mathias pushed off the ground and blasted through the hole into the morning sky.

Night did not last long on Vega, and the sun had already begun to creep back over the horizon. It was a truly breathtaking view as Mathias soared above the lush vegetation. The calm before the storm.

Hold on, Ardy. I'm coming. However, much to the Grand Master's dismay, the Sky Warden did not respond. Instead, an ear-splitting cry pierced the quiet of the morning air. Mathias knew he was running out of time. He continued to rapidly push through the air, propelling himself ever forward. Within a matter of minutes, Mathias had closed in on the Longshot. The ship didn't appear to have suffered any exterior damage. He scanned the clearing for any sign of Ardemis, finally homing his eyes in on a burning patch of grass. He landed quietly beside the flames when another cry, this time far more desperate, echoed throughout the valley. He turned his head toward the sound and flew off in its direction. Twigs and branches snapped in rhythmic succession as Mathias blasted through the jungle.

After only a few seconds, the Grand Master popped into another clearing, only this time it wasn't empty. On the far side of the tranquil grove, dimmed by the elongated shadows of the massive trees in the morning light, Pius stood tiredly over an unmoving body Mathias could only assume was Ardemis. With a heart wrenching cry of fury, Mathias charged across the clearing towards Pius.

The Raven, exhausted from his brawl with the Sky Warden, turned his head slowly towards Mathias but, before he had any time to react, the Grand Master's fist slammed with incredible force into Pius's jaw. The Raven writhed in agony as he felt the bones in his face crumble to pieces. He tried to scream, but found it nearly impossible as his body was sent flying into the jungle. He was airborne for only a moment before he collided with the unyielding trunk of a giant oak tree. Again, the man tried to make some sort of noise to dampen the pain of his back shattering against the wood, but still no sound came out. His body lingered against the tree for only a second before it began its rapid descent to the hard ground below. The Raven could barely see as the swelling in his face forced one of his eyes shut, but he realized it no longer mattered. After only a few seconds, the Raven hit the ground hard. The man known as Pius was no more.

Mathias breathed heavily as he stood over Ardemis. He didn't care to watch the Raven as he flew through the jungle, knowing the power of the blow would be enough to end the man. Instead, his attention was solely focused on the man on the ground. The once bright green grass Ardemis rested on was now painted a dark red, and more blood was oozing out of him by the second.

"Shit, Ardy," Mathis began, doing his best to mask the sadness in his voice. "What the hell happened?"

Bastard got the jump on me. Mathias was surprised to hear the voice in his head and not from Ardemis's mouth. *Stuck me with that damned blade while I had my back turned. Lost me ability to fly. I could feel the power seeping out, but still managed to make it difficult for him.*

Mathias winced as the Sky Warden let out a gurgling cough, blood bubbling from his lips. He was no doctor, but he knew the little man didn't have long.

"Ardy, I'm so sorry. I should never-"

Don't you dare blame yourself, laddie. We knew something was off about those two, and I let me guard down. It's me own damn fault. Ardemis tried to sit up, but groaned in agony as more blood suddenly gushed from the wound in his back. Mathias rested his hand on the Sky Warden's shoulder and gently pushed him back down.

"Stay still. You'll only make it worse." But Mathias knew there was nothing he could do to stop what was coming.

I need you to do something for me, lad. Ardemis coughed again, and more flecks of blood spewed from the man's mouth.

"Anything."

Don't let me die down here. The dirt is cold, and I can already feel the bugs nippin' at my flesh. A collection of tears dripped slowly down Ardemis's cheek. *I would take my final breaths amongst the stars, only I can't get there on me own.*

Mathias knew what the Sky Warden was asking, but he didn't think he had the ability to accomplish such a task. He knew how to manipulate the wind around him, but flying into space where there wasn't any air was a completely different story.

Don't doubt yourself, lad. Ardemis's words of encouragement echoed sadly in the Grand Master's head. *No one has ever picked up this power as quickly as you have. Remember the vacuum trap I caught ya in? Do you remember how you escaped?*

Mathias did remember the trap. He remembered being unable to breathe or move. He wasn't even sure if he knew how he ended up getting out.

It's actually easier to fly through nothing than it is to fly through something. I know you can do it, laddie.

Mathias smiled down at his friend, thinking back to the ashwolf. He had spared the creature because he didn't believe that any being of the sky deserved to die on the ground. Ardemis was certainly no exception.

"Of course, I'll help you, Ardy." Mathias scooped the Sky Warden into his arms, wincing as Ardemis grunted in pain. Blood still oozed from the open wound, and his skin was growing paler by the second. The small man didn't have much time. Mathias pushed off the ground hard and blasted into the sky. Higher and higher he climbed, the jungle rapidly shrinking below him. The air became easier to push through and, much to his surprise, the Grand Master realized it wasn't getting any harder to breathe. A couple minutes later the pair passed through the last bit of atmosphere Vega had to offer. Then there was only blackness.

Mathias drifted easily through the abyss and found that wisps of air swirled gently around him. Each time he would go to take a breath, the air would drift into his nose and then dissipate into nothing. The trick of breathing in space was finally made clear.

I knew you could do it, laddie. Ardemis's voice was full of pride, and he beamed as Mathias looked down at him.

I had an awesome teacher.

As did I, lad. Another tear dripped down the Sky Warden's face. *Keep the others close, they'll need you now more than ever.*

Of course. Say hi to Emily for me, will you? Mathias hadn't forgotten about the young woman whom Ardemis had spent most of his life with. He was finally to be reunited with her.

She'll be flattered. The smile plastered to the Sky Warden's face wasn't enough to mask the sadness dancing in the man's eyes. *Time to go, lad.*

Mathias nodded at the Sky Warden and released his grasp of the man's limp body. Very slowly, Ardemis began to drift into the dark expanse, and Mathias finally broke down. Tears streamed down his cheeks and immediately crystalized.

This is not the end, Mathias. It is the beginning. And then the bond between the two of them was gone.

Matthew Louwers

26

Even after the body had completely vanished from his view, Mathias continued to stare blankly out into the daunting black abyss. He was only minutely aware of how cold his own body had become, and the gentle breeze that surrounded him had grown dangerously thin. He was going to run out of air if he didn't pull himself together.

Mathias had never had the opportunity to truly appreciate the serene beauty of the emptiness of space. Stars twinkled in every direction while the emerald glow of Vega radiated dimly behind him. It was a sight many would never see. The Wardens were far more resilient than normal beings when it came to the dangers of space, but even a Warden would eventually succumb to its enveloping darkness. The Grand Master knew this but, at that particular moment, didn't seem to care.

The day Ardemis transitioned from simple pilot to Mathias's teacher, the two developed an intense bond of friendship, a connection immensely dissimilar from the link he felt with the other Wardens. However, as the darkness swallowed Ardemis into nothing, that bond shattered. Mathias had never felt a pain like this before. Even the loss of his father hadn't weighed as heavily on him. It was a sadness no living creature should ever have to bear.

It was in that moment, as Mathias's emotions dropped to the lowest point they had ever been, that the pain inside of him changed. It was as if someone had flipped a switch that removed his sadness completely and replaced it with unbridled rage. His fists were so tightly clenched that his fingernails dug deep into his palms, and his body was shaking uncontrollably. A fire was growing inside of him, the same fire he had felt stirring after Monk died. He had suppressed those feelings then, afraid of what they might mean. However, as the reality of his situation set in, he chose to let the fire grow. It began in his chest and quickly spread throughout his entire body, eliminating any remnants of the cold that had consumed him. Mathias closed his eyes as he felt the power rushing through him. He let go of all his worldly emotions and allowed himself to be completely and utterly consumed by the fury within.

The moment he opened his eyes he could tell something was different. The blackness of space around him was flooded with searing white light, and the stars and planets that once merely twinkled in the darkness were now as visible as the giant planet behind him. The power pulsed through his veins, and the brand on his back burned fiercely. He felt stronger and smarter than he ever had before, and his confidence soared. It was as though nothing in the universe could stop him.

No longer hindered by trivial emotions, the Grand Master turned his attention toward Vega. Taking a deep breath from the last of his air reserves, Mathias released

himself from suspension and began his drop back to the
planet's surface. In his twenty seconds of uninterrupted
freefall, Mathias had never felt more alive. He broke through
Vega's atmosphere with ease and then altered his course for
the Well of Travelers. He had yet to hear from Mira or Joel,
but he knew that they would have felt the Sky Warden's
passing as well. He hoped they wouldn't blame him for it.

    Is anyone there? Mathias reached out hoping the
others would finally respond.

    Kid! Where the hell've you been?! Joel's response
was almost instantaneous, and Mathias was surprised to
detect a vast amount of fear in his voice.

    I went after Pius, Mathias explained. *I told Marcus to
inform you of that when-*

    Ain't time for detailed explanations or apologies.
Joel's thoughts in Mathias's head were spoken with urgency.
Something was wrong. *Pietrus is still alive. Marcus and I are
locked down here with him and a bunch of clones or
somethin', those damn daggers at our backs. Mira's in some
sort of trance. She tried to use her power, but Pietrus stopped
her 'fore she could. I think she's fightin' with the emotions
inside her.*

    I'll be there shortly. Don't do anything stupid.
Mathias had had just about enough of the two Ravens. With
his newfound power, he pushed against the wind harder than
he ever had, propelling himself forward with lightning speed.
It took only a few seconds to reach the stone walls
surrounding the well. The hole in the ceiling had grown since
Mathias left, and he decided it would be the perfect entrance
to catch Pietrus by surprise. He pulled at the wind around
him and then blasted through the crumbling rocks. As
Mathias slammed into the ground, the room was shrouded in
dust and other debris kicked up from the gusts of air that

followed the Grand Master in. The grey cloud lingered only briefly before settling back into the grass.

As his vision cleared, Mathias was surprised to find a whole swarm of men standing around the room. Each man was identical to the next, and none of them flinched at the Warden's entrance.

"Better late than never, I suppose." Pietrus's nasally voice rang out behind Mathias. He whirled around and immediately saw Marcus and Joel looking up at him with looks of sheer surprise. The two were kneeling uncomfortably on the ground, and both men had blades at their backs. Then his eyes fell upon Mira. She was sitting cross-legged in the grass, her eyes burning with bright red light. It was the same ruby glow that had emanated from her back on Ravendra. Then Mathias noticed the red splotch of blood steadily expanding on her shirt.

I don't know what happened to you, kid, but there's too many of 'em. Unless you can miraculously find the original. Joel's voice was barely audible, however, as it rattled around inside the Grand Master's head. Mathias's attention was focused solely on the illusions scattered about the room. He knew what he needed to do. The power crackled at his fingertips; he merely needed to call to it.

"The anger radiates from you, Warden," Pietrus continued.

"It's clear to me now why Jax was so adamant about taking you alive," another man spoke. His voice and appearance were identical to that of the first man.

"He'll be here soon, you know." The voice came from behind him this time, but he knew it was the same as the others.

"You can surrender to me now..."

"Submit yourself to Jax when he arrives and your friends will go free..."

"Or you can try to stop me..."

"I will destroy the two Wardens and this pathetic Shifter while you stand helplessly by..."

"And then deliver you to Jax anyway." Each man suddenly smiled in horrific unity. Marcus, once again naked and drenched in hair, lowered his head in defeat, but Joel never took his eyes from Mathias. The Grand Master hadn't flinched as the army of identical Ravens threatened him. In fact, Mathias hadn't reacted in any way. He just stood calmly before the swarm of clones, waiting.

"The choice is yours." Every man spoke the final four words in unison.

For Mathias, though, the choice was a simple one. The power coursed fiercely throughout his body, and his mind had never been clearer. Each man stared smugly at him, silently hoping Mathias would attack. The Grand Master knew, no matter what he did, Jax would never let his friends go.

Without fully understanding how or why he was doing it, Mathias raised his arm. The power inside of him burst with excitement and raced for the man's outstretched appendage. In the fraction of a second, the energy that had been swirling around inside of him since the Sky Warden's death exploded forth from the Grand Master's open hand. A blinding flash illuminated the room followed by a searing arc of white lightning that struck one of the Pietrus clones square in the chest. At that moment, had the Raven had any time to react, Pietrus would have slain Mathias's friends on the spot. However, as the bolt of electricity struck the clone, it immediately branched out and chained to the closest men standing nearby. The lightning continued to arc from man to man, disintegrating each one before bouncing to another. In a matter of seconds, the entire army that had stood before Mathias was no more, and the smoldering carcass of the real Pietrus was sizzling in the corner of the room while the blades of grass beneath him burned to a crisp.

Mathias didn't so much as flinch as the bolts of lightning returned to his outstretched hand. The power once again coursed through his veins.

"What the hell..." Joel muttered under his breath, but Mathias ignored him completely. Instead, the Grand Master ran to Mira. He sat down in front of the Warden, her eyes still glowing with bright red light, and gently placed his fingertips on the girl's temples. Just as it had before, the power inside of him answered his call and raced to his fingers. However, instead of a massive burst of electricity, Mathias released only a small dose of energy. The effect was instantaneous as his consciousness was ripped from his own mind and hurled into the Warden of Fury.

At first everything was black, and Mathias was afraid that something had gone seriously wrong. But a world suddenly materialized around him, and he was blinded by sunlight.

He was in a park. Enormous bluish green pine trees sprung forth from the ground while a marble fountain spewed crystal-clear water into the pond behind him. He stood on a grey cobblestone path that appeared to twist and turn throughout the entirety of the park.

The cheerful laughter of a child in the distance snatched the Grand Master's attention. Without hesitation, he followed the path deeper into the park. The further he went, the greater varieties of trees and flowers there were. Birds chirped happily in the open, blue sky above, and the laughter grew louder. The whole place was incredibly serene, and way too good to be true.

Eventually the path came to an end and opened into a small clearing. It reminded Mathias a lot of the clearing he had found Joel in the night before, but he was far more interested in the four children running through the grass. One of them, a young girl, seemed to be chasing the other three boys in a rigorous game of tag. Just behind the children was a beautifully crafted wooden bench, and sitting peacefully upon it was Mira. She wore a loose fitting, white t-shirt and a short pair of blue shorts. Her red hair was a choppy mess atop her head, and she sported a sad smile as she watched the children playing before her. Her brown eyes slowly moved past the kids to Mathias, and her smile vanished. She leapt from the bench and pulled a knife from her waist. The group of children instantly vanished.

"You can't be here!" Mira yelled as Mathias walked across the clearing towards her.

"Yet, I am," the Grand Master replied. His voice was deeper than it had been before, echoing against the trees and ripe with confidence. He came to stop a few feet from the woman. He didn't know what would happen to him if he died in here, but he wasn't exactly jumping to find out.

"What... What happened to you? How are you here?" Mira asked with uncertainty. She was eyeing the Grand Master suspiciously.

"I could ask you the same thing," Mathias replied smoothly. "Quite the sanctuary you've built for yourself. If it were me, I'd give myself over to the power as well just to escape to this place."

"You don't know anything about this place!" Mira yelled angrily, the red blade clenched tightly in her fist.

"I know that, instead of accepting the power inside of you, you retreat here every time you can't control it." Mathias took a slow step toward Mira, but she held her ground.

"The power can't be controlled!" Mira was growing angrier. "How dare you presume to understand anythi-"

"But, I do understand, Mira," Mathias interrupted. "I, too, have felt the power inside of me, the same power that you feel. I first felt it on Ravendra when Monk fell, but I buried it, afraid of what it might mean. I felt it again when Ardemis passed."

Mira simply stared at Mathias in stunned silence.

"This time, I accepted it as a part of myself, and used it to save you and the others. I wanted vengeance for Ardemis's death, and the power answered my call."

"So, it's really you in there?" Mira lowered the knife and took a step forward to examine the Warden.

"It's me," Mathias replied with a smile, his voice ringing angelically throughout the grove. "It's time to go back, Mira."

Mira looked at the man nervously. Very carefully, she reached up and placed a gentle hand on the side of his face. "I don't know how," she said sadly. "The darkness has control. I can only keep it restrained for so long."

"That's where you're wrong." Mathias took another step toward the Warden, the space between them now almost nonexistent. He was minutely aware of the warm, rough hand against his cheek as he looked deeply into Mira's eyes. He had never realized just how beautiful they were. The different shades of red and brown danced in artistic harmony in the sunlight, while the reflection of his own eyes stared back at him. "You have to stop fighting with yourself and embrace the power as a part of who you are. Only then will you regain control."

314

"You make it sound so easy," Mira replied, a stream of tears cascading down her cheeks. Mathias knew how much she hated what her power had become. It would take everything she had to accept the darkness as a part of herself.

"That's why I'm here." Mathias placed his arm around Mira's waist and pulled her to him. Her eyes grew wide with fear, but she let it happen. "You don't have to do this alone."

It was at that very moment, as she stood warmly in the Grand Master's arms, that Mira finally felt at ease. The emotions that once terrified her now greeted her with open arms. With her hand still on Mathias's face, she began to pull his head towards hers. She lingered only briefly, as his warm breath brushed against her cheek, and then finally brought her lips to his.

Unfortunately, the kiss lasted for only a second before Mira's mind exploded with energy. A concussive blast knocked Mathias away, while the very fabric of Mira's dream world was ripped to shreds. Within a matter of seconds, the refuge the Warden had created for herself was gone.

Mira was finally free.

The Grand Master slowly opened his eyes as he returned to his own body. Mira remained opposite him, only now the red glow in her eyes was gone, and she was smiling.

"You did it," she said with immense relief.

"*We* did it." Mathias couldn't take all the credit. It took a hell of a lot for Mira to accept her power.

"The hell you talkin' about?" Joel butted in suddenly. Mathias jumped in surprise. He had completely forgotten about the others.

"He just helped me to understand my power," Mira replied, continuing to keep her eyes and smile fixed on Mathias. "I'm in control now. I can feel all of the emotions flowing through me, and none of them are vying for dominance."

"Well, I'll be damned," Joel said with a shrug. "Can't believe the kid pulled it off. Ain't ever seen anythin' like it."

"I'm still not exactly sure how I did it. Just seemed like the right thing to do. I'm glad it worked. And, about Ardy-"

"We know, Mathias," Mira said sadly, her smile finally starting to fade. "He was a great man, and a wonderful friend. He's finally found his peace amongst the stars."

Joel simply nodded in agreement.

"What'll you do now?" Marcus asked impatiently. The Shifter had been unusually quiet.

"Pietrus said that Jax was on his way, and he knows the Well of Travelers is here." It pained Mathias greatly to say it. "We're going to move against him, intercept his ship if we can and destroy him."

Marcus sighed deeply. Everything he had worked towards to keep the well safe was now, quite literally, crumbling down around him.

"You could come with us," Mathias continued.

"What?" Marcus's face suddenly lit up with excitement.

"Longshot could use 'nother pair of hands, or four dependin' on what animal you turn into next." Joel slapped the Shifter on the back.

"The Ravens know of the well, you said? Perhaps my time as guardian is finally ending." Marcus almost seemed sad to be abandoning his post. "The creatures here will defend it, as they always have. But, eventually, the power of the well will fade, and all those who are bound to it will die. But, I suppose coming with you allows me to perform my duties off world. I'd be honored."

"Excellent!" Mathias extended his arm to shake the Shifter's hand but Marcus, instead, went for a hug. He was still naked as he pulled Mathias in. Mira and Joel chuckled in unison as the Grand Master struggled for air. "You've no idea how much this means to me, Warden. Being a protector has been unbearably lonely."

"I think I do," Mathias gasped as the Shifter finally ended the awkward embrace. "Make any preparations and then meet us at the ship. We'll leave as soon as you're ready."

Marcus simply nodded at the Wardens, a smile still plastered to his face, and then he quickly transformed into his eagle form and took off through the hole in the ceiling.

"Guy's weird, but I like him," Joel said with a chuckle.

"You two will get along then," Mira replied. The group laughed for a few moments together. It felt good to laugh after everything that had happened.

"So, we really goin' after Jax?" Joel asked in anticipation.

"We are," Mathias replied. "Get the ship ready. We leave as soon as Marcus arrives."

Matthew Louwers

27

The commander was pacing. When he first set his plan in motion, he had hoped the Grand Master would lead Pietrus and the Ravens to the Warden refuge. Instead, Blackbird, the commander's personal vessel, was en route to Vega and the Well of Travelers, and Jax couldn't have been more excited. The well had eluded him and his people for some time, and now, thanks to his ingenious plan, they had found it. The mission had cost him two of his finer soldiers, but he had others. The Grand Master wouldn't be able to stop him now.

"Sir," a voice buzzed over the ship's intercom. "We'll arrive at Vega shortly."

"Excellent," Jax excitedly said to himself. His moment had come. He would dispatch of the Warden pests and then submit his crew to the well's power. With a gait that could only be described as childish, Jax skipped out of his quarters and quickly made his way to the cockpit.

As far as ships in the Raven fleet were concerned, Blackbird was one of the biggest. Equipped with a vast assortment of weapon systems, a fully stocked medical facility, and several escape pods, the commander's starship was nothing to joke about. Jax even considered it the flagship of the Raven armada, but there were others who would refute that opinion regularly.

The Commander's Quarters were located around the middle of the ship, so it took only a few minutes for Jax to reach the crowded cockpit. A man and a woman sat behind the ship's control console, both of whom immediately straightened their backs when they heard their superior enter the room. A group of three men were chatting off to the side, while a young boy sat at the navigation computer. Jax cleared his throat and the chatter stopped immediately.

"Commander!" The room sang in unison.

"As you were," Jax replied with a wave of his hand. "How much further?"

"Disabling boosters now. Standby..." The female pilot pulled back on a large lever and a giant green planet appeared just off in the distance.

They had arrived at Vega.

Jax sported a childlike grin as they drifted through the dark area before them known as Dead Space. Many a ship had met its doom to the dark recesses of Dead Space, and any pilot worth his salt knew that boosting through it was a deadly mistake.

"Sir," the boy at the navigation panel yelled hesitantly. "There's s-something showing up on radar."

"What is it?" Jax asked in annoyance. He didn't want anything to spoil his moment.

"It appears to b-be another ship, sir. Warden vessel, f-fighter class."

"So, they're trying to escape-"

"Actually, sir, t-they're flying straight for us."

"What?" Jax said curiously. He was intrigued by the Grand Master's tenacity, but it was time to end this game. "Set up a connection with them. I wish to speak with the boy."

"Establishing link. S-standby..." The boy said. Jax watched patiently as the child typed away at the console in front of him. "Link established. Shall we p-proceed?"

"Yes," Jax replied hastily. The men in the corner, who had been whispering amongst themselves, now watched the commander intently.

The monitor just above the giant window crackled with static. After a brief moment, the static subsided and a clear picture of the Warden cockpit was visible. There, standing in the center of the frame, his friends not far behind him, was Mathias. However, this was not the same Mathias he had met on Ravendra. The Warden, instead, had glowing white eyes and looked far more powerful than the boy he captured only some time ago.

"Commander Jax," the Grand Master said firmly. His voiced echoed harmoniously, and he spoke with a confidence that sent shivers up the Raven's spine.

"Grand Master," the commander replied. "I hope I'm not inconveniencing you, but I require a moment of your time."

"And I require a moment of yours. You've taken much from me in the short time I've known you, Jax. My brother, Monk, Ardemis. Even my father died because of you, and I'm afraid I can no longer allow those acts to go unpunished."

"Is that so? You are hardly in a position-"

"You sent bounty hunters after me. You imprisoned me. You killed my friends and family. All of this because of your lust for my power, and I'm here to tell you that you will never have it."

Jax was flabbergasted. Here he was, the commander of the Raven army, spoken down to by this mere child. He glanced anxiously around the room. He couldn't show weakness, not when he was so close to achieving victory.

"You think you can stop me?" Jax asked firmly. He needed to show the others that he was still in control. "We will crush you before you even have the-" but the commander stopped himself. Mathias was laughing. "What is so funny?!"

"I seem to have to led you to the assumption that you still have a chance." Mathias ceased his laughing and grew dangerously serious. "I *will* stop you, Jax, and there is nothing you can do about it. We've suffered enough at your hands and, before I go, I want you and your people to know that your desire for power has caused you to lose everything." And with those final words, the channel went black.

"Bring him back!" Jax roared angrily. He would not allow this child to speak to him in a such a way.

"T-the link is gone, sir! I can't f-find it," the young boy yelled as he frantically tried to re-establish the connection.

Jax roared ferociously and, in his fury, raised his right hand and blasted the poor boy with a ray of dark energy. The black beam pierced the Raven's chest and exploded into the machines behind him. The boy instantly fell to the floor, a smoldering hole where his heart used to be. The communications panel danced with sparks for a moment before fizzling out. Blackbird wouldn't be calling any other ships anytime soon.

"Is there anyone else that can't do their job properly!" Jax demanded. The rest of the room was dead silent, no one wanting to even breathe in a way that would make the commander angry. "That's what I thought. Prepare all weapons. We're going to show this child who the hell he's dealing-"

"Uh, sir?" The male pilot said hesitantly. He hadn't wanted to interrupt the commander, but what was transpiring before them warranted the man's full attention. Jax slowly turned his head to the young pilot and glared at him fiercely without saying anything in reply. "Look." The pilot extended his hand and pointed a single finger out into the darkness of space. Jax followed the man's appendage, but he could hardly believe what he saw. There, hovering between Blackbird and the Longshot, was the Grand Master.

"What in the hell..." Jax said. The Grand Master was floating in the empty space between the two ships, his eyes burning with white, piercing light. Jax could even see small wisps of air circling the man in gentle, rhythmic orbits.

"How is he-" one of the men who had been standing silently in the corner began, but Jax immediately cut him off.

"Fire everything," Jax said sternly through gritted teeth. The pilots both turned to face him, unsure if they had correctly heard the man's orders. The commander had spent a great deal of time and effort to retrieve the Grand Master alive, but it would all be for naught if they blew him to pieces now.

"Sir?" The female pilot asked, her voice trembling.

"Fire everything! Destroy him!" Jax pushed passed the two pilots and slammed his fist down onto a red button on the console. He might not have understood all the navigation and communication systems, but he knew what the big red button did.

A soft whirring hum suddenly echoed throughout the ship's long corridors and then the blaster cannons unloaded shot after shot of burning yellow bolts of energy into the lone Warden. However, instead of finding their target, the beams were simply deflected off into the space. Not once during the entire barrage did a bolt of energy hit its mark. Jax allowed the guns to fire for nearly a minute before calling off the strike. When the cloud of smoke left behind by the blasts finally dissipated, the Grand Master continued to hover before them, completely unharmed.

"I don't…" Jax began but trailed off as he noticed a sudden change in the boy. He watched fearfully as the Grand Master raised his hands towards Blackbird. A bolt of white hot lightning escaped from boy's fingertips and streaked across the blackness towards the very cockpit in which Jax stood. The commander flinched as the bolt collided with his ship, but the explosion he was expecting never occurred. Instead, the lightning began to race through the ship's electrical systems. Within seconds, Blackbird was without power.

"Primary and secondary systems are all offline!" The male pilot yelled frantically.

"What about the backups?" The female pilot replied immediately. She was not going to be the next one to take a blast to the heart from the commander.

"Offline as well!"

"How is that possible?!" Jax yelled angrily. He was in such a fit of rage that you could see the dark, violet energy radiating off him.

"He's managed to hit us with some sort of electromagnetic pulse. All electrical systems are offline, including life support. If we don't get it restored-" But the pilot was suddenly cut off as a beam of white energy pierced through the glass and tore through his chest. His co-pilot screamed in horror as she was violently sucked out of the room. The air in the cockpit was rapidly pulled into the blackness, as well, along with bits of debris and other unsecured objects. The others quickly fled the room, while Jax remained motionless. His grand plan was quickly spiraling out of control. He stared angrily at the Grand Master, who was already preparing another attack. Jax knew the cockpit would likely be ripped to shreds. Giving the Grand Master one final glare, he spun on his heels and bolted out of the room.

He had only taken three steps when the cockpit exploded behind him. The ship shook violently in response. It wouldn't be able to sustain many more attacks. Jax continued to run at full speed through the cruiser, pushing and shoving his way past several other crewmen all heading for the same place: the escape pods.

Blackbird was equipped with ten, single-rider escape pods, and Jax needed to make sure he was in one of them. While they primarily ran on electricity, the pods also contained a manual release mechanism that Jax was fully prepared to use.

He rounded a corner just beyond the medical bay when another explosion knocked him to the floor. His face stung from the collision with the cold ground, but he quickly jumped back to his feet and winced as the hall behind him collapsed and burst into flame. No other Ravens would get through, but Jax could no longer go back. With the inferno quickly growing out of control, Jax took off in the only direction he could. Another blast shook the ship, but he maintained his balance. Unfortunately, the commander was running out of time. The Grand Master was going to tear Blackbird apart.

As he rounded another corner, just beyond the crew quarters, Jax came to a screeching halt. He had reached the escape pods, but there were several other men and women before him arguing about who would get to take the last pod.

The last pod!

Without a single ounce of hesitation, Jax released an arc of dark energy from his fingertips. The black bolt of lightning blasted through each Raven's chest before chaining to the next one. Within mere seconds, the crowd that had stood before him was nothing more than a steaming pile of carcasses upon the floor. The last pod was his.

As he stepped over the lifeless bodies beneath him, a beam of white light pierced the ceiling and exploded in a shower of sparks and debris. Jax was once again thrown from his feet. However, and conveniently, he was launched in the direction of the final pod. Unfortunately, the hole in the ship immediately began sucking everything out into the darkness of space, Jax included. He grabbed at the jagged knife at his hip and thrust it into the floor. It cut clean through, but refused to hold as Jax was quickly pulled towards the blackness. He was dragged a few feet before the knife finally caught against a beam in the floor. Jax let out a yell of surprise when his arm jerked as the knife came to stop. Most of the oxygen had burned up in the explosion and the rest had fled into space. He took as large of a breath as his body would allow, but he knew he wouldn't last much longer. He needed to get to that pod.

With his free hand, he pulled at a pair of bodies stuck in the nearby doorway leading off towards the bathrooms. After a few good tugs, the bodies broke free and were pulled towards the hole. Exactly as he had hoped, the bodies hit the

hole in such a way that they plugged the burning gap.
Knowing that his plan would only buy him a few seconds,
Jax leapt from the floor and sprinted as fast as he could
across the room towards the escape pod. He could hear the
snapping of the contorting bodies behind him as they were
sucked through the opening in the ship. Fortunately for him,
Jax managed to reach the small cabin just as the blockage
was ripped out into space. He could feel his body growing
sluggish from oxygen deprivation, but he managed to yank
the sliding door into place and then pulled down on the
emergency release valve. Normally, a robotic voice would
have told him to fasten his safety harness and prepare for
launch, but with the electrical systems down, Jax would have
to make do without it. After only a few seconds, the small
pod propelled itself away from Blackbird and zipped into the
blackness.

The sudden hissing of a nearby vent signaled the
release of oxygen into the pod, and Jax desperately began
gasping for air. The precious resource filled his lungs and he
was finally able to breathe a sigh of relief. He was still alive.
The Grand Master's sudden surge of power had surprised the
commander for sure, but it wasn't something he couldn't
handle. Jax had kept his true abilities hidden from the
Warden, letting the boy have the upper hand and hoping to
take him at this pivotal moment. However, Jax was currently
alone in an escape pod, watching his precious ship crumble
to pieces, as he drifted helplessly toward Vega.

A sudden blinding light illuminated the blackness of
space as Blackbird exploded in a giant ball of flame. The fire
dissipated almost instantly, but a massive wave of energy
collided with the escape pod sending it flying in the opposite
direction. Jax was suddenly in a state of panic as Vega grew
smaller and smaller. He clambered about in his seat and saw

that he was instead descending rapidly towards the desert world, Mal'Rashim. His eyes grew wide in horror as he recalled the dangers of the Dead World: sweltering heat, no water or life, and sand as far as the eye could see. How could he possibly survive in a place like that?

Slowly returning to his seat, Jax noticed a streak of white light bearing down on his pod.

It was the Grand Master.

A wicked smile spread across the commander's face. He knew the Warden and his friends would follow him to the planet's surface where they would no doubt attempt to end his life. They would assume that he would be weak and beaten from his narrow escape from Blackbird, but they would be wrong.

Dead wrong.

Jax fastened himself back into his uncomfortable, metal chair and watched as the pod was enveloped in flame as it entered Mal'Rashim's atmosphere. Soon, he would finally have what he had longed for all these years, and the Wardens would be destroyed in the process. All he had to do now was wait.

28

A massive cloud of sand exploded around Mathias as he slammed down onto the planet's surface. He shielded his eyes from the debris, but nothing could stop the grains of sand from burying themselves in other places. He vigorously brushed the flecks out of his short hair and then opened his eyes to the harsh sunlight bearing down on him. He'd heard the stories of how dreadfully hot the planet was, being the Dead World closest to the system's star, but they paled in comparison to actually standing on the surface. He had only been there a few seconds and was already drenched in sweat.

A hiss of steam echoed across the dunes, and Mathias was quickly reminded why he was there. He suspected Jax would never go down with his ship and would do everything in his power to survive the attack. Mathias's newfound ability had enabled him to sense the presence inside each of the pods as they had escaped Blackbird's destruction, and it wasn't until the final pod launched that Mathias sensed the commander. He instructed Mira to fire upon the other pods, blasting them out of existence before they could reach Vega and the well.

Mathias hadn't anticipated Blackbird to explode in the fashion that it had, so he was forced to chase Jax's pod as it fell rapidly to the surface of Mal'Rashim, saving his energy as he broke through the planet's atmosphere. His power, as well as his thick Warden skin, protected him from the descent, but it had taken a lot out of him. He only hoped his friends were close behind.

The other Wardens had, at first, been much opposed to the Grand Master's plan, everyone except for Joel, that is. The hulking behemoth of a man was actually in favor of the idea from the start. Mira, on the other hand, had practically begged Mathias not to go through with it. She pleaded with him that there had to be some other way, but the Grand Master's mind was made up. He stepped through the airlock after his brief conversation with Jax and had done exactly what he said he was going to do. The only downside of his plan had been the escape pod that he now trudged slowly towards. He would end this struggle with Jax, here and now, or perish and be lost in the shifting sands forever.

The pod was smoking heavily as Mathias made his way across the shimmering dunes. He could taste the dryness in the air around him, and he knew that controlling it would be far different from what he was used to. Luckily, the power continued to flow through him and guided his every move. He had never felt more alive.

A black shadow slowly rose from the burning pod. Mathias had to squint against the blazing sunlight to see that the Raven's shirt was ablaze. However, the commander just allowed his clothing to burn away as he stood and waited for Mathias. Bits of cloth slowly dropped to the ground and disintegrated until there was nothing left. Fortunately, the

man's black pants remained intact, but the penetrating
sunlight would certainly murder the commander's pale skin.
Mathias was slightly unnerved by the man's complete
disregard for what had just happened to him. Even through
the shimmering waves of heat emanating from the planet's
surface, the Grand Master could tell that the Raven's azure
eyes were glued to him. His confidence wavered slightly, but
for only the briefest of moments, before Mathias finally came
to a stop about ten yards away.

"This ends now, Jax!" Mathias said. His voice was
scratchy, and the moisture in his mouth instantly dried as it
made contact with the arid desert air. He didn't sound nearly
as threatening as he wanted to.

Jax ignored the Warden's taunt, and continued to
seethe in the hot sun.

"Do you have nothing to say in your defense?"
Mathias continued but a black ball of energy was suddenly
flying straight towards him. Mathias jumped out of the way
just as the orb smashed into the ground where he had been
standing. The sand exploded like a column into the air, and
Mathias had to once again shield his eyes. When the dust
cleared, Mathias could see Jax with his hand outstretched.
The Raven's eyes now glowed a deep purple, and he was
shrouded in an ominous violet hue.

"The time for talk is over, Warden," Jax replied
dangerously.

"Very well," Mathias said sadly and then, without
hesitation, raised his right arm and released a stream of white
lightning from his fingertips. The bolt collided with Jax's
outstretched hand but, instead of searing the target like it had
before, the lightning disappeared into nothing. Mathias
cocked his head to the side, confused at the lack of a result.
He prepared to launch another attack, but Jax acted first,

releasing a black bolt of lightning from his own fingertips. Mathias barely had time to shield himself from the blow, calling what little wind there was to deflect the arcing blast away. The sheer force of the attack launched Mathias back a few feet, but he managed to keep his footing in the soft sand.

"Did you really think it would be that easy?" Jax said with a chuckle. Like Mathias, the Raven also seemed to have undergone a transformation. His voice was deeper than it had been before and far more sinister, and he was clearly much more powerful than Mathias had anticipated. "I've had years to perfect my abilities, carefully sculpting their very essence to my will. To attack me in such a way is insulting and only shows me that you are indeed nothing more than a child learning to walk!" Jax launched another ball of dark energy at Mathias. The Warden dodged the blow again and sidestepped the pillar of sand that exploded nearby. He tried to retaliate with another blast of lightning, but Jax absorbed the attack again and sent it flying back. Mathias deflected the blast again, this time sending the bolt downward. As the scorching hot streak struck the ground, the sand immediately crystalized, forming an arcing glass sculpture. The sight of it was eerily beautiful as it reflected the sunlight over the nearby dunes.

"Do you truly believe that you, alone, can defeat me?!" Jax roared and readied another blast of energy. However, much to the Raven's surprise, a barrage of green energy bolts suddenly rained down on Jax's location. The commander was shrouded in a cloud of dust and sand as the beams continued for a few seconds. Mathias smiled to himself as his plan began to unfold.

The Longshot had arrived.

After delivering its surprise counterattack, the ship landed just behind Mathias, and the other Wardens came streaming out. Joel led the pack, the brands on his legs shining brightly through his beige pants, while Mira and Marcus followed closely behind.

"I can't believe that actually worked," Mira said as she came to a halt next to Mathias.

"Never doubted ya for a second," Joel said happily and slapped Mathias on the back. Marcus simply smiled at the Grand Master and nodded approvingly.

"How touching," Jax snickered as he emerged from the cloud of sand still swirling about. There wasn't a scratch on him, and he even appeared larger than he had only moments before. The smiles on the Wardens' faces vanished as they were suddenly reminded why they were there. "I want to thank you for saving me the trouble of tracking the rest of you down." Jax was twirling a small, purple wisp of smoke between his fingers as he spoke, never taking his eyes from Mathias.

"You were right, Jax," Mathias began. His confidence radiated outward as he spoke, and the others closed in tightly beside him. "I would never have defeated you on my own. I underestimated you, but what you fail to understand is that I am never truly alone and, with the help of my friends, I will stop you."

"Your honesty is admirable, Grand Master. It's a shame that I have to kill you." Jax raised his hand again and immediately fired a blast of dark energy at the group of Wardens. This time, however, Mathias was ready for it. He called upon the wind around him and caught the blast just as it was about to hit. Then, using the attack's momentum, the Warden spun around and flung the dark matter back at Jax. The Raven simply sidestepped the counter attack, and then smiled wickedly as he raised the purple wisp still blowing gently around in his palm. Mathias watched in wonder as it

twisted and snaked into a beautiful long and narrow sword.
The hilt was jet black with the same small purple gem inlaid
at the base, while the blade protruded nearly five feet and
glinted radiantly in the piercing sunlight. It was the most
magnificent weapon Mathias had ever seen.

"Enough of this!" Joel roared ferociously. He pushed
angrily past Mathias and charged for the Raven commander.
Jax waited patiently for the Warden, readying himself to
counter whatever was to come his way. Joel closed the gap
between them almost instantly, the brands on his arms and
legs glowing brightly in the sunlight, and prepared to ram the
commander, but Jax leapt to the side and avoided the blow
with ease. Joel, however, remained unwavering and, even as
his first attack missed, he was already preparing his second.
The Warden planted his right foot firmly in the sand then
spun with nearly as much force as a high-speed train. The
light of the brands on his left leg and left arm went out and
the one on his right arm suddenly glowed even brighter. Joel
yelled again to bolster his strength and felt his fist connect,
but the outcome was not what he expected. Jax stood firm,
completely un-phased by the attack, and held the Warden's
fist tightly in his grasp. Joel tried to pull his arm away, but he
was locked in the Raven's hold.

"Is that it?" Jax laughed, clearly amused. "Surely you
can do-" But before Jax could finish his taunt a monstrous
roar resounded across the desert and a massive shaggy fist
slammed into the Raven. Jax released his grip on Joel as he
was thrown through the air. He landed on his feet a fair
distance away, his elegant longsword still firmly in hand. He
almost seemed to hover in the air for a moment before he
turned back to the Wardens. He was immediately met with a
dagger flying straight for his face. Jax raised his sword and
easily deflected the projectile away. A wisp of the man's

blonde hair dropped in front of his eyes, and Jax casually brushed it back into place with his free hand. He then raised his sword again and waited as the Warden of Fury sprinted across the desert towards him. The Grand Master and the Warden of Strength were just behind her, and the Shifter, currently in the form of a gargantuan gorilla-like beast, brought up the rear. Finally, the battle Jax had been waiting for was to begin.

Mira reached the Raven first, her eyes glowing red with rage, and immediately stabbed at him with her two ruby hilted daggers. Jax deflected the first blow with ease, but Mira didn't falter. She continued to attack, spinning around the man in a graceful dance with death. Jax parried each strike, fluidly dodging each thrust before making a return attack. The two were intertwined in battle only briefly before Mathias and Joel arrived. Mira did her best to draw the Raven's attention from the newcomers, and Joel took the opportunity to launch an attack of his own.

The Warden of Strength once again diverted the power from his legs to his arms and leapt into the air. He came down hard behind Jax, hoping to land a decisive blow, but the Raven was ready. Jax sidestepped the blow at the very last moment, forcing an imminent collision between the two Warden combatants. Mira had to roll backwards to prevent the hulking man from crashing into her, and Jax exploited that weakness by swinging his sword at her. The blade would have landed had Mathias not intervened.

With incredible speed, the Grand Master blasted a wave of hot air, not at Jax, but at Mira. The Warden of Fury was propelled backwards and away from the Raven's deadly swing, but there was no time to celebrate. Jax turned his attention immediately to Mathias, bringing his longsword around and nearly slicing the Warden's head clean off.

Remembering his training, Mathias dodged and dipped with each thrust of Jax's blade, but it wasn't enough. Jax was too fast, and the sweltering desert was wearing on Mathias. That's exactly when Marcus arrived, slamming into the Raven at full speed. However, he now resembled a large, black jungle cat, the very cat that had attacked Mathias and Ardemis back on Vega.

The beast launched itself at the Raven, claws and fangs bared and ready to strike. Jax was unable to fully avoid the creature, but managed to evade just enough to keep from being torn apart. The Raven was knocked back a few feet, right into the waiting arms of Joel. The Warden of Strength threw two punches in quick succession, both of which successfully connected with the commander's exposed back. Jax roared in agony and swung his blade viciously around him, forcing Joel to leap away in defense.

Mira took this gap in the commander's concentration to hurl a pair of daggers through the air. Jax heard the whistling of the blades and turned to deflect the projectiles, but one managed to make it through his defenses, embedding itself deep in the man's leg. He howled in rage as he quickly pulled it free and tossed it aside. Blood seeped from the open wound, but the Raven commander didn't seem to care.

A blast of hot wind slammed into Jax and he suddenly found himself flying through the dry, desert air. He tried to stabilize his landing but, as he came down, Marcus, in full gorilla form once again, was waiting. The shifter launched a colossal fist at the Raven and sent him flying back towards the others. Mathias channeled the power inside of him, while Joel and Mira readied themselves to defend their leader. The moment Jax hit the sand Mathias unleashed his fury, sending white hot bolts of lightning arcing across the desert.

The Warden

Jax, knowing he would never survive if he kept this up, immediately dropped his sword and began to absorb the Warden's attack as he had earlier. However, as he was about to release the pent-up energy, Mira and Joel attacked the man from the sides. The Warden of Fury slashed at the man's already injured leg, sending him to his knees, while Joel channeled all his power into his right arm and then slammed it down on the back of the Raven's skull.

Mathias was sure he heard something crack.

Jax slammed face down into the sand, coughing up blood and spitting it into the dirt around him. It was at that moment, when the Warden's felt that they had finally achieved victory, that something unexpected happened.

Jax started to laugh.

The four quickly raised their defenses, but nothing could have prepared them for the blast of energy that followed. In an explosion that could have leveled an entire city, the group was launched into the air. Jax released a devastating blast of violet energy, presumably the stored attack he had stolen from Mathias.

The Wardens landed hard in the dunes some ways off, but quickly returned to their feet.

"What the hell was that?" Mira asked as she rubbed her neck.

"I don't-" Mathias began, but stopped when he noticed the Shifter struggling to stand next to them. The Grand Master ran to his new friend and grabbed his arm, helping him to regain his balance.

"Thanks," Marcus said, his voice raspy and dry.

"I think we should be thanking you," Mathias replied.

Just as the blast went off, Marcus shifted into a huge beast with an impenetrable shell on its back and jumped in front of the explosion. The creature's thick hide managed to protect the group from being consumed by the purple energy.

"Don't worry about-" but the man was cut off as a nail biting screech echoed across the desert and a beam of dark, purple light shot up into the sky from where Jax had been only moments ago. Black clouds swarmed out of nothing, and the sun completely disappeared, sending the harsh desert world into cold darkness. Black bolts of lightning arced across the sky and a violent wind threw sand everywhere.

"What's happening?" Mathias yelled as the storm continued to swell.

"Nothin' good," Joel replied. He was staring up into the sky, never taking his eyes from the dark shape growing inside the clouds. The rest of the group followed Joel's gaze, and Mathias's eyes grew wide in horror as he recognized the being.

"It's a Dread Raven!" Mathias yelled. It was just like the one he'd seen in his vision, and he was sure he didn't have to explain to the others what a Dread Raven could do. Only the most powerful of Ravens could assume the form, and Mathias knew their battle with Jax was only just beginning.

Mira turned to face Mathias, but the Grand Master could barely see her in the blowing sand. However, he knew the look on her face was the same as his.

"How do we fight it?" Joel yelled.

"*We* don't," Marcus said as he stepped in front of Joel. He stood in front of the group now, his back a scarred, smoldering mess. His eyes were fixed on the Dread Raven, the monstrous bird continuing to grow as it consumed the storm's power.

"What're you talkin' 'bout?" The Warden of Strength asked in confusion.

"I've got this," Marcus said definitively without turning around. Then, and much to everyone's surprise, the shifter began to grow. His skin grew darker and a layer of thick black scales enveloped the man's entire body. His torso elongated, sprouting black spines every few inches along his back. His arms and legs gained pounds of muscle as giant claws appeared where his hands and feet had been. His neck stretched steadily and his mouth became a deadly maw of razor sharp teeth. Finally, a black tail, complete with a clubbed, spiky tip, and a pair of jet black, webbed wings sprouted from the creature's back. Mathias could hardly believe his eyes.

Marcus had transformed into a dragon.

Dragons were only creatures of legend, and Mathias knew that Chiede was the only dragon ever known to truly exist. To see one, standing before him now, was breathtaking. The creature was as majestic as it was deadly.

"You can stop staring now," Marcus said calmly, his voice booming with each word he spoke, but it did little to diminish the awe plastered to the Wardens' faces.

"Finally!" Commander Jax's voice reverberated through the raging storm. "A worthy opponent!" The Dread Raven let out an ear-splitting screech and swooped out of the sky. Marcus reared his head back and roared in response, sending a scalding blast of raging fire hurtling into the sky. Each grain of sand the fire passed through crystallized into glass and dropped to the planet's surface, twinkling with the light of the inferno.

Jax rolled through the air to avoid the flames and continued his dive. Marcus, knowing that simply breathing fire wouldn't be enough to stop the avian terror, flapped his enormous wings in rapid succession and pushed off the ground. Sand billowed everywhere with each beat of the dragon's wings, and the Wardens had to take a few steps back to avoid getting in the Shifter's way.

It had been a long time since Marcus had taken the form of a dragon, but he eased into it like a professional. Higher and higher the beast climbed, the gap between him and Jax diminishing rapidly. The Raven flew sporadically, never allowing Marcus to get a fix on its movements. Fortunately, Marcus was large enough that it didn't matter.

The Wardens watched in stunned silence as the dragon and the Dread Raven collided in midair.

Marcus gripped the giant bird in his claws and then threw it back into the night, following up his attack with another blast of fire. Jax quickly regained his equilibrium and arced over the flames. He then tucked his massive, purple wings in and dove with incredible speed straight for Marcus. The Shifter hadn't anticipated such a maneuver and was unable to do anything about Raven's counterattack.

Jax slammed into the dragon's back, being careful to avoid the spikes. He clawed at Marcus's neck with his razor-sharp talons, ripping bits of the creature's scales away and revealing the tender skin underneath. Marcus roared in agony as he desperately tried to throw Jax from his back, but the Raven had dug its talons in deep and wasn't going anywhere.

"This isn't good," Mira said anxiously as she watched the dragon getting torn to shreds. "Mathias, we need to help him!"

"I know," the Grand Master replied. Even though Marcus had taken the form of a dragon, Mathias knew that Jax was too powerful for the old Shifter to handle on his own. "I'll need a boost."

"I got ya, kid," Joel replied, knowing exactly what the Grand Master needed in order to fly through the storm raging around them. Joel planted his feet firmly in the sand, directed his power to his right arm, and waited.

"Go get him," Mira said confidently, never taking her eyes from Mathias.

The Grand Master simply nodded in reply and then ran some ways off before stopping and turning back to face the two Wardens. Even in the dark storm, Mathias could see the glowing brand of Joel's arm shining like a light at the end of a long tunnel. He briefly looked up into the sky where Marcus was trying desperately to shake free of the Raven's hold, before lowering his gaze back to Joel and then sprinting as fast as he could towards him. Mathias knew that he would need more than just a swift push off the ground to break through the raging winds and sand that dominated the skies.

Calling to the storm around to aid him, Mathias ran faster than he ever had. He reached Joel within a matter of seconds and leapt into the air. Joel grabbed Mathias by the arm and, with as much strength as he could muster, flung the Grand Master high into the darkness. The maneuver had the desired effect as Mathias soared upwards at an alarming rate. He would reach the rampaging sky terrors sooner than he would like, but Jax would never see him coming.

Marcus, Mathias reached out using his mind. He knew the mental link didn't work on ordinary individuals, but the Shifter was far from ordinary. *I'm coming for you. You'll see me shortly. I need you to launch a ball of fire at me.* Mathias knew it was the only way to do any real damage to the Raven, and he also felt that, just as Monk had, he could control the fire before it consumed him.

Marcus roared viciously, a sign, Mathias hoped, that he had received the message. A few moments later, as Mathias finally came into range, Marcus took his attention from the Raven on his back and fired an immense ball of boiling fire straight for Mathias.

The heat from the blast was instantaneous as it consumed the sky around them, and Mathias was suddenly unsure of his ability to control it. He tried to summon the power inside of him and to connect with the blaze hurtling towards him, but nothing seemed to work. A wave of fear washed over the Grand Master as the inferno raced towards him. But then another thought crossed his mind, and he remembered that he was, first and foremost, a Warden of the Sky.

Mathias called to the wind around him, which had become increasingly devoid of sand the higher he climbed and, with incredible force, used it to reflect the attack back at its host. The spell had taken much of the Warden's momentum, so Mathias simply hovered in the air as he watched the raging inferno race towards the winged terrors.

Marcus, seeing that an opportunity had presented itself, continued to command Jax's full attention. He was in serious pain, but he only had to endure it a little longer. Within seconds, the inferno collided with the creature on Marcus's back.

Jax screeched in horror as his dark, violet feathers went up in flame. He released Marcus from his clutches and flapped his wings rapidly to put the fire out, but to no avail. Marcus took his momentary victory to fly over the Raven and then dropped in a freefall. The dragon collided with the flaming bird and latched on with his massive claws. Mathias watched in stunned silence as Marcus and Jax fell rapidly back to Mal'Rashim's dusty surface.

Jax screeched in terror as he tried angrily to escape the dragon's grasp, but Marcus only strengthened his hold. He held the commander so tight that he probably could have

342

squeezed the life from the Raven then and there but, as the ground neared at lightning speed, Marcus continued to fall. Only when there was no chance of Jax escaping did Marcus finally release the Raven. With a grace only a creature of the sky could muster, Marcus pulled up just as he was about to hit the ground.

Jax, on the other hand, was not so lucky. The Raven slammed into the earth, spewing bits of sand in every direction and shaking the ground beneath the Wardens' feet.

Marcus roared triumphantly as he came to a firm landing beside the smoldering bird, then quickly transformed back into his humanoid form. Mathias landed gently beside him, while Mira and Joel ran across the desert towards them.

Jax no longer screamed in pain. Instead, the bird slowly shrunk as Jax reverted to his original form, the dragon's fire continuing to consume the man.

"Is it over?" Mira asked nervously.

"Yes, Mira, I think it-" but Mathias was unable to finish his thought because, at that moment, the Grand Master's world exploded.

Matthew Louwers

29

When he opened his eyes, the world around him had completely changed. There was still coarse sand beneath his feet, but he now stood inside a swirling purple dome of mist. Dark lightning arced across the dome's surface, but the wind seemed to have vanished. Mathias turned to Mira to make sure she was okay, but he was met with a bizarre sight. The Warden of Fury stood, unmoving, with her arm outstretched, as if she was reaching for him. She didn't blink, nor appear to be breathing in any way. It was almost as if she was frozen.

"Mira?" Mathias asked nervously, but she didn't respond. In fact, she didn't acknowledge the Grand Master at all. Perplexed by the situation, Mathis looked beyond the Warden of Fury to the others and found them in that exact same stasis.

"They can't hear you," said an icy voice that caused the Grand Master's hair to stand on end. Mathias spun on his heels and was immediately met with the half-melted face of

Commander Jax. "You'll have to excuse my face. I'm afraid it's no longer as dashing as it used to be."

"What did you do to them?" The Grand Master demanded as he took a step forward.

"Do you like it?" Jax asked seductively. "It's the only power in my arsenal that was ever truly mine. You see, Mathias, I was once a Warden of Time."

The two slowly circled each other, each one preparing for an attack from the other.

"A Warden of Time?" In all his readings, Mathias had never heard of the Time Wardens.

"The ability to start and stop time as I see fit," Jax continued. "We could do what we wanted with the current flow of time, but we could never travel through it. And so, we were tasked with the role of jailer, trapping our prisoners in an eternal cell of the mind. You see," Jax stopped and pulled his purple hilted knife from his side. "They have no idea what is happening around them. They can't see or feel a thing, and they're powerless to protect themselves." And, without warning, Jax stuck his blade deep into Mira's arm.

"No!" Mathias yelled and prepared to fire an arcing blast of lightning at the man, but he found that his power no longer heeded his command.

"Hurts, doesn't it, knowing that you're powerless to stop something from happening?" A smile was plastered to the Raven's face as he pulled his knife from the Warden's skin.

"I'm going to kill you," Mathias said through clenched teeth.

"No, Warden, you're not. You see, the only reason I haven't locked you in this stasis as well is because I want you to know that, even with all your hope and power, you can't do a damn thing to stop me." Jax moved his knife to Mira's throat and began to slice very slowly.

However, before Jax could complete the execution, Mathias slammed into him. The Raven went flying and landed a few yards away. Mathias quickly checked Mira's neck and found only the slightest hint of a scratch. He had saved her, but just barely. His rage fueling him now, Mathias turned his attention to the commander.

"I always knew you would put up a good fight, Warden. I could see it in your eyes back on Ravendra. You're a fighter, always willing to put the lives of others before your own. And that is why you will *always* lose." Jax charged at Mathias, his gleaming dagger in hand. Mathias was ready for the attack, however, and dodged the first slash with ease. The second strike came as quickly as the first, and then the third. On and on it went, Mathias sidestepping and rolling to avoid each attack Jax threw at him. The man was faster than anyone Mathias had fought before, and his sporadic attack patterns kept the Grand Master guessing at every turn.

The dark mist around them continued to spin, growing in speed and releasing bolts of dark energy in random directions. One of the blasts exploded near the two combatants, forcing Mathias to leap away from his foe.

"Impressive," Jax said dangerously. "But I grow tired of this game. This ends now!" The Raven charged at Mathias once again, but the Grand Master was ready. Mathias dodged the first attack, and then the second, but, as Jax swung in for a third strike, he vanished into a cloud of smoke and instantly reappeared behind the Warden, his attack still moving through the air.

In a sudden explosion, Mathias felt his back rip open. The Warden howled in agony as he fell to his knees. Blood gushed from the open wound and dripped into the sand around him. But there was more to the pain, something that frightened Mathias more than the loss of blood. He was losing his power.

"There it is, that helplessness," Jax said as he slowly walked around Mathias, savoring his victory. He stopped at the Warden's side and slammed his foot into the Grand Master's stomach. Mathias buckled as his knees gave out and his face fell into the sand. "You know, I'm almost tempted to release your friends so they can watch you die. But, then I'd have to fight them and, well, let's be honest, that all seems a bit tedious." Jax stuck his foot under Mathias's stomach and kicked, rolling the Warden onto his back. The sand painfully stuck to the open wound, and Mathias cried out once again. Jax stepped over the fallen Warden and kneeled so that his face was only inches from the boy's. He pulled out his knife and held it before the Warden's eyes, eyes that no longer glowed with light. "Goodbye, Mathias." Jax raised the knife into the air and brought it down hard, but the blade never reached its target because another dagger, one red in color, collided with it and sent it flying from the Raven's hand.

"Get away from him!" A woman's voice yelled. Jax stood slowly to face the attacker and noticed that the Warden of Fury had broken free of her stasis.

"Impossible!" Jax yelled angrily. No one had ever escaped the stasis. "How-"

But Mira was in no mood to chat. She pulled two blades from her waste and immediately charged at Jax. She collided with him in seconds and sent him flying across the sand. She chased after him, not wanting to give the man any time to formulate a plan, but Jax was ready. As soon as Mira arrived, he vanished in a puff of dark, purple smoke and reappeared some ways off. Mira turned to face him and found that the Raven, once again, held his thin, long sword in hand.

"Come, girl. Come and meet your end!" Jax roared as he readied his sword, a wicked grin slowly spreading across his face. This time, however, Mira returned the smile. And then, much to Jax's surprise, the Warden's eyes changed from a deep red to a vibrant white glow.

Mira was in control.

She let out a blood curdling scream and charged at the Raven, who was suddenly not as confident as he would have liked. This time it was Mira doing the attacking, slashing and jabbing with each blade, one right after the other, in a seemingly endless dance of knives and swords. This went on for only a few moments before Jax grew tired of the Warden's attempt to harm him. He knew the swirling vortex around them would eventually collapse and he needed to be far away when that happened.

In the exact same way as he had done with Mathias, Jax vanished from sight as Mira threw an attack his way. He reappeared just behind her and shoved his shining silver blade straight through her chest.

The Warden of Fury howled in agony, but didn't falter. She spun rapidly, yanking the sword from the Raven's grasp. Jax, caught completely by surprise at the Warden's resilience, stumbled forward and immediately found himself on his knees before the Warden. Mira, fueled solely at this point by her power and lust for vengeance, brought her dagger up and plunged it deep into the Raven's left eye. Jax roared as his sight immediately left him and blood spurted everywhere, but that didn't stop the Warden of Fury. With the sword still wedged in her chest, Mira spun with her other dagger and sliced the Raven's neck clean open.

Jax was immediately silenced as he fell to a crumpled heap on the ground. Black blood poured from his neck and the violet light in his eyes went out, but Mira's attention was elsewhere. With Jax's sword still stuck in her back, she limped to Mathias and fell to her knees at his side. The Grand Master's eyes were shut, but he was still breathing, just barely alive.

Mira stood and began to pull the blade from her chest when Jax's dying body exploded. The blast sent Mira flying, the sword still firmly in place. She landed in the sand not far from Mathias and was unconscious in seconds.

30

"What the hell?" Joel said to himself as he opened his eyes. He was lying face down in the sand with no recollection of how he got there. He desperately tried to remember anything that happened after the Dread Raven fell out of the sky, but he was coming up with nothing.

"Joel!" A voice yelled in the distance. Joel swore he recognized it, but his brain was so fuzzy that he couldn't place the owner. "Joel, are you alright?" A large hand grabbed the Warden by the arm and flipped him over onto his back, and then everything became clear.

It was Marcus.

"Remind me never to have you-," Joel started, but the look on Marcus's face stopped the jab in its tracks. "What is it?"

"See for yourself." Marcus extended a hairy arm and pulled the Warden of Strength to his feet, and that's when Joel saw his friends. Mathias was lying on his back in a pool of his own blood, while Mira laid on her side with a sword protruding from her back, also in a puddle of blood.

"No..." Joel said quietly, the color draining from his face. He sprinted over to his friends, completely ignoring the swirling purple vortex that was spinning rapidly around them.

"I'd leave that sword in there if I were you," Marcus said as he came up behind Joel. "It's the only thing keeping her alive." But, just as the words were spoken, the Raven's long sword vanished in a wisp of purple smoke and drifted up into the rampaging storm.

"Well, shit..." Joel muttered under his breath.

"What the hell is this storm?" Marcus asked as he examined the dome around them.

"It's all the power Jax has accumulated over the years," Joel said matter-of-factly. "I'm guessin' Jax was a Time Warden, which is why we missed everythin' that just happened, and all his power got trapped in here when he died. I'd say we only got a few minutes left 'fore it implodes."

"There has to be something we can do, mate," Marcus yelled, refusing to accept defeat. "We can't just give up!"

"Oh, I ain't givin' up," Joel continued. "I got an idea, but they ain't gonna like it." Joel motioned towards Mathias and Mira and then looked back to Marcus. "I might be able to rip a hole in the wall of the vortex which'd give you enough time to get them outta here."

Marcus looked past Joel to the dark purple storm swirling around them and wondered if what the Warden suggested was even possible.

"Listen to me!" Joel yelled. "This is gonna happen, whether you like it or not. All you gotta do is get 'em outta here." Marcus nodded as Joel continued. There was no way he was going to interrupt the Warden with his objections. "If Jax really was a Time Warden, then things are about to get a lot worse out there. Tell the kid that he needs to find Damien. He'll know what it means. Tell him, Damien is the only one who can stop what's comin'!"

"What *is* coming?" Marcus yelled in response, but Joel had already stood and was making his way towards the rotating wall. He placed his hand against the purple mist and was met with a painful jolt that arced through his entire body. There was no way he was getting out of this alive, but he could still save the others.

"You ready?" Joel yelled at Marcus across the sands. The shifter had taken on his gorilla form and held Mathias and Mira tucked under each arm. He simply grunted in response and Joel turned back to the raging storm. Summoning as much energy as his power would let him, the Warden of Strength slammed his hands into the mist. The Warden was immediately overcome with pain as the storm poked at him, sending electrical surges throughout his entire body. He roared in agony as he ripped the wall apart. The storm instantly lashed out, angered at the disruption, and launched Joel into the air. He landed some ways off, his back completely crushed as he slammed into the ground.

As he felt the power in him fading, Joel turned his head towards the opening. It was already closing rapidly and Marcus was doing his best to get to it. The giant gorilla stampeded across the desert sands, keeping the Wardens close to him. He reached the wall of the storm and, without stopping to look back, leapt through the tiny opening. A small smile of victory spread on Joel's face as the breach in the wall closed.

His friends were safe, and that was all that mattered now. The Warden of Strength laid his head back into the sand and closed his eyes. All he could do now was wait.

31

There is only darkness. No dreams, no visions, nothing. Only the never-ending abyss of black that goes on eternally in all directions. This is death, and it calls to me. It is comforting as it embraces me, enveloping me in a cocoon of shadow. It isn't cold, but neither is it warm. It simply is, and it is nothing more.

No!

A voice? There are no voices here. There is only silence in the darkness, an eternal quiet that is never broken nor disturbed.

Don't you die on me!

The voice grows more impatient as I drift towards the darkness. What does it want? What could it mean? I want to find out.

Death clings, fights to keep me in its grasp, but my will is strong. My will to live. I push away from the shadowy tendrils coaxing me further into the abyss. They fight back, but I ignore them.

Please! Come back to us!

It's a woman's voice. Caring and full of emotion. It drives me onward, my curiosity growing with each push. The tendrils below weaken the higher I climb, and a light appears. A light that pierces the endless black of death. I see it and continue to press forward. Higher and higher I go.

The darkness tries one final time to pull me back into its never-ending hold, but I am resilient. Death will not have me this day.

*   *   *

Mathias awoke in a violent coughing fit, spewing phlegm all over himself. Fortunately, there was no longer blood in the mix.

"Easy! Easy! Slow breaths, mate," Marcus said as he laid a hand on one of the Warden's shoulders. "That's it, nice and slow."

Mathias caught his breath, heeding the Shifter's advice, and the coughing subsided. He could breathe again, but that's when he noticed the pain. A streaking hot burning sensation ran up and down his back, and he moaned in agony as he collapsed back down in the bed.

"I was beginning to think you'd never wake up," Marcus said sadly. It was clear the man had gone through great lengths to keep Mathias alive.

"Mira-" Mathias began but found it painful to speak.

"She's fine." The smile on Marcus's face was enough to make Mathias melt with relief. "Took that bastard's blade straight through the chest, but she'll live. Never seen anyone fight off death like the two of you."

Mathias was overcome with joy, but that happiness disappeared when the Shifter's smile vanished. Something was wrong.

"Mathias, I... I'm so sorry." Marcus could barely form the words as they stumbled out of his mouth. He tried to keep eye contact but was forced to avert his gaze.

"Tell me," the Grand Master said, his voice raspy and dry.

"After you and Mira finished off Jax, his power was released and trapped inside the storm, and the only way we could get out before it imploded in on us was-"

"Joel," Mathias whispered sadly. Marcus only nodded in response. Tears streamed down the man's face, but he did his best to maintain his composure. "If I know Joel like I think I do, then I know there was nothing you could have done to help him. It's not your fault, Marcus."

Marcus nodded again and wiped his face clean. "There's something else..." Mathias figured there would be more. "Your brand has been severed. You'll likely have lost access to whichever of your abilities had already manifested."

Mathias's heart sank. He would never fly again, and his power of emotion was lost to him as well.

"Marcus, where are we?" Mathias asked, changing the subject.

"The Longshot, believe it or not." Mathias didn't believe it. "After I squeezed through the hole in the vortex, I shifted into a giant bird and carried you two back to the ship. I strapped both of you in the med bay and then prepped the ship for takeoff, knowing I only had a short window before the vortex collapsed. I was only inches off the ground when the storm imploded. It shrunk to the size of a grain of sand and then released one of the most devastating shockwaves

I've ever seen. Luckily, I was able to get above it and into space before any damage could be done."

"You can fly this thing?" Mathias asked in surprise.

"My friend, there is quite a bit I can do that you don't know about." Marcus smiled, but only briefly.

"Where are we heading?" Mathias sat up again, enduring the pain as it came, but refusing to lie down.

"Before he died, Joel told me to find someone called Damien." At the mention of Joel's brother, Mathias's eyes lit up. "I told Mira and she immediately charted a course for Malador. Apparently, this Damien fellow runs a top end science facility there."

"Damien... Why would we need to go after him?" Mathias swung his legs out over the bed and prepared to stand.

"Joel said something about Damien being the only one who can stop what's coming? Mira didn't seem to know what that meant, and frankly neither do I." Marcus seemed worried, his voice shaky with uncertainty.

"Thank you, Marcus." Mathias smiled and then pressed his feet to the floor.

"I would advise against that if I-"

"I need to see her." Mathias said forcefully. He stood up, his legs wobbly at first, but he eventually found his balance.

"Fine. I'll be in the back if you need me." And then the Shifter left, somewhat annoyed at Mathias for ignoring his advice.

Very slowly, Mathias took a step. Pain shot through his back and he almost collapsed to the floor, but he stood firm and took another step, and then another. Eventually, and very slowly, Mathias made it to the cockpit. Mira was sitting quietly in Ardemis's chair, her hands resting gently on the control panel in front of her. Mathias took the seat opposite her, and remained silent.

The two stared out into the starry sky for what seemed like an eternity before the silence was finally broken.

"I loved him once, you know," Mira said sadly, keeping her eyes forward.

"I know," the Grand Master replied. To be fair, Mathias only suspected a relationship had once existed between the two. It was all clear in the way Joel would look at her and how he acted around her. He was always so protective. "What happened?"

"We grew up. We realized there were more important things than our personal interests." Mira slowly turned and faced the Warden, locking her eyes with his. "We're warriors, Mathias. We don't get to have the luxury of distractions." Mathias knew she was talking about him, and it nearly ripped his heart in half.

"What happens now?" Mathias asked, not wanting to linger on the subject any longer.

"We continue what we set out to do. We find Damien, as Joel requested, and continue our war against the evil in the universe. Jax was the commander, but there are far more dangerous adversaries in the Raven army." Mira turned away from Mathias and stared, once again, out into space. "We need to keep fighting."

"It was you, wasn't it? The voice I heard?" Mathias already knew the answer to his question, though.

"It was."

"Thank you." Mathias took Mira's hand in his and squeezed it to show his appreciation. She allowed the gesture and, as he went to pull away, considered keeping him in her grasp, but that thought drifted away into nothing as his hand left hers. "We're going to be ok, Mira."

"I know," she replied, punching a few commands into the console before her. The vibrations of the boosters starting up rattled the cockpit, and Mathias sat back in his chair as the Longshot disappeared into the starry abyss.

Epilogue

"Sir! We found him!" The small voice echoed over the intercom. The huge man at the desk dropped his pen, stood immediately, and left the room, not bothering to close the door behind him. With massive strides, the man walked down the long corridor, a slight hop in his step.

It's about damn time, he thought to himself as he neared the cockpit. They had scoured the desert world for days and come up with nothing, and he was beginning to lose hope. But now that hope was restored.

"What've you got?" The man asked as he entered the cockpit, ignoring standard protocol.

"There, sir," said the pilot, who was no more than sixteen years of age, as he pointed out through the glass. There, poking through the sand, was an arm with a glowing yellow brand.

"Makers be damned, kid's still alive..." The large man muttered to himself. "Set the ship down immediately and prep cryo. I want everyone ready, no excuses."

"Yes, sir," the boy replied diligently and then began to radio the ship's staff. The huge man, however, was not focused on anything the boy was saying anymore. Instead, he took off down the corridor towards the ship's cargo bay. Within seconds, the huge man reached the loading door and lowered it. The moment the gap was big enough, the man jumped through, not bothering to wait for the ramp to make its full descent.

It only took the large man a few seconds to reach the arm poking through the sand. He quickly began digging around the exposed appendage, slowly revealing more and more of the buried man's body. After a couple minutes or so, the man in the sand was completely exposed, his other arm also carried a brand of yellow light, but the glow was fading.

"Hang in there, kid," the huge man said as he hoisted the body into his arms. The victim was barely breathing and completely unconscious. His hands were also fried to a crisp and his body was covered in severe, jagged burn marks. He didn't have much time left.

The huge man sprinted across the sand, being careful not to drop the man in his arms, and he reached the ship within a few seconds. He strode through the corridors, avoiding each turn with care and finally arrived at the med bay.

"Sir! The cryo chamber is prepped and ready for storage," said a nearby technician, another young boy still in his teenage years.

"Perfect." The huge man laid the body in the stasis chamber and then watched as the technician input a string of commands into the console. The sliding door sealed itself shut and a blast of icy air surged into it.

"Will there be anything else, sir?" The technician asked.

"Yea," the huge man replied continuing to stare at the man in the tube. "Inform Stonewall of my return, and check in on the machine's progress. And tell them..." The man hesitated for a moment before making his final request. "Tell them my brother is comin' home."

To be Continued...

Made in the USA
Columbia, SC
29 June 2019